ELLIE SIMMS

PHOENIX

Published in the United Kingdom by:

Red Falcon Publishing, an imprint of
Blue Falcon Publishing Limited
The Mill, Pury Hill Business Park,
Alderton Road, Towcester
Northamptonshire
NN12 7LS
Email: books@redfalconpublishing.co.uk
Web: www.redfalconpublishing.co.uk
Copyright © Ellie Simms, 2020

A CIP record of this book is available from the British Library.

First printed 2020
ISBN 9781916321601

Thank you for all the support...
... you know who you are x

PHOENIX

ELLIE SIMMS

Preface

None of this seemed right, Briana thought as her eyes searched for answers. She could see nothing and her arms, pinned behind her for some reason, were of no help. Her head hurt, throbbing horribly on her right side. Had she fallen, a car accident? Her mind was a fog; her thoughts cryptic. She tried again to move her arms to no avail. Were they bound behind her? It didn't make any sense. She lay on her side, that much she could tell, but there was nothing but darkness; 'pitch-black' her mind repeated to her.

Her other senses sprung to life. The smell of wet paper, burlap maybe. Something abrasive on her wrists, rubbing against her skin as she tried to move her arms. Her breathing hampered, but not impossible. She had a metallic taste in her mouth, copper maybe, the taste of blood.

Definitely, blood.

Her heart raced. She shifted her legs, trying to pull them up under her, to sit up. They didn't move freely. Her mind had figured something out, but her body was still working through the situation, rationalizing, adjusting like a child in the dark. A naked woman, a tiger in the jungle. The low rumble of an engine and the occasional bounce of her body indicated to her that she was in a moving vehicle.

She shook her head, trying to clear the fog, something shifted in front of her. She moved her head again. Sniffing. Wet burlap. Copper. She drifted off once more, a painting of a beautiful woman sitting on a horse. She pulled hard at the restraints on her wrists, feeling them cut into her skin this time, the pain jolting her back to reality. She was bound. What the fuck? Take stock, Briana. Think through this. Wake up! The club, the dance floor. Esteban.

"Huh?" she said, her voice, muffled, echoed back to her. "Help!"

She pulled again at the ropes behind her, kicking her feet trying to break free. Why couldn't she see? She shook her head. She felt it this time. Sliding in front of her, pressing up against her face, her neck. The smell. Her heart raced. Tears spilled from her eyes as she began to sob. Reality was a rude awakening. I was naked. In his bedroom. Everything came together in a fraction of a second presenting a stunning revelation that was much too horrible to conceive.

"Nooo..." she heard herself cry out, kicking and tugging futilely at the restraints, her body bucking.

Her sobs increased, her breathing coming in gasps as she inhaled, tasting the burlap bag that covered her head. Briana writhed on the floor of the moving vehicle, her mind racing with images, realities, memories of movies and her mother's own words of warning, "trust no one!" All for naught, she thought. All for naught. Focus. Get a grip. It was too much. The car ride; the champagne. She lay on the floor and cried, her mind playing back the last memories she had.

She had been with Esteban. At his home. After the amazing time at the club, and the incredible ride in the back seat of his limo. They were admiring his art collection. He was glib about it, she remembered, proud of his work. She felt lucky to have met him. He offered her another drink, and as she lost herself in his eyes, those amazing eyes, she remembered swallowing down the champagne and then him taking the glass from her, leading her to the bed. That was it. There was nothing else. Fear gripped her body, froze all of her save her tears and cries.

Chapter 1

As the plane lifted into the air, Briana breathed a sigh of relief. All of her planning, discussions, and decisions had led to this moment. She closed her eyes, leaning back in her chair, belted in as the ever-present hissing noise of the forced air moved through the pressurized cabin. A long flight, but one that she hoped would land her in a world filled with adventure and challenge. The first step in her adulthood. A huge leap in her independence.

The arguments at home had been fierce at times. Both her mother and father had encouraged her to begin college immediately, put off her crazy plans for a gap year of adventure, beginning with a three-week trip to Brazil. Her father, a teacher and professor preached education above all else and could not imagine why anyone would deny themselves the opportunity to avail themselves of higher learning. Briana would not relent, first engaging them in videos, catalogs, brochures of Brazil and all it had to offer.

"These three weeks will help me to understand my independence, my ability to adapt," she had stated. She had practiced almost everything she said beforehand, hoping to be persuasive, influencing her parents to accept her actions as those of someone who had done her homework.

To her father specifically, she spoke of the learning possibilities of being abroad, untethered, absorbing culture, nature and people in their element; not through books and movies. She spoke of her passion for languages, several of which she had excelled in secondary school. How it could possibly be her career, something she could earn a living out in the future. She spoke of working with the underprivileged, possibly in foreign countries, maybe it was her calling.

Briana had eventually concluded, if they would not let her go willingly, that she would sneak out in the middle of the night and head out on her own. Gradually and thankfully, she broke down her parents over several months getting them to not only understand her desire to delay her schooling and travel to Brazil, but to also foot the bill for her plane fare as her graduation gift. She remembered just before she left, her father whispering to her that they would be there to help her should she need their assistance. "Anything, you need," he said, in tears, "anything."

Now, as she watched the ground disappear out the window, she closed her eyes thinking of the opportunities ahead of her. She had managed to secure a few interviews during her adventure in hopes of finding a position teaching English to students that could pay her rent if she decided to return; which she fully expected to do. A friend of a friend of her mom had helped her to secure a no-obligation apartment for the three weeks in the outskirts of Rio De Janiero. Everything had fallen into place nicely just weeks before she was to leave, but in plenty of time for her mother to feel like her daughter wasn't just going off to play in a foreign land filled with drugs and kidnappers.

That hadn't stopped her though. Just as Briana had provided documents of adventure, learning and growth opportunities to secure her parent's consent, her mother did the same with news stories of murders, kidnappings, and politics meant to change her only daughter's mind. This went on through most of the summer, well after airlines were booked and arrangements had been made.

"Enough, mom," Briana had said to her one morning as they were eating breakfast.

Her mother looked at her with a blank stare as if she didn't understand her daughter's exclamation. She had littered the table moments earlier with copies of news stories that she had printed from the Internet. 12 Dead in Hospital Shooting, Rival Drug Lords Battle It Out in São Paulo, Rio Safety Levels Fall to a Three-Year Low the headlines read. It was her mother's biggest haul yet of negative articles about the country, and while she feigned ignorance about Briana's push-back, she pointed to the articles as proof of her concern.

"I'm already booked, mom. I'm going. Please don't make this any harder than it has to be. You and dad should be encouraging me at this point, making sure that I have everything together so that I have a successful trip instead of making me feel bad, and," she looked down at the headlines, "scared at the prospect of traveling in another country all by myself."

Briana broke down then, tears rolling down her face. Her mother pulled her into her arms holding her tight, patting her back.

"It's okay, Bree," she said. Then added, "I'm sorry. We just want you to be safe and I thought it would help…"

"It doesn't help mom," Briana said, pushing back from her mother. "Not at all." She was still crying, but she was also mad. "Reminding me every day that I might be making a major mistake or that I am going to be harmed or murdered doesn't help at all!"

"I'm sorry, Briana," her mother said.

They two stared at each other silently for another minute before Briana turned away, pouring cereal from a box into a bowl. She worked to get her crying under control. She promised herself that she wouldn't break down in front of her mother, but she couldn't take it anymore. When she turned back to the table, her tears had subsided.

Her mother sat down next to her. "I'll make you a deal," she said, pushing the hair on Briana's forehead out of her eyes. "I won't dig up any more stories before you go. But, if I do see something that is alarming, I can't promise you I won't tell you about it." Briana nodded her head. "You have to promise me that you will call me every night to let me know you're okay."

"Every night, mom?"

"How about every couple of nights? Definitely, daily when you first get there. And, then maybe every couple of days," her mother said. "Never more than a week."

"Okay," Briana said, hoping to satisfy her mother's concern.

"If your father and I don't hear from you at least every week, we send in the Calvary."

"Mom!"

"Just... just keep us informed about how things are going and, well, you'll have a lot to tell us about. We just want to know you're safe and that we're here for you, honey."

"I know, mom, I know." Briana turned to her mother and patted her hand. "At least once a week," she said. "I think that's fair."

"More if you want to..."

"More if I want to," Briana responded. "You'll have my number too, mom."

After that breakfast conversation, the rest of the summer flew by. Conversations about Briana's trip were suddenly very positive. Her mother would cut out articles about beautiful places to visit in various cities. Together, they would all talk about day trips she could take, safe day trips to crowded tourist areas.

When her parents dropped her off at the airport, they stayed with her up until she went through the security line, her mother holding her tight. All three were tearing as she waved goodbye. She knew her mother would be inconsolable on the ride home, but that she would find a way to get through it. Her dad would see to it.

As the plane continued to climb, Briana couldn't help but notice the symbolism as it rose through the clouds and leveled off, speeding toward the first stage of her new life and all that waited ahead.

"Would you care for a drink, Miss?" Briana turned to see the young flight attendant staring down at her, as she broke out of her thoughts.

"Ah, no thank you," she said, looking up at the handsome man. His blue eyes sparkled as he smiled back at her.

He pointed to the call buttons above her head. "My name is Marco." He said, pointing to his name badge. "It's a long flight, feel free to call for one of us if you need us." Flight attendants could always make out first-time solo flyers. It was to their benefit to make them comfortable. For many of them, it was also to their individual benefit to seek out the more attractive guests, and Marco had singled out Briana the moment she stepped onto the plane. "I am at your service, Miss...?"

He specifically left the question hanging and Briana eventually picked up on it. "Oh Briana," she said, smiling, revealing a perfect set of white teeth.

"Briana," Marco repeated, "Very nice. I don't believe I have ever met a Briana." He bowed his head and smiled. "If you need anything." Marco turned and stepped down the aisle with full intentions of returning once his flight responsibilities were behind him. He very much wanted to get to know more about the young woman.

Briana smiled to herself as he stepped away. She was no stranger to men flirting with her, and she wasn't sure that was what had just happened. Marco was quite a bit older than her 18 years, but she sensed he was more than just trying to make her comfortable. She had plenty of boys come onto her during her high school years, but it was different when it was a stranger. It was more exciting in some ways, she thought.

Briana leaned back in the airplane seat and thought back to her coming of age in high school. She had always considered herself attractive, but her friends and family had told her she was beautiful almost all of her life. It wasn't until she was in the 10th grade in high school when she realized that she stood out from many of the girls at school. Her body seemed to mature at a faster rate, taking on a much more shapely form by the time she turned 15. At age 16, she had developed the figure of a young woman, complete with large breasts and shapely hips. This caught the eye of most of the young boys at school as well as some of the teachers.

Her science teacher was the first adult outside of her parents to vocalize the noticeable change in her figure in a creepy way that caused her to steer clear of him when there were no others around. Briana would catch him leering at her during testing periods or when others were focused on the board in class. She remembered at graduation when he walked up to her as she was leaving the school for the final time. He said something to the effect that she had 'turned into quite a woman' over the years and that if she ever wanted to 'talk about her future studies' with him, he would readily make himself available. Briana thanked him for the offer and quickly made her way toward a crowd of her friends, distancing herself from him for hopefully the final time.

Briana dated several boys her own age during her high school years; none of them particularly seriously. Her first real crush came in the form of Ben Helmsly, a tall upperclassman who approached her and her friends as they hung out in the backfields of the school after classes. He and his friends played Frisbee and football on the fields late each day and Briana and her friends made it a point to watch them play. Briana liked watching the boys play hard, sweat and rough it up with one another; it stirred feelings in her that she hadn't known she had. When she became more of a permanent fixture after school watching the boys play, Ben took notice of the group of girls and Briana felt like he picked up his game, maybe played a little harder when she was around.

When Ben first approached her, she found herself blushing and speechless as he stood in front of her, shirtless and sweating. He spoke to her and her friends, but she felt that he was speaking directly to her when he asked if they wanted to join them throwing the Frisbee around.

"Okay," she blurted out, and the rest of the girls laughed.

He had been speaking to the whole group, but now he turned his attention to her, leaning down and offering her his hand. "You can be on my team," he said. "What's your name?"

"Briana," she heard herself say as he lifted her from the ground with his strong arm. "Briana Campbell."

"Hi, Briana. I'm Ben. C'mon."

The other girls laughed once more as she followed him out into the large field. They joined her shortly and together the two groups merged throwing the Frisbee about in various degrees of expertise. Briana was surprised how bad she was at throwing the disc but didn't seem to mind at all when Ben came up behind her, his arms loosely wrapped around her and helped her throw resulting in a much better toss.

Gradually and casually, the two groups began to meet daily, and Briana got to know Ben quite well. He was set to go off to an upstate college at year's end, but they had a whole year ahead of them to get to know one another better. After several weeks of flirting and meeting up after school, Ben asked her out on her first official date. She said yes before he was even finished with the sentence. She was in 10th grade and her first real date would be with a 12th grader. She wasn't quite sure how that would fly at home but had grown quite fond of Ben quickly and he made her feel 'different' when she was around. Her parents would just have to get used to the idea, she thought – well, eventually.

Briana didn't tell her mom and dad about the first date with Ben. She lied and told her parents that she would be staying the night with her friend Patricia. Patricia and she had worked out a sophisticated alibi that would allow Briana to be out until at least 11 p.m. with Ben before he had to bring her home. She would ultimately stay with Patricia, but she had arranged for Ben to pick her up at her girlfriend's at 7 p.m.

When Ben arrived in his white Mustang, she was all goosebumps and shivers as she stepped into the front seat and closed the door behind her. She waved goodbye to Patricia and then turned to face Ben, who leaned across to her and kissed her on cheek. She smiled as they drove a way to a small restaurant. At dinner, she remembered smiling so much that her face hurt by the time dessert came. She had eaten more than she thought she would, her stomach so nervous, but she still managed to slide down a small ice cream after their meal.

"Wow!" Ben said. "You have quite an appetite."

She blushed. "I'm sorry," she said. "I just..."

Ben's hands reached across the table and covered hers. "No," he said, cutting her off. "It's cute. I hate when girls pretend they're not hungry. I mean you have to eat, right?" He laughed a loud laugh and Briana found herself laughing with him.

She noticed then that his fingers had entwined with hers and her stomach was a thousand butterflies all flying at the same time. Briana wasn't sure where the night was taking them, but she was so into the ride.

"Let's get out of here," Ben said, and she was on her feet in an instant, her smile still plastered across her face, as his hand slid into hers and they walked out of the restaurant.

The captain on the plane made a quick announcement giving his name and their current altitude. Briana opened her eyes to look out the window of the plane, noticing the clouds below them as they soared. She settled back in and closed her eyes, quickly bringing back the night of her first date with Ben.

When they left the restaurant that night, she could feel the heat coming off Ben's body. It was different between them; even different than before they walked into the restaurant. Their quiet conversation at dinner, his lightly touching her hand, the way he looked at her as she laughed; all of it seemed to make them closer. She never wanted to be closer to anyone more than Ben. When he pulled his car over to the side of the road outside a small county park, she sat in her seat as he turned off the key.

"Briana," Ben said as he turned to her. She stared forward in the car, almost in a trance. She wasn't sure what to do; she hoped he would make the first move. "That was a nice dinner, wasn't it?"

She turned to him. Nodded, not ready to trust her voice. "Yes," she managed finally.

"I really enjoyed it," he said. "Especially because you were there."

Could he see her blush, she wondered? Did she glow in the dark in the car?

"Hey?" he said. "Look at me." She turned to look at Ben as she heard him unclick his seatbelt. "You are so beautiful, Briana. So very beautiful."

She remembered thinking that she knew he was going to kiss her, right there, right then, even before he said those words. She was ready for it; she was sure of it. That was what she had wanted; why she had come on this date. She looked up into his eyes as his head leaned forward. He bent down and his lips brushed up against hers. She could feel his breathe on her as she gently kissed him back, tasting his lips; the lips of another boy for the very first time. Her body was on fire, every nerve taut as his fingers slid onto her cheek and he held her face as they kissed.

Even as she sat on the plane now, Briana remembered that first kiss as if it happened only yesterday. Her body reacted so completely, straining against the seatbelt of the car. She never felt the way she did at that one particular moment before he had kissed her. It was hard to recount what exactly it was that was different, but she knew when their lips parted, that everything had changed, as it had when he first took her hand and picked her up off the grass field back at the schoolyard.

She was sweating and dizzy when Ben pulled away from their kiss, the seatbelt holding her tight against back of the seat. Briana's hand reached for the button to release it, and when she couldn't unbuckle it, she felt herself trapped inside of the seat, suddenly needing to get out as her hand searched for the red button. Then she felt Ben's hand on hers, guiding her slowly over the release and she depressed it until the belt popped free.

"Relax," he said. If he hadn't known it was her first kiss before, it was clearly evident now. "Briana, relax,"

He leaned his head back across the seat, blurring in front of her as his face came closer to her. They were kissing again, her body shifting in her seat, toward him as she felt his tongue slip between her lips and into her mouth. A moan escaped her, unintentionally as her tongue first hid, and then met his as she reached up around his neck to pull him close. It was the most exiting emotional moment in her life and, as she leaned into the kiss, she knew it was something she would never forget.

Briana's eyes opened once more, this time without the prompting from the plane's PA system. Her lips were curled into a smile at the ends as she let the memories of that first romantic moment with Ben drift away. She would treasure that memory forever. She fumbled in her bag for her phone and opened her ToDo list. She put in a small note to remember to send a note to Ben that she was travelling abroad in Brazil. They were no longer romantically involved, but they remained friends over the years. When he graduated from high school, they stayed together for another year before they separated, and he made his way into the big bright world.

Their courtship grew during those two years, but Ben

was always a gentleman, allowing Briana to take it a little further on more than one occasion, but ensuring that they never went all the way. He reminded her that he should not be her first; that she should find someone that she loved and could remain in love with always intimating that he would be moving on. She was forever grateful for Ben's love and treatment and all that he taught her over the years.

"Hmm," Briana said aloud as she slid her phone back in her bag, still smiling.

She shifted in her seat and stared out the window. After Ben, she remembered, she had moved onto two other boys from school. First Danny, who she really only dated once, when he made it very clear that he wanted only one thing from her. That relationship ended quickly after he told her that all girls her age were 'putting out' and if she wasn't doing it yet, then there was probably something wrong with her. She treasured her one-date relationship with Danny, however, because the breakup brought her directly to Tom Drysdale.

When Tom had heard she was going on a date with Danny, he made it a point to find Briana and tell her she was making a mistake. "You can do much better," were his exact words. And he was right. Less than two days from her quick-split with Danny, she and Tom went on their first date which lasted through the whole of 12th grade. Tom took her to the prom and that night, nestled together in bungalow that Tom had secured through a member of his family, he took Briana to a place she had never been before. Briana remembered crying out into the night in the small wooded-shelter over and over again as they made love together for the first of several times. He was patient and kind with her, and she returned the favor.

Briana shifted in her seat thinking about that night. His

hands, so strong, so soft. Never had anyone made her feel the way he did. She and Tom dated lightly for the rest of the summer and then, since they knew they would not be together once he went off to school and she to her adventure, they shared one last night together, less than two weeks ago, in the same bungalow where they first consummated their relationship. It was another incredible night. He left the following morning for college and two weeks later Briana boarded the plane she currently sat on reliving those moments.

Chapter 2

On the ground in Brazil, Briana quickly got the lay of the land. She had become a quick-study over the summer on Rio di Janiero and the surrounding areas. Once they were laid out in front of her, she quickly found ways to navigate the streets and to identify key landmarks that helped her to get around. Taxis seemed to be the best mode of transportation during her first week, although there were some awkward times when cabbies actually fought over her for pickup.

The apartment that her parent's friend had helped arrange for was not much an apartment, but it served as a bed and a place to have a quick breakfast. That was all Briana was really looking for, and certainly all she could afford. She assumed, once she established herself somewhere, she would look at alternatives that would meet her budget. Right now, her budget consisted of the money she had managed to save over her last semester of school and the summer.

On the second day in town, she had her first interview. It was in the small town of São Conrado. During the trip to the interview, the taxi driver, Jose, told her – in perfect English – that she should not ever take a job in the small city and that he would stay with her as long as he could should she want to continue into town.

"Is it that bad?"

"It is your Detroit," the driver said. "From what I understand, it is very bad in Detroit."

Briana laughed at the reference, but also understood what the driver was trying to say. "I understand," she said.

As they continued unabated toward the area, she noticed a large mass of colorful buildings that climbed the side of a nearby mountain.

"What is that?"

"Rocincha," the driver said. "Don't let it's colors fool you."

"It's beautiful," she said. In front of her hundreds of houses of various degrees of construction rose alongside the face of the mountain. Pastel colors of orange, blue, green, yellow all mingled together as if it was a painting. "People live in those houses."

"What you Americans call 'Shanty town,'" he said. 'Drugs and violence. Stay away, lady. I tell you now!"

"It's like a painting," Briana said out loud.

"Not for you, miss," the driver said.

"Okay, okay. I get your point. Please, turn around. I'm sorry for the inconvenience."

The driver stopped and made a quick U-turn on the main road. "It's no inconvenience to me. But, you. They would eat you up in a place like that."

Briana thanked him again and wondered about the rest of her interviews. She had two more tomorrow both in different towns outside Rio. She pulled out her phone and looked up the addresses.

"Can you tell me if Santa Teresa is a place I should be concerned about?"

"She is the most beautiful city," the driver said. "I will

drive you there every day if you wish." He laughed and Briana laughed with him, lightening the mood in the car.

"Thank you," she said. "Then I will take that job and look no further."

"Dios Mio! If you have a job there, why would you look to Rocincha?" the driver asked.

"I don't," she said, "but since you tell me it is safe, I will make sure that my interview there goes well and that I land that job."

"Very good, miss. Very good," the driver said.

Back home, Briana picked up a sight-seeing book and plotted her plans for the weekend. She very much wanted to see as much as she could over the short three-week period, but she had every intention of staying once she was able to land a job. If she couldn't get to everything, then she would when she was more settled.

She spoke to her mom a little after dinner, choosing to leave out the almost-trip to Rocincha and certainly didn't mention the job interview she was going to the following day. Why dwell in the supposition, she thought. Once she landed the job, she would let her mother know and then there would be nothing either of them could do about it.

After a quick dinner from a local take-out place, Briana settled into bed early for the night. She wanted to get a good night's sleep so she would ace the interview tomorrow and nail-down the job so she could get started with her life abroad.

The next morning, the same taxi driver waited outside for her as she stepped out of the apartment. He whistled as she approached the car.

"My lady, you are very beautiful," he said making Briana blush. He held the door for her as she stepped into his cab. Once back inside, he continued. "I don't know what you are interviewing for, pretty lady, but I'd hire you on the spot."

"Thank you, Jose," she said.

"I'm serious, mamma. You are a picture. How did I not notice it yesterday?" He let that hang in the air as if she was supposed to answer it. "Let me take a picture of you so I can tell my friends that an American movie star was in my cab."

"Shut up, Jose," she said. "But, thank you. It's very helpful on a day like today."

"The day you get your job, yes?"

"Yes, Jose. The day I get my new job."

As they drove along, she realized she was very confident that if the description of the job was right, she was properly qualified and could sell herself well. She felt good about her prospects and equally good, not that Jose had chimed in, about her selection of clothes. For the interview, she had chosen a long, white dress that contrasted against her tan skin. It was tight at the top, accenting her large chest, but still remained conservative. There was no doubt it hugged her slender figure, but in this town where women were paper-thin and showed more skin than she had ever seen before, she didn't feel likes she was overdoing it. Still, Jose's comments made her feel kind of sexy, which, although she hadn't planned it, she thought may give her the edge that she needed.

When they arrived outside what looked like a squat office building, Jose came around and opened her door. His eyes walked up her legs as she first slid them out from inside the car and then stood up alongside of it. He slowly finished taking her all in and then looked into her face.

"Muito bonito," he said, perhaps not realizing he was speaking out loud.

"Jose," she whispered.

"Eu sinto Muito," he said, and then in English. "You have

28

great beauty miss. I hope it works well for you in your interview."

"Thank you, Jose," Briana said, stepping away from the cab. She turned to him and he smiled.

"Yes," he said. "I'll wait."

"Thank you, Jose," she said.

Briana gathered her confidence once more and stepped into the building. Stepping up to the reception counter, she suddenly felt like everyone was looking at her. Damn you, Jose, she thought. At the counter, the woman, clad in glasses looked up at her. She said nothing.

"I'm... I'm here for an interview," she said. Still, the woman remained quiet. Get it together, Briana, she thought.

She was getting a traditional dose of nose-down reprimand from the woman behind the counter. Was she dressed wrong? She thought she had dressed appropriately, but still conservative. Finally, the woman looked up at her.

"Mr. Souza will be out for you in a minute. Have a seat," the woman said, her right hand indicating where she thought Briana should sit.

"Thank you," Briana said, and she walked over to the nearby lounge and sat down. She crossed her legs very lady-like and looked back at the receptionist who still stared back at her as if she was an irascible child. Stay on task, she thought to herself as she looked about the room.

The building did not appear old by local city standards. Everything in Rio, besides the modern skyscrapers, seemed to be 300 years old or more. This office seemed to be relatively young, or at the very least, modernized. She tapped her hand against her thigh to an unknown tune as she waited. When she stopped her hand from fidgeting, she heard a door open and she looked back behind the receptionist.

A young man stepped out, perhaps in his mid-30's. He was thin and good-looking. She wondered if this person was her interviewer. She watched as he leaned in close next to the receptionist and then he looked in her direction. He stood up straight, fixing his suit jacket and walked in Briana's direction.

"Ms. Campbell?"

"Yes," Briana said, standing up to meet him. She turned and accepted his extended hand, shaking it. "It is so nice to meet with you, Mr. Souza."

"Walk with me, Ms. Campbell." He turned and began walking away from her at a brisk pace. She did her best to keep up as they walked past the receptionist who shot her a glance and then they stepped into the offices behind her. "You are qualified for this role?"

"Yes, sir. Very."

"Good. Do you like children?"

"Yes?" Briana answered, not realizing it came out sounding like a question. "Yes," she said more matter-of-factly.

"Good. How is your Portuguese?" He moved down a long hallway, actually accelerating in pace.

"Fluente." Fluent, she said, following close behind. Briana was studying languages and was fluent in both Portuguese and Spanish.

"Excellent. Your real first name is Briana?"

"Yes, sir," she said.

"Very good," Mr. Souza said as he stopped in front of a room at the far end of the hallway. "Inside here, Briana... may I call you Briana?"

"Of course, sir."

"Inside here," he continued, "are 30 of the most precocious children in all of Brazil. Their parents are titans of industry, CEOs of companies, one is actually a high-ranking government official, and one," he lowered his voice to a whisper, "is the son of a prominent member of a large drug cartel. Despite his profession, he is an honorable drug lord – we have both here in this country."

Mr. Souza stopped speaking for a moment taking Briana in for what seemed like the first time. His eyes washed up and down her body before he continued.

"You are quite beautiful, Ms. Campbell, but that's not what I require for this class. What I require is someone who can stick to the curriculum. They need to speak English with confidence within the next six months. Is this something you can do?"

Was he offering her position, right here, right now, here in Rio for the next six months? Could she do it? Of course, she could. Was this the right role for her?

"Ms. Campbell? Briana?" he said, his arms were crossed, his foot tapping impatiently, as he waited for an answer.

"I've no doubt if given the time and the right tools..."

"You'll have whatever you need at your disposal," he said.

"Then, I don't see why that would be a problem at all. You have your girl, Mr. Souza," she said with confidence this time.

He looked at her, his right eyebrow arching as he gave her a more formal once-over. "Excellent. Follow me and we will work out the details." He started to walk down the hall. "You have all of your paperwork to work in this country?" She nodded. It was something she had to do on the sly back home so that she could get a temporary job in Brazil. "Very well," he said as he opened a door when they reached the other end of the hallway.

They both walked in through the door. He offered her a seat. She sat and he pulled out paperwork from a manila envelope. He pointed to a few words on the contract that was written in Portuguese and he asked her if she needed anything translated. Briana shook her head, took a moment to read what she considered the salient points of the agreement, noting that it was for a period of six months and a specific clause that said she could not work for a competing organization as long as she worked for this particular firm.

At the very bottom was the weekly salary they would be paying her, which was at least twice as much as she anticipated. She looked up at Mr. Souza.

"This salary," she said. "It is well above what this position should get." He nodded. "Is there a reason it is so much?" He was silent for a moment and Briana opened her mouth to ask another question.

"Briana," he said. "These kids come from such wealth that they think they don't have to learn anything. Their parents have come to realize that it is important for them to speak your language so that they can be worldly and carry on the family's name. They don't care how much money they spend."

"Do they have the ability to learn?" she asked.

"As much as any child does," he answered.

"Then, I see no problem in getting done what you need me to do." She leaned forward and signed the papers.

"Very well, Briana. You start tomorrow," Mr. Souza said. He handed her a large book across the desk. "This is the curriculum plan book. You should review it tonight. It tells you what is expected of our teachers and what you will be teaching the children. There are methods in there also, but every teacher is different."

"Thank you," Briana said, taking the book. "I'll review it tonight."

"Is that your taxi waiting for you?" Mr. Souza said, looking out the window onto the street.

"Yes," she said.

"Be careful, young lady. The men in this country are not always as they appear."

She smiled. "Oh, Jose. He is more of a protector."

"Everything is not as it appears, Briana. Keep your wits about you. Most men – especially men, are duplicitous at best.

Briana looked at him wondering why he offered such a warning. "Does that go for all men?" she said, looking directly into his eyes.

"I assure you – you are safe with me. But I am a rare person. I see beauty for what it is, not for the taking. Other men are not so kind."

"Well, thank you, Mr. Souza. For both the opportunity and the wisdom," she said as she pulled her pocketbook together. "Will there be anything else today?"

"No, Briana, no. Mrs. Alves will give you all of the other information that you need. Please see her on your way out." Briana nodded. "Don't worry," he added, "her bark is worse than her bite." A small laugh escaped him. "In a battle, you would do well to have her on your side."

"Thank you, Mr. Souza."

"Call me Marcos," he said.

"Thank you, Marcos."

"I will see you in the morning."

Briana left his office and made her way to the receptionist. She explained that she had gotten the job and the receptionist seemed to soften a little as she went about the motions of pulling out more paperwork and instructing her as to what she needed to do to get started. When they were done, almost a half-hour later, Briana thanked the woman and walked out of the office.

Jose saw her coming and slipped out of the taxi, opening her door for her as she stepped up to the car. He ran around to his side and jumped into his seat.

"Senhorita, you were inside for a long time. How'd it go?"

"Very well, Jose. Very well."

"Excelente!"

"I got the job, Jose. I start tomorrow." Jose let out a loud cry. Briana smiled to herself. "Is there a place we can go to get a beer, Jose? To celebrate."

"I have something better, senhorita," he said as he started the car.

They drove for no more than five minutes while Briana worked through her head the events that had just transpired and whether she should be telling her mother yet about the position. No, she thought, not until I see my class and get my feet wet. She decided she would give it a day or two before she would spring the news on her parents. No sense in getting them all worked up until she was sure of what she had landed.

Jose pulled the taxi to a stop in front of a small turquoise-colored cantina. It looked seedy from the outside and not a place that Briana would have stepped into unless Jose had brought her there. He turned the car off and got out of the cab. As he opened the door for her, she stood up and stared at the bar.

"Are you sure, Jose?" She looked down at her own outfit and then back at him. His smile was from ear-to-ear. He wanted to show her off. She let out a giggle and he laughed with her. She smiled back at him. Marcos Souza's words floated through her head as she looked back at Jose. He was harmless, she thought. "Okay," she said to him. "But promise me that you will protect me if anything crazy happens."

Jose's smile left his face, his grin turning sincere, his hand crossing his heart. "Okay, amiga, lead us inside."

Jose took her by the arm and led her into the cantina. When they crested the doorway, everything but the music stopped. Every head turned and looked in her direction and she slid her arm around Jose's neck. If standing next to him would make him a rock star in his friend's eyes, she was happy to do so. She felt his arm slide around her back, and she smiled back at him and to the waiting crowd.

The two of them had a couple of beers and she had a single shot of tequila. Briana had planned on paying for the small outing with Jose to thank him for his assistance, but her money was no good in a place like this. Her presence was payment enough as he spoke to his friends in rapid Portuguese. She heard the word girlfriend, 'namorada', passed about as he spoke to his friends and she smiled broadly when they looked back at her.

When they left the bar, Jose had been lifted to new heights amongst his peers. She instructed Jose to drive her home.

After picking up a quick take-out dinner from a local place, Briana got ready to pack it in for the night. Before she fell asleep, she called home and told her mom that she had had a wonderful day, letting her know that the sights of Rio were incredibly beautiful. She told her nothing about the cantina and of course, news of the job would have to wait until she had a couple of days work under her belt.

Briana lay in bed with the curriculum plan book on her lap, reviewing the lesson plans. Nothing in the book seemed too difficult and she felt confident that she could carry out most of the plans without issue. When she fell asleep that night, she thought, for the first time, that her dream of living abroad might actually come true.

Chapter 3

Day one in her classroom was eye-opening for Briana. She had arrived early, dressed more conservatively than the day before. Mrs. Alves nodded her 'approval' as she stepped into the office. Briana smiled back and headed into her class. She had about a half-hour to kill before the children showed up.

As she walked about the class, looking at the desks and small library at the back of the room, she noticed that everything was written in English; there was no Portuguese anywhere.

"We believe in complete immersion," Marcos said, stepping into the open doorway.

"I see that," she responded. "So, no Portuguese at all?"

"Not unless it is necessary. The moment they walk through this door, they will be speaking English and you will be encouraging them through conversation." Briana nodded. "You will, of course, have a few children who will need some coddling, but the less the better, I always say."

"What are their ages? I realized I never asked yesterday."

"Three, four and a few five-year-olds. All ripe for learning."

"Very good," Briana said. She had come to the class early

to get settled and she was glad to have had this quick conversation with Marcos. She hadn't realized how nervous she was.

Marcos sensed her concern and nervousness. "You will do fine, Briana. Just stay confident and in control."

Briana nodded and he left the room. Before the children came into the class, she had a few minutes to sit at her desk and to look at the whiteboards in the classroom. Ten minutes later, her class was filled with 20 young, well-dressed children who flitted about the room until she called for their attention.

It took a few minutes, but very quickly, she established herself as their teacher and for the most part, the class went well. Most of the children adapted easily and throughout the morning, she brought them through a number of lessons following the curriculum plan book.

Just before lunch, the class was dismissed, and she watched as parents and what appeared to be security teams took the children from class and loaded them into Mercedes Benz cars, BMWs, and other luxury vehicles. At least one of the children were escorted into the back of larger SUVs by a team of men that all looked like they were carrying concealed weapons. Interesting clientele, Briana thought.

Her second class arrived about a half-hour later. She realized just before they arrived that she had not properly prepared for lunch and that beginning tomorrow, she would need to bring a sandwich or something light to eat between classes. In her short downtime, she jotted notes down about the children from the first class to serve as reminders for the following day.

As the second class arrived, Briana watched out the window as a new parade of luxury vehicles made their way up to the building. Each shiny car was nicer than the previous, clearly standing out amongst the common vehicles that rode alongside them on the streets. She also noticed the larger SUVs pulling in last and the children of those vehicles being escorted into the building by what she could only imagine was a security team.

Her second class was larger – about 30 children. All well-dressed like the earlier class. They sat in their chairs attentively and worked through each of the lessons as required. Briana felt as though the bulk of the class enjoyed learning new things and she was more confident, as the class came to a close, that she would be able to meet her objectives of having both classes speaking fluid English by the end of her 6-month stint.

As she walked the last of the children out to the main area for pick-up, she watched the parents, nannies, or security teams pick up their charges and lead them out to their vehicles. The last to leave was the larger security team who surrounded three of the children – all boys and walked them out of the door while still in a circle. The men, suspicious and alert, looked up and down the street as the children were loaded into the cars. Once the boys were inside, two of the men stepped inside of the SUV and another moved to the car behind them and slid into the backseat. Together, the cars sped down the block.

"Not the government children," Marcos said from behind her. She turned to face him, still floating on adrenaline from the last class. "They are very fortunate children – of the FDN, the Familia do Norte. The kids do not know of the family business, and the parents would keep it that way if they could."

"Their fathers..."

"Yes, all heads of families within the cartel. Very powerful men," Marcos said.

"Very powerful. To be feared," Mrs. Alves said from behind the reception desk.

"Yes, Mrs. Alves, but here... in our classrooms, they are just children. And, they should receive no special treatment and have the same opportunities as the other children."

"Of course," Briana said. "Doesn't it present a problem that they are here with the children of government officials?"

"Our countries are very different, Briana. Here, the cartels are much wealthier than the government. They have to work together in many cases to get things done." Briana nodded, not quite understanding. "When our country was suffering under huge debt, it was the cartels who loaned the money to the government to help us get back on our feet."

"Not the banks?"

"The cartels control the banks and much of the money in the country." Marcos offered a small laugh. "Well, we're not as bad as Mexico in that sense, I guess. Right Mrs. Alves?" She laughed with him, both of them understanding the inside joke that confused Briana even more. "No, not as bad as Mexico, but still, our government has no control over the cartels."

"I see," Briana said, soaking in the current events lesson.

"And, how were the classes?" Marcos said.

"Wonderful," she responded. "Everything went extremely well."

"Excellent," Marcos said, and he turned to Mrs. Alves as if to say 'I told you so.' She merely shrugged and look over at Briana before looking back down at her desk. "Then, you are all through for the day, Briana," he said. "Enjoy the rest of your day."

Marcos turned and walked back into the offices and Briana went back to her class to grab her bag. She packed up the plan book and then sent a quick text to Jose who told he would be available to pick her up when she was ready. Didn't he have other clients, she wondered?

Day two at the office offered much of the same. The students had quickly come to know her, and she was beginning to learn each of their idiosyncrasies. She had never really taught a class before, so this was all new to her in a way also. She did have the upper hand – she was the teacher. Some of the children even hugged her as they left the class, which both embarrassed her and at the same time, touched her emotionally.

When the second class finished, she watched the luxury car parade as it glided up to the building trying to match each of the children with their respective cars. It would take some time to do that, but it seemed like a fun game to play. The security team was still in the office; three men getting ready to circle around three of the boys. One of the members of the team looked over at Briana and, for the first time, she noticed something other than a stern look on his face. It may have actually been a smile. He said something to the other men and then he broke from the group and walked over toward Briana.

Her eyes went wide as he walked toward her. She found herself looking behind her for a means of escape if necessary. She felt herself begin to shake as he approached. What could he want? She pulled herself together as he stood in front of her. He was at least a head taller than her and he looked down at her.

"You are the new teacher, yes?"

He was solid from head to toe; she could tell by the way the air in the room changed as he stood in front of her. She could smell his aftershave, which she found strange as he was a bearded man.

"Yes," Briana said.

"Good," he said, stepping back. His eyes swept her up and down and he smiled once more. "Quite pretty for a teacher."

Briana felt like a piece of meat in a butcher shop on display for this man's purpose only. She was about to say something when he smiled at her. His face softened and for a moment, his weathered mercenary persona disappeared.

"There is a club," he whispered quietly to her, "a very exclusive club for women who are as beautiful as you are." He pulled a card from his pocket and covered its words as he handed it to her as if it was a secret. "You should come one night. They will show you the real Brazil, and how a lady of your beauty should be treated."

Briana blushed at his words. No one had ever spoken to her like that. Certainly, not a man like the one that stood before her now.

"Friday night," he whispered, his voice softened. "Think about it. You would be welcomed there."

"Thank you," she managed.

The card was in her hand now and she looked away from him, down at the card.

"For you. You alone," he said.

The man stepped back, still smiling and then he turned back to his security team and together they surrounded the children and walked out of the building. Briana looked down at the card. It read: A Flor Dourada, The Gilded Flower. She pushed the card into her pocket and was about to head back to her classroom to get her things before heading home. She was met with Mrs. Alves's gaze.

"What?" she said.

"Do not be fooled by a handsome man's charm, young lady. They are not good people."

"I know," Briana said.

"They have money, but money is not everything."

"I know, Mrs. Alves. I'm a big girl."

"You are a young girl in a strange country. And young girls do not always make the best decisions."

Briana wondered if Mrs. Alves had made some bad decisions when she was younger. Perhaps that was why she was so down on her. "Thank you, Mrs. Alves. I'm going to head home for the night." She nodded at the woman and then went back to her class to collect her bag before heading back to the reception. She smiled at Mrs. Alves and said goodnight as she headed outside.

At home that night, Briana did a quick look-up on the Internet for The Gilded Flower in both Portuguese and English and found no reference to it. She thought that was odd but didn't dwell on it. What she did dwell on, was the phone call she was about to make. She procrastinated for about a half hour before she finally picked up her phone and called her mother.

"Hi, mom."

"Hi, honey, how are you?" Her mother sounded cheery on the other end of the phone. It was around dinner time and she expected she was toiling about the kitchen getting supper ready.

"I'm good. Actually, better than good."

"That's nice, honey. What did you do today?"

Briana braced herself as she was about to drop the bomb. "I, ah... I started a job today, mom."

"That's nice. A job? Wait, what do you mean you started a job?"

"An opportunity came up here, and I applied for a job teaching English to a bunch of rich kids and, well, I got it."

"What does that mean, Briana? If you're working there,

when will you come home?"

"That's just it, mom. I won't be coming home in a couple of weeks. I'm going to stay here – for six months." Briana started to speak very quickly then, getting out everything she had practiced in her head. "It's a great opportunity, mom. I can learn so much here. So much. They are paying me quite a bit also, because all of the kids are rich, and they have to speak English fluently before the end of the semester. I'll have enough money to travel more... if I want to, but more importantly, I can continue to see sights here, and learn from the people and the surrounding areas. It's good, mom. Really, it is."

Briana stopped to take a breath. There was only quiet on the other end of the phone. She waited, letting her words sink in. She knew that what she just told her mother would hurt her, but there was no easy way to say it. Finally, after a full minute, Briana spoke again.

"Mom?"

"Yes, Briana."

"It's good for me. Really good."

"I know, honey. I had just gotten used to your coming home in a couple of weeks, now you tell me you're not going to be home for six months. You've never been away for that long. Now, I have to worry for another six months."

"You don't have to worry, mom."

"Of course, I do. That's all I do, Briana. With you in another country. That's all I do."

Briana had a thought at that moment. "Why don't you and dad plan to come visit. You can see how beautiful it is here and..."

"I don't know, honey."

"No, seriously," Briana pressed, wishing she had thought of the visit earlier. "It would be great if you came over. You can see for yourself that it is safe and that there is nothing to worry about. And we can travel together for a long weekend or something. Think about it."

"Sure, Briana."

There was quiet on the phone once more.

"Mom?" Still quiet. "Mom. It's really what I want to do."

"I know, but I miss you."

"I miss you too, and dad. I miss you all of the time, but I will never get another chance like this again. Ever." Briana started to cry.

"I know, baby," her mother said. She began to cry also.

"I'll be okay, mom. And, the school is great; the kids are great."

"I know," her mother said.

"Thanks, mom. For understanding. Please tell dad for me. I'm not sure I can go through this on the phone with him."

"Sure. I will tell him."

"Mom?"

"Yeah, honey."

"Are you going to be alright?"

Her mother sniffled into the phone and then cleared her throat. "I'll be fine, honey. So will your dad. It will just take some getting used to."

"For me, too. It will take some getting used to over here, also."

"I know."

"I'm going to go now, mom. I need to get some sleep."

"I love you, honey."

"I love you, mom."

Briana hung up the phone and burst into tears. She grabbed at the bottom of her t-shirt and wiped the tears from her cheeks. She had taken a huge step over the last couple of days; huge steps actually. Now, she had taken the hardest step of all: informing her mom that she wouldn't be home for another six months. Briana was surprised at her own reaction and tears. But she knew it was the right move for her at this moment in her life. She was proud of herself for taking the initiative.

Chapter 4

The next couple of days were more of the same at work. Briana settled in and she and the children – in both classes, began to establish a rapport with one another. She found it quite fulfilling, coming home after a hard day, sitting in her small apartment with a glass of wine and a take-out dish. The children were learning quickly, and she felt that they were giving back quite a bit to her also.

One of the children, Romeo from her earlier class, had decided to act out a little. He was one of the 5-year-olds and he was a bit of a troublemaker. At one point, on Thursday morning, he had drawn a picture of Briana that he passed between two of his friends. When Briana heard a small group of the children laughing, she asked what was so funny. Romeo turned bright red in front of his classmates and tried to hide the drawing. Briana walked over to him and he sheepishly handed the folded paper up to her, looking down at his desk.

Briana slowly unfolded the drawing to find a picture of a woman – a stick-figure woman, presumedly herself, with massive breasts. The figure was drawn in blue crayon and it showed the woman also wearing a short skirt. She looked down at Romeo, not quite sure how to admonish him for his drawing but knew that she should. She asked him to follow her out into the hallway which he did, reluctantly.

"Listen," she said. "It's not nice to draw pictures of people like this."

"Why not?" Romeo said, in perfect English. "Do you not like it?"

She decided to change tactics. "Why were you all laughing at the picture?" Romeo's face turned red once more. "That's why you don't draw pictures of your teacher."

"Eu sinto Muito," he said; he was no stranger to apologizing.

"Romeo?"

"I'm sorry," he repeated. His eyes crept up to Briana's breasts as if to say, I thought my picture was pretty accurate.

"Let's not do this again, okay?" He shook his head. Briana stared down at him. She thought at age five, it was a little too young for children to be thinking like Romeo was, but she was in a different culture. Maybe she was being too hard on him. She reached down and rubbed his head with the palm of her hand. "Let's get back into class, okay?"

"Okay," he said, a smile re-appearing on his face.

They stepped back into the classroom and the two other boys looked over at Romeo. His face still contained a smile, but she hoped he would pass the message onto the other boys in one way or another. The rest of the day went without incident. Briana walked the children out at the end of the day. Standing in the vestibule, she was once again approached by the security man. This time, she held her ground.

"Ms. Campbell," he said standing next to her, looking down. She could smell him. "We will see you tomorrow night, at the club, yes?"

Briana looked up at him. There was something about this man, his power, his confidence. She didn't like it, but she didn't want to push him away either. She had never been around someone like him before.

"I haven't decided," she said. His eyes went wide. She suspected most woman did what he asked of them. She wasn't that type of person.

"Well," he said, exhaling slowly. "I would consider it a personal favor to me if you did show up. There are some people I would like you to meet; very influential people."

"Thank you," she said, not sure what else to say to him.

"Good," he said, whispering now. "Then it is settled. I will expect you at 7 p.m." He turned from her and clapped his hands. "Vamos la," he said to the men and they circled around the children as they left the school.

Briana watched as they left and then turned to go back to her class. Mrs. Alves caught her eye and Briana just rolled her eyes at the woman. She was not in the mood for another lecture.

She sent a message to Jose to see if he was around for a pick-up. He showed up 10 minutes later to take her home. As usual, he was outside of the car waiting for her as she stepped out of the building.

"Jose," she said, as they got underway. "Are you familiar with a club called, A Flor Dourada?" He didn't answer right away, and Briana was about to ask a second time.

"I'm familiar with it, senhorita. Why do you ask?"

"I've been invited there. Tomorrow. I was wondering if you knew anything about it."

"It is very expensive. Top of the line club. Hidden, they say."

"Hidden?"

"Yes, only people with a card can get inside. And, they move the whole club at different times of the year."

"Move the club?" She reached into her bag and pulled

out the card, noticing for the first time that it had no address.

"Yes. It is there one day. And then not there the next day."

"That doesn't sound very good for business."

"Very special club. They don't need money in this club."

"Do you know of anyone that has been there?"

"No. And, maybe you should not go there either."

"Do you think it is dangerous?"

"I don't know, but the people... the people that run these clubs... they are not the nicest people."

"You mean the drug cartel," Briana said, fishing.

"Maybe. Maybe them and the mob people. They are not nice people."

Briana thought of how the invitation was delivered and who actually delivered it. She couldn't disagree with Jose. At the very least, there was some element of danger there.

"Thanks, Jose. I appreciate the info."

They were pulled up in front of her apartment now, and Jose was out of the cab. He held her door for her as she got out and she thanked him once more. He said he would take her to work in the morning, but was tied up later in the afternoon, so she would have to take a different cab home after work.

Inside, Briana fished around on the Internet to see if she could find out any more about the club. There wasn't a single word about it. She knew that she probably shouldn't go to the club, but at the same time, the prospect was intriguing. Just the fact that she could not find out anything about it made her wonder what was inside.

After dinner, she settled into bed before calling her mother. She didn't expect that her follow-up phone call from the previous night was going to go any better, and she was right. For the most part, it was a rehash of the night before with less crying. Her mother did tell her that she was seriously considering coming to visit just before she hung up, which was a little uplifting for both of them.

That night, Briana dreamed of visiting a glorious night club, high on a mountainside, with dangerous men and fabulously dressed women. There was tremendous amounts of food and champagne for everyone to drink and a massive orchestra that played all night long while the men and women danced the night away.

In the morning, as she slipped into Jose's taxi, still undecided about the club later that night, she remembered the dream and wondered if it was a premonition.

"All set for work, senhorita?" Jose said.

"Yes," she said, smiling at him. She was looking forward to today. It would be the last day or a very long work week and she had the whole weekend in front of her. She had pulled together plans before she had taken on the job and she expected go traveling in the morning.

Jose dropped her off at the office and reminded her that he would not be around later in the day. She thanked him and went off to class.

Inside the school, she realized that she had quickly become comfortable with the students and the surroundings. Even Mrs. Alves was bearable – in small doses. Marcos had decided to let her do her own thing since it seemed like the children were getting along well with Briana. He appeared before and after each class, asking her if there was anything she needed. As they were about to get into English writing, she had asked that Marcos provide small pads for each of the children so they could keep their work separate from one another. He liked the idea and told her that they would be ready by Monday.

When classes were over on Friday, Briana waited with

the children for their pickups. Romeo was one of the last to leave, and he gave her a big hug, telling her that he would miss her over the weekend. She responded in kind and then watched him step into a brown Porsche 4-door Panamera. Last to leave, as always, were the three boys and their security team. Briana noticed that the man who had approached her earlier in the week was not with the team this time; another man was standing in his place. They circled around the children and walked them to their car as she waved goodbye.

As she looked out the window, she saw the door open on the lead SUV and a man stepped out. It was the man who had asked her to come to the club. She watched him as he made his way to the office and stepped inside. He carried a box in his hand and walked across the lobby to hand it to her.

"For you," he said. "Should you decide to come tonight. Just call the number on the back of the card." Briana was about to object, but before she could, he turned and walked away leaving her standing there holding he box.

She turned and headed back to the classroom, thinking she would open the box inside, but decided against it. The box could wait until she got home. She rang for a cab and waited in her classroom so as not to get the third degree from the receptionist. When the cab arrived, she told Mrs. Alves to have a good weekend and she left the office without turning back.

At home, she was barely inside before she opened the box, depositing it on the couch as soon as she closed the door. There was a tight red bow around the box, and she tried to untie it but gave up, instead, sliding it off the side of the box. When she opened the lid and parted the tissue paper, she found a beautiful red dress which she promptly lifted from the box.

The material was silk and soft. She held the dress up in front of her and thought it might actually fit her. How could he have done that, she thought? Quickly, she undressed in her living room and slid the dress up over her underwear. It fit rather well, and the fabric felt incredible next to her skin. She stepped into the bathroom and looked into the full-length mirror. It was beautiful.

The dress was short, like a cocktail dress, but it covered her ass. The front, had small ruffles on it and opened into a V. The top of her chest could be seen with a generous cleavage, but she didn't think it was any worse than what she wore to the prom. Of course, her mother didn't like what she wore to the prom, and she wouldn't like this dress either. Clearly, it was showing too much skin. But, when Briana looked in the mirror, she knew she looked beautiful. She would be quite a presence in this dress at the club, she thought.

Had she made up her mind then? Up until she put the dress on, she still had no idea if she would go to the club. In fact, she hadn't even thought about what she would wear if she did go. Now, that part was decided for her and as she stared back at herself in the mirror, adjusting her breasts, looking at her white smile, she realized that the other decision had been made for her also. She would be going to Club A Flor Dourada!

Chapter 5

At 6 p.m., already showered and dressed, Briana dialed the number on the back of the card. A male voice answered and asked for her address. She willingly gave the address and waited for a response.

"Ten minutes. Red sedan. Driver's name is Carlito." The phone went dead.

Briana giggled to herself. It all sounded so cloak and dagger. She had a small purse and her phone – that was all as she went outside to meet the car. It showed up promptly and the driver got out and opened the door for her. His eyes looked her up and down as he stood by the door, and then he closed it after her.

"Comfortable?" he said, once he was back in the car. His voice had a slight accent. Not Portuguese, maybe Russian.

"Yes," she said. She was giddy, a little high on all of the luxury and pomp.

"Very well. It is a short ride – maybe 15 minutes," the driver said. "Please let me know if you need anything."

"Of course," she said, realizing how formal it sounded.

They drove out of the main city and took a turn up into the mountains. It was just like in her dream, she realized. She remembered how much food was at the club in her dream, and she heard her stomach growl as she thought about it. She was quite hungry. She fiddled with the bottom of her dress and stared down at her long legs, her feet tucked into a pair of silver heels – the ones she had actually worn to her prom. She didn't have any other dress shoes. With her first paycheck, she thought she should probably buy another pair.

The road in front of the car suddenly turned dark as they continued their ascent up into the mountains. Fifteen minutes turned into 20 and, for the first time, Briana was beginning to worry. She reached for her phone and quickly texted Jose that she was going to the club. Before he could respond, she threw her phone back into her small purse. At least someone would know where she was – if they could find the place.

"Sorry, miss," the driver said. "It's just up ahead."

"Thank you," Briana responded."

As they made their next turn, the road was flooded with lights and through the windshield, she could make out a grand house in the distance. It was a massive mansion and they were on the lighted approach toward its entry gates.

"Wow!" she heard herself say.

"Beautiful, isn't it?" the driver said.

"Yes," was all she managed as the car made its way along the path.

When they were outside the gates, they swung open in front of them and the car pulled into a small rotunda before stopping. The driver stepped out of the car and made his way around to her door. She knew enough to sit tight until the door was opened and then she slowly stepped out of the car. There were not many people outside of the mansion, but those that were there turned to look at her and smiled. She felt like royalty or a movie star. The driver took her arm and led her to the large door that opened into the house.

"Enjoy yourself, Ms. Briana," the driver said as she stepped into the club. When she turned back to look for him, he was already heading to his car. She wondered briefly how she would get home that evening. When she swung her head back, she no longer cared about the driver.

Briana had stepped into an open foyer area. To her left and right were tuxedoed men who moved quickly to her side. Each of them took one of her arms and led her forward toward a 20-foot wide marble staircase that she presumed led up into the club. They escorted her to the top of the steps and then parted once she was on the red carpeted floor. She noticed people staring at her as she stood at the top of the steps, but she ignored them as she took in the splendor of the club itself.

To her right, what looked like a casino was set up in the distance. It was not overly crowded with people, but she could see men and women mingling by the tables. To her left, a number of small dinner tables dotted a marble floor and then a large glass and brass bar took over the entire back wall. She wasn't sure what direction to move in, so she held her space consuming the enormity of the club.

"Briana, yes?" a man's voice to her left said.

She turned to face the voice and a pleasant-looking man, stared back at her. "Yes," she said.

"Follow me, please."

He took her gently by the arm and guided her to the bar near the back of the room. She looked about, hoping to recognize someone, but she had no idea who she should be looking for. The man brought her to a seat adjacent to the bar and asked her to sit.

"Champagne?"

"Please," she said.

Immediately, a glass was placed in front of her. The man nodded and then he spoke once more.

"I am aware this is a lot to take in," he said. "Our host would very much like to meet you tonight. I will let him know you have arrived."

"Your host?" she asked. "Who is he?"

"I will let him tell you himself, but please, for now, enjoy the champagne. Rafael will provide more if you need it."

"Thank you," Briana said.

When the man left, she spun her stool so she could look out over the club. From the spot she was in, she could see almost the entire floor, the bar at her back. She looked about the room. The club was not crowded, but there could be twice as many people as there were now and it still would look unpopulated; the floor was immense. All of the men that walked through the club had beautiful, well-dressed women on their arms. She continued to watch the couples and she was sure that she had never seen this many beautiful women in one place. How was that possible?

Briana downed the remainder of her champagne as she continued people-watching. When she turned back to the bar, a new, chilled glass awaited her. The bubbles and lack of dinner were going straight to her head. She knew she needed to slow down before she was completely buzzed.

"Quite beautiful," a voice from her side said.

This time she jumped. They had to stop appearing out of nowhere in the club, she thought. She turned to see another dark, handsome man at her side. He was well-dressed and he carried himself differently. She could tell just by his look.

"You scared me," she said.

"I assure you, I did not mean to," he said, his voice deep and melodic. He reached out his hand. "My name is

Esteban."

Briana shook his hand, feeling his warm fingers as he brought her hand to his mouth and gently kissed her fingers. No one had ever done that to her before and she felt her face flush.

"Briana," she said, trying to maintain her poise.

"I know." He took a step back from her now, still holding her hand. His eyes soaked her in, and he smiled. "Patrick was right," he said. "You are quite beautiful."

"Thank you," Briana said, pulling her hand back and placing it awkwardly at her side. She assumed Patrick was the security man who had provided her with the club's card.

"You are probably wondering why you are here," Esteban said. She nodded. His eyes were brown and when she looked up into them, they sparkled in the light. He was tall and thin. Serving as a front man for various factions of one of Brazil's largest cartels, Esteban was well-known and wealthy. He was considered untouchable by many – he was a Made man. Highly respected in the inner circles and a sought-after bachelor. "How about we discuss it over dinner. You must be starving... unless you have eaten already."

"No, I can eat," Briana said, laughing and Esteban laughed with her.

"Good. Food is very important. You don't know that until you don't have any."

He took her hand once more and he lifted her up off of the bar stool. Together they strode across the dance floor. This time, she didn't imagine everyone looking at her; it was clear that they were.

When they approached the dining room, a waiter met them and showed them to a secluded table in the rear. Briana sat down while Esteban whispered something into the waiter's ear. Moments after Esteban sat down, a bottle of red wine was placed at the side of the table. Esteban lifted the bottle and poured each of them a small glass. Then he lifted his glass. Briana did the same.

"To new beginnings in a foreign land... and, to your beauty," he said.

Briana flushed once more and then he tapped his glass with hers and took a small sip as she did the same. The wine was incredibly tasty, and Briana took another sip before she placed the glass back on the table. She looked around for a menu so she could both busy herself as well as get something to eat sooner than later.

"There's no need for a menu," Esteban said, reading her thoughts. "Food will be here soon. In the meantime, let me tell you about myself."

Esteban started by telling Briana a little about the club and why it was formed. How it had become difficult for people, people like himself to find safe places to enjoy themselves. This club, and several others like it, allowed men like him to relax without any fears. He mentioned that it was important to have a retreat, to have some downtime because they all led a very hectic life. When he was silent for a minute, Briana broke into the conversation.

"Who are people 'like you'?" she asked.

Esteban smiled. "Interesting question. I see you get right to the point. I like that. People like me are the very wealthy. Together, we are very powerful, but we are still simple men who want the best things in life just like any normal man – or woman, no?" Briana nodded because she felt it was the right thing to do. "We pursue beauty in all forms. Cars, boats, homes," he said, his arms indicating their surroundings. "For me, it is art. I am an art collector. I have a very large collection and with it has come wealth." He took a long sip of his wine. "And women," he added as he placed his glass on the table. "Beautiful women are my passion. You, Briana, are most beautiful."

Briana had heard the words so many times that night that she hardly blushed when he said it again. It was either repetition or perhaps the wine that dulled her reaction to the compliments. She had formed a question in her mind but lost her train of thought as a team of waiters and waitresses circled the table sliding various plates between the two of them. When they stepped away, they had deposited at least six different types of food and salads on the table.

"My God!" Briana said, remembering her dream from the previous night. "I don't think I've ever seen such a presentation."

"Please, eat," Esteban said. "I am sure you can find something to please your palate."

Briana surveyed the table and chose to sample first the fish and then something with a brown sauce. Esteban took from the different plates and filled his own. They both ate in silence for a few moments until Briana exclaimed how wonderful the fish dish was.

"All of the food they serve here is wonderful. We employ some of the country's best chefs."

"Full time?" she found herself asking.

"Yes, full time. We make it worth their while to stay with us."

"I'm sure you do," she said, giggling to herself. The small sips of wine between bites were definitely getting to her.

"You find that funny?" Esteban asked. She nodded, her mouth filled with food. He let out a loud laugh. "I admire your... what do they call it, moxy?"

Briana almost spit out her food, but instead pulled her napkin up to her mouth and covered it while she coughed.

Esteban smiled back at her as she pulled the napkin away from her face. "Moxy," she said. "That's funny. I don't think anyone back home would say I had moxy."

"You are a strong, confident woman in a strange country," he looked around the room once more, "definitely a strange place. I would call that moxy, no?"

Her wine glass was in her hand again as she took a sip. "Thank you, Esteban. You say the nicest things."

They continued to eat for a while with Esteban asking her what her weekend plans were, what sights she intended to see. Briana told him all of her plans and how she hoped, at the end of the six months, that she would be able to travel into eastern Europe before she returned home. He asked if her plans were to attend college back home, and she told him she intended to, but that she wanted to leave the door open in case something wonderful happened while she was abroad. He told her he thought that was a good idea, and that he would be more than happy to show her around his country when she had the time.

As the plates from dinner were cleared, Esteban switched to discussing desserts, telling Briana that she would be remiss if she didn't try the various delicacies the club had to offer including the Brigadeiro samples, a variety of truffles, and the Mousse de Maracuja. Both, he said, were the finest he had had in the country.

"Well, I would not want to waste a recommendation like that," she said.

Before her sentence was finished, dishes of both desserts were on the table. "Oh, my," she said as she brought one to her mouth. Esteban stared at her lips as she devoured the truffle. She realized for the first time that he was starting at her, and also that she liked when he looked at her. When dessert was over, Briana was incredibly full. She had eaten more than she expected during the main meal and completely overdid it during dessert.

"Care to dance, Briana," Esteban said, as he stood up from the table, unbuttoning the top button of his suit jacket.

She looked up at him. He was quite handsome, she thought. His body was thin and long and as he lent his hand to her to lift her from her seat, she noticed the length of his fingers and felt his strong hands.

"I'm not sure I will be a very good dancer here," she said.

"Nonsense," Esteban said. "Everyone is a good dancer in Rio. You just have to let the music move you."

He took her hand and led her out of the dining room. She briefly thought that someone needed to pay for the meal, but quickly dismissed that as she caught up with Esteban and he pulled her alongside of him. Briana tucked her hand behind his arm as he led her across the large marble floor. Everyone in the place stared at them as they entered a large dance floor almost completely on the other side of the club, passed the casino. There was no orchestra, Briana noted, but there was a DJ who was playing club music at a respectable level.

"First, drinks," Esteban said as they glided over to the bar. He was handed two champagnes and he offered one to Briana. "Are you enjoying yourself?"

"Yes," she said, nodding her head. She was enjoying herself quite a bit, she realized.

"Good," he said, tapping her glass. "That is what life is all about."

Briana and Esteban finished their champagne as he stared into her eyes. She didn't know this man, but she felt attracted to him. She couldn't recall that happening to her before, but she decided to go with the feelings. He was wealthy and well-known. She was certainly enjoying his company.

"Let's dance. I want everyone to see me dancing with the most beautiful woman in the room." He took her hand and led her to the dance floor.

The music in the club, despite it not being loud, had a deep bass beat that seemed to vibrate anything on the floor. Briana could feel the beat and she was swaying slowly to it as they entered a small section of the dance floor. Esteban took her by the hips and pulled her toward him. She placed a hand on his shoulder and the two of them began to dance slowly to the music. He pulled her tighter against him as they moved slowly across the floor.

Briana could smell Esteban now. His aftershave and his manly scent were very apparent. She slid her arms around his neck as they danced and she felt his hands slide down her back, just above her ass. He looked into her eyes as they danced, and she smiled and lost herself in them. The music, the food, the drinks, were all so much. She inhaled, as she rested her head on his shoulder, breathing him in. He smelled good, very good. This all felt so good, she thought.

As the song they were slow dancing to came to an end, a new song with a similar beat was mixed in. Esteban picked her head up off his shoulder and looked into her eyes once more. This time, he leaned in to kiss her and Briana met his lips with hers. She felt an immediate electricity as their lips touched and his hands slid down over her ass and pulled her tight against him. She could feel his hardness against her as she slid her tongue into his mouth.

They kissed as they swayed on the floor for a long time. His tongue was thick and warm, and she swallowed it into her mouth. Her hand slid behind his head pulling his mouth closer to hers as she licked and sucked on his tongue. She could feel her body break into a sweat as he gently grinded against her, his strong fingers kneading her ass through her dress.

When they finally broke from their kiss, Briana pulled her head back and smiled at him, her breathing coming in short spurts. There was no mistaking that he was as excited as she was as he held her tight against him. He smiled back at her and the mouthed the word, 'beautiful.' She leaned forward and kissed him again sliding her tongue back between his lips.

Time seemed to stand still as they kissed and swayed on the dance floor. She no longer heard the music, at least not the music played by the DJ. Instead, she heard her own pulse, in her ears and chest as her heart beat faster and harder. This time, Esteban pulled his head away and he stepped back from Briana. He looked into her eyes, his palm making small circles on her ass. He led her back toward the bar, and he picked up two more glasses of champagne. He handed one to Briana and toasted her once more, his hand never leaving her bottom. She looked into his dark brown eyes as she lifted the glass to her mouth and swallowed it down.

"Who are you?" she said.

He turned her so her back was facing the bar and slid his hand up under the bottom of her dress as he sipped his drink. Briana could feel his fingers slide across her underwear and she let out an audible moan. She knew she should stop him; they were in the middle of the club, but she almost melted at his touch.

"Take them off," he said.

"What?"

"Take them off. No one will know, but us."

"I will know, Esteban."

His hand squeezed her ass through her thin panties, his

thumb pressing hard against her. Briana had never done anything remotely like what Esteban was asking, but his hand felt so good on her body. Her entire body was on fire. She shook her head; no, she would not take them off.

He looked into her eyes. "Take them off, Briana. Slide them down."

Slowly, with her eyes looking past Esteban onto the dance floor to see if anyone was watching, she moved her hands to her sides and one side at a time, slid the waistband of her underwear down over her hips. Esteban helped her by sliding his hand into the back of her underwear and pushing them down over her cheeks. While she continued to look out at the dance floor, she felt her panties slide down her thighs and come to rest at her ankles. His hand and his warm fingers slid onto her flesh and cupped her cheek.

"Excellent," Esteban said. "Now, let's dance once more."

She didn't put up a fight as he pulled her onto the floor. His hand slipped out from under her dress and fixed the dress, so it covered her ass. They drifted out to a corner of the floor and she slipped her arms back around his neck once more. She wanted to feel him grind into her again.

Esteban wasted no time, his hand sliding down to her hips and ass. He pulled her tight and she moaned as she looked up into his eyes. Briana felt naked without the protection of her underwear, but she also felt free, and incredibly sexy. She knew others were watching them and that was okay with her. She was with the sexiest man in the room, and he had told her she was the most beautiful. They should be staring, she thought. They were a couple to be stared at.

She leaned forward and covered his mouth with hers. At some point, as their tongues wrestled, she felt his hand creep back up under her dress, but it didn't matter, she wanted it there. She gently grinded into him as his hand ran across her smooth skin and she sucked on his silken tongue. Her body was one with his and as far as she was concerned, there was no one else in the room. Her own hands slid down from his neck, over his back onto his ass. She pulled him toward her, his hard member pressing up against her. She repositioned herself to feel him better, through her dress, rubbing up against him.

Briana pulled away from his kiss and stared into his eyes. Her insides were smoldering. She felt sexy and dirty. Her eyes implored him to take her off the dance floor while her hips and hands contradicted them. He smiled at her and he stepped back from her, his hands quickly fixing her dress. They were both breathing heavy and he took a deep breath.

"Perhaps, we should get out of here," he said, taking her hand and leading her over to the bar. "One for the road?" Briana nodded and accepted a glass of champagne from him. Tipping his glass, she smiled. "To your beauty," he said.

They both swallowed their champagne and he slowly walked her across the floor. Every head turned to look at them and Briana never felt more excited. Her nipples were hard, and she was wet down below, wearing no panties as this crowd looked on at them both. She felt free, and sexy and beautiful. She never felt more beautiful in her life. She held onto Esteban's arm as he led her down the big marble staircase. The tuxedoed men opened the large entrance doors and the two of them stepped out into the large courtyard.

While they waited, for what Briana assumed was his car to arrive, Esteban lifted her chin so she looked up at him, and placed a gentle kiss on her lips. He smiled at her as a car pulled up next to them. The driver moved around the car and opened the door for them. Briana slid in first, holding her dress down and Esteban slid in next to her. She slid across the seat, so she was tight against him and he slid his arm around her shoulders as the car sped away. She had no idea where he was taking her, but she didn't care. As long as they were together at this moment in time, that was all that mattered.

She felt Esteban's free hand move onto her thigh and slowly push the end of her dress up. She looked over at him as he lifted his arm out from around her neck and with both hands, slid her dress further up her thighs. Then, she watched as he slid down off of the seat onto his knees and he buried his head into her lap. Briana only hoped that the window between the driver and the rear seat was soundproof because she moaned loudly and cried out several times during the ride to Esteban's home, her hands holding his head tight between her spread legs.

Chapter 6

When Briana and Esteban arrived at his home, she had recovered from the pleasure he'd administered. By the time the driver came around to open their door, she had her breathing under control and was ready to leave the car. An ear-to-ear smile spread across her face; one she knew she would have trouble soon removing. Esteban stepped out of the car, and took her hand lifting her up and out of the seat. She hugged herself tight against his arm as they walked down the long path to the front of the enormous house, his arm wrapped around her shoulders.

No one had ever made her feel as Esteban had made her feel during the car ride home. She found herself giving into him wholly and completely, something she had never done before. Now, as she walked through the entrance and into his home, she pushed him up against the wall, and kissed him deeply. Her body was ready to return the favor in any way he wanted. They kissed for a long time, her hands running up and down the sides of his body. When they broke from the kiss, he stared at her.

"I have something to show you," he said.

She tilted her head. Her hands were around his neck now and her mind focused on only one thing. "And what is that, Esteban," she said, her voice low and sultry.

He stepped away from the wall, grabbing her hand. "You asked what I do for a living and I told you I collect art and beautiful things." Briana nodded as he spoke. "I'd like to show you part of the collection I have at this home."

He pulled her up a short set of carpeted steps that led to a main living area. As they reached the top of the steps, the lights came on revealing a large room filled with many colors. Adorning the walls were various pieces of art that reminded her of museum pieces, most of which she was not familiar with. Esteban smiled at her confusion and led her across the room. He detailed each of the many paintings as they walked along the long wall, identifying the artist and the period in which the piece was painted. He seemed very at home talking about his collection and Briana saw something different in him as he paced about the room. When they reached the far end of the room, Briana's head swimming with all of the information, he stopped and turned toward her.

"All of this art – and three more floors of it, and still the most beautiful thing in the room is you." He pulled her toward him and kissed her softly as she melted into his arms.

Briana felt her excitement returning as she pressed her body against Esteban, her arms reaching around his neck. She felt his hands slide down over her back and she willed them down to her ass. When he reached the base of her dress, she gently grinded into him. They were back on the dance floor again, but this time there was no music and no one there to watch them. They could do whatever they wanted. She slowly began to slide down to her knees.

He let her slide halfway down, her hands on his belt, working the buckle before he stopped her. "Wait," he said.

She looked up at him, her big eyes staring into his. She wanted to do this for him. "Let's go upstairs where it is more comfortable." She smiled and fought him briefly, but his strong arms pulled her up in front of him.

Briana visibly pouted as he turned her around, his hands on her hips, leading her out of the room. She giggled, still buzzed as he stepped to her side and took her hand. As they walked to another set of steps across the room, Briana felt her body reacting to all that had happened. She wanted nothing more than to be with this mysterious man who had set her body on fire. As they approached the steps, her fingers folded into his and she leaned into his arm. The sound of her phone suddenly broke through her haze.

Flushed, she let Esteban's hand go and reached into her small bag. She looked at him, embarrassed that her phone had broken the mood and then stared at the screen. It was her alarm, set to remind her to call her mom. Damn, she thought. Not now. But she knew if she didn't call now, she would not be in any position to call later.

She stopped walking and turned to Esteban. "Do you mind?" she said. "I need to make a quick call."

He stared at her and then he smiled, stepping back, releasing her hand. "Of course," he said. "But you will not get any service in this house. If you like, you can use the blue house phone," he pointed to the side of the room. "It will allow you to make calls anywhere."

"It is to my mom," she said.

"That's fine, Briana," he said instructing her how to make the overseas call. "I will get you another champagne as you make your call and then we can relax, yes?"

"Yes, Esteban," she said, stepping close to him and kissing him softly. "That would be very nice. I promise not to be long."

Esteban stepped away from her and walked across the long room to a bar that sat in the corner. Like everything else, it was beautifully curated. When he stepped behind it, she walked over to the blue phone and dialed her home, using the directions from Esteban. When her mother answered, she was surprised she had gotten it right the first time.

"Hello?" her mother's voice said.

"Hi, mom, it's me, Bree."

"Hi, Bree, where are you calling from."

"The office," she said, creating the lie on the fly. She didn't need to get into the reason why she was not calling from her own phone or, worse yet, a man's phone.

"Are you okay, honey? Your voice sounds funny."

"I'm sorry, mom. Just tired is all," she consciously raised the level of her voice while cupping the bottom of the phone with her hand. She felt foolish that she was calling her mother when she should be wrapped in the arms of the handsome man across the room. Still, she had not been away long and that it would be better to get the call out of the way.

"Is the new job hard?" her mother said, recognizing her new role for the first time.

"No, not really. Just a lot of hours this first week. I'm hoping that I settle in next week and that everything becomes easier. Everyone is very nice there," she added.

"Good." There was a short pause and then her mother said, "Your dad says hi. He stepped out to get some ice cream for me. He knows the way to this woman's heart."

Briana laughed and her mother laughed with her. It felt good to laugh with her mother again. The last couple of calls had been very tense; this call seemed to be lighter. There was an audible pop across the room and Briana watched as

Esteban poured champagne into two fluted glasses.

"I spoke to your dad about coming over and he thinks it's a great idea. We've been looking at flights and hotels."

"That's good, mom. It would be great to see you. And, I can start looking for places to stay; maybe even a bigger apartment since I am making some money now."

Briana realized that she needed to move the phone call along. All of the magic that she and Esteban had shared was quickly slipping away.

"Hey, mom. I'm pretty tired. I just wanted to call and say goodnight. I'm off tomorrow, so I can call, and we can discuss plans for your trip here."

"Okay, honey," her mom said.

"I love you mom. I'll call you in the morning."

"I love you too, Briana. Have a good night."

Briana hung up the phone. She dwelled briefly on how nice it was to be able to have parents that loved and cared about her so much. She started her walk across the long room. She felt Esteban's eyes watch her as she approached the bar, and she never felt more beautiful. He stepped out from behind it, holding two glasses in his hands. He smiled at her and she smiled back as he offered her the glass in his right hand. The phone call with her mother was quickly forgotten as she stepped close to him and kissed him gently. They tapped glasses took a small sip, and then Esteban took her hand and started to lead her back toward the steps. She reached back to the bar and grabbed the bottle, giggling as she followed him, the electricity in her body building once more.

At the top of the steps, the turned down a wide hallway. It was dimly lit and Esteban told her that it was necessary to protect the paintings that hung on both sides. She glanced at them as they walked, noting the gilded frames and different sizes. At one point, Esteban stopped walking and turned her toward a painting. He took a deep breath as he admired it. The painting depicted a woman, alone in a jungle setting. She was completely naked. In the distance, a tiger lurked, his eyes staring in her direction. She looked peaceful, unknowing; the muscles and texture of her skin visible on the canvas.

"This painting is by José Maria de Medeiro from the early 1900's. Most people believe it was lost in a fire some years back, but this is the original. It has no name. The woman is drawn so perfect. Yet, she is unsuspecting, no?" Briana nodded. "Soon, the tiger will take her, and she will never see it coming. Natural selection is God's plan, and it is beautiful." He turned to Briana and smiled.

"Is it worth a lot of money?" she asked, not knowing how to respond to his comments, but wanted to be part of the conversation.

"It is priceless, Briana. As many of the paintings in this hallway are." He looked at her and at that moment, she felt like a piece of art, a sculpture. She saw the way he stared at her, consuming her with his eyes. "Come," he said.

They walked the short distance to a room near the end of the hallway. Esteban opened the door to a large bedroom. In the center of the room was a massive four-post bed, its posts extending up to the raised ceilings. Along the top, rested a colorful tapestry that captured Briana's eye as she moved further into the room. She felt Esteban step up behind her as she admired the furniture and the room. His fingers slipped the zipper down in the back of her dress and she let out a quiet moan. Esteban turned her to face him.

"Finish your drink, Briana."

He tapped her glass with his. He watched as she swallowed it all down and then he did the same with his. He took her glass and placed both of the them on the dresser at the side of the room. When he turned back, Briana was slowly slipping out of her dress in front of him. She swayed her hips as she had on the dance floor, humming to a song in her head as she stared at him. As the dress fell to the floor, she stepped out of it. She stood in front of Esteban in only her bra, her panties left long ago at the club. His eyes walked down the front of her body slowly and she felt herself shiver as she reached behind her to unclip her bra. One of her hands held it in front of her as she released the clasp. Slowly, she peeled it off of her chest revealing her large, perfect breasts. She could see in Esteban's eyes his appreciation for her beauty and she smiled at him as she stepped closer.

Esteban slid his hand over one of her breasts, his fingers warm, and gently circled her nipple as Briana let out a quiet moan. He pulled himself still closer still, his arms wrapping around her back as her breasts pressed into him. She wanted to feel his chest against hers, his warm skin next to her. Briana pulled herself back and began to work the buttons on his shirt, slowly and methodically unbuttoning as she gently swayed before him in the large bedroom.

The first button opened easily, but she had trouble with the second. It was out of focus, the champagne having more of an effect on her than she thought. She giggled, refocusing her thumb and forefingers and worked opened the second button. Esteban's hands were on her hips watching her fingers move to the next button. Why were there so many buttons, she thought as she pulled his shirt tails out from his pants?

"I'm sorry," she said, as she fumbled with the next button. Esteban covered her hands with his and helped her with the buttons, working his way down his shirt. "Thank you," she said as the last button opened revealing his sculpted chest. "Wow!" Briana said aloud, even though she meant to keep it to herself. She giggled once more.

Her hands slid up his chest and she looked up into his face. Esteban stared back at her as her hands slid down over his abs to his belt. Both of her hands worked the buckle and this time he did not stop her. It took longer than she expected, but she finally pulled the ends apart and unclipped the top of his pants. Briana fumbled with the top of his pants. What's wrong with me? His hand undid his pants at his waist.

"I'm sorry," she said, her words slurred. Christ, she thought. Am I wasted? Standing naked with this beautiful man in front of me. Her hands reached into his pants clumsily. "I'm sorry," she said again, looking up at him.

Briana thought she saw a smile and then his hands reached for her. "Come, Briana," he said. "Let's get you over to the bed." She walked alongside of him as he guided her to the big bed in the middle of the room. It was raised several feet off of the floor. Esteban bent toward her and lifted her up into his arms. He placed her on the side of the bed, onto her back. "There you go," he said.

"I'm sor..." she tried again; the words just didn't come. Her head raced. She felt her muscles relax and she tried to lift her arm. She looked at Esteban as he smiled down at her on the bed. Her vision was blurry. "Esth..." she could not say his name. She tried to lift her arm to reach for him, but nothing happened.

Esteban stared down at her naked body. He ran his fingers down the side of her face, over her long neck and gently prodded her breasts, her nipples reacting to his touch. She stared up at him, a silly smile planted on her face, her eyes opened wide. He knew she could hear him, feel his touch, and he also knew that she could not move, her

74

muscles were totally relaxed. The drug he had given her in the glass of champagne was not designed for human consumption. Administered properly, it would render the patient immobile for hours. Coupled with the alcohol Briana had consumed throughout the night, it would also dull her mind to the point where she might black out. He hoped that would not happen; it would only make what he had to do more difficult.

Esteban took his time admiring her body, his hands running along her smooth skin. He was extremely hard as he traced a path over her stomach, down between her legs and finally down the length of her right leg. Stepping back from the bed, he smiled. She was incredibly beautiful. He looked into her face as a tear fell from one of her eyes. Her mind was trying to rationalize what was happening, but it would not be able to. The drug he had given her would ensure that. He leaned forward and kissed her gently on the lips. Her vapid eyes watched him pull his head away. Then Esteban got down to business.

Chapter 7

Esteban stepped away from the bed slowly moving across the room. He picked up a blue phone on the dresser and made a quick call. Stepping back to the bed, he reached into the bottom drawer of the bedside table and pulled out a small box. Reaching inside, he pulled out two sections of rope and some clothes. He placed them on the bed and pulled on a pair of latex gloves.

He climbed onto the bed onto his knees alongside of Briana. He fanned out the material from the box. It was a short, grey coverall. Gently, he lifted her feet and worked the grey material up her body and over her ass. Then he manipulated her arms into the sleeves of the outfit and then zipped it up over her chest watching her amazing breasts disappear. He rolled Briana's body onto her stomach on the mattress. She grunted as he turned her, and he fixed her head so it was sideways on the pillow. He could hear her breathing normally which was very important. Esteban pulled her arms behind her back. With the first piece of rope, he bound her wrists together, checking his knots to make sure that they were tight. She didn't struggle; she couldn't.

Next, he slid his hand down her back, over her shapely

ass, dragging his fingers down her long legs. With the other rope, he tied her ankles together, once more checking his knots. Briana lay there before him, her eyes opened. He gently closed her eyelids and stepped back from the bed. The clock showed 11 p.m. He had about another 10 minutes before his team showed up. He made his way across the room, still wearing the gloves.

Esteban slid the gloves off his hands and deposited them in a plastic bag. The bag would be sent separately with the extraction team. Her clothes, the sheets and anything that could identify her would be placed in a separate bag and would also leave with the team. They would burn the contents of both bags somewhere far away from Esteban's home. He stared down at Briana's body. Her long legs extending from the grey outfit, her arms and legs trussed up as he waited for the team.

****

The extraction team consisted of two men; two very strong men. They knocked at the door and entered the apartment on his orders. They swiftly moved about the house; their moves rehearsed. They had done this more than once. They spoke little as they collected items about the house, directed by Esteban. They lifted Briana off the bed, placing her on the floor next to it before they stripped the sheets. They sprayed something on the bed and then did a final sweep making sure they removed the glasses, and her pocketbook. They handed her phone to Esteban and he reached in and pulled the SIM card from it. He knew that the phone would be crushed and burned along with the other items. He also knew that there would be no trace of her phone ever having been at his home as he used sophisticated equipment to block all signals starting more than a mile away. The same was true of the club. He made sure the blue phone was used as he knew it would not lead back to his home as it was routed through many different places show up as a withheld number.

When the team was satisfied that they had properly swept the apartment, they nodded to Esteban. He nodded back and they moved to the side of the bed to reach down and pick up Briana. One of the men, lifted her over his shoulder and turned to walk toward the door. The other followed looking about to make sure that nothing else was left behind. At the door, he picked up three white plastic bags. He followed the man carrying Briana's body out the door. Esteban closed the door behind them and then walked to the bar and poured himself a glass of whiskey. He had added to his collection this evening. A beautiful piece. In the case of Briana, it would not hang on his wall, nor would it be hidden from view to only be seen by a few. Briana, he knew would be seen by many.

****

Under the cover of darkness, not that it mattered, Esteban's home was set deep in the mountains, the two men spoke Portuguese as they slid Briana's body into the back of a large SUV. They drove for about two hours to the small area of Botafogo, an ocean city with views of the mountains. They stopped along the perimeter of the half-moon bay. Another car was to meet them here. Both of the men were tired and rested their heads back as they waited for the other vehicle.

"Acorde! Acorde!" Wake Up! Wake Up! The words were accompanied by a pounding on the window. Tacito, the driver, was the first to wake up. Startled, he grabbed the wheel with one hand and his gun with the other. He turned to the source of the sound, men pounding on the window and he raised his hands in the air.

"Basta!" Enough, he screamed back at the men who calmed down when they saw he was reacting.

Across from him, Oson, the other man who 'cleaned' Esteban's home opened his door and stepped out of the car. Tacito did the same. There was some argument amongst the men then finally, they moved to the back of the SUV.

One of the new men spoke before they opened the door. In English, he said, "She is blindfolded, yes?"

Oson and Tacito looked at one another. They had not remembered to put a blindfold or a bag over her head. If she was awake when they opened the rear of the car, she would see their faces. Their silence and confusion were a solid indication that they had not taken that step. The man looked at them both, told them they were worthless and that he would report their slip-up back to Esteban. Tacito begged the man not to do so.

"Help us with her and perhaps I can overlook this," he said, in perfect English.

Tacito went to the side of the car and pulled out a burlap bag. He looked at Oson and told him to open the hatch on the SUV. Oson opened it and Tacito slipped the bag over Briana's head. Luckily for him she was sleeping from the effects of the drug and alcohol. He tied it at the base making sure that it kept the bag on her head but did not cut off her breathing. He stepped back from the car and looked at the hand-off men.

"Now bring her over and put her in the van."

Neither of the transporters wanted to touch Briana if they didn't have to, and the one who did the most talking seemed to be getting a kick out of ordering Tacito and Oson around. No one seemed concerned that this was all happening while a woman lay drugged and bound in the car beside them.

Oson started to protest, but Tacito hit him on the side. If they moved the body and put it in the van, perhaps the driver would forget about their mistake. They moved to the car and lifted Briana slowly, one from her feet, the other from her shoulders.

Briana wasn't sure what was happened, but she thought she felt her body being lifted into the air. She had no idea where she was and when she tried to open her eyes, they didn't seem to respond. Nor, for that matter did any of her limbs. It could all be a dream, she thought, but something in the back of her mind told her that was not the case. She felt herself being carried and she tried to struggle. Nothing. She concentrated, hoping to buck her body a little since she couldn't move her arms or legs.

The men carrying Briana were half-way between the two vehicles when her body shifted, on its own and then bucked between them, the head coming up first and then the knees buckling.

"Fuck!" Tacito said and they both moved quicker between the two cars.

The rear doors were open on the black van and they slid her inside. She moved once more as Oson dropped her legs. He stepped back out of surprise and then punched her hard in the face. Briana felt only the blow and nothing after.

Tacito pulled Oson back and they closed the doors. The two men, the new drivers, shook their heads. It was the worst hand-off they had ever been part of. There was so little to fuck up, but these two managed to do it more than once. Oson started to defend himself, but Tacito once again cut him off.

"Completo," Tacito said, and they both walked to their SUV, never turning their backs on the two men.

Inside the car, Oson started to complain, but Tacito shot him a look that shut him up immediately. They drove in silence for most of the trip back.

The men double-checked the back of the van to make sure that Briana was still properly bound and that the bag remained on her head. They didn't trust the two idiots who brought her to them. When they were sure she was secure, they got into the van and left. They had another hour's drive before they would be able to deliver the woman and the night was growing longer.

Chapter 8

None of this seemed right, Briana thought as her eyes searched for answers. She could see nothing and her arms, pinned behind her for some reason were of no help. Her head hurt, throbbing horribly on her right side. Had she fallen, a car accident? Her mind was a fog; her thoughts cryptic. She tried again to move her arms to no avail. Were they bound behind her? It didn't make any sense. She lay on her side, that much she could tell, but there was nothing but darkness; 'pitch-black' her mind repeated to her.

Her other senses sprung to life. The smell of wet paper, burlap maybe. Something abrasive on her wrists, rubbing against her skin as she tried to move her arms. Her breathing hampered, but not impossible. She had a metallic taste in her mouth, copper maybe, the taste of blood. Definitely, blood. Her heart raced. She shifted her legs, trying to pull them up under her, to sit up. They didn't move freely. Her mind had figured something out, but her body was still working through the situation, rationalizing, adjusting like a child in the dark. A naked woman, a tiger in the jungle. The low rumble of an engine and the occasional bounce of her body indicated to her that she was in a moving vehicle.

She shook her head, trying to clear the fog, something shifted in front of her. She moved her head again. Sniffing. Wet burlap. Copper. She drifted off once more, a painting of a beautiful woman sitting on a horse. She pulled hard at the restraints on her wrists, feeling them cut into her skin this time, the pain jolting her back to reality. She was bound. What the fuck? Take stock, Briana. Think through this. Wake up! The club, the dance floor. Esteban.

"Huh?" she said, her voice, muffled, echoed back to her. "Help!"

She pulled again at the ropes behind her, kicking her feet trying to break free. Why couldn't she see? She shook her head. She felt it this time. Sliding in front of her, pressing up against her face, her neck. The smell. Her heart raced. Tears spilled from her eyes as she began to sob. Reality was a rude awakening. I was naked. In his bedroom. Everything came together in a fraction of a second presenting a stunning revelation that was much too horrible to conceive.

"Nooo..." she heard herself cry out, kicking and tugging futilely at the restraints, her body bucking.

Her sobs increased, her breathing coming in gasps as she inhaled, tasting the burlap bag that covered her head. Briana writhed on the floor of the moving vehicle, her mind racing with images, realities, memories of movies and her mother's own words of warning, "trust no one!" All for naught, she thought. All for naught. Focus. Get a grip. It was too much. The car ride; the champagne. She lay on the floor and cried, her mind playing back the last memories she had.

She had been with Esteban. At his home. After the amazing time at the club, and the incredible ride in the back seat of his limo. They were admiring his art collection. He was glib about it, she remembered, proud of his work. She felt lucky to have met him. He offered her another drink, and as she lost herself in his eyes, those amazing eyes, she remembered swallowing down the champagne and then him taking the glass from her, leading her to the bed. That was it. There was nothing else. Fear gripped her body, froze all of her save her tears and cries.

Briana wasn't sure how long she sobbed or laid unmoving in the back of the moving vehicle. Her thoughts forged her new reality and she remained unable to address it. Lay here, someone will help, she thought, but she knew that to be untrue. As she lay there, she came to understand that no one would come to help her; only she could save herself. Think, damn it! Think!

Rational thought was impossible. Too many unknowns; too many scenarios. Until she knew more, she was confused and useless. Breaking out of the ropes that cut into her wrists and ankles was the only thing on which she could focus. She tried first to make her hands as small as possible. One free hand was all she needed. Making a fist with first the left hand and then the right. Then, loosening up her fist, pointing her fingers, she tried again to no avail. The rope tore at her skin as she tried to break free. So what? If tearing at her skin would get her out of this predicament, so what? She pulled harder, pain exploding in her elbows as she lifted her arms, pulling against the ropes. Nothing. Frustrated, Briana resorted to crying once more, her head resting on the floor of the van bouncing up and down as it continued on its journey.

Where could they be taking me? Who was taking me? What did they want with me? All of these questions flashed through her head. Headlines of the stories her mother presented her before the trip appeared in her mind. She tried to slow her thoughts down; to bring them under control, but it was no use. It was all so futile. How did she get herself into this situation?

The van took a hard-right turn and Briana felt herself sliding to one side. Without the ability to protect herself, she rolled across the van and smacked into the opposite side. The wheel-well of the van struck up against her back, her bound hands breaking part of the blow, but the pain was sufficient enough to elicit a loud cry. Briana bit her lip as she clamped her mouth shut, conscious that she might attract unwanted attention from whomever was driving the van. As she cried to herself, tightening her back muscles to absorb the pain as best she could, she worked herself up against the side of the van, by pressing her feet against the back wall and scooting until her injured back was pressed against the van.

She felt the vehicle slow down and she inhaled deeply as she pulled her wits about her. Then the car sped forward once more; this time over what she assumed was a poorly paved or dirt road. As the van bounced up and down, Briana felt herself slide back down the side of the van and back onto her back. Through a variety of twists, turns and bumps, she was tossed about the back of the van like a large piece of meat. When it finally came to a stop, the momentum of the van propelled her against the back of the front seats causing once more a jarring blow to her back. She let out a loud grunt as she heard the engine of the van shutdown. Despite the pain, her eyes opened wide and started to think once more about her own survival. She remained still, attempting to control her own breathing and sobbing as she heard the voices of men outside the vehicle.

The rear doors of the van opened and despite the burlap sack over her head, she saw light from outside and felt the wind rush around her in the van. She didn't move, not sure what she should do. She felt a hand on her ankle and involuntarily pulled her feet away. She heard laughter and some muffled conversation. A hand fell on each of her ankles and her body was pulled across the base of the van. Her head banged on the metal floor as the strong hands pulled her to the open doors. She grunted as her body was lifted and grunted louder as she was thrown over the shoulder of one of the men, her head smacking into his muscly back, jarring her neck as he began to carry her away from the car.

"Where... where are you taking me?" she muttered, not sure if her voice could be heard outside of the bag surrounding her head. She inhaled deeply and the bag was sucked into her mouth that she quickly spat out. "Help!" she yelled, and she heard laughter once again.

"Quieto!" growled one of the men. She now knew that they could hear her.

"Help!" she screamed once more, finding her voice. "Someone help me!"

"No one can hear you. Save your strength," a man's voice said. "You're going to need it."

Briana was carried a little distance further before the man holding her stopped. She heard keys, her aural sense compensating for her lack of sight. Then a door opening. There's a woman's voice and then Briana felt herself floating in the air as she was hoisted off the man's shoulder and flipped on her back, onto a mattress or couch. Her landing was soft. She laid there motionless for a moment and then once again, tried to free her hands.

"This one has spirit," said one of the men. "Deal with her."

Quickly, Briana sucked in her cries and stopped pulling on her ropes. She heard some more conversation that she couldn't make out and then some shuffling in the room as she laid still on the bed or the couch. Finally, she heard a door close and, thinking she is alone, she began her futile struggle once more. Her sobs returning.

"Stop, stop," someone said. A woman this time.

"Help me! Untie me! Get this fucking thing off of my head!" Briana sobbed.

"Stop struggling. It will only make it worse." Briana listened to the voice. It was clearly a woman.

"Then help me or I will scream until someone comes to help me!"

"Okay! Okay." The voice was closer now and Briana could feel someone touching her shoulder. She recoiled and the voice told her to stop moving.

"Let me help you."

Briana held still and soon felt the bag being lifted up over her head. Light came into focus and she shook her head. She squinted, trying to gain focus on the woman in the room. She saw a young woman.

"Untie me!"

"Easy. Slow down and I will help you," the voice said. Briana thought the words were slurred, but she knew it could be her own perception having just been freed from the bag.

Briana took a deep breath. She was ready to break, but she held herself together. Let this woman free you from these ropes and then you can find a way out of here.

"My God! Look at your face," the woman said, slightly slurred with a slight giggle. Briana was sitting up now. She could feel her fingers working the knots on her wrists. "What did they do to you?"

She looked around the room. It was a hotel room of sorts. There were two beds, a mirror on the wall and a bedtable between the beds. There was a door to the outside and another door inside the room which she assumed was the bathroom. She turned to face the woman who was freeing her arms. Young, blond, she noticed. Her fingers worked the knots.

"Hurry!" she urged.

"We have time," the girl said. "I can't get the knots... stop moving!"

Briana held still. Finally, after another minute, her hands were free. She pulled her arms forward, feeling the pain in her shoulders and biceps. Immediately, she reached down to untie her ankles. She was crying now, almost free, she thought. Once she got these off, she and this woman could go, get away. She would figure all of this out once she was away and safe. The knots on her ankles were not coming free. She pulled and tugged at them as tears rolled down her face, her breathing coming in short gasps.

"Let me help you."

"Get away!" Briana heard herself say to the woman who had helped free her arms.

The woman stared back at her, shook her head as if clearing it and then tried again. "Let me help you."

Briana let her hands fall to her sides and the woman slowly worked the knots free on her ankles. When she did, Briana didn't stand up immediately. She didn't break for the door. Her mind knew more than she did. Instead, she bent her knees and pulled her legs up close to her as she sat on the bed, her arms wrapping around her legs. Tears freely flowed down her face as she cried, looking at the other woman.

"I'm Lily," the woman said. "Do you want some water?"

"Yes," Briana said. She watched as Lily went into the small room next to them and returned with a plastic glass of water. "Thank you," she managed.

She drank through her sobs, managing half of the glass

down before she began to cough and choke. Lily took the glass away from her.

"Small sips," she said.

Lily stood up from the bed and walked around it, looking down at Briana. Together, they reviewed each other, both wary of one another. Lily was dressed in a pair of blue doctor's scrubs – both top and bottom. Her hair was a mess and her eyes were wild, her pupils black and large, like she was drugged.

"You're pretty," Lily said. "Not right this moment, but you are very pretty."

Briana had gotten her breathing under control. Now she was trying to figure out her situation. Who was this Lily? What did she have to do with anything?

"Who are you? Where are we?"

"Don't know," Lily said.

"Can we get out of here?"

"Armed guards at the door. I'm here to get you cleaned up."

"Have you been you kidnapped too?"

"Yes. Some time ago. I don't know how long."

"Do you know what they want?"

"I don't think about that. They keep me drugged-up and I keep quiet." Lily sat down on the end of the bed and stared into Briana's face. "We should clean you up. There are some clothes here for you also."

"You knew I was coming?"

"No. I don't know anything, but you need to get out of those clothes."

Briana looked down to find that she was wearing a grey romper of sorts. Where did it even come from? Esteban?

"Did you meet Esteban?"

"Who?"

"Esteban. I was with him and I don't remember much else. Now, I am here." Briana stood up from the bed. Her legs were wobbly, but she steadied herself and moved to the door of the room. She turned the handle and pulled on it. Nothing. She banged on the door, repeatedly, screaming for someone to let her out of the room. Nothing.

"It's no use. I tried it all. Everything. The window in the bathroom, the door. When they first took me, I even thought about slitting my wrist with glass – so they couldn't have me, but everything they give me is made of plastic."

Briana banged again and then turned from the door, tears rolling down her face. Lily walked over to her and took her hands, leading her back to the bed.

"Let me help you clean up." She disappeared into the bathroom for a minute and came back with a wet towel. Slowly, she administered to Briana's face, blotting and wiping. "They hit you," she said, as she gently touched a bruise on her cheek. Briana pulled away. "Sorry."

When Lily pulled the rag away, it was covered with blood. Briana stared down at it and then looked into Lily's face. "What do you mean: 'have you'?" her face hurt, and she was sobbing once more.

"Forget I said that."

"No. Tell me."

"For sex. Like their slave," Lily said quietly. Briana's eyes went wide. "Sorry, I've said too much."

"You don't know that's what they want," Briana defended for her own sake more than anything.

"No – I don't. I don't know what they want."

"We have to find a way out of here, Lily. We can't stay here."

"What's your name?"

"Briana," she said. "We have to find a way out of here,

Lily."

"There is no way out, Briana. I'm here to take you along with the others."

"Others?" Briana asked, her chest rising once more, her sobs beginning all over again.

"If you play by their rules, Briana, they won't hurt you."

"What do you mean?" Briana screamed.

"Listen to me. We are going to get you cleaned up. You are going to change into these clothes. Tonight, in a couple of hours, you and I are going to get into a car and the driver is going to drive us away from this hotel. Like friends going out for a night of fun." Briana's eyes opened, she held her breath. Was this an escape plan? "But they will be following us. And, we won't be going out for fun. We will be going to their prison camp where they have kept me since they took me."

"I won't go," Briana said.

"You will go. And you will do everything that I told you, or they will beat you, or maybe worse, kill you."

Briana just stared at Lily, too afraid to react.

"Now, let's get you cleaned up the rest of the way and get dressed."

Lily stepped up from the bed and took Briana's hand. She led her into the bathroom. "You need to shower. You smell awful. Do you want some help in here?"

Briana shook her head. Lily started the shower, checking the water and then she stepped out of the bathroom, leaving the door open as she stood outside. Briana turned her back on Lily, worked her way out of the gray romper, the pain in her arms and back reminding her of her journey, and then she stepped into the tub. As the warm water ran over her body, she imagined it washing away all that had happened to her that day. Esteban, the ride in the van, the pain she felt in her arms, face and back, and the situation she was currently in. She let the water wash over her hair as tears flowed down her face; her situation could not be imagined away. When the water was turned off, she would still be kidnapped and she would have to find a way to escape.

After several minutes, she turned the water off. Her mind could not help her without more information. She would do her best to play by her captor's rules until she could find a way to escape.

"Much better," Lily said when Briana stepped out of the bathroom. "You are very pretty. That bruise will go away in a few days."

Absently, Briana touched her face where she was punched and then winced. She wore a pair of purple scrubs, much like the blue ones that Lily wore. Lily stood up next to her and smiled.

"Twins," she said, and smiled. "We have to go soon. Here are some socks and sneakers. Put them on."

Briana had so many questions. Why was Lily working for them? Where were they going? Who were they? She started to ask Lily when there was a knock at the door.

Lily stood up and walked to the door. She opened it slowly and spoke to someone outside. She closed the door and looked back at Briana.

"Come," she said. Briana didn't move. Lily walked closer to her and took her hand. "C'mon Briana. They will hurt us both – really hurt us if we do not follow their rules. Right now, we just have to get in a car and go for a ride. Like friends. Okay?" Briana nodded her head. "Good girl. And, no screaming or crying. At least until we get in the car."

Briana stood up and slowly followed Lily to the door. She knocked on the back of it and it opened. Together, they stepped out into the night air. Lily took Briana's arm and directed her to the nearby waiting car. When they got near the door, the driver opened it and Lily prodded Briana to get inside. She followed behind her. The driver closed the door and walked around the car. There was a glass wall between the driver and the passengers, much like in Esteban's car. Briana was sure this would be a very different ride.

Lily reached over and took Briana's hand. She held her fingers up to her lips, reminding Briana to be quiet during the ride. Tears slid down Briana's face, but she held back her sobs as the car pulled away from the hotel. She tried to find where she was based on the surroundings, but it was nighttime, and she was in a strange place. The car drove through the dark roads.

Lily's grip on Briana's hand loosened and when Briana looked over at her, she saw that the woman was sleeping. How could she sleep under these conditions? Had she just learned to accept it? As the car inched along, Briana's mind raced – so many thoughts, so many confusing, intersecting thoughts. None of them helpful. She leaned her head back as the car drove on.

Chapter 9

Lily awoke when the car came to a complete stop more than an hour later. She had slipped into a deep sleep, even snoring lightly as if nothing was going on. She looked over at Briana as soon as she woke and offered her a small smile.

"Remember," she said. "Be obedient and all will go well." Whatever slurring that Briana thought she had heard in Lily before seemed to be gone.

The door to the car opened and Lily was lifted out of the car by her arm. Briana didn't move at first and the driver reached into the car and grabbed her by the upper arm, squeezing hard as he pulled her across the seat. He was rough with her and she pulled herself to her feet as soon as she was out of the car. She stared at Lily as the man released her arm; a new bruise already forming.

"Come with me," the man said, leading them to a large building across a grassy field.

They followed him closely, Lily seeming to know the way already. When they got to the building, the man opened the door to the large structure and Lily stepped inside. Briana didn't move and the man pushed her from behind. She stepped inside. Inside it was dimly lit and Briana quickly saw that the building had been transformed into a prison of sorts, with make-shift floor-to-ceiling cells in the center of the room.

"You know the way," the man said, and Lily stepped forward toward the center of the room.

Briana followed reluctantly, but she knew she had no choice. Lily stepped in front of the corner of the large cell structure and waited. The man opened the door to the cell and stood back as the two women stepped inside.

Briana stepped slowly and the man smiled at her. What the fuck, she thought, and she spit in his face. He slapped her hard across the face as she stepped through the door. She lost her balance and fell to the floor. She turned back to the man, her face stinging, tears in her eyes as he slammed the cell door shut and locked it.

"Look away from me," the man said, "or I will show you real pain. And nothing for you tonight," he added, his comment meant for Lily.

Briana stared for a moment, stoically and then turned her head to look down at the ground. She could taste blood in her mouth, but she was glad she had spit in his face. Lily was at her side a moment later, her arms on her shoulders as she helped her up from the ground.

"Stupid, stupid, girl," she said. "I told you to be good."

"Fuck him!" Briana said. "Fuck this whole place!"

"Okay, okay," Lily said as they sat on the ground.

"What did he mean 'nothing for you'?" Briana asked.

Lily didn't answer right away, then she said, "Nothing, I don't know."

Lily wrapped her arm around Briana's shoulders as Briana began to sob once more. Lily pulled her tight against her, trying to sooth her as the woman broke down. Lily let her have this moment; it was inevitable. She needed to be angry, to cry, to breakdown. Lily let Briana get all of it out of her system; didn't even try to quiet her. They were to be partners which meant they needed to work together. For now, she would have to be Briana's friend. Tomorrow would be a rude awakening for Briana, but for her to survive, she would have to play by their rules.

****

At some point, Briana fell asleep, exhausted and spent from the trauma of the kidnapping as well as the toll it took on her emotionally. When she woke up, she was on a blanket on the floor in the corner of the cell. She knew before her eyes opened that it had not been a dream. The pain in her back, her arm, and the side of her face was a clear indication that the events her mind presented her with did indeed happen. Her eyes only sold the deal, the weight of her situation rushing in on her as she lifted herself up to a sitting position.

She looked about the cell, the door first – maybe it was open. No chance. Then for Lily, her only friend since the whole ordeal. The cell was small and there was no sight of Lily. She stood up, her body one large bruise, and grunted as she made her way to the cot across the cell. She ruffled the sheet as if doing so would reveal Lily, but she was not to be found. Briana climbed up on the cot and pulled her legs up underneath her. She wrapped her arms around her legs and began to cry once more. Tears rolled down her face as she sobbed. She didn't know how to control it.

There was a sound in the distance suddenly, and she inhaled deeply, wiping the snot from her nose with the back of her wrist. She let her breath out quietly, listening for the sound. She knew she heard something and as she thought about it, it made sense. They were probably not the only people imprisoned in the cells. She was sure she saw several cells last night when she was brought in. Maybe Lily had been moved to a separate cell. She wanted to call out, but she held her tongue. She didn't know who was out there. She remained quiet.

"Hello?" It was a woman's voice. Briana didn't answer. "Help? Is someone out there? I think I heard someone. Hello?"

Briana was about to call out to her when she heard another voice, shushing the first one.

"Hello…" the voice said.

"Shh…" the second voice said.

Brianna could hear sobbing then, which she assumed was from the first woman. She tried to identify from which direction the voices came and guess how many people might be in the cells, but she had nothing to base her answers on. Instead, she waited for the woman to speak one more time. She obviously spoke English, at least one of them did. Was she young like Briana and Lily?

A loud noise broke the silence of the cells and Briana sat up on the bed. It was the sound of a door opening then closing. A cool wind rushed through her cell as voices stepped into the building. She looked up to see if she could see anything out of the small window in the door to her cell. Nothing, but the voices continued.

"Doesn't matter what you do to me, you know…" a woman's voice said.

"Stand up straight," this time a male.

"You can't hurt me anymore. I erased you in my mind…" the woman again, her voice coming very close now.

Briana heard keys enter the door of her cell and she stepped back from the door, jumping up on the bed, in the corner of the room. Was that Lily's voice?

"Erased. That's what you are. All of you. You can't hurt me if I don't let you in. If I don't remember you."

The door opened and Lily was pushed inside. Her hair was a mess, her scrub top torn. The front of her pants were wet around the crotch. The door slammed shut behind her and Briana heard the bolt lock.

Lily turned to her and half-smiled. "They can't hurt me," she said. "Erased." She collapsed to the floor in a heap.

Briana moved to her quickly, shaking the other woman by the shoulders. Lily didn't respond.

"Lily, Lily, wake up," Briana said, keeping her voice low despite her concern. She shook Lily again. Lily's face was all wet, her eyes puffy as if she was crying; her lower lip split and bleeding. Her neck was red, possibly bruised and where her shirt was ripped, at the base of the v-neck, Briana could see that her chest was also red. The woman stunk. "Lily. Wake up."

Lily's eyes opened slowly, half-way. "Can't hurt me," she said, her words slurred.

"Lily, it's me. Are you okay?"

"Briana?" she said, a small smiled appeared on her face.

Her eyes closed once more, and she was out. Briana checked her pulse and breathing – both were strong, but Lily was passed out or asleep. She tried to wake her one more time and then went to the bed to grab a blanket. As she pulled it over Lily, she adjusted her body, so she was more comfortable on the hard floor. That's when Briana saw the tracks on her arms. Initially, Briana thought it was dirt or something else, but as she took a closer look, she could tell that they were needle marks; many needle marks. They were drugging Lily, she realized for the first time, and her own reality set in once again. After she covered Lily with the blanket, Briana climbed back onto the bed, pulled up her legs underneath her and returned to her sobbing.

As tears flowed down her cheeks, she searched for solutions to her problem. Somehow, she needed to get out of here. Find a phone. Call the police. What would she tell them? She had no idea where she was. She thought of her family back home. What would they do when they didn't hear from her later today, tomorrow, next week? It could be days before they took action, especially because it was the weekend. It was only Saturday, right? She hadn't lost track of time yet. Just last night was when she was abducted. On Monday, two days from now, when she didn't show for work, would Marcos report her missing. No. He'd call her phone and when she didn't answer, he would cover her class. No help was coming for her. Not now. Not yet. She would have to do this all on her own. Stay tough. Stay strong.

But she was far from strong as she sat whimpering on the bed. She was doing nothing to help herself; nothing to bring about a resolution. In front of her, on the floor she saw her fate. She saw what would happen to her if she didn't stay strong. Her sobbing continued; this was all too much to take in. All too much to come to grips with. Three days, she reasoned through the myriad of thoughts that were going through her head. Three days she had to stay tough. Then someone would begin looking for her. Three days...

Briana let her thoughts take her away. She rolled to her side on the bed, helpless save for her thoughts. She let her mind wander, searching for a solution, one that she knew was not there. Marcos, her parents, Jose – could Jose help her? Mrs. Alves – Briana's eyes opened briefly as if her brain had stumbled across something important. Mrs. Alves had seen the exchange between her and the bodyguard back at the school. Maybe there was a shot there. Mrs. Alves coming to her rescue. Fat chance. But she did see. And, Briana remembered asking Jose about the club. Her parents, her mind reminded her. They could be coming to Brazil for vacation. To visit her. But they never finished those plans. Hadn't really made plans. She cried for her mother now. She would be so worried when she didn't hear from Briana. Her father was strong, but her mother would break into pieces. She had warned Briana; warned her so many times.

At some point, all of this thinking exhausted Briana to the point where she fell asleep. In her dream, she saw Esteban and asked him why he had done this to her; why had he had her kidnapped. He just smiled at her and told her she was beautiful. Hours later, Briana woke up on the cot in the corner of the cell. She had no idea what time it was. Lily still lay on the floor, wrapped in the blanket. Briana turned to the wall and stared at it. All was lost, she realized. All was lost.

The sound of the door, cool air once more. Someone was coming into the big building. Voices. Men's voices. Briana stayed in her position; her head turned away from the cell door. She put her hands over her ears. If she didn't look, didn't listen, maybe it wasn't happening. The voices grew closer. Definitely, more than one person. The key in her cell door. She heard everything. The door opened.

"Get up!" the accented voice said. She ignored it. Maybe they were talking to Lily. They could take Lily. "Get up now!" A rough hand pulled her shoulder. She turned to face the voice. "Get up, I said. Now!" Her body pulled itself up into a sitting position, her arms wrapped across her chest. "Stand up!" Briana was shaking. Slowly she slid off the cot, standing alongside of it. Her sobs started once more. She said nothing as she stared back at the large man that stood before her. "Come. We need to get you cleaned up."

The man bent down in front of her. Briana felt his hand

touch her ankle and she pulled away.

"Stay still!"

She stopped moving and she cold metal being wrapped around her ankle. She sobbed loudly. Her other ankle was cuffed. The man stood up, placed his hand on her arm and pulled her forward. She could only walk slowly as a result of the shackles. They walked past the puddle of Lily on the floor out of the cell, toward the far side of the large building. Briana sobbed as she looked around, searching for a way to escape, a place to hide.

At the far end of the building, they stopped in front of a set of wooden doors. The man opened the doors and he pushed Briana inside. "Showers," he said. "Clean up quickly." He handed her a set up clean scrubs, this time green. "Put these on when you are finished." The man bent down and unlocked the shackles on her ankles. He stood up once more and nodded past her, to the showers on the far wall of the large room. "Don't worry, I'll be watching," he said, this time smiling.

Briana stepped away from the man, happy to add distance between them. He remained by the door, the shackles in his hand. There were several showers on the wall; she chose the one furthest away from the door. Several white towels hung from the wall. She reached for the single handle on the shower and turned it first one way then the other before the water came on. She adjusted the temperature, wasting time, hoping he would leave. The man stayed where he was, watching.

Slowly, Briana, sobbing once more, stripped out of her scrubs, dropping them into a heap away from the running water. Keeping her back to the man, she slipped under the running water, letting it run through her hair and over her body. Her hands rubbed her sides pushing the water in different directions. There was a large bottle of soap which she used to wash her hair and body. Despite her being watched, she felt somewhat invincible in the shower. The sound of the water drowned out everything else including her sobs. She stole glances back toward the door feeling the stare of the guard's eyes on her body.

Finally, she raised her hand and turned off the water. She reached for a towel off the hook and wrapped it around her, feeling the crusty cloth press against her skin. Briana briefly questioned how many people had used the towel before her, but she pushed that out of her mind. The guard continued to stare at her from a distance. She was happy to be wrapped in whatever was available. She turned her back to him and quickly pulled on the green scrubs over her half-dry body. When she was done, she ran her fingers through her hair to shape it; more a force of habit than anything else.

"Come," the guard said. Slowly, she walked toward him. "You did good. Put these on."

He handed her the shackles. A moment of trust passed between them. Briana wanted to spit on him, take the shackles and beat him with them. He was a pervert. A pig. His eyes stared into hers. She took the shackles and stepped back, bending to her knees, she locked one around each ankle. When she stood up, he smiled at her. A look of pure domination. He was pleased with himself that he had trusted her, and she had done what he wanted her to do.

"Come," the guard said, opening the door of the showers. He led Briana to the door that led outside the large building. "There is someone you now must meet."

Briana froze.

"Come," the guard repeated, more insistent now. "You will give him what he wants, and he will give you food."

Tears began to roll down Briana's face once more.

Chapter 10

"I would have thought she would have called by now," Briana's mom said to her dad.

"Leave her alone, Claire. It's the weekend. She's probably out enjoying herself."

"I texted her and she didn't respond."

"Maybe she's in the mountains and out of range," he stood from the table and stood behind her in the kitchen. "Don't worry, she's fine."

Briana's mother texted her once more: "Please call me to discuss vacation plans." She thought she'd keep it light, not letting on that she was worried because she had not heard from her. She put the phone down and tucked it under a dish towel on the counter to prevent her from thinking about texting again, at least for a short while. She put dinner on the table and sat down to eat.

****

Briana stepped out of the large building into an open lot. The sun was setting. She had thought it was morning. How much time had passed? Across the large lot was a large house which seemed out of place. She didn't remember seeing it when they brought her in. The guard led her to the house and they walked up a set of steps that led to a set of wooden doors.

"Wipe your feet here." Briana wiped her bare feet on the mat that sat in front of the doors. "You listen to what you are told. Good."

The man opened the doors and motioned Briana inside. Several guards were in place inside the home by the doors and in front of a large staircase. They all turned to look at her as she shuffled by them. Her guard led her to the staircase and together, they slowly climbed up two flights. The stairs continued up at least another two flights. On the landing of the second floor, the guard led her down a long, carpeted hallway. Briana's head moved from left to right, noting the art on the walls. She hadn't noticed, but her pace had slowed, almost as if she didn't want to get to wherever the guard was taking her. He put his hand on her arm and dragged her forward. Briana reluctantly fell into step.

At the end of the long hallway, the guard opened a door and motioned for Briana to step in. She stepped through the door into a massive room. On one side there was a large desk with a computer setup on it, almost like an office. At the far end of the room, there was a large bed with a canopy on it. The sides of the canopy were closed, draped with colorful tapestries. On the other side of the room, there were counters, filled with fruits and food. Her stomach growled at the sight of the food; she couldn't remember the last time she ate.

"Welcome," a soft voice said. Briana turned her head to see a man standing on the rug in the office area of the room. He walked toward her. Looking at the guard, "You can remove those."

The guard bent down and removed the shackles from Briana's ankles. He stood up.

"That will be all," the man said to the guard.

The guard stepped out of the room and closed the door behind him.

The man walked around Briana slowly. She did her best to contain her sobbing but tears still ran down her face. Her body shook as he walked behind her. She held her arms across her chest. A sob escaped her. Who was this man?

"My name is Nicolau," he said. "I am one of Esteban's most trusted assistants. You will call me Sir or Master. Do you understand?"

Briana nodded her head.

"Put your arms down to your side."

Briana didn't move.

"Please," he said.

She dropped her arms. Nicolau stood in front of Briana now. His eyes walked down her body and then back up to her face. She sobbed again and he tilted his head.

"You must be hungry, yes?" Briana felt herself nodding. "You've not had much to eat in more than a day. You must be very hungry." She nodded again. "Speak!" he said, his voice raised.

Briana jumped at the change in his voice, her eyes wide as she looked down at the ground. Her arms crossed her chest once more.

"Speak," he said, quietly this time.

She was openly sobbing now, her body shaking. "Please let me go. I won't say anything to anyone." She inhaled deeply, trying to harness her voice, control her cries. "Please, please. I won't say anything. Let me go. Please!" she pleaded.

"Very good. Get it all out now," Nicolau said. He walked across the room and pulled tissues from a box. He handed them to Briana. She took them from him but continued to plead with him.

"Please! Please!" She walked toward him as if to get his attention, pleading with him. "I want to go home." Briana's face contorted as she cried, her hands shook, reaching out to him.

Nicolau let her go for a full minute, before he stopped her. "Enough!" he said, his voice raised loud enough to cut through her cries. "Enough."

Briana sucked in her sobs, wiped her face with the back of her hand. She tried to control it. "Please," she said, almost in a whisper as she looked to the ground.

"Look at me," Nicolau said.

Briana lifted her head.

"You should know a few things right now. First, for now, this is your new home."

Briana started to sob again, "No..."

"Yes. This is your new home. Your new home is with us. You will do what we say when we say it." He stepped forward and with his finger, he lifted her chin, so she was looking into his face. "Do you understand?"

Briana nodded.

"We will take care of you as long as you do what we say. If you don't, we have ways of making you comply with our wishes. Don't make us resort to those."

Nicolau removed his finger from her chin and stepped back. He slowly started to walk around her once more. Her shaking was maybe more pronounced now than it was earlier. Briana tried to contain herself. Her mind tried to wrap itself around the current situation. It was no help.

When he completed his circle, standing in front of her once more, he smiled. "There, that's a good girl," he said acknowledging her attempt to get her sobbing under control. "Very good. Would you like something to eat now?"

Briana nodded her head up and down.

"Good. Yes, some good food is very important. We need to keep you from getting sick, rundown." Nicolau motioned with his arm to the side of the room where various plates of food were laid out on tables. Briana's stomach growled again, loud enough to betray her need. "Yes, you shall have some food," he said. "It is all very good. But first, I would like you to undress."

Briana looked up into his eyes. Undress? Her arms crossed in front of her.

"Please," Nicolau said, his request more a command. "What have we discussed? You will do what we say when we say it, yes? Now, please undress."

There was no choice, she realized. She would have to undress for this man. Then she would eat and then go back to her cell where she could try to figure out her next move. That's it. She stared back at him and then his eyes walked down the front of her shirt. Briana reached down to the bottom of her shirt and slowly lifted it over her head. She thought of turning around, away from him, but she knew that would only be temporary. Rip the band-aid off, her mind said. Get it over with. Her body shivered as her breasts were revealed. She pulled the shirt over her head and dropped it to the floor. She stared back at Nicolau with a defiant glare, her arms crossing over her chest, hiding her breasts.

"Now, the pants," he said.

Her sobbing had started once more, tears rolled down her face. Slowly, she uncrossed her arms and pushed her pants down over her hips. As they slid down her legs, she felt the coldness of the room settle in on her. Her nipples sprung to life against her will. She crossed one arm in front of her and placed her hand in front of her crotch.

"Modest. I like that," Nicolau said, as he walked around

her once more. "You are beautiful. Precious," he said. "Now, put your arms down, let me look at you."

Reluctantly, Briana let her arms fall down to her sides. Her body shook, covered with goose bumps. She could feel the tears dripping from her face onto her chest. She looked away from him, across the room toward the food as Nicolau stared at her body.

"Very nice," Nicolau said. "Come. We shall eat now." He reached his hand out to her and when she didn't take it, he stepped closer and grabbed her hand, leading her across the long room toward the food table.

Briana walked slowly at Nicolau's side as he explained the types of food that were laid out before them. He spoke to her as if she was a friend, not naked, as they stepped up to the tables.

Nicolau handed her a dish. "Please take what you wish, you can have as much as you want."

Briana's eyes washed over the table. Her need to eat, for this moment, surpassed her need to be clothed. She reached for what looked like a sausage, brought it to her mouth taking a bite. She was ravenous, she found, as she pulled other foods onto her plate. Chicken, tomatoes, other meats. She heard Nicolau laugh, but she didn't turn to him. She took a bite of a plantain, swallowed it and then dropped another onto her plate. At the end of the long table, she looked back at Nicolau and the plate he had before him. He carried a small salad. Nicolau took her hand and escorted her to a table in the corner. He pulled out her chair and she sat down.

Briana ate quickly as if the food would be taken away from her. She would look up occasionally and find Nicolau staring back at her, his fork in hand as he toyed with his salad. He poured her a glass of water from a large pitcher and pushed it in front of her. When she saw it, she stopped eating and took a long sip, choking on it. She used a napkin her handed her to wipe her mouth.

"Very good," Nicolau said. "Very good. I like to watch you eat. You are very beautiful."

Briana had finished eating now. She took another sip of the water and looked back at him. She knew she needed to eat and if getting undressed allowed her to do that, then she reasoned it was okay.

"You now go by the name Phoenix," Nicolau said to her.

Briana's eyes squinted as if she was confused.

"Yes, your name is Phoenix. Your old name does not exist anymore." She stared at him. "Do you understand?"

She nodded in agreement, not at all accepting what he had said. She knew not to argue.

"What is your name?" She didn't answer. Nicolau's arm shot across the table to grab her wrist. He squeezed it. "What is your name?"

"Phoenix," Briana said. "My name is Phoenix."

"Very good, Phoenix. Very good. Now, stand up and let me look at you."

Briana stood up from the chair slowly. She used the napkin to wipe food off her breasts that had fallen while she was eating. Her arms crossed her chest once more.

"Put your arms down. Good. Now, turn around slowly. Very nice. Come sit on my lap, Phoenix."

She didn't move at first, feeling the sobs starting to return. She choked them down. Be strong, Briana. Nicolau pushed his chair back, turning it slightly. He patted his thighs.

"Come. Come sit on my lap." Briana slowly walked toward him. When she stood in front of him, she heard him tap once more. She sat down on his lap, looking out across the room. "Very good," Nicolau said. "Very good."

He reached his hand up to her breast and his fingers lightly traced her skin. Briana looked up into the air, at the ceiling, inhaling, holding back a cry. Nicolau's fingers slid over her breast and squeezed her gently.

"Very nice," he said.

Then he slid his fingers around her nipple, circling the nipple before he ran his thumb over the tip, back and forth slowly. Both of Briana's nipples hardened as he touched her, betraying her true feelings. His other hand moved to her other breast, his fingers sliding across her smooth skin. He ran the back of his hand over her nipple as he gently pinched the other. She continued to look away, her nakedness quickly becoming the least of her concerns. What if her body reacted to his touch? Could it? Would it?

"Very nice," he said once more. "Very nice..." he was whispering now as one of his hands slid off her breast and down between her legs.

Briana let out a gasp as his fingers touched her just below the waist at the top of her pubic hair. She felt tears sliding down her face as his fingers moved through her hair and touched the top of her vagina. Please, God, she prayed silently, but she knew 'He' was not listening right now, or none of this would have happened. Nicolau's fingers continued south past her vagina and down to her thighs. She let out a quick sigh of relief, no matter how temporary. The hand on her thigh spread her legs apart. Briana started to sob now as his fingers traveled up her thigh and slid back between her legs.

"Shh," Nicolau said as she slid his fingers between the lips of her vagina. Briana jumped as he touched her. "Shh," he repeated. "Relax."

Nothing could make Briana relax at this moment. His

one hand was on her breast and his other was between her legs. Her body was rigid, the complete opposite of relaxed. She wanted no part of this situation. Yet, her body was reacting.

"That's it," he said. "We can take it slow for now."

Briana could feel herself getting wet despite her not wanting any part of this. It was the body's natural reaction; she could not control it. She whimpered as his fingers slid further down and then back up again.

"Very good. It's important that you accept this, Phoenix," Nicolau said. "You're doing very well." His hand squeezed her breast hard making her look down at him. "Yes," he said. "I want you to look at me when I touch you. Just like that."

Briana stared at Nicolau. Her eyes wanted to burn a whole through his head. She stared into his eyes as his fingers slid up and down. Should I play along, she thought? Is that what he wants?

"Does that feel good?" he said.

Briana didn't respond at first.

His fingers slid up to the top of her vagina. "How about now?" he said as made small circles just below her clit. "Does that feel good?"

She could not comprehend this man violating her and expecting her to enjoy it. She knew she needed to get through this situation as quickly as possible and find a way to escape She nodded dumbly as Nicolau continued to violate her.

Nicolau applied pressure with his fingers, making small circles at the top of her vagina. He moved his fingers faster now, pressing harder.

Briana wanted to push his hand away, but she knew that would do no good. She thought of her mother, home, worrying about her, hoping to focus her mind on something other than his fingers, to distract her. She looked away, back up at the ceiling.

"Look at me," Nicolau said, his fingers drumming a beat on her.

Briana looked back into his face, a tear escaping from her eye.

"That's a good girl," he said. "Very good girl. Now cum for me."

Tears flowed down Briana's face as she tried desperately to hold back, to dismiss his touch, but it was no use.

She let little moans escape her giving a false impression of enjoyment. Her body twisted in his lap, her hands still at her sides. His fingers moved faster and then he slid them up further, making larger circles now, applying more pressure. When she thought she could put an end to it she arched her back and pretended to orgasm. Briana stared into his eyes hoping to transfer the hatred she had for this man directly into his brain even as her body shook and shuddered under the touch of his hand.

When her faked orgasm passed, she immediately started sobbing. His fingers moved away from her body. She wanted to stand up. She wanted to throw up, but there was no place for her to do so. She hated this man who had touched her without her permission. She looked away from him suddenly afraid that he might see that hatred and hurt her for how she felt. She inhaled, trying to gain control of herself once more.

"Very good, Phoenix," Nicolau said. "You passed the first test. Very good. Now, stand up."

Briana stood up slowly, backing away from Nicolau. She wanted to go back to her cell now. She felt dirty and cheap and she wanted to be away from him. Her sobbing started once more.

Nicolau remained in his chair looking up at her. He smiled at her, despite her sobbing in front of him. It gave him more power to see her in this weak state. He watched the tears fall from her face, her chest rising and falling as she cried, gasping for air. Snot ran from her nose. His eyes walked up and down her body. Despite her state, she was still beautiful. A tremendous find, he thought. Normally he would have the choice here and now whether the girl would be sold or sent to the training camps to train and please. But this one was different as Esteban had taken a personal interest and already determined her fate. Either way they would do well because of her. Once she was trained. Once she understood how to please a man or a woman the way they needed to be pleased. He took one last look at her long legs, her large, firm breasts and her pretty face. Yes, he thought, she was a good find.

"Come, Phoenix," he said. "Get down on your knees in front of me." His hands reached down as he unbuckled his pants. Briana froze as she watched him open his pants, lift his hips and slide them down. His cock, long and hard stood erect as he looked up at her. "Come," he said. "You know what to do."

Briana didn't move. Tears fell down her face, she gasped for air, sobbing.

"Phoenix," Nicolau said. "Come."

Briana stepped forward slowly and slid down to her knees in front of Nicolau.

"That's a good girl," he said.

Chapter 11

Briana moved as fast as she could with the shackles around her ankles. She couldn't get to the bathroom fast enough. She would have thrown up outside of the main residence, but her guard would have none of it. Instead, she was shackled and paraded out of the house in her green scrubs. Now, in the rear of the big building, where she had showered before, the guard pushed her into a section on the far side of the room. She immediately dropped to her knees and threw up.

Sobbing into the bowl below her, she let go of everything she could. All of the food inside of her, all of the fear and agony that she had felt since her abduction, and then Nicolau. His taste, his smell, she let it all out as she vomited into the toilet her tears splashing down on top of it. It was too much, too much for one person to handle. She cried and cried until she heard the guard outside urging her to hurry.

When she was finally able to wrestle control of herself, Briana pushed up off of the toilet and stood up. She needed to bury what had happened to her today deep in her brain so that she could think clearly; so, she could find a way to escape.

The guard led her back to her cell, stopping in front of

the door to remove the shackles. He opened the door and she stepped inside half-expecting to see Lily still in a bunch on the floor.

"There you are," Lily said, running over to her, taking Briana into her arms.

Briana wasn't expecting it, but welcomed the hug, her head falling down onto Lily's shoulder as she started to cry once more.

"I thought you were gone," Lily said.

"It was so horrible," Briana sobbed. "So very horrible." She wanted to tell Lily what she had done, but she was too embarrassed to say it out loud. "So horrible, Lily."

Lily patted her on the back as she comforted her. "I know, honey. I know."

They stayed like that, hugging in the middle of the cell for a while until Lily picked her head up and looked into Briana's eyes.

"Do you want to talk about it?"

Briana put her head down once more and cried out. "I never want to talk about it." She thought for a moment. "Wait, you knew. You knew all along what was going to happen, and you didn't warn me."

"I told you what I was told to tell you, Briana. I didn't want them to hurt you if you didn't listen. I was protecting you."

"Protecting me? Do you know what I had to do in there?" Lily nodded.

"You didn't warn me. You said you didn't know what they wanted with us..." Briana was crying again.

"I know," Lily said. "I know. I was trying to protect you..."

"You didn't protect me. He made me... what he did to me..."

Lily reached for Briana once more and pulled her into

her arms. Briana sobbed on her shoulder, gasping for air. She was inconsolable at first and then she slowly began to calm down. Lily patted Briana's hair as she slowly stopped sobbing. Finally, Lily broke from the hug and went to sit on her cot. She knew she had lied to Briana, didn't in any way prepare her for what was about to happen, but she had had no choice. She stared over at Briana. Lily had eaten from the food that was delivered to the cell. There was some bread left over and she offered it to Briana.

"It's not good, but it will fill you up."

"I'm not sure I can ever eat again," Briana told her.

Lily stared at her. "It gets better."

"Better? How can any of this get better? We have to find a way out of here, Lily."

Lily was shaking her head. "There's no way out. There's nothing we can do. This is who we are now."

Briana wasn't going to take that; wasn't going to give in. She couldn't give up. Not now. Not ever. She was crying again, but this time she shook her head and wiped her nose. She stopped. She walked toward Lily.

"What have they done to you to make you this way?"

"There's no way out. Listen to them, do what they say, or they will hurt you. Sometimes really bad."

Briana grabbed Lily's arm. "Like this?" she said. "Did they do this to you or were you already broken when they took you." Lily pulled her arm away and walked to the corner of the cell. Briana waited. "Lily?"

"It doesn't hurt anymore now, Briana. Nothing hurts anymore. They dulled the pain. There is no pain. I do what they want. I don't get hurt..."

"And they keep you drugged, like this? So, you can't feel anything. I won't let them do that to me, Lily. I won't let them drug me."

"The pain all goes away. I erase each and every one of them." She turned and pointed to her head. "They don't live in here anymore, Briana. They can't hurt me if I can't remember them."

Lily was crying now, and Briana opened her arms to her. She let Lily put her head on her shoulder and she patted her back. This poor girl, she thought. This poor, broken girl. Lily cried for a little bit and then she picked her head up off of Briana. She pulled out of her embrace and took Briana's hands.

"Look at us. What a sorry pair we make, huh?" Lily offered Briana a smile and Briana smiled back. "Eat the bread, Briana."

Briana bit the bread and swallowed it slowly. Her throat still hurt from vomiting, but she was able to swallow small bites. The two of them talked a little more; Lily telling Briana all she knew about the cells, which wasn't very much. She said she had thought of escaping before, but there just didn't seem a way. Even if she did escape, Lily told Briana she had no idea where she was or where she would go. Briana knew she was right. Unless someone came to get them, there was really no escaping.

****

The girls slept in their cots that night. Briana was surprised that she could sleep at all, but she was exhausted from the vile day that she had had. She drifted off quickly. She didn't dream at all. When she woke up, Lily was once again missing from the room.

Briana busied herself in the cell for the first part of the morning, at least what she thought was morning. Some food was slid under the door a little while after she woke up. It was bread and a pasty vegetable dish of some sort. Briana wolfed it down and drank the water that accompanied it. While she ate, sitting up on her cot, she tried to remember how long it had been since she was abducted. Was it Monday yet? Would people be looking for her because she didn't show up at work? Her mother must be going crazy; her father too now. She knew he was more reasonable, but after not hearing from Briana for two days or more, even her dad must be worried. They would do something. She knew they would try and find her. Briana found herself crying silently thinking about the pain her mother must be going through.

"I'm sorry, mommy," she said aloud. "I'm so sorry."

Briana pulled herself together. She was not going to sob through another day. She needed to get control of herself, her body and her mind. She needed to take care of herself. She needed to stay disciplined or she would end up like Lily.

At some point during the day, she heard keys in the cell door, and she expected Lily to be pushed inside. The door opened but only the guard stood in the doorway. Briana froze.

"Come," the guard said.

She remained still. He nodded and took a step forward. Briana relented, walking toward the cell door. The guard handed her shackles and she bent down to place them on her ankles. She was shaking, not knowing what was in store for her once she left the room. When she stood up, she had gotten her shaking under control. She walked slowly, taking in all she could, mapping it out in her mind so she could remember.

The guard didn't walk her back to the showers this time, instead he walked her directly out of the building toward the main house. Briana had thought she had time, but now that they had skipped the showers, her fears of Nicolau crept back in. She felt herself shaking again.

Inside the house, they climbed the stairs to the second floor once more. Flashbacks of the day before consumed Briana. Her pulse increased as she neared the door at the end of the hallway. She didn't want to go back in the room. Still, she shuffled forward.

Inside the room there were two men this time. They both had their backs to her, but she was sure one of them was Nicolau. She recognized his voice when he asked the guard to remove her shackles. The guard did as he was asked and then left the room. One of the men stood up and the other followed. Nicolau was on the right and he smiled at her.

"This is Phoenix," Nicolau said. "Please, disrobe."

Briana stared back at him and then slowly pulled her top off and slid out of her pants. She felt her body shake, and she did her best to control it. Both men looked her over, from head to toe. Then the other man, heavyset and bald, walked closer to her and then slowly walked around her. Nicolau held Briana's gaze while the man walked around her. She felt his touch on her back, pulling away at first, and then she held steady as his fingers gently slid down her arm.

"Muito agradavel," very nice, the man said.

He came to a stop in front of her and stared into her face. He had a tic that made his left eye twitch every few seconds. Briana tucked that into her mind. His hand reached up to touch her. Briana inhaled deeply to prevent herself from sobbing or worse screaming.

"Ah, Oalo, please," Nicolau said. Oalo dropped his hand before he touched her skin. "You know we have strict rules here."

Oalo turned to Nicolau and nodded. "She is quite

beautiful."

The two men walked away, toward the office on the other side of the room. Briana stood in her place, not knowing what else to do. After a short while, she heard them laughing and she turned to watch them. She could smell cigar smoke and she watched a plume of smoke rise from where they were sitting. They held their glasses as they toasted. Both men drank down whatever was in their glass and then they stood once more. They returned to where Briana was standing.

Oalo took a long look at Briana. His eyes walked up and down her body several times. Finally, he turned to Nicolau. "I should take her now," he said, laughing.

"In time my friend." Nicolau patted Oalo on the shoulder and walked him to the door. Behind her, Briana heard the door open and then close. She held her place and waited. Nicolau walked back into her view and stood in front of her. He smiled at her.

"You did good, Phoenix. Very good. That man is very important and after seeing you today, we can go forward with our plans. Very good, very good. Are you hungry?" Briana shook her head no. "You're sure?"

"I'm not hungry right now, Nicolau," she said, her voice was stronger than she thought it would be.

"Very well. Tomorrow, you and Lily will start your training. It will be away from here, so sadly, I will not see you for a while." Briana nodded as if she understood. She had no idea what kind of training Nicolau had intended for them, but she knew not to ask. "You will miss me?"

Was there a right answer for the question Nicolau posed to her, she thought? He stared at her and she knew there was only one right answer.

"Yes," she said.

"You will," he agreed. Then his eyes slid down over her breasts and he smiled once more. "You are different today. Prettier when you are not crying. I like you better like this. Much better. I will give you a choice today since you were so good for our guest. Do you want to be on your knees in front of me or on your knees on my bed?" Briana felt herself beginning to shake and she tried to keep it under control. "It doesn't matter which of your holes I put it in, they are all beautiful." His eyes traveled down the front of her body again. "See, Phoenix, I am not an unreasonable man. You choose."

Briana swallowed hard and then she stepped forward toward Nicolau. She had no intention of letting him put himself inside of her body if she could help it at all. She fell to her knees in front of him. Her fingers worked his belt, opening it. She unzipped his pants and slid them down over his hips, hearing the belt buckle hit the floor. Her hand reached for his member, feeling it grow harder as her fingers clasped around it. None of this was acceptable, but this was much better then him penetrating her. She felt his hands on her shoulders and she was about to slide him into her mouth when she felt his hands slide around her neck. She looked up at him as he squeezed her neck and lifted her up from her knees as if she was a doll.

When she was face to face with him, her face turning red as her oxygen was being cut off, he stared into her eyes. "Be very careful with those teeth. Don't get any ideas, Phoenix." He released the pressure on her throat and slid her back down to her knees. His hands moving to her shoulders once more.

Briana coughed as she inhaled deeply, catching her breath once more. She swallowed the spit that had built up in her mouth when he choked her, tasting blood from where she bit the inside of her cheek. She reached for him, not wanting to delay this any more than she needed to. She wrapped her hand around him. He was incredible hard, bigger than she remembered. She swallowed him into her mouth, her tongue sliding over him.

"Look at me," Nicolau said.

Briana looked up into his eyes as her hand worked him in and out of her mouth. Her eyes were watery and teary from the choking, but she wouldn't give into crying. Instead, she concentrated on bringing him to a finish. The faster she could get him out of her mouth and back to her cell the better. Part of her wanted to bite down, bite down hard, make him bleed and suffer the consequences, but she knew they would be severe, and her survival reflex held her back. She moaned loudly as she sucked on him, hoping that would expedite the process. Her free hand reached for his scrotum, tugging on it, harder than she should, squeezing his balls. She stared into his eyes daring him to complain as she stretched his sack, sucking him deep into her mouth.

Briana could feel him thrusting into her now. She pulled her head back when he did, but his hands held her head as he pressed into her, gagging her. When she tried to pull away, he held her steady until he was ready to release her. When he did, she spit him out, working to catch her breath and then slide him back in. This went on for a while, her eyes widening as she stared at him each time he gagged her. He got off on choking her with his cock. She tried to control him by pulling on his balls, but that only seemed to get him more excited. She could hear him moaning now above her and she focused on bringing him over the line, making him finish so she could be done, go back to her cell.

Nicolau pulled on her hair, pulling her off him completely, holding her head back. She let go of his balls, letting her hands fall to her side as he stared down at her. They were both breathing hard. Then he pulled her head toward him and slid himself back into her mouth. He guided her head back and forth while holding her hair as he thrust in and out of her mouth. She had very little control of the situation. He stared down at her as he pulled her head onto him sliding deep into her mouth, holding himself there. Briana coughed and gagged, but he held her steady, choking her. She implored him with her eyes to let her free, and when he did pull out, she coughed and spat a wad of saliva on the ground. He looked down at her, giving her a minute to catch her breath and then he held her chin with his hand and pushed himself back into her mouth. This time, he slid himself in and out repeatedly, his hips pumping into her mouth as he worked himself to a climax.

When he was ready, he pressed himself inside of her again, holding himself there as he swelled inside of her mouth. Briana stared up at him; she knew it was almost over. Then she felt him pull himself out of her mouth and step back as he jerked himself in front of her shooting his load all over her face, neck and breast. He moaned loudly as he let go, watching his stream as he painted her body and hair with his seed. When he was finally done, he stepped close to her one more and he lifted her jaw with one hand and slipped himself inside her mouth again.

"Clean me off," Nicolau said. "Make sure that there is nothing left inside."

Briana sucked and licked him until she was sure he was empty and then she pulled her mouth off of him. He stared down at her, covered with his spunk, and he smiled.

"I think your mouth was a good choice today," he said, stepping back as he pulled his pants up. "Next time, it will be my choice." Nicolau finished buckling his pants and smiled at her. "You are a mess. Get dressed, but no wiping it off. Not tonight. I want you to sleep with me on you all night tonight."

Briana stood up and walked over to where her clothes were. She dressed quickly, pulling her clothes over her sticky body. When she was finished, Nicolau called for the guard. The guard entered the room moments later with the shackles. He bent down to put them on her ankles and then stood up. He looked at Briana and then turned away. She was sure her face and hair told the story of what had just happened in the room.

"Take Phoenix back to her cell. She will be leaving us tomorrow for training. Make sure that she and Lily are ready bright and early." Nicolau started to walk to the office side of the large room. "Oh," he said, turning back. "This one will need a shower in the morning. She's covered with my sperm."

Briana flushed at Nicolau's last comment as the guard looked her over. It was his final shot at humiliating her and it had hit home. What did she care at this point? The worst part of this day, she hoped, was over.

****

Back in the cell, Briana found Lily, high as a kite. She offered Briana food which she ate willingly. Briana told Lily that they would be going for training the next morning which didn't seem to mean anything to her. Most likely the drugs had dulled her mind and Briana would have to wait until she came down to have a real conversation with her.

When Briana was finished with her food, she slid the tray to the side of the cell and sat down on the edge of her bed. She tried to commit to memory everything she had seen today. Places, locations, Oalo and everything from Nicolau's room. Lock it away. It could come in handy someday. She heard Lily giggling and making noises on the opposite side of the cell, but she ignored her as she committed her day to memory.

At one point, Lily walked over to Briana's cot and looked down at Briana.

"What is in your hair?" Lily reached up to a clump of hair that was stuck together. "Is this... and it's seeping through your shirt also? Are you covered in spunk?" she laughed.

Briana tried to ignore her, but Lily kept asking. Finally, Briana nodded her head and that was enough to push Lily over the edge. She fell onto her bed and buried her head in her pillow muffling her laughter so that she did not get into trouble. Briana found herself laughing at Lily's laughing and picked up her pillow to cover her mouth. Nothing was laughable about any of their situation, which she realized was what made it so funny.

Chapter 12

Jose pulled his taxi up to the school in Santa Teresa. He was there earlier than he would normally expect to see Briana, but he wanted to see her arrive. To say he was smitten with her was an understatement, and he knew she would never go for a guy like him, but he still was worried that he had not heard from her in more than three days.

Now, as he sat outside the school, he expected to see another cab pull up in front at any moment to drop off the lovely Briana. He waited 10, then 15 minutes and still no cab arrived. Perhaps she was inside already, he thought, but he was sure that was not the case.

Within another 15 minutes, the expensive cars pulled up dropping off the children of the wealthy and powerful. Each of the kids walked into school wearing clothes which were worth more than Jose's whole wardrobe, including the one suit he owned for weddings and funerals. He didn't look down on them though. You cannot choose whom you are born to, he knew.

The last car unloaded two children and he saw the guards circle around the young boys and lead them into the building. To live like that was a curse, no matter how much money they had. He waited until the three men walked out of the building and watched as their two SUVs left.

Where was Briana, he thought? Could she be sick? The food itself could get to someone if they were not careful. Or, maybe she got called home. There could be many reasons. Jose decided he would wait another day before asking more questions. He did not want to become a burden to Briana; he wanted to be her friend – or more.

****

Back in the states, there was no such concern about becoming a burden on Briana, the US Consulate in Brazil, or even the local state senators. Briana's mother, after 24 hours, had tried to file a missing person's request with the police department who told her that there was nothing that they could do and they she would have to reach out to government officials. Briana's father then reached out to a few of his friends who were attorneys and they suggested reaching out to their local politicians. They helped of course, but the wheels of the government move slowly – especially at weekends.

It was not until Monday afternoon when Senator Marshall initially returned Briana's mother's call – through an assistant. The assistant listened to the panic and worried mother and told her he would do all he could to try and get the senator's attention, but it might be difficult because there was a big budget vote happening which might go well into the night. Briana's mother hung up the phone and looked over at her husband.

"Phil," she said, "they are not taking this seriously. They think I am being hysterical, and they won't even bring it to the senator's attention."

"Did they say that?"

"Not in so many words. But, there's a big budget battle or something and well... who the fuck knows when they will help us!" she said, turning red as the words came out of her mouth.

Briana's mother rarely cursed, and Phil had never heard her spill the f-word. He walked over to her and took him in her arms. He pulled her tight against him as she sobbed.

"I'll talk to my lawyer friends, Claire. They have some friends up in Washington. We can find a way to get their attention." He patted her back. She continued to sob.

"We're not doing anything," she cried. "Nothing to help. Can we call the consulate directly?"

"I'll find out," Phil said. "As soon as I can, I'll find out."

Claire put her head on his shoulder and continued to cry. Her tears would not abate for several hours.

****

When morning came, Briana was surprised to find Lily in the room when she awoke. Lily was already out of her cot and she smiled at Briana.

"Guards were here. I told him you definitely needed to shower. So, he'll be back shortly. He likes to watch, but he's harmless."

"None of this is harmless," Briana said.

"Our guard is. I think his dick would explode if he touched any of us," she laughed at her own statement as they both heard a knock on the door.

When the door opened, Briana saw the familiar guard's face as he entered the room. He didn't smile; he didn't frown. He looked emotionless, she thought. Probably how Hitler's captors looked during WWII.

"Come," he said, pointing at Briana. She stood up. "You

– be ready in 10 minutes also. We have to leave very soon."

Briana looked over at Lily and watched her nod. Then she followed the guard out of the room. He didn't bother to put the shackles on her. Briana wasn't sure if that was because he trusted her – he never put shackles on Lily – or if they were in a rush.

When they got to the showers, he handed Briana some plain panties and a new set of scrubs, blue this time, then motioned for her to shower.

Briana moved to the showers, pulling a crusty towel off a hook to wrap herself in quickly if needed. She turned the water on and then undressed quickly keeping her back to the door. After testing the water, she stepped inside, washing her body with the shampoo or soap that sat in a bottle on the floor. When she bent, she did so at the knees so as not to put on more of a show for the guard. After shampooing and rinsing her hair, she let the water rinse off her back and then turned the water off and picked up the towel at the same time. She dried off and was in her scrubs managing to show as little skin as possible to the guard.

When she returned to the door, he had a small smile on his face which made her think he wasn't quite as emotionless as she thought and that she had not done that good of a job covering up. They hurried back toward the cells at the other end of the large building and just as they were getting to Briana's cell, a loud whistle sounded off behind her.

Briana turned to see a large man; obese was really the appropriate word. He blew the whistle once more and several guards approached the cells, opening each of them one at a time. Briana watched, for the first time realizing there were many more cells than she imagined. Watching the guards go from door to door, she estimated there were maybe 20 cells all together. When the doors opened, women stepped out into the large open space. At least two women from each cell, each wearing blue scrubs, stepped out of the rooms. It wasn't just Briana and Lily and maybe one or two others. There were at least 40 women trapped – presumedly kidnapped and held in this prison. She felt her jaw tighten at the enormity of the operation. Something in the back of her mind made her think that the size of the kidnapped group could maybe be a good thing at some point.

"Listen carefully," the fat man said. He had a Russian or Eastern European accent. "You will all be boarding buses shortly. There will be no talking. Our ride is some two hours and when we arrive, you will be taken to new holding cells – with your partners. Then we will commence training." He stopped to look amongst the many woman in the large room. "I will say this only once. You will listen and obey all orders – or..." he clapped his hands "or you will be dealt with appropriately. There are many of you. If I lose one or two of you over the course of training – which is likely, that doesn't mean anything to me." He walked closer to the group of women now. "But I warn you. The pain we inflict on you for not listening will not be swift. Some of my men take great pleasure in stretching out their punishments. Do you understand?"

The women nodded and muffled their responses. Briana looked over at Lily who stood in front of their cell door. She wanted to go to her, be next to her so they could protect one another, but she was afraid to move, less this monster make an example of her.

He turned his back on the women and walked back toward the door of the large building. "During your training, you will be asked to do things most of you have never done before. You will do them willingly and with great enthusiasm. Remember the women you are partnered with. They too can pay for failure to cooperate. And... one of you, I can almost guarantee it, will be given away to the team of trainers at the end of the week for their sport. Let's board the buses like good girls. You all have a lot to learn."

What the hell did that mean, Briana thought. For sport? She looked at the group of women as they started to move away from their cells. They carried no pocketbooks, no phones, nothing. They all were scared, as was Briana. All of the women were young, slim, pretty and many of them were Asian, she noticed. She thought that was interesting. Briana waited for Lily to get close and then she fell in next to her.

"This is crazy," Briana whispered, "and all fucked up." Lily nodded. "Are they going to train us as sex slaves?" When Briana said it out loud, it almost sounded laughable, impossible. But it also sounded horrible and inhuman. Lily's face provided the answer that Briana didn't want to hear. "We have to stop them, Lily. This is ridiculous. I'm not going to submit to..."

"Shut up, Briana!" Lily whispered loudly. "Nothing he said to us was untrue. Just remember that whatever they do to you doesn't have to hurt you if you don't let them get in your mind."

"There's like 40 of us. We could rise up..." she looked around at the women who all looked broken and demoralized. "Even if we can't, there has to be people looking for all of us. There's too many of us not to go unnoticed."

"Some of us have been here for a while, Briana. You have only been here for a short time but look what they've done to you in a couple of days. Your parents will be made to believe that you are dead. They will stop looking for you. You need to listen and obey, I've seen what happens when you

131

don't. Just play along. It will be better for all of us."

Briana wasn't ready to give in; to be broken and demoralized. They didn't get to own her body and they certainly didn't get to own her brain. She would find a way out. She just had to be smart. To play along just enough to earn their trust – like she had with the guard. Just be smart.

When they were all loaded on the buses, they rode in silence for a little over an hour before the buses went off road and eventually pulled over into an encampment in the jungle. It was hot and humid. They were escorted from the buses into a series of green tents, separated by rooms within the tents; grouped back with their partners. It was still early morning, but it looked like dusk as the sun did not penetrate the dense jungle. The empty buses drove away, leaving the women behind in the dark and sweaty tents.

Briana and Lily each moved to their respective cots and sat down. There were dim lights in each tent. In the corner was a mirror, a bowl of water, toothbrushes, toothpaste, and a hairbrush. Lily was the first to rise and brush her teeth swishing the brush in the water and rinsing her mouth before spitting it on the floor.

"Feels good to have clean teeth," she said.

Briana was slow to get up but knew that it was the little things that they needed to cherish. She brushed her teeth quickly also spitting the water on the ground. There was a loud whistle which drew their attention toward the front of the tents. Briana and Lily stepped out of their tent onto the hard ground.

"You will be fed two meals each day when you are in camp – if you are allowed to eat. They will be lunch and dinner. When the whistle blows, you will go to the table in the front, get your food and then go back to your tent and eat it inside your room. You will only come out to relieve yourself and to eat, unless requested to come out by a guard. Do you understand?"

The group of women responded with a mix of murmurs and nods.

"Very well, welcome to camp. You may get your lunch."

A sudden frenzy erupted amongst the women as they all made their way toward the large tables at the end of the room which contained the food. They knocked into one another as they reached for their food and then fled back into their tents to eat. Briana watched, knowing that it would be difficult to pull this group of women together to complete any task, much less an escape. It was every woman for herself. She would have to come up with a better plan. When the crowd died down, she reached for a plate and piled on what looked like two pieces of chicken and some bread – much needed protein and carbs. She took a cup of water and headed back to the tent. Lily was already inside when she arrived.

"What a bunch of animals," Briana said.

"Keep someone in a cage, they become an animal," Lily responded.

Briana nodded her head as she began to eat, taking the time to savor the food not knowing when she would really get another meal. When they were finished, they collected their plates. When they next left the tent, they would deposit them in the waste cans that were outside.

"Do you think we will ever get out of here, Lily?"

Lily didn't respond, instead turning her head away. Briana was sure that she heard her crying. Soon, they found themselves laying down on their cots resting, dreaming, plotting, planning, worrying, and rationalizing – all at the same time. None of this was absorbable, Briana thought. It was too much for one person to comprehend.

Chapter 13

The next morning, Briana awoke on her cot. Lily was not in the tent. She didn't remember hearing her leave; she didn't remember anything after going to sleep the night before. Her body, exhausted, must have shut down. She busied herself in the tent walking the length back and forth many times, counting her steps. Fourteen steps one way, 10 steps the other. She then walked standard lengths, not toe to toe and realized it was roughly seven steps one way, five steps the other – half the number of steps; something she had never known.

She wondered where Lily was, where they had taken her and what she was doing. She thought about the training – sex slave training. What the fuck was that? Who would be willing to do that? Well, no one, she realized would willingly do any of this. She thought about her mom, her dad. Even the kids at the school. Anything to take their minds off what was happening in the place that she had found herself. There was crying too. And she wasn't alone. She was sure she heard others crying and occasionally raised voices. Briana kept to herself during the morning waiting for lunch, so she could get outside, better understand her surroundings and plan her escape.

At one point, as she found herself huddled up on Lily's cot, praying and crying, there was a commotion at the front of her tent. She inhaled and held her breath as she heard the zipper open. She watched as Lily was pushed into the tent, onto the floor. She waited for the zipper to close and then she went to her.

"Lily. Are you okay?" She shook her. "Lily?"

Lily looked up at her, smiled and her eyes rolled back into her head. Briana looked her over as she shook her. Her lips were bruised, and her hair was a sweaty mess, pushed back onto one side of her head, matted down. She called her name again and Lily briefly opened her eyes and then closed them again, her body like Jell-O on the tent floor.

"C'mon, Lily. Wake up." Then Briana remembered and she picked up one of Lily's arms and sure enough, there was a puncture wound, still bleeding a bit where they had administered the drugs; the drugs that made Lily compliant. "Fuck! What did they do to you?" She held Lily's head in her lap as she ran her fingers through her hair trying to separate the matted mess as she tried to rationalize what was happening. Neither pursuit was fruitful, and Briana found herself crying as she tried to console Lily.

Gradually she pulled and dragged Lily as best as she could, without hurting her, over to the cot and lifted her onto the small mattress. She laid her down and fixed her clothes, so she didn't look so disheveled, and then she went to pull her sheet up over her. That's when she saw the blood on her pants in the area between her legs. Briana let go of the sheet and slid down the front of Lily's pants. Her underwear was all red between her legs. Briana looked up at the ceiling of the tent as she started to cry, keeping her mouth shut to muffle the noise. She pulled Lily's sheet up and placed the sheet over her, up to her neck. She sat on the side of the bed, gently massaging her cheek as tears sobbed quietly. Lily lay silent on the cot.

The tent zipper suddenly opened startling Briana. Before she could even compose herself or get up off the cot a man entered the room. He was tall – another guard she assumed. He stared down at her, nodding as he looked at a clipboard in his hand.

"Phoenix," he said.

She found herself nodding even though she had not heard the name since she had left the prison camp.

"Come with me."

She didn't move.

"Now!" he said, his voice conveying a need to obey him.

She stood up, taking a last look at Lily who rested comfortably on the cot. The man took her by the arm and led her from the tent. She protested at first, and then she followed him as he led her across the courtyard. Briana took it all in; every aspect of it, trying to commit it to memory. Saving it to a map she was creating in her head. All part of her escape plan which had no shape or design at all. They walked for a about five minutes completely across the compound. It was much larger than Briana thought. There were small buildings and another large tent setup similar to the one that she and the other woman were brought into the day before. There were jeeps with mounted guns and other larger vehicles, buses as well as at least one tank that she noticed before she was led to a large wooden building.

Outside the building the man turned to her. His eyes walked up and down her body as if she couldn't see what he was doing. He smiled when their eyes met once more.

"You are very pretty," he said. "Do as you are told; do what you are told, and you will remain pretty. Understood?"

Briana couldn't make out his accent. They all sounded

Russian or Eastern European, but it made no sense, not out here in the Brazilian jungle.

"Understood?" he repeated.

"Yes," she said, surprised by her own voice. It was shaky and nervous, but it was deeper than she expected, almost as if she had rehearsed.

"Very good. We will go inside now. Remember: speak only when asked a direct question and do whatever you are asked. Do you understand?"

Briana nodded her head.

Chapter 14

Jose, the taxi driver, had made himself a prominent fixture outside of the school where Briana was supposed to be working. It was more than two days, plus the weekend where he had not seen or heard from her. He had decided that if she did not show up, he would march into the school to inquire about her whereabouts. He waited for all of the students to arrive and even for the guards to walk the cartel children in before he decided he would approach the school. When Briana still had not appeared, he stepped out of his cab and went inside.

Mrs. Alves's eyebrow lifted as the taxi driver stepped into the school. She looked him up and down and stood up from her chair.

"Can I help you?"

"My name is Jose. I am a taxi man. For Ms. Briana. I have not seen her for days and I want to find out if she is okay."

Mrs. Alves looked at Jose. The poor man, she thought. He was a cab driver and had probably fallen for Briana and all of her charms. Alas, it got him nowhere, just as it had not gotten Marcos anywhere. He hired her for her looks, not her skills and she took off on him. She decided she would not be the one to deliver the news to this taxi driver.

"I am not at liberty to disclose any information about our teachers."

"She has not been here. Is she still a teacher?"

Mrs. Alves shook her head. It is not my place to discuss this with a taxi driver. For all I know you could be responsible for her disappearance."

"So, it's true. You have no idea if she is okay. And, she has not been in contact with the school."

"What is all of this?" Mr. Souza said as he came out from the doors behind Mrs. Alves.

Jose was surprised, but he held his ground. "I am inquiring about your teacher, Ms. Briana."

"What business is she of yours?"

"I am her driver. Jose. I was her driver every day since she arrived here. Now, I hear nothing, and I know she was happy about taking this job and now I do not see her anymore." He stared at Mr. Souza.

"Come," he said, indicating that Jose should follow him.

Jose followed him into his office in the back where he was told to sit down.

"You know Brazil is a dangerous place, yes?" Jose nodded, sitting up in his chair, expecting bad news. "We can never be too careful. Briana was a beautiful girl."

"Has something happened to her?"

"That's just it. We have not heard from her. Not a note, not a call. She doesn't answer her phone. Nothing."

"Polícia? Have you reported her missing?"

"We have, but we do not know much about her. We can only tell them her name, where she said she was living and that she is a US citizen. It is being reported to the embassy soon."

"Soon?" Jose said. He stood up from his seat. "Why does it seem like no one is concerned."

"Please, sit down," Mr. Souza said. "We have done what we can; it is out of our hands."

"Because you are scared," Jose said. He remained standing, his finger pointing at the administrator. "You are scared that one of the cartel or other people whose children you teach did something to her or will do something to you if you ask too many questions."

Mr. Souza had had enough of Jose. "You should be scared too! Do you think these people care about a taxi driver or a school administrator? They will kill you just for asking questions. I did what I had to do. I am sorry that Briana is not here and I cannot tell you where she is. She was a nice person; a good teacher."

"You speak of her as if she is already gone." Mr. Souza did not respond. Jose backed his way toward the door. "I will report this on my own; tell the polícia what I know. Maybe that will help."

"Be careful, Jose," he said. "Mind my words."

Jose opened the door and stepped out into the hallway, slamming the door behind him. As he walked past Mrs. Alves, he shook his head. He turned towards her before he left. "You should be ashamed of yourself. Briana is a good person."

He turned and left the building heading back to his taxi. Jose drove to the police station to report Briana missing. He hoped whatever information he gave them would help them find her safe somewhere – maybe even back home. It was all he could hope for.

****

Briana's parents were beside themselves. It took two days before they could even make any headway and that was after calling in as many favors as they could. Finally, with the help of prominent lawyers that her father knew well, they were able to get their senator, Senator Marshall, to listen to them. When they finally described the situation, the senator told them he would inquire of the embassy and put out a missing person's report with the Federal Police of Brazil. It was now two days later and they had heard nothing despite repeated phone calls.

Briana's parents drove to Senator's Marshalls office, more than two hours from their home with the intention of confronting him and making him take action. What they thought would be a battle turned out to be quite the opposite.

"Come in, come in," the senator said to them.

"Why haven't you returned our phone calls?" Briana's mom said immediately.

"I've been working on a solution for you."

"You've found our girl," Briana's father said. His wife took his arm and held it.

"No, no," Mr. Campbell. "Unfortunately, it is a difficult situation."

"What are you telling us?" he asked.

"Listen – without boots on the ground, it's difficult to get any traction on this kind of thing. We've been calling and reporting, but nothing." Mrs. Campbell started to cry again. "But we have a plan. We're sending you two over to be our boots on the ground. You can work directly with the embassy, provide them all of the information that they need. They will assign a caseworker to work with you and the police there. This way, we can bring the most important people to the investigation. You."

He smiled when he finished his sentence and Briana's dad had to hold her mom back.

"That's it? You worthless piece of shit! My daughter is lost overseas and the best you can do is send us over there, assign us a caseworker?"

"Now, now, Mrs. Campbell. Remember who you are talking to."

"I know who I am talking to, you asshole!"

The senator seemed non-plussed by her words. "Are you sure your daughter didn't just sneak off with the first Hispanic man she met?"

Briana's dad almost leapt across the table at him; it was her mother's turn to do the holding back.

"Careful now. I can revoke my offer at any time. Your plane leaves in the morning. Here is the information. I suggest you pull some pictures together of your daughter and get some rest. My assistant will see you out."

The senator pressed a button on his desk and the door opened. The Campbells followed the man out the door, Briana's mom clutching her husband's arm as she cried.

Chapter 15

The guard led Briana by the arm into the large white building. They walked up a small set of steps. He knocked on the outside door and it opened up in front of them. There were two guards manning the doors as they stepped inside. He led Briana to a room buried in the complex as she flashed back to her visits with Nicolau.

Her body started to shake and her walk slowed down as they moved forward. The guard squeezed her arm and pulled her forward, looking down at her as she involuntarily resisted.

"Por favor," please, he said.

Briana straightened up and stepped forward. At the end of the hallway, they stopped in front of a door and Briana began to shake once more.

The guard opened the door and he led her into the room.

Inside, a small, dark woman stood up looking at Briana and then turned her back on her as she walked across the room to a rack of clothes. The small woman took a pole with a hook on it and she lifted a single item off the long rack of clothes. She dropped the item onto a table, replaced the pole against the wall and then carried the item she selected over to Briana. On her way, she stopped to pick up a pair of shoes.

"Undress," she said.

Briana didn't move.

The woman stepped forward and repeated the word.

Briana stared down at her, into her eyes and then slowly lifted the sides of her top up. She pulled the shirt over her head and dropped it to the floor. She wore no bra. She crossed her arms across her chest.

"The rest," the woman said.

Briana reached down, slowly sliding her pants down over her hips. She stood, nearly naked, as the woman looked her over. Once more feeling like a piece of meat on display, Briana crossed her arms over her chest.

"Lower your arms. Take off the panties."

Briana stared down once more. Who was this small woman giving her orders? The woman looked into her eyes and then punched her hard in the stomach. Briana doubled over before she knew what hit her. When she did, the woman slapped her across the face, hard with an open hand.

"Fuck!" Briana said as she held her stomach and then her face. Her head was spinning as she tried to get her bearings. Her stomach hurt tremendously where she'd been punched and her face stung. She wasn't sure which one was worse.

"The panties," the woman said.

This time Briana didn't look at the woman, instead she reached down to slide her panties off. When she was done, she stood with her arms at her side as the woman walked around her, nodding and scratching her own chin. When she completed her circle, she stood in front of Briana and smiled.

"Put on the clothes," the woman said, pointing to the shoes and the robe she had selected from the rack.

Briana reached for the short, red satin robe and slid her arms into it. She wrapped it around her and tied the belt tightly across her waist. The knot pressed against the pain in her stomach from the punch. She pulled the knot away as she tried to lessen the pain. She stepped into the red stilettos suddenly feeling very tall next to the small woman.

"Very well," she said. "She's ready." The woman turned and walked away. "Get these filthy clothes out of my sight."

"Pick them up," the guard said as he grabbed her arm.

Briana bent down and picked up her clothes.

"Good, now put them in this trash over here." He walked her over to a large trash bin, filled with similar clothes, some blue, some purple. "Now, let's go."

The guard led Briana out of the room, closing the door behind her. As she walked past, guards turned in her direction watching the robed woman being led across the long hallway toward a set of double doors. Before they even got to the doors, they opened, and the guard walked Briana inside. They walked up three steps and then down another small hallway. At the end of the hallway, in a large throne-like chair, sat a man waiting for their arrival. The guard led Briana up to the man and let go of her arm.

The man stayed in his chair as he looked Briana over. "Her name?" he said.

"Phoenix," the guard replied.

"Hmm. Look at me."

Briana looked up at the man in the chair.

"Very nice. Very nice." The man was dark-skinned, and he spoke with a Latin accent. He was a big man, not fat, but big. His hands were very large, Briana noticed. "Do you know why you are here?" Briana shook her head. She had a good idea of what she would be asked to do, but she thought playing dumb might buy her some time. "You are here for training. You will learn to do much with me and others so that you can be part of our elite team. Do you understand?"

Briana nodded as she stared down at the ground.

"Look at me."

She looked up.

"Remove the robe."

Briana slowly untied the knot on the robe's belt. She could still feel the pain in her face where the woman slapped her, and her stomach reminded her of the punch. She did not want to go through that again. Her fingers worked the knot open and then she slid the robe off her body, letting it fall to the floor.

The man stared at her. His head moved up and down looking for any imperfections. She shook silently but visibly. "Stop shaking," he said. "You are not welcoming if you look scared. Stop shaking."

Briana willed herself to stop shaking.

"Better. Now, let me see you smile."

Briana looked up at him. He wanted her to smile, to pretend this was not happening. Her mouth was not cooperating; she could not smile. Her face shook, her lips trembled. Tears fell from her eyes.

"Not very good at all," the man said. "You will learn. A client wants his woman to be happy, willing to please him... . or her, at all times. A client wants there to only be one thing on your mind – their happiness. You will learn to do this, I promise you. Shall we try again?"

Briana looked up at him. A client? Man or woman? Happy? He wanted her to appear happy that she was doing this. As she thought of all of this, she curled the ends of her mouth into a smile. It was not at all a pretty smile, but it showed effort.

"See, you almost did it," the man said. Then to the guard. "Leave us. Wait outside the door for my call."

The guard turned and left. Briana heard the door close

behind her.

"Now. Lesson one is learning how to please someone when you do not want to." Briana looked up at him with her arms crossed across her chest. "I assume you do not want to please me, right?"

She didn't answer.

"Good. Then it is perfect."

The man stood up from the large chair and walked down two steps until he stood in front of her. He wore nothing but a thick black robe. He reached down and took Briana's hand.

"Cold," he said. "No man likes a woman with cold hands. You should rub them together and warm them, so they are not cold."

He let go of her hand and Briana rubbed her hands hard against one another to warm them. The entire time she was doing that she thought of wrapping them around the man's neck and squeezing them tight.

He reached for her hands after a short time and smiled at her. "Better. See, you are already learning."

He folded her hand in his and he slowly turned her as they walked down a side hallway. He opened a door to a room which contained a large bed in the center. He walked Briana into the room and closed the door behind her. When he turned his back on her, Briana thought about attacking him, but she didn't move, didn't even face him.

"Good. You see, your urges to hurt me, to resist, are of no use. Please, put them out of your mind. Concentrate on pleasing your charge. That is your job. Whatever they need, you will provide. Do you understand?"

Briana nodded slowly. Her eyes welled up with tears and she could feel them dripping over her cheeks.

"You need to control your crying. You only cry if you are asked to, understood?" This time she nodded quickly out of fear that he might strike her. He sounded as if he was losing his patience and she didn't want to be struck by those large hands. "Very good," he said.

The man held her hand up as he walked around her taking another look, this time much closer. He smiled when he completed his examination and then he let her hand go, stepping back and admiring her.

"Now, normally, I would take my subject to the comfortable bed over there," he said pointing to the massive bed in the center of the room. "But you have not been as willing a subject as you need to be." He stepped forward and lifted her chin with his finger. "You'll not even smile for me."

Briana began to shake once more as he stared into her eyes. She would need to do whatever he asked. She would need to do that to survive. She would have to put it out of her mind. Like Lily had said, erase their actions, don't let them into your brain. Erase everything. She reached up her hands to put them on the man's arms as she slowly looked back into his face. She exhaled, trying to get control of her shaking and then she managed a small smile.

"Very good, Phoenix, very good," the man said. "But I am afraid that is too late for today. Remember it for next time. You need to learn faster and to listen the first time."

Briana felt the man's hands on her sides as he turned her around. His one hand found the small of her back as he pushed her, walking alongside of her across the big room. She tried to stop him from pushing her, but she was no match for his strength. There was a table against the far wall, and he positioned her in front of it. Then he pulled both her arms back and up behind her. She involuntary bent pushing her chest onto the table as one of his large hands held her arms tight. She tried to pull away, lift herself up from the table but there was no fighting him. Her head was turned to the side resting on the table as she tried to look back at him, but he held her down.

Then she heard him spit loudly, as his legs kicked her legs apart, spreading them as he held her down on the table. She knew what was coming next and she closed her eyes, tried to fight against him, feeling the pain in her arms and her shoulders Then she felt his cock head push up against her, spreading her lips open as he rubbed himself up and down her pussy. She screamed out and he lifted her arms to quiet her as he pushed the head of his cock inside of her, entering her slowly at first and then pulling out quickly before she heard him spit once more. This time, he found her hole and pressed inside of her. She cried out once more as he pushed into her, burying himself deep inside.

"Learn to please, Phoenix," he said. And then he started to fuck her. Holding her arms behind her, lifting them when she cried out, he rammed in and out of her over and over again. His balls slammed against her as he drove himself in and out unabated by her cries.

Briana tried to focus on something else, but it was impossible. The pain in her arms where he held her, her shoulders as he bent them back, was nothing compared to his cock slamming into her over and over again. She tried to pull away, but his large hand held her wrists forcing them up over her back. She didn't move. Merely a receptacle for his dick. She closed her eyes hoping that he would cum soon and pull his massive member out from inside of her.

The man leaned down over her, his weight pressing down on her back. "This is not the worst thing that can happen to you, Phoenix," he whispered into her ear. "There is much worse. I decide between pain and pleasure." He lifted her arms once more; Briana cried out. "There can be so much more pain." He loosened the pressure on her arms and then pressed himself deep inside of her once more. "And there can be so much more pleasure. It is up for you to decide. Do you understand?" She didn't answer. He slid his cock out of her and rammed it back inside. "Do you understand?"

"Yes," Briana cried out. "Yes. You're hurting me."

She felt the pressure lift off her back as the man lifted himself off of her. He released her wrists and slid his hands down to her hips. The relief was immediate, and Briana pulled her hand up by her sides feeling the excruciating pain as she brought her arms up over her head. He was still inside of her, his hands on her hips. Then she felt him pull himself out and step back from her.

Briana looked back, afraid to lift herself from the table; afraid to move at all, but she knew she could not stay in this position. She placed her palms on the table and slowly lifted herself. When she was standing, she turned to him, shaking still, tears falling from her eyes.

"Please let me go," she cried.

"Enough," the man said He was still wearing his robe which hung open, his large cock hanging down in front of him "We will spend the next several hours together, learning the difference between pain and pleasure." He started to walk away. "That is really up to you. You will learn that you are here for my pleasure and those I tell you to pleasure. Nothing else. If you do that well, there will be no pain." He stopped and turned around. There were 20 feet between them. "I don't mind administering punishment. I don't mind it at all. Do you understand?"

Briana nodded.

"Good. Now, there is a sink in the corner over there." He pointed to the far wall. "Go clean up your face. We will have some breakfast together."

Chapter 16

Lily had learned long ago that being submissive was a way of extending her life. The drugs, when they gave them to her, were just enough to take the edge off while her captors did horrible things to her body. Just enough to dull her senses, but not enough to prevent her from engaging sexually. She tried to do it without the drugs, but she found herself beaten on a regular basis. Her true self – un-drugged and lucid, couldn't take what they were doing to her, couldn't stomach the way they treated her and other women. Her true self got her into trouble. The drugs helped her escaped the horrible reality forced upon her.

Lily thought back to the early morning when the guards had taken her from the room, in the dark and pushed her into a room with three other women. They waited, naked for a long time before they were squirted down with firehoses and told to wash themselves with soap that was thrown into their room. When they were done, they were asked to dry off and dress in dresses that were handed to them by a very small woman. She had sized up each of the woman and presented them with a dress. Two other women were there to comb out their hair, roughly until most of the knots were removed. Lily remembered the tears in her eyes as they tugged on her hair.

When they were dressed and presentable, they were ushered into a small van and driven a distance from the compound. Lily watched out the windows to see if there was any sign of life outside the camp, but not until they were a distance away did she even see any streetlights. When they finally stopped, they were taken into a darkened room, but not before Lily was given her dose of drugs, injected just below her elbow. The man smiled as he gave it to her, taking her hand and placing it between his legs as he pushed the drug into her veins. She remembered him being hard beneath his pants and she traced its shape until the drugs took their initial effect on her. When her hand dropped, he lifted her up and led her inside with the other girls. Lily shook her head to gain control over the drug; she had to focus, or it would take her over.

The girls held each other's hands as they were lined up against a wall. The men who brought them into the room reminded them that someone was always watching and that if they tried to escape, they would be killed. The men left; two of them remained outside on guard, as the lights gradually brightened in the room. As the room became brighter, Lily heard clapping and cheering. She looked out across the room and saw at least 20 people packed into a small auditorium of sorts. They appeared to be on a stage.

Several people from the audience screamed out to them in different languages, none of which Lily understood. One of the women, reached for another woman's hand and pulled her to the center of the stage. She must have understood Portuguese. When they reached the middle of the stage, the first woman took the second woman in her arms and pulled her close to her as she kissed her on the mouth. The crowd cheered loudly. Lily stood with her back to the wall as the women kissed on stage and then watched as one of the women slowly undressed the other, sliding her out of her dress. Another loud cheer. When the woman was naked, the other woman bent her head to her breast and pulled her nipple into her mouth.

Were they to put on a show for these people, Lily wondered? As she thought that, the drugs swirling through her brain, the other girl, the one who stood next to her reached for her hand. Lily swatted the hand away before the woman took it again. When she had a solid grip on Lily's hand, she pulled her onto the floor amid the cheering of the crowd. Now, they stood next to the other two women as words were yelled out from the crowd. Lily was able to make out some English, and all of it was filthy. She looked over at the first two women. Both were naked now and one was on her knees before the other. What the fuck, she thought?

Moments later, the girl who pulled her to center stage leaned her head in and kissed her on the lips. The crowd cheered even as Lily pulled away.

"What are you doing?"

"What we have to do to stay safe. You know the rules," she said. Neither of them had to whisper because the crowd was so loud. "Now kiss me back; I don't feel like getting another beating."

The woman leaned her head in and this time, Lily kissed her back tentatively. As she did, the crowd roared, and the other woman placed a hand behind Lily's head as she pressed her tongue inside. Lily protested at first, but then she kissed her back, meeting her tongue as the woman's hands slid up over her breast. She was going to do the same thing, Lily thought. She was going to strip me naked in front of this crowd of people. Her head tried to get a grip on what was happening, but by then, the other woman had slid the zipper down on the back of Lily's dress. Lily felt herself slipping out of the dress as directed by the other woman and the crowd broke into a huge cheer.

Lily turned naked to the cheering crowd and then back to the woman who had also slipped out of her dress and stood naked, her head bending down to Lily's breast, sucking her nipple into her mouth as her tongue circled it. The reaction of the crowd was predictable, but Lily could only hear a dull roar as the drug pulled her deeper into its grasp.

Lily succumbed fully to the drug and let the roar of the crowd engulf her and her actions. She stared over at the other two girls who were down on the stage now, their heads buried in each other's crotch. Even with all of the crowd noise, Lily could hear them both moaning. She placed her hands on one of the girls shoulders and pushed her toward her own crotch. The woman did not hesitate, her tongue sliding up and down her wet lips. Lily arched her back and pulled the woman against her. Her tongue was pure heaven.

The crowd was going crazy as she slowly started thrusting against the woman's mouth. Everything seemed to be getting louder. The crowd, the moaning she could hear from herself as well as the other women, and her own heart beating in her ears. The drugs, the tongue, the crowd, all swirled together in Lily's head as she cried out loud, climaxing unexpectedly into the other woman's mouth. As she came, Lily held her the woman's head tight against her body, thrusting into her until she was finished, staring at the crowd as they cheered her on.

When her orgasm was complete, Lily guided the woman up from her knees in front of her, again looking at the crowd as if she was the star of the show and then she kissed the woman hard on the mouth. Her tongue pressed into the

154

woman's mouth. The crowd cheered once more, and Lily slowly started to lower herself down the woman's body. Her mouth moved down past her nipple and the woman pulled her close to her. Lily opened her mouth and sucked the nipple inside.

What happened next seemed to happen all at once. Lily remembered that the woman in front of her, the one whose nipple she was sucking on, was pulled away from her. She watched as the woman looked at her as she was pulled away. She reached out to her as an arm wrapped around her waist. Lily turned to her side to see several people coming in her direction. She reached down to the hand that that held her and looked back to see a man behind her. He smiled at her as his hands reached up to cover her breasts. She looked out at the crowd, but it was no longer assembled. It had collectively moved to the stage and as she watched, the men were pulling off their clothes. She shook her head thinking that the drugs had conjured an image of 30 naked men in one place. As her head cleared, she realized it was not her imagination at work.

Next, she was pushed to the floor as she felt someone's hand on her ass, and then she felt a hard cock sliding up against her. She turned to look at what was happening, but before she could say anything or stop it, the cock was inside of her, deep inside of her. Strong hands held her by her hips as she tried to pull away. She let out a scream which was greeted with a slap. She looked up at the person who slapped her. He smiled down at her and shook his head. Then he pressed his cock up against her mouth. Lily slowly began to realize what this was as she opened the mouth to let the man slide his cock inside.

For the next several hours, the four women were used and abused by the men from the audience. Lily had no idea how many people were inside of her during this time; inside her mouth, her pussy, her ass, but she remembered starting to erase all of what was happening after the first person came inside of her mouth. Everything else became a blur as all four women took on the 30 or so men who never seemed to tire of using their bodies.

When the allotted time was up, the guards who had brought the women to the event, had trouble pulling the men away from the stage. Lily remembered the guards pushing and shoving the men to get them to leave the stage and, ultimately, the women alone.

When the crowd was cleared, the four women dressed slowly. They helped each other into their dresses, careful to work around the bruises perpetuated by the men who had used them for the last several hours. When the guards escorted them from the stage, the crowd cheered once more, loudly with sustained applause. Lily look back at them as the men sorted through the clothes that were strewn across the stage. Back in the car, the other three women cried to themselves, nursing their own wounds. Lily didn't make a sound; she closed her eyes and let the drugs swirl around her brain.

Lily knew that if she thought about what she allowed herself to do, what she allowed all of those men do to her in the early morning hours, she would hate herself; couldn't live with herself.

Hours later, when the black van pulled back into the compound, Lily woke from her foggy sleep. She looked about the van, getting her bearings. When she saw the other three women, the gang rape, or whatever you want to call it, came flooding back into her. How could anyone treat another human like that? When was this all going to end? Her mind flashed back moments from the morning in bits and pieces. All of the scenes were ugly, unforgettable, but that wouldn't do; she needed to forget, she could not carry this with her.

The side doors of the van opened, and the daylight shined in. Behind it, two men reached into the van and pulled on the women's arms, urging them to follow them back into the camp. The other three women listened to their orders, standing up as the men prodded them. They left the van willingly. When one of the guards touched Lily, she saw him as one of the men who had accosted her on stage earlier that morning. She pulled her arm way. He gave her another chance.

"Don't fight me, Lily," he said.

"Get your fucking hands off me!" she said, shocking the guard which had always known Lily to be obedient and peaceful.

The guard stepped out of the van and spoke to another guard. Then two of them boarded the van each taking one of Lily's wrists.

"Come now. Don't fight us. We don't want to have to hurt you. He's going to give you something to calm you down, to make you forget."

Lily continued to fight until she felt the pin prick in her arm. She knew what came next. She knew that it would all go away soon once the magic medicine slipped into her veins.

"That's it," she heard the guard say. "Nice and easy."

Minutes later, she followed the guards out of the door willingly, a silly grin on her face.

"Erase it all," she said aloud. "It never happened."

They led Lily back to her tent as the initial jolt of the drug passed. She was lucid again, if only for a short while before the drug kicked in big time. She closed her eyes as she lay on her cot and cried, her subconscious doing its best to conceal from her the unthinkable. But before then, it needed to reveal to her once more all that happened.

She was not surprised that Briana was gone, and she wondered how she was getting on. Briana had not fared well back at the prison camp; she was practically broken when they put her back in the cell. This, she knew, was much worse. Lily had been around for a much longer time and it was known that with the right amount of drugs, she could be very compliant; very submissive. That's what they liked; she had learned. They wanted something they could fuck, whichever way they wanted, as often as they wanted. They wanted someone who could moan and scream when they came inside them or on them. And, when they didn't get what they wanted, they would beat you, maybe even kill you.

She wondered if Briana was okay as she lay down on her cot. The medicine was about to take effect on her. She knew because everything around her had a blurry edge to it and her mouth went dry. She knew because she was already starting to forget. Even though she cried, her mind was compartmentalizing what had happened. To protect her; to keep her alive. Her hand fell to her sides as she lay on the mattress. She probably couldn't lift them right now if she tried, but she had no desire to try. Take me, she thought, closing her eyes, thinking of the drug inside of her that helped conceal the horrors to which they all had been subjected.

Chapter 17

Inside the white house, Briana quickly separated herself from the man when he gave her permission. He had done something so horrible; violated her, cold-fucked her on a table, ramming into her as she cried out for him to stop.

She'd been raped.

She knew now he was ruthless, worse than the man Nicolau she had met in the prison camp. She had to keep her wits about her to stay alive.

Briana moved across the room, to the sink, to clean-up as he had asked. Nothing could ever erase how dirty she felt. Erase, she thought, that's what Lily was telling her. You have to figure out a way to erase what they do to you. She had said it repeatedly. Maybe she was onto something. How could you erase the physical pain and the emotional pain that she felt right now? She had no idea. Keep your wits about you, Briana, she thought.

She turned the water on in the sink, cold and dipped her hands into it. It felt good, clean; so different than she felt. How will I last the couple of hours with this man; he is ruthless? He was right across the room, waiting for her. For God knows what. Where was God now; it was not the first time she asked herself that question. She filled her hands and washed her face, rubbing her eyes and cheeks clean. She was still crying, sobbing to herself. She blew her nose and washed her face once more. There was a rag on the corner of the sink, and she wet it with the water and wiped down below, hoping to wash his scent off of her. She wasn't sure if she did, but it felt good to try and be clean again. When she was finished, she turned off the water and dried her face. Briana looked in the mirror. Her days in the jungle had not been kind to her. Her hair was a mess and she did her best to tame it. She gave up after a minute; it was no use. She turned back toward the man who was at the far end of the room.

Pull yourself together, Briana, she said to herself. Act the part. It's just a role. Fill the role he needs you to fill and then it will all be over. Be smart. You don't want pain from this man. He would just as soon kill you then put up with your shit. Do what he wants.

She slowly started to walk toward the man who now sat down at the end of the big bed. When she got closer, the man smiled. In his left hand he held a bunch of red grapes. His large fingers picked a grape from the cluster and he pushed it into his mouth. She stopped when she was about 10 feet away.

"Much better," he said. "Do you care for some grapes?" She nodded and he waved her closer to him. He plucked a grape and held it up to her mouth. She sucked it in, bit it and swallowed it. He smiled and offered her another.

The grapes were cold in Briana's mouth. As she bit them, their juices burst into her mouth offering her a reminder of home, of a good meal. She savored the grapes two and then several more, eating them from the man's hand as he offered them.

"Very good," he said. He patted the bed and Briana

pulled herself up into a sitting position next to him. He reached for a piece of cheese and some bread and offered it to her. She took it in her hands and ate it slowly. "My name is Rey, I run this camp and I have orders to take special care of you. I want you to be happy here, Phoenix. You are a beautiful girl, but you have to learn our ways or there will be much pain." Briana ate the cheese and nodded as he spoke. "Do you think I like administering pain?"

She shook her head indicating that she didn't think he did.

"Oh, you are so wrong, Phoenix. I like it very much. I think women like it more than they let on, also."

Briana started shaking again. He patted her arm. Offered her more cheese. She took it, hoping to make the breakfast last as long as it could.

Rey stood up from the bed as she ate. He walked a few steps away in a circle as he spoke. "We have a small community of women here that are very important to us. But... there is no shortage of women. I learned that very quickly, as will you. If you do not do what is asked of you, we have no use for you, Compreendo?" He didn't wait for an answer this time. "Have you had enough breakfast?"

She nodded.

"I would like for you to speak to me, Phoenix."

"Yes," she said, afraid to ask for some more.

"Are you sure? There is plenty of food here." He was back by the food now, lifting bunches of grapes and other fruits. "All you need to do is ask."

She stared at the food basket, not at all satisfied by the small amount of grapes and cheese she had eaten.

"Go ahead, tell me what you want."

"May I have some more bread and cheese?"

"Of course," Rey said. He reached for a small plate and

161

added some cheese and several pieces of bread to it. He handed her the plate and the poured her a glass of water. "It is important that you eat; keep up your strength. When someone offers you food, you always take it. Enjoy it. Consider it a gift. Now, eat your cheese."

Briana did as he asked, doing her best not to get it on her naked chest as she sat on the end of the bed. She could not get a read on this man at all. He stood, covered in his robe not far from her at all, watching her eat as she sat naked on the end of the bed. He could be kind and he could be brutal; the extent of his brutality she was sure she had not yet seen, nor did she want to see it. When she finished the last piece of cheese, he stepped closer to her and handed her the glass of water. She traded the glass for the empty plate.

"Good," he said.

"Yes." She realized she needed to thank him. "Thank you, Rey."

"You are welcome. I can see that there is a smile not too far from the surface now. You must learn how to show that more, Others will want to see it. You have a very beautiful smile, a very beautiful mouth. Come, let me see your mouth."

Briana wasn't sure what he meant and then he waved his hand indicating that she should come to him. She slid down from the bed and slowly walked toward Rey. She began shaking as she got closer to him. It was involuntary and seemed to get worse with each step. As she closed the gap between them, he opened his robe. She stopped and he smiled at her.

"Get on your knees, Phoenix."

She stared at him and then lowered herself to her knees in front of him.

"Very good. Now, nice and slow, I think you know what

to do." He stepped closer to her and felt her hand reach up for him. "That's it, nice and slow. This is very important."

Briana slid Rey's cock into her mouth. He was very hard, but as she sucked him between her lips, she felt him swell even more. Tears rolled down her eyes as she pulled him into her mouth, reminding her of her time with Nicolau back in the prison camp. She felt Rey's hand on her shoulders, holding her in place as he thrust himself in and out of her mouth. His hands slid up to her face and, holding her head as she worked her head on and off of him.

"Slower, use your tongue. Up and down my shaft. Just like that. Very good, you are a quick learner, Phoenix. Very good. Ah! Yes, swallow as much of me into your mouth as you can. Very good. Again."

They stayed like this for several minutes. Rey instructed her and she followed his instructions. He gagged her a few times by holding her head on him as he pressed deep inside of her and then he pulled himself out and slapped her in the face with his member several times before pushing back inside. He encouraged her the whole time and then, without any notice, he pulled himself out of her mouth and instructed her to get up off of her knees.

"You did well, Phoenix. Now, we are going to teach you how to fuck." Her eyes opened wide and he walked past her and climbed up on the bed. He patted the mattress. "Come," he said.

She did as he asked and when she climbed up on the mattress, he smiled at her. "Fucking is a two-way street. Not all of the time, but it is so much better when both parties enjoy it, no? Our clients require participation; complete participation. So, you will now learn how to fuck and, how to enjoy fucking. Do you understand?"

Briana didn't understand. This man was going to fuck

her, no rape her again, and she was supposed to enjoy it; fuck him back. She took too long to answer. The slap was loud and painful, her head twisted at the force of it. She looked down at the bed, her hand rubbing her cheek where she was just slapped.

"Obedience is very important, Phoenix. Now, spread your legs."

She was sitting up on the bed and did as she was told. Her face hurt from his hard slap, but she let it go so she could use her arms to hold herself up.

"This is for your own benefit – I don't care either way. I think it is much better for you – and our clients, if you are wet. So, I want to watch you make yourself wet for me."

What? Jesus, if this was not humiliating enough, Briana thought, now he wanted her to touch herself. She didn't know if she could do it. Didn't know if she could make herself wet. She didn't want to be slapped again. She slid her right hand down between her legs.

"That's it, Phoenix. All of this is what our clients may want to see. Now, open your lips for me. Very good. We'll have to get that all shaved soon. Good, slide your finger up and down. Very good. Look at me when you touch yourself."

Briana turned to him.

"Think of my fingers on you, inside of you. Very good."

Briana's fingers slid up and down her slit. She was still wet from the washcloth or for some other reason, but she used that to help lubricate her more. She looked up into Rey's eyes. She wondered if he could see the hatred in her eyes. She looked away afraid that he would see what she was feeling.

"Now, slide them inside of you. Get them nice and wet." Briana slid her fingers down to her hole, circling it, pressing it against the edges. "Push them inside," he said, his voice more forceful as he watched her fingers slip into her pussy. "Good, very good." Briana glanced down between his legs, his robe opened once more. He was hard again; very hard, very big. "Good, now slide them in and out, fuck yourself. You know that feels good. It's okay to feel it, Phoenix. It's okay."

Nothing about this felt good, Briana thought. Being forced to finger herself in front of man she didn't know did not turn her on in the least. Still, she slid her fingers in and out despite her not wanting to give into him.

"Deeper, deeper – like a cock. Press them deep inside of you. Very good. You have another hand, Phoenix. You should use it to help you along. To make you more wet." He looked up at her and nodded.

Briana shifted herself and then slid her other hand between her legs. The fingers of her left hand slid up and down her slit slowly while she fingered herself with her right hand. More tears rolled down her face.

"Slide them up. You know where to touch. Yes, just like that."

Briana had slid her fingers up to her clit. She made small circles with the tips of her fingers as her other fingers slid in and out of her.

"Very good. See, you can listen well. I bet you are all wet now. Getting wetter."

She looked at Rey. He was smiling as he stared down at her, his hand slowly pumping his own cock. Briana slid her fingers out from inside of her and slid them up the front of her pussy, making her lips wet. Her left hand slid down from her clit to get wet and then slid back up. The fingers of her right hand moved down between her legs and then slipped back inside of her. She let out a small grunt and then bit her lip.

"It's okay," Rey said. "I want you to feel this now. Get nice and wet for me. It will be better for both of us."

Briana's fingers moved faster on her clit. She was desperate to get this humiliation over with and was ready to start faking the climax. If he wanted her to get excited, to cum for him, she was going to make him believe he had got his wish.

"Slow down now. You need to put on a show for me. I want to see you squirming."

Briana was no longer listening, desperate to end this ordeal. Her hips were slowly thrusting up against the fingers pressing in and out of her. She could feel the sweat on her back and her upper lip. Despite how she felt, she was going to make this monster think he'd made her cum. Her eyes closed and her fingers moved as if by their own will.

"Stop!"

Her eyes opened. Whatever she was feeling was instantly replaced by fear. What had she done wrong? Is this not what he wanted?

"I told you to slow down. I didn't tell you to cum. You will do that when I tell you to. Now, move your hands."

Briana was stunned and still breathing hard. There was no pleasing this man which she knew, meant pain. Out of fear of retribution, she pulled her hands to the side.

"Lay down on your back."

She did as she was told. Rey climbed between her legs, shifted his robe around him and positioned himself on his knees in front of her. "Now, put me inside of you."

She didn't move; he stared down at her. Slowly, Briana lifted her hand and found his hard cock as he leaned forward. She slid his head down her wet slit and then guided it toward her hole. When it was there, she felt him push forward and, involuntarily, she lifted her hips toward him.

With one thrust, he slid himself deep inside of her. She grunted as he leaned into her. She felt his hand slide under her ass, pulling her toward him as he started to drive in and out of her. Briana closed her eyes and thought of happier times. Times with her family back home. Times back in high school.

"Look at me, Phoenix."

She opened her eyes, the past drifting away.

"I want to hear you cum while I fuck you."

She stared up at him. Moments before, he admonished her for thinking about an orgasm, now, as he rammed into her, she was supposed to cum?

"That's not a request. I will fuck you like this until you cum, do you understand?" She stared back at him, slowly nodding. "I don't care if it takes all day."

Briana closed her eyes. She could feel his cock sliding in and out of her. Not like before, when it was dry and scraping against her pussy walls. Now, he was thrusting easily in and out of her, filling her up. His hands were on her ass, pulling her on and off of him, sliding her all the way down his cock until he could go no further. Like he had with her mouth. When he was fucking her mouth earlier. She could fake this. She just needed to get the timing right.

Her eyes sprung open and she stared at Rey. This big man with his big cock driving into her - for his pleasure. Her hands reached up from her sides and she reached for his arms, the arms that pulled her on and off of him. She found his wrists and she held onto them, lifting herself as he thrust into her, thrusting back even as he pulled her over his cock. She focused on his face and then looked down between them, watching his cock piston in and out of her. His big fat cock as it pressed against her walls, spearing her, touching all of her nerves. She purposely let a moan escape her. He wanted to hear her cum. Wanted to hear her scream. Every man wanted to know that his dick was the cause of great pleasure for a woman. That's what Rey wanted and that's what she would give him.

"Fuck me," she heard herself say. "Just like that. God, that feels good." He looked down at her as he thrust himself deep into her. She was thrusting back against him, arching her back off the bed. "God, you are so fucking big. You are splitting me in half." She didn't know where the words were coming from, they were just spilling out of her.

"Very good," Rey said as he stared back at her. He drove deep into her and then he slid himself all of the way out. "Turn over. Up on all fours."

Briana didn't give it a second thought. She rolled onto her stomach and lifted herself up to her hands and knees. As she turned to look back at Rey, he pressed himself deep inside of her. She rocked back against him, driving him even deeper as they worked to find a rhythm. Once they did, they moved like a machine on the bed, his hands on her hips sliding her back and forth over his dick as she rocked against him. She moaned loudly.

"Faster, faster," she said. If he wanted a good fuck, this was the best she could do.

Rey increased his speed. Briana started to make her body shake. She moaned out loud, saliva dripping from her mouth as she rocked back and forth, her pussy swallowing up his big cock. Finally, she arched her back and cried out as he continued to pump into her.

Briana's pretend orgasm rolled through her body. She shook her body as it took her and spasmed at the end as Rey continued to pound her. She yelled, screamed and rocked back on him to complete her ruse. She dropped down to her elbows and worked to regain control of her breath as she felt him continue to drive into her. As she started to come back to reality, a tremor took her and her whole body shook once more. She looked back at him as he slowed down, expecting him to withdraw, but Rey kept going, his hands on her hips as he slid in and out of her. She closed her eyes, resting for a moment, regaining her strength.

"Very good, Phoenix," Rey said a few minutes later.

He pulled himself out from inside of her and sat down beside her as she slid down to her stomach. She could still feel him inside of her as her body started to recover. She looked over at him as she lay still, hoping to recover as much strength as she could. Her eyes fluttered; despite her predicament, she felt as if she could sleep right now.

"Don't think about sleeping, Phoenix," he said. "We have much more to do."

He slapped her on the ass to make sure she got the message. Her eyes sprang open as much from the sound as the pain. She looked at him, her situation immediately flooding back into her mind. What was she going to do?

"Turn over." Briana looked at him and then slowly rolled to her back. "Good. Now, slide over to the end of the bed."

Briana didn't get what he was saying but it didn't matter. Rey took hold of her shoulders and directed her body in the direction he wanted. When he was finished, she was on her back with her head hanging off the end of the bed. She watched him get off the bed, and then she saw him approach, upside down as her head hung down.

"Open your mouth," he said.

She did as he said, and he slid himself inside. His hands found he side of her head and held her there as he pressed himself in and out of her mouth. When she gagged, he pulled out, only to push back on further the next time. Briana's eyes teared as he choked her with his cock, turning

169

her head to spit and catch her breath each time he pulled out.

"You need to learn to take more of it inside. All of it inside."

Briana's eyes went wide thinking about swallowing his massive cock. More than once, as he gagged her with it, she thought of biting down on him, but she knew that the pain would be swift and sustained. She wasn't willing to take that chance. She relaxed her throat, shifted her head a little. When he next pressed in, she felt him slide a little further down her throat before she choked.

"Better," he said. "There's plenty more to go."

His hands let go of her head and slid down to her breasts. He kneaded them roughly and circled her nipples with his fingers as he pressed himself into her mouth. The weight of his body was controlling how deep he slid in now and only after she gagged, did he pull out. Briana's eyes and nose were running as she tried to catch her breath. He relentlessly continued to press into her mouth.

"More," Rey said, not indicating at all how much more.

Briana guessed that he had been fucking her mouth for at least 15 minutes. His fingers were on her breasts now, pulling at her nipples; a welcome distraction from the cock that was choking her. She chose to concentrate on them as she shifted her head, relaxed her throat. Nothing was going to make this any better. She needed to busy herself to take her mind off of what was really happening.

Rey tugged on her nipples, pinching them, pulling on them, watching them harden and soften under his touch. He leaned hard into her mouth, feeling her swallow his cock deeper and deeper inside of her. She was a quick learner, a survivor, he thought. A shame, because he would really like to see her pretty face in pain. He pinched her nipples hard and she grunted as he pressed his cock into her throat, gagging her. There would be time for pain, he thought, no matter how pliable and compliant she became. Always time for pain. Now, it was time to cum.

He pulled himself out of her mouth completely. Briana gasped for air, turning her head and spitting a wad of saliva to the ground. She tried to lift her head, already light-headed from the position, but he held her there, his cock pushing against her lips. She gasped for air knowing that he would soon put it in once more, collecting as much air into her lungs as she could. She didn't have much time before Rey pressed himself deep inside her mouth.

"Very good," he said as he slid himself deep into her mouth, down into her throat. "You are a quick learner. Now, I want to feel it inside of your throat as you lick around my shaft."

Rey placed his hand on her throat as he drove his cock back into her, watching as its shape was visible from the outside. When he felt it, he gently squeezed, cutting off any air that Briana might have had. When she choked, he released his grip and slid himself out once more.

"Very good. Again." He pressed himself in deep once more, repeating the steps with his hand on her throat, feeling his cock as he saw it slide deep into her. "Excellent."

He was choking her with his cock and Briana felt herself ready to pass out. To give into whatever force was trying to pull her away. When he pulled out, she coughed, gasping for air turning her head, trying not to swallow the saliva that was built up in her mouth. Just as she thought she had enough wind, he would thrust back into her, squeeze her neck, rubbing up and down with his hand and then she would gag all over again. It was brutal, taking her back from the brink of passing out over and over again.

"You did good," he said.

Briana could barely hear him through the fog of conscious and unconscious that she was drifting in and out of as she tried to catch her breath. Her head was turned to the side and she waited for his hand to turn it back, for him to jam his cock back into her mouth, but this time it didn't happen. Maybe it was over; maybe she had done something wrong.

"My father would say you are an apt pupil," Rey said, his voice suddenly clear, her mind coming back into full consciousness.

She could hear him breathing hard as he spoke. She continued to spit and choke. Her throat hurt, both inside and out. Her eyes tried to bring the room into focus, amidst the tears that puddled at the base of her eyelids. She was no longer gasping for air, but every breath seemed like a gift and she inhaled deeply as she listened to the monster breath loudly next to her.

"Open your mouth," he said.

Not again, she thought. I just caught my breath, but I am still having trouble, still foggy. She knew not to argue; she opened her mouth.

"Very good," he said as he stepped closer to her; standing over her now as her head hung off the bed.

She watched as he pulled on himself, stroked his big cock. He was breathing hard and some moans escaped him. She didn't move, but he didn't press inside of her. Another gift she thought as she worked to bring her breathing back to full strength. Take it where you could get it, she remembered one of her friends saying. Who was that? A stray thought. Then back to Rey who was jerking himself off over her face. She watched his hand slide up and down. She didn't know why she kept her eyes open.

"Open your mouth," he screamed out.

She hadn't noticed she closed them. Then she felt his hot load squirt into her, across her tongue, down her throat. She wanted to turn away, but something instinctively told her not to do so.

It would get her another hard slap, another bruise, more pain.

He shot several more times before he placed the head of his cock just inside her lips and then he milked whatever remained inside as she painfully held her mouth open. When he finally stepped away, she closed her eyes and swallowed slowly, feeling his cum slide down her throat, knowing that spilling it onto the floor might warrant another punishment.

Rey stepped back, his cock spent. He pulled the robe around him and he tightened the belt.

Briana lay on the bed, naked, head hanging down, broken. Her eyes fluttered as she watched him, upside down as he moved further away from her. She heard a match strike, smelled smoke from a cigarette. She tried to lift her head. Her jaw and back hurt. Her throat was on fire. She was sure that was only the beginning of the wounds she would find. She heard some voices and then she watched as Rey came back toward the bed. She was helpless; she would do what he wanted.

"You may get up now, Phoenix. Go get your robe and then come back here."

Slowly, as fast as she could go, Briana lifted her head, feeling the pain in her back and neck. She twisted herself until her legs were hanging off of the bed and then took a deep breath as she stood up. She did not want to stay on the bed any longer than she needed to, but her body wasn't cooperating. Slowly, she lifted herself, turned away from him and walked across the room to pick up her robe from the floor. When she bent down, she felt new pains, in different parts of her body. Still, she was alive, she thought as she pulled on the robe. She made a knot in the bow and then turned around and slowly walked back toward Rey, standing in front of him with her head down.

"Very good, Phoenix. You did very good this morning. The guard will be taking you back to your tent now. You should be proud of yourself. You did very well." He reached out and patted her on the shoulder; Briana recoiled from his touch at first and then held herself steady as he rubbed her shoulder. "Very well. Go, have some lunch. They will give you a shower. It will feel good." His finger slid under her chin and he lifted her head as he had done earlier. He looked into her eyes. "You will come back here after lunch. I have some friends I would like you to meet. We share everything."

Rey stepped away from her and walked across the room to where the sink was.

Briana stared after him, wondering what he meant, but was too tired try and figure it out. There was something important in what he said. She heard a knock at the door and turned as the guard walked in, took her by the arm and led her out. She shook as she left the room, happy to be leaving, but knowing she would soon return. "We share everything..." was what he had said.

Briana walked head-down as the guard brought her back to the tent. When she stepped inside, she immediately went to Lily. She needed Lily. She needed to tell her what happened; what she had gone through.

"Oh, Lily, it was fucking horrible," she said as she grabbed Lily's shoulder, turned her over on the bed. Lily opened her eyes and looked up at her. She seemed to be looking right through Briana. She wasn't there; she had

174

checked out once more with the drugs. She let Lily fall back onto the mattress. Useless, she thought. Briana walked to her own cot; her words caught in her throat. The words she needed to tell Lily so she could get them out of her system, out of her memory. She crawled up onto her mattress, pulling her legs up under her, staring at the zippered tent door. Tears fell from her eyes as she sobbed quietly. Her whole body hurt. She bent her head down to her knees. Silently, she said her prayers to a God she no longer believed in.

Chapter 18

Briana faded in and out. Her eyes, when they were opened, never left the zipper. When it opened, she knew she would crawl back against the wall behind her. The guard would have to pull her out of the room before she went back there to see that horrible man and whatever he had planned for her. So, what if he beat her? It was better than what happened in that room.

At some point, she fell asleep, remaining in her sitting up position, her chin falling down onto her chest. The sound of the tent zipper opening, a sound she would never forget as long as she lived, woke her and she pulled her legs tight against her as her eyes opened wide. Would she fight, she wondered?

"No, no, no," she muttered to herself as a guard stepped through the door.

She wasn't ready. Not ready to go; not ready to fight. She looked to Lily, still crumpled on her mattress across the room. Helpless. Maybe they came for her. They could take her, Briana thought. She wouldn't know what happened. That would be best. Lily was used to this. She had prepared for this, insulated herself against whatever they threw at her with the drugs. The man called her name when he stepped into the tent. She didn't budge.

"Phoenix, don't make this hard. It's been a long day."

A long day. Was he fucking kidding her? Nothing could have been longer than the day she had, and it was still light out. It's been a long day – fuck you, she thought. She still didn't move, and he took a step toward her. She recoiled when he reached out his arm, pulling herself closer to the wall then she thought possible, hoping to dissipate into it as he watched.

"One last time. You are too pretty to hurt," he said.

He reached out his hand. Briana slowly lifted her arm, letting him pull her up from her mattress. She followed him to the opening in the tent. She didn't blame this man for what happened to her, but if a number of them stood up to the really bad men, they could probably put an end to this. She held no hope that would happen until someone – like herself – escaped and exposed the compound to the entire world.

The guard led her out of the tent and zippered it back up. She followed him across the yard, thankfully in another direction providing her with a reprieve – even for a short while. He opened the door to a building and escorted her inside.

"Shower," he said. "Quickly, but thoroughly."

The guard handed her a bar of soap, a towel and a rag.

"Aren't you going to watch?" she said to him, remembering how the guard at the prison camp seemed to get off on that.

This guard shook his head and turned the other way. She made a mental note about his behavior. It could come in handy at some point. Briana moved across the room to one of the showers, stepped inside and pulled the curtain. She undressed and then turned on the water, testing it, expecting it to be ice cold, but it wasn't. She slipped under the shower and tried to wash all of the day away, all of Rey away and all of her thoughts away.

As she dried herself off, she realized, she had no clothes to change into. She wrapped a towel around herself and pulled the curtain. She was onto the guard; he wanted to look at her naked after she was clean. He had turned to her when he heard the curtain. She stood there with a smug look on her face. There were no good men in this jungle. He smiled and then he nodded to his right. Next to the shower, on a hanger hung a pretty red dress. Below it was a pair of black heels. She wondered if they would fit her. She knew she would have to wear them anyway.

Briana took the dress from the hanger and slipped back behind the shower curtain. She pulled it on over her head and zipped up the back. It fit perfectly. She was a little concerned there was no underwear, but she knew she couldn't really request any. She stepped out from behind the curtain and stepped into the heels. They also fit perfectly. She wondered if the small lady was responsible for picking out her clothes again.

When she was finished dressing, thoughts of where she was heading clouded her brain. She had promised herself that she would fight them when they came for her, but here she was dressed in a red dress and black heels. She had put up very little of a fight. The guard smiled at her from across the room and held out his hand. It was time to go. Would she fight when she was inside, or would she let them do whatever they wanted with her? She walked slowly toward the guard and followed him out of the room. He led her across the grounds toward the big white house; toward whatever fate awaited her.

****

Lily woke up in time to see Briana being removed from the tent. She wanted to call out to her, but something inside stopped her. She didn't want to be noticed. Not yet. The longer she remained under the spell of the drug, the more invisible she felt. She wanted to remain invisible for as long as she could.

The drugs had taken a much larger toll on Lily than she ever expected. When Briana first noticed, Lily didn't agree with her assessment that she was being controlled by the drugs, but the more she had thought about it, the more she realized that while it was her escape, it was also keeping her from taking stock of the situation and trying to figure a way out. It masked the pain and the horror – that's what it was for, but she couldn't let them use her this way forever. No one was going to stand up for Lily; she had to stand up for herself.

To that end, she had done her best to limit her drug intake, pushing away the shots, slowly letting the reality creep in when she was pulled from her cell. It left her a little more lucid and focused so she could conceptualize a plan, any plan to get away, to get a message to someone. Today, she knew, was totally different. When they pushed her in the back of the black van, she knew she would need the drugs just to get through the trip lest her mind conceive the worst things that could happen to her. And, then after the deeds became reality, she willfully accepted the shot once again to push away the horrors she'd endured.

Lily knew she needed to do better. Like Briana. Briana seemed to be thinking through her actions. Like all of the imprisoned women, she was upset and afraid. But Briana, from what she could tell, was holding it together. She had not witnessed Briana being brought back to the cell or the tent, except for that one time, and even though she complained about the horrors she had experience 'too horrible to discuss', she seemed to let them wash off her back by the next morning. Lily needed to be more like Briana. Together, she thought, they could find a way out of the compound.

Soon, they would come to take Lily to lunch, and she would eat as much as she could. Begin to rebuild her strength. She would start pushing away the needles, telling the guards that she didn't need their drugs anymore. She imagined she could control her own mind, suppress what she needed to, compartmentalize the evil. That must be what the others did.

At lunch she would drink a lot of water, hoping to cleanse her body, free it from the toxins of the drugs. She would pee out the drugs. Get them all of out of her system. Start anew. That's what she needed to do. Then she would bond with Briana. She realized she knew very little about the woman, where she came from, what she did. Lily knew only what they had told her when they sent her to that hotel room, to help move Briana back to the first camp. In exchange for that deed, Lily was fed well and given an extra shot of the drugs that made her forget.

Eat a big lunch, drink lots of water, start anew. Get your mind in the right place to handle these horrors so you can find a way out. Lilly's mind shifted. She knew that she couldn't drink too much water. She was sure that the water had been treated with some sort of birth control. She wasn't sure how she knew that – maybe she overheard it from someone at the other camp, but it made sense that they would distribute birth control through the water or food. The guards never ate or drank from the same sources as the prisoners, she noticed. And, they couldn't afford for the women to get pregnant, and God knows, no one was wearing any protection. Lily thought back to the morning where any number of men could have unwittingly impregnated her; none of them caring where they deposited their seed.

Not too much water, Lily, she thought. Everything in moderation. One day at a time. Mentally prepare yourself for what you knew was going to happen. Strengthen yourself. Your mind and body needed to stay sharp – at all times so that you can work with Briana to find a way out.

When she'd finished taking stock of herself and her situation, Lily smiled to herself. She was taking a preemptive step to save herself. Very important. Her mind was still sharp. She sat on her cot and waited for them to come and get her for lunch. She was a new person. In control. She didn't need their drugs. She would not let the horrors of this camp or outside of this camp bother her. She was confident.

A half-hour later when she heard the zipper of the tent open, Lily's body began to shake, and she felt her confidence break even before the guard stepped into the tent. It was only lunch, she thought – get a grip, but it was no use. As the guard summoned her, she could only think of the pinprick of the shot that sent that heavenly medicine into her arm. The medicine that clouded her mind and allowed her to forget.

Lily climbed down from the cot and followed the guard out into the compound. He took her arm and administered a shot before they left the tent. The fog came quickly, along with the warmth. She felt sweat beading on her upper lip, and she licked the salty water away. She nodded at the guard and he led her over to her lunch. She was compliant, obedient. Just like they taught her.

Chapter 19

Jose's trip to the police station was worthless. He presented his concern and was led to one of the investigators in charge who basically told him that all that could be done was being done. The taxi driver didn't believe it for a moment. A young woman, overseas by herself. The Brazilian police assumed that she was shacking up with one of the many handsome men from Rio – like in the movies.

Jose presented his findings – the lack of communication for more than four days from a woman who spoke to him each morning and evening since she'd arrived in the country. He considered himself her personal driver, he told the investigator who laughed off Jose's claim.

"She is tired of you, is all," he said. "She's found someone better, no doubt."

"It was not like that," Jose insisted. "Her school administrator has not been able to locate her either. No communication."

"Exactly," the investigator reiterated. "She is getting laid on the beach somewhere. When she is finished shacking up, she will find her way back to work, beg for her job back. I see this all of the time."

"You do?" Jose said. "Young women from the states come

over here, get a decent paying job, and then go off and meet someone and never return to work?" He shook his head.

"I don't like your tone," the investigator said. "In fact, I don't like your attitude at all."

"I don't appreciate you ignoring my concerns," Jose said. "This is a young woman we are talking about. A young, helpless woman."

"None of them are helpless. Now, you are testing my patience and it is quickly running out. I have your name and number. I will call you if anything develops. Do not hold your breath."

Jose stared at the man and then turned and left the office. Outside, in his cab, he tried to figure out his next steps. Was there nothing else he could do for Briana? He headed back toward the school in hopes that she would come out as the school day ended; allay his worst fears. He would be mad at her, but relieved that she was safe. He parked across from the school and waited for the children to be picked up. As usual, the last pickup was the cartel family security guards. He watched as they entered the school and then as they surrounded the two children on the way out of the school. They drove away in their SUVs. There was something about the sight of them that caused Jose to pause. Something Briana had said.

As he tried to work out his thoughts, he decided to follow the SUVs at a safe distance. Driving was calming for Jose and it allowed him to concentrate. He navigated the streets easily as his brain worked through complex problems. Briana was the only problem he had had on his mind for the last few days. What was it she had said to him about the security team?

He followed the cars past the crowded, close-together houses and up into the mountains. They were driving for more than a half-hour when Jose's mind prized out what he had been looking for. Briana had said that one of the men had given her a card to one of their night clubs. What was its name? Something golden. No gilded. Yes - A Flor Dourada, The Gilded Flower. He remembered her asking him about it and he had said to stay away. That might be information that the police would want to investigate, he thought. Maybe she did go to the club despite his warning. It would have been late at night. She was in a strange country – he knew she did not know her way around. Anything could have happened to her.

Jose was deep in thought, mulling over his find, thinking he might be onto something when the SUVs stopped up ahead. He pulled his taxi over to the side of the road and waited for them to move again. He could wait, he thought, or he could now just drive away. The trip had allowed him to figure out what he needed. He could leave now and report the mysterious club to the police. Hopefully, that would give them a lead they could pursue. He thought about calling the station but decided it would be better to deliver the information in person. This way, he could answer any questions, and maybe even get an apology from the investigator. Fat chance, he thought.

He was about to pull away from the curb when there was a knock at his window. Surprised, Jose looked up to see a man standing alongside his car. At first, he thought it was the polícia, but as his door was opened from the outside, he thought it might be something much worse.

"Get out of the car," the man said in English.

"What is it you need?" Jose said, his mind racing. He had done nothing wrong, but this man was insistent.

"I will not ask you again."

Jose looked up at him and slowly unbuckled his seatbelt.

As soon as he was free, the man lifted him up by his arm out of the car. Jose planted his feet under him as he came out of the car. He pulled his arm away from the large man. Who did he think he was?

"Who are you?" the man asked. He wasn't just large, he was massive. Wide and tall.

"I could ask you the same thing," Jose said, his voice filled with false bravado.

"Come with me." The man turned expecting Jose to follow him.

"Where are we going?" Jose said, standing his ground.

"To my car."

Jose looked behind his own car to where a third black SUV was parked. How had he not noticed that before. His brief bout of bravery receded.

"Please," the man said.

Jose followed the man past his car toward the black SUV. What did they want with him? Behind him, he heard his taxi start and when he looked back, he saw it driving away.

"Hey, where are you taking my car?"

"If you don't want to get hurt, get in the car."

Jose hesitated and the man stepped behind him. He climbed up into the SUV. Inside there was one other man and a driver. The man who had approached him at his car climbed in alongside of him and pulled the door closed. The SUV drove away from the curb. Jose became very concerned.

"Was there a reason why you were following us?"

"I was not following you; I was thinking. Driving helps me to think clearly." The man did not say anything. Jose looked from left to right at the two large men that bookended him in the rear seat. "I mean it. I have no reason to follow you. I don't even know who you are."

"Our friends in the Policia have told us you've been

asking questions... and now... you are... following us. That is very troubling."

"I was not following you. I tell you I was just following the path your cars were taking because it helps me concentrate – being on the road. I guess I picked the wrong cars to follow," Jose said, as he let out a nervous laugh.

"You sure did. You sure did," the man to his left said.

The SUV drove up further into the hills, continuing along the same path they had followed earlier. Jose knew he was in trouble, but he had no idea what kind of trouble he was in.

"Listen," he said, hoping to talk his way out of the problem. "If I did something wrong, it was unintentional, you see. I didn't mean to bother you or whatever it is you think I did. Please, just let me out here. I will find a way home and that will be that. I can give you whatever you want; tell you whatever you want to know, but I was not following you and..."

"Enough," the driver yelled from the front. His accent was thick, his voice was deep. "You've been asking too many questions about a certain school teacher."

Jose started to say something once more. He was incapable of keeping quiet when he was nervous.

"I don't know..."

"Shut him up."

The man to his left, elbowed him hard in the stomach and Jose doubled over in pain. He couldn't remember ever being in so much pain. He coughed and spit out as he tried to recover. He kept his head down as the car continued up the mountain. Jose remained quiet; his mind worked to find a way out of the situation. He would just play by their rules; bide his time until he could find a way out.

When the car came to a stop, Jose began to sweat. He

had so many thoughts going through his head. He was in a state of confusion, which led to a state of panic. The doors of the SUV opened, and Jose was pulled by his arm out of one of the doors. The big man held onto his arm as Jose stood up. The panic that had been rising in him, was now becoming more apparent. He tried to breathe through it, to calm his thoughts, his urge to run, his confusion.

They were walking Jose out to an open field; a man on each side of him. In the distance, Jose could see a small structure, that looked like a cabin. His body slowed down as it became apparent what was going to happen to him. For following their cars, he thought. There must be more to it. It was then he started talking and sealed his own fate.

"What did you do with her?" he asked. "Did you hurt her? Where is she? The police will find out. I told them everything about you. If you let me go, I can lead them in a different direction." There was no response. After a long pause he tried a different tact, contradicting himself. "It doesn't really make a difference what I told them. They wouldn't believe me anyway. Who would listen to a taxi driver?"

"Too late my friend, you've asked one question too many."

Jose stared back at the man. "I... I didn't tell them anything. Believe me. I don't know anything about who you are or what you do. I was only concerned for my friend. I swear, I didn't follow you. I mean I was following you, but I didn't mean to. It was an accident."

"We believe you," the other man said, his voice full of impatience. "Do you see that garage over there?" He pointed to the structure in the distance. Jose nodded. The man let go of Jose's arm. "Your taxi is parked in the garage there. I think you've learned your lesson. Don't follow us ever again. Do you understand?"

"Yes," Jose said. "Yes. Oh, thank you." He turned to the other man. "Thank you."

He started to walk away. Slowly at first and then more quickly. Jose sped up hoping to put a greater distance between him and the men. He was breathing hard, the panic slowly receding, but not quite quitting on him yet. He might just get out of this, he thought as he got closer to the garage on the far end of the field. Would he tell the police what he knew about the club? He wasn't sure. He thought it may be better to leave things as they were. He had no business trying to find Briana on his own. That was a job for the police. He would leave it with them. Well, the information about the club could be very helpful. He wasn't sure what he would do. He was only sure of one thing. He would get to the garage, get in his car, and get as far away from this place as possible. If he never saw the cartel men again, it would be too soon.

Jose was less than 50 yards away from the garage when two shots rang out. The first bullet tore through his thigh. Before he could feel any pain, the second bullet blew open the back of his skull. Jose fell face forward; he was dead before he hit the ground. A team would come and take care of the body later. They would keep his car and body hidden for a while in case they needed it. By morning, there would be no trace of Jose or his cab.

****

A few hours later, a private plane carrying Briana's parents, an assistant to the senator and a single member of his security detail, landed at the airport in Rio Di Janiero. A limousine waited to whisk them to the US Embassy less than 20 miles away. It was to Senator Marshall's benefit to get them to the embassy quickly and keep them off the streets of Rio; keep them from creating waves that would give him something else to manage. He had arranged for an agent to meet with them, to placate them as the local police continued their investigation. The senator was sincere in his belief that the pretty young lady had gone off somewhere with a Latin stud.

When the Campbells arrived at the embassy, they were met by the Ambassador, Richard Johnson, and escorted to a dining room where a lavish meal had been prepared.

"Please eat. You are my guests. You must be tired after your flight."

"Thank you, Ambassador Johnson," Briana's mom said. "We would like to start immediately. We have no time to waste."

"Please," the ambassador said. "Eat something. We will start in the morning when the agent arrives." He saw the look on Briana's mother's and father's faces. "Believe me," he said, "nothing can happen until the agent gets here. You should get your rest today. It will be a long day tomorrow."

Briana's mom started to open her mouth, but her husband took her hand and led her to the table. She whispered something loudly to him.

"Calm down," he said. "We need their help and it won't help to get off on their wrong side. We will eat some food, get some sleep and then we can start early in the morning."

She looked at her watch. "It's dinner time. We will lose the whole night, while our daughter is out there somewhere..." she started to cry, and he pulled her into his arms.

Briana's dad looked over at the ambassador who shook his head, as if his hands were tied. He offered his apologies before he left the room, not wanting to sit and listen to them while they ate.

Mr. and Mrs. Campbell sat down and ate silently. They had taken a huge step. They were now in the same country where their daughter was. They would do whatever they had to do to find her.

When they finished their dinner, they were shown to their rooms. As they retired for the night, Briana's father heard his wife cry for several hours as he lay awake next to her. It was their new ritual; one they had performed every night for the past several days.

Chapter 20

Briana followed the guard across the compound. The white house stood alone in the distance and she knew once she got inside, there was no telling what would happen. She had compartmentalized her last visit and refused to let it out of its box. For now, she looked about the compound, searching for weaknesses and avenues of escape. Her mind took pictures of each area as she looked deeper into the fencing, the woods, where the jeeps and vans entered and exited. She took it all in, storing it for future reference. It would all go in a separate box in her mind.

As they neared the house, Briana's step faltered, but she quickly regained her composure, refusing to let the guard see that she was afraid. He reached for her arm, but she pulled it away calmly as if to let him know she did not need his assistance. When they got to the steps, she climbed them steadily in her heels. The doors opened before her and before she stepped inside, she took a look out across the vast compound, noting the house's proximity to the exits, along with other important locations that she thought might come in handy. She entered the house noting the eyes of the inside guards moving up and down her body as they closed the doors.

Briana's bravado was weakening the further she moved into the house. As they started down the long hallway, she swallowed hard thinking about what awaited her behind the doors at the long end of the hallway. She remembered her slowing down the last time she walked the length of the hallway, fearful of what would happen to her.

"Please stop," came a voice from behind her.

Both she and the guard stopped. Briana didn't turn around, recognizing the voice. She realized that she was not ready to see the man again.

"Turn around."

She hesitated at first and then slowly turned around. Rey stood some 20 feet away from her.

"My, you are beautiful. Will we see that smile now?"

Briana tried to smile, at least a little, just to appease him, but her face wasn't cooperating – just the corner of her lips raised.

"No matter," he said. "Still very beautiful." He extended his hand. "Come."

Briana slowly walked toward the man who had raped her earlier. The man who had total control over her. His hand was still extended, and she saw her own arm reach up, presenting her hand to him. He nodded, took her hand and then said something quietly to the guard. The guard walked past them and then down the steps and out of the house.

"Very good, Phoenix. Very good." He held her hand up and looked over her body, slowly walking around her. "Most excellent. We will be going out this evening." He laughed. "I hope you didn't have anything planned." He turned to her. "You will do everything I say tonight. Remember what we discussed this morning and what I can do to you. Yes?"

Briana nodded.

"Good. Now, when we walk, you will walk one step

behind me at all times, unless I tell you to be at my side. Understood?"

"Yes," Briana said. "Understood."

"Very good. Now, follow me."

Rey led her out of the house and down the small set of steps. When the doors opened this time there was a waiting car. The driver opened the door for them, and he let her slip inside first. He stared at her long legs as she pulled them up inside the car. He sat down next to her and moments later, the car pulled away from the curb and left the compound. Briana noted the proximity to the exit from the house as well as how many guards were located near the gates.

"We will be going to a private club tonight. You will have a fine dinner, I assure you."

Briana didn't say anything. She stared forward, happy to be out of the camp, wondering if an opportunity to slip away would present itself.

"I know what you are thinking, but please know that there is no place for you to go, and nowhere for you to escape to." He paused. "I see something in you, Phoenix. Something I do not see in the others. You are smart. You learn quickly. You can adapt. That's good," Rey said, his hand patting her thigh. He left it there and gently rubbed her as he continued to speak. "We will see how much you adapt tonight. Yes?"

Rey was quiet for a minute, lost in thought, then he said, "Relax for now. It is good to relax."

He patted the flesh of her thigh as he leaned back against the seat, closing his eyes. Briana did the same, hoping to mentally prepare herself for whatever was to happen later. The car drove on for a short while over twisting roads and then came to a stop. The driver turned the engine off. Briana felt her panic beginning to rise. She took some deep breaths to control it.

Rey's door was opened from the outside and he stepped out. He reached in for Briana's hand and guided her out of the car. He stood next to her as she looked over the club which seemed all alone up on a hill. Her quick view showed no other buildings in the area. The club, however, was large. Rey touched her elbow as he moved past her, indicating to her that she should follow him. He walked the few steps to the door of the club. The doors opened for him and he stepped inside. She followed him in, standing behind him, waiting for him to acknowledge her as she took in her surroundings.

They stood in huge open area. There were some 20 or 30 people milling about, all wearing the same uniform. They must be workers, Briana thought. One of them, a pretty, older woman approached Rey and bowed before him. She smiled at him as she rose and then nodded. He followed her and Briana followed behind. They entered a large room with a big stage in the center of the room. Lights from the ceiling focused down on it. There were large tables surrounding the stage and one was set with four places.

Rey walked to one side of the set table and pulled out a chair, his hand indicating that Briana should sit down. She sat and looked about the room. Rey sat down next to her and patted her thigh once more; she noted that she no longer recoiled from his touch.

"This is my favorite room in the club," he said. He seemed different, more animated. "The area in the center is a stage." He said it as if it was a wonderful treat. "First, we eat, though, yes?" Rey stared at Briana and she nodded her head. "Excellent. I am sure you're hungry for quality food."

"I am," she said, thinking he wanted a reply. Her voice seemed to echo in the room, coming out a lot louder than she expected. He eyed her, almost as if she should not speak, but it did not deter her. "Thank you," she said, hoping to appease him.

Rey seemed satisfied and clapped his hands together. Immediately, uniformed servants came from all sides to place dishes on their tables. They retreated as quickly as they came. The presentation flashed her back to her dinner with Esteban which she quickly dismissed. Rey took food from the various service dishes and placed it on her plate first and then filled his plate.

"Eat," he said, "you'll need your strength."

Briana leaned forward and slowly began to eat. The food was delicious. Everything that touched her mouth was wonderful. She didn't realize that she was ravished until she found herself shoveling food into her mouth.

"Easy, easy," Rey said to her. "Slow down. Nice and slow."

Those words stopped her cold, remembering when he had said them to her earlier, when they were alone in the white house. Briana closed her eyes and put her fork down, indicating to him that he had heard her as she tried stay in control of her emotions. She turned her head to him giving him a small smile.

"Very well. I know you must be hungry. The tea is incredible also." Rey pointed to a glass of blue liquid with a small flower in it. "Please, try it."

He was being so generous; so much different than he was back at the house. She picked up the glass and drank from it. He was right; the tea was incredible. The sugary drink hurt her still-swollen throat a little, but the cold felt good. She continued to eat, taking her time this time so as not to cause any concerns. She made sure that she ate the meats that looked like they could provide protein as she knew that would help her strength. She tried to stay away from anything starchy.

There was a knock at a door on the far side of the room and Briana looked in the direction of the sound.

"Enter," Rey said, standing from his chair.

The door opened and a man and a woman stepped inside. As Rey went to greet them, he turned to Briana – "Our guests are here," he said, a wide smile on his face.

Briana place her fork next to her plate, wiped her mouth and looked on as the guests entered the room. She remained in her seat as she thought that is what he would want and watched as an extremely striking man and a gorgeous young woman walked into the room. They were all white smiles as they shook Rey's hand. They had met before, she noted, and they seemed very comfortable with one another.

After he kissed the woman on both cheeks, Rey turned to Briana to introduce her.

"This is Phoenix," he said.

He held both of his hands out in front of him indicating to her that she should stand. She stood from the chair and took his hands. She was his to show tonight, she knew, and she would play the part, especially if that was all there was to it. She smiled and watched his eyes light up when she did.

"Ah Phoenix, the pleasure is mine," the man said as he bent down to pull her into his arms and kiss her on both cheeks before Briana even realized what was happening. When he let her go, the woman did the same, pulling her tight against her chest, kissing her on both cheeks and then letting her go.

"Very good, very good," Rey said. "Please sit, eat. Phoenix, this is Gentry," he said, pointing to the handsome man. "And, this beauty is Santana." The woman smiled and waved across the table at Briana who had reseated herself.

The guests reached for the food and filled their plates. Rey poured wine for himself. Each of the two guests drank the same blue tea that Briana was drinking. Rey refilled Briana's glass with the tea when it was empty.

Briana took a long drink from it. As she watched the new couple eat, she picked at her food, suddenly full after eating so fast earlier.

Rey spoke to Gentry in a language that Briana didn't understand. The three of them erupted in laughter so she assumed that Santana knew what they were saying. If Briana were home, she would tell them it was rude, but she was in no position to do so and, while she was concerned with what they were saying, she appreciated the chance to think on her own.

She stared over at Santana. She looked to be maybe 20 years old and she was absolutely stunning. Her chest was large, her eyes bright blue, and her hair was honey gold. She wore a low-cut dress that showed the top of her breasts. Briana's eyes were drawn to her ample cleavage more than once. Briana looked across Santana at Gentry. If ever there was a sculpture of the perfect man, he could be it. He was tall, his skin olive. His chin was square, and his eyes were dark blue. He also had blond hair, but it was short, not like the long locks sported by Santana. He wore a tight black shirt that indicated that he had muscles on muscles across his chest and his biceps tested the strength of the fabric that made up his short sleeves. Perfect, was the only way she would describe him.

The three of them spoke for 10 minutes or so, excluding Briana from their conversation. On more than one occasion, Rey pointed to her, including her as a subject in the conversation. As their discussion died down, he turned to her and smiled.

"It was good to see your smile," he said. "They are a beautiful, are they not?"

Briana nodded her head.

"You may speak."

"Yes, they are stunning," Briana said.

"Stunning," Rey said loudly. He turned to Gentry and Santana. "That from the American girl. She thinks you are stunning." He laughed and they joined him. Briana felt herself laughing a little also.

The table grew quiet as they finished eating. Rey picked up his wine glass. "To the stunning couple," he said. The three of them raised their glasses together and smiled, each taking a drink following the toast. "Very good, very good. Now, it's show time."

He clapped his hands as he had done before. The room filled with servants who removed their plates before exiting once again. The lights that lit up the area around the table began to dim as the lights on the stage grew brighter. Low music, which gradually became louder, started to play and a curtain opened up on the far side of the room. Briana watched as a woman climbed the steps onto the stage walked to the center. She looked at each of them and bowed to Rey before stepping back a foot and slowly started to dance to the music.

Briana was immediately entranced by the woman. She was young, pretty and captivating as she danced methodically to the rhythmic beat and low bass. She raised her arms as she spun, undulated her hips as she danced and ran her hands over her body. It was sensual and very personal, Briana thought. There was a smell in the room also, incense of some kind. The smell was familiar, but she couldn't place it. She continued to stare at the woman as she began to undress.

The music continued to play as she removed the top of her garment, revealing a large set of breasts that appeared to defy gravity. Rey clapped as they came into view. The others followed. He looked over at Briana and she began to clap also. He nodded at her.

The volume of the music increased slightly as drums seemed to join in. The woman now shook her bottom to the beat as her hands gently massaged her breasts. Her fingers slid over her nipples and she pulled on them as she stared into Gentry's eyes. Her other hand reached behind her and moments later, her skirt fell to the floor revealing her naked body beneath. Briana's eyes widened as she saw the smooth, dark skin of the woman, shaved clean, her body undulating slowly before her. She looked over at Rey who began to clap loudly. The others joined him. Briana clapped as she stared at the woman whose hand slid down in front of her, her fingers sliding up and down her lips.

"Excellent," Rey said. "Excellent."

Rey turned to Santana who stood up from her seat. Briana watched as she circled the stage and then climbed the same set of hidden stairs and walked out onto the stage. Santana stepped up in front of the woman and stared at her, watching her dance methodically. They were less than a foot away from each other and Briana watched as Santana reached for the woman's breast, kneading it in her hand as she slowly slid down in front of her. Still massaging her breast, her fingers tugging and circling her nipple, Santana put her head between the woman's legs and slowly began to lick up the front of her pussy.

"Excellent," Rey said, clapping effusively

Reluctantly, Briana joined in. She couldn't pull her eyes away from the stage. There was something alluring about the two women as they pressed against each other, Santana's head sliding up and down. Santana pulled her head away from the woman; her face shined in the bright lights covered with the woman's juices. She smiled briefly towards the table before she pressed her mouth back between the woman's legs.

After a small while, Santana lifted herself from the stage, her tongue licking up the front of the woman before her mouth clamped on her breast. The woman pushed her away and Santana turned around slowly in front of her. The woman unzipped her dress. Santana stepped away and slowly began to work her way out of her dress. She turned her back to the three seated at the table as the woman continued to dance slowly. Santana swayed her hips as she stepped out of dress, revealing the perfect ass that Briana had expected.

Rey clapped loudly and Briana and Gentry joined in. Out of the corner her eye, Briana saw Gentry stand up, but then she turned her attention back to Santana who was slowly turning on the stage, ready to reveal those amazing tits. When she did, Rey clapped loudly as Briana's eyes widened. She clapped absentmindedly as she knew to do, but her focus was not on Santana's chest, but instead on the massive penis that protruded from between her legs. Santana's hand slid down to the cock and began to stroke it slowly as Gentry walked up onto the stage.

Briana thought she was going to pass out as she watched the beautiful man join the two women on stage. She finally looked up to see the incredible breasts that she expected in Santana, but her eyes were repeatedly dragged down to her large cock. She looked over at Rey and he smiled back at her as he clapped once more.

"It gets better," he said. "Much better."

Briana swooned once more. She wasn't sure if it was the lighting in the room, the incense, or the beautiful woman with the massive cock, but she felt light-headed as she continued to stare up at the stage. She felt Rey's pat on her thigh, which she ignored once more and watched as Gentry approached the two women.

Gentry first approached the dancing woman, who pulled him close and lifted his shirt up over his head. Briana had been right; he was incredibly well cut. She found herself clapping as she watched the dancing woman unbutton his pants and push them down over his hips. He wore no underwear and Briana strained to get a look at what was between his legs as he turned toward them. His cock was hard, and big. Not quite as big as Santana's, but she knew it was large once the dancing woman wrapped her hand around it.

Rey was clapping once more, and Briana had joined him. She smiled as she watched, having forgotten where she was as she enjoyed the show. She didn't know what to expect next as Santana walked closer to the others on stage. Then her eyes widened once more as she watched Gentry slide down to his knees in front of Santana and swallow her cock deep into his mouth.

"Fuck!" Briana said under her breath, not having expected that at all.

Her eyes stared down at the beautiful man as he swallowed Santana into his mouth. Rey clapped loudly and looked over at Briana to make sure she was watching. He nodded to her and she clapped loudly also as Gentry sucked Santana in and out of his mouth. At one point, he slid her cock out and looked back at the table to smile. Then, he tilted his head, slid her back inside and swallowed her completely inside his mouth. He made it look effortless as he slid her out and then back inside again. Rey clapped louder than ever at this feat.

Briana thought back to what Rey had done to her, how

he had slowly pushed more and more of himself into her throat until she could take all of him in. It was incredible to watch Gentry's mouth swallow all of her in and out as his hands played with the Santana's massive breasts.

The lightheaded feeling was back, reminding Briana of her time with Esteban. Her head started spinning and she felt Rey's hand on her thigh once more. She felt herself clapping as she watched the stage, the incredible act on stage, but she also felt faint. She also felt Rey's hand slide up under her dress, it was something she had expected all along and thankfully the drugs dulled the thoughts of the brazen assault. She turned to him and offered the expected smile as his finger slid between her legs.

"Very good, Phoenix. Very good."

On stage in front of her, Gentry continued to blow Santana, her cock slipping deep into his mouth each time. Santana moaned quietly, her voice louder than the music. The dancer stepped closer to the couple on stage. She covered Santana's mouth with hers, cutting off her moans as her hands roamed over her large breasts.

Briana let out a moan as she watched the dancer's fingers pull at Santana's nipples.

Rey no longer clapping, worked his fingers into Briana's hole sliding deeper as she slipped down in her chair. She stared at Santana wondering what her tongue would taste like as Rey slipped another finger inside of her.

On stage, she watched as Gentry stood up from his knees. Santana's large cock stood straight out from her as Gentry's mouth covered hers. The dancer slipped down in front of him, sliding Gentry's cock into her mouth. Briana cheered them on as the drugged tea took full effect, Rey's fingers sliding in and out of her pussy. Gentry pulled the dancer up, off of his cock. He didn't want her there. What did he want, Briana wondered? She watched as he turned Santana around in front of him. Spun her so that she was facing away from him, looking off to the side of the table, and then he bent her over. Briana watched him spit on his hand, slide it behind Santana and then he moved his hands to her hips.

Briana knew what was going to happen next. She moaned loudly as she watched Gentry slide his cock into Santana's ass. She let out a loud cry and then stood up in front of him, her back arched as he reached around her, his hands sliding up over her tits. Gentry's hips slid back and forth as he started to fuck Santana, his cock buried deep in her ass. She rocked back and forth against him as they fucked. She looked back at the table smiling and then Briana watched the dancer step in front of Santana. Santana bent her over and buried her large cock deep inside of her and pulled her close to her by her hips.

That was more than enough to put Briana over the edge even without Rey fucking her with his fingers. She stared over at him as she stared felt a tremor, his fingers continuing to slide in and out of her. She began to swoon once. She saw Rey's face, and then the threesome on stage, fucking one another, all connected, and then she heard her heartbeat in her ears.

The lights in the room began to grow dark.

"What did you do to me?" Briana slurred.

"You're up on stage next," she thought she heard, but it was muddy. It could have been her imagination. "You're going to be wonderful. Excellent," said the same voice.

Her body was shaking. Was she having an orgasm? Her eyes caught a glimpse of Santana's head bent back, screaming. Was she cuming too?

Then it all went dark.

Chapter 21

Claire Campbell couldn't sit back and wait while her daughter was missing any more.

"Fuck them, she told her husband. I'm not waiting until the morning when I am in the same country as my missing daughter, for some agent to arrive when I can do something on my own."

"Calm down, honey," her husband said. "We have come a long way."

"Yes, and we are still doing nothing." It was 8 p.m. local time. They had eaten their dinner, bided their time, but she wasn't ready to rest. "Let's go to the police station; they will have to talk to us, we're her parents."

"We don't even speak their language," Phil said.

"They'll speak English. Jesus, Phil, we have to do something! I can't sit on my hands anymore while my daughter is God knows where. She took a job here, she lived in an apartment here. Let's go there, then. Something! How can you just sit there?"

Phil wasn't sitting on his hands, but he was a realist. He knew that there was no way, no conceivable way that his daughter was okay. He had known her for too long, spent too much time with her, frankly, taught her too well. She would never go three or four days without contacting her mother, and certainly not a week. All of Claire's concerns were real and he knew, especially after speaking with his international attorney friends, that there was a very real likelihood that they would never see Briana again. He was in no rush for Claire to come to the same conclusion. He could not tell her what he was thinking.

"You're right, honey. Let's go to the police and then to her apartment. We can provide them with additional information, pictures and anything else they need. Maybe we have key information that they need," he said, standing next to Claire as he spoke. He took her hands. "Come, we'll go tonight and explain to the agent that we just couldn't wait."

"Thank you, Phil," Claire said.

They left the embassy after talking to a guard who provided them with the whereabouts of the police station. The guard questioned their need for the police and Phil gave him a bogus answer, telling them that he knew someone there. Outside, they hailed a cab to the station and when they arrived 15 minutes later, Claire was already a disheveled mess, crying as they stepped inside.

Phil asked to speak to someone who was working on the Briana Campbell case. They were bounced from person to person at the station for the better part of an hour before he was informed that the inspector who was working on the case, had gone home for the evening. The officer who provided this information told the Campbells that they should inquire in the morning – after 10 o'clock.

Phil turned to Claire and shrugged his shoulders as if there was nothing left to do. Claire looked past him and addressed the officer.

"Where is the captain?" she said.

"The captain, ma'am?" the officer replied.

"Who is in charge tonight? Here. At the station!"

"Ma'am, please. The inspector will be back here in the morning. That is your best hope for a discussion."

"Don't tell me about hope!" she screamed. "I've been living on hope for the past week! Now, I want action! Go get us someone to talk to! Now!"

Several officers in the station were standing now, making their way over to where Claire was making a commotion. Two had their hands above their hips, over the weapons. The officer stared at her. She stared back, her chest rising and falling. She was seething. He thought about going back at her, but then thought better of it. He did not want to be made a fool of in front of the squad.

"Very well," he said. "Please, have a seat and I will find someone you can speak with."

"Thank you," Claire said, her voice breaking as she tried to control it.

The Campbells waited another 30 minutes before the officer returned with someone who looked more official. He was introduced as Captain Benito Baritz. The captain carried a folder and he asked them to follow him and then stepped into a small conference room.

"First, Mr. and Mrs. Campbell, I want to say I'm sorry you are having difficulty getting in contact with your daughter." He smiled at them as he spoke. He had a strong accent, but he was easy to understand. "You understand, these things are tricky – especially when we are talking about a young girl."

"She's our young girl," Phil said.

"Of course, and I too am a father and understand your concern. If I was in your shoes, I would also want to know that many women come here to celebrate Rio and all it has to offer, yes? Sometimes, they get caught up in the festivities." He nodded as he spoke. "Ah, especially the young ones. They meet our men – our handsome men, and it could be days before they come up for air."

"Captain Baritz!" Phil said.

"Yes, yes. I am not speaking necessarily of your girl, please. But we need to consider this. Could she have met someone, eh? Maybe gone on a small vacation. She is here to see Brazil, no?"

"Yes," Claire said. "I mean no – that's not what happened. She would have called, sent us a text. She knows I am worried. We are both worried."

"Of course," the captain said. "And, it is good you have come to us." He looked first to Claire and then to Phil, as if he could appeal to Phil. "Let me tell you what I will do for you. I will put a special team on this. My best men that are available to me. I will instruct them to focus on your little girl and to investigate immediately."

"Does that mean no one has been looking for our Briana?" Phil said, standing up, looking down at the captain.

The captain shook his head. "It does not work that way here. Not here in Brazil."

"She's been missing for days, and you have done nothing. I know it was reported," Phil said. "The embassy told us they reported it."

"Yes, yes. We have the report. We even had another report from a taxi driver who said he could not find her. Claims, he was her personal driver. Hmm. Perhaps, we should start with him. Sometimes, the guilty want to get caught, yes?"

"What does that even mean?" Claire said. "I want to know what you are doing to find my daughter. Are you doing anything?"

"Yes, yes. As I have told you, we have assigned an inspector. He is not here until tomorrow. He has the most information. He spoke to me about the taxi driver. Said we should investigate him. Perhaps he has."

"Is there nothing in the file. Can we have a name?"

Captain Baritz held his hand up, waving his finger. "You will not come here and take law into you own hands, Mrs. Campbell. You may have friends in high places, but this investigation will be conducted my way. So, no, I will not give you the driver's name. I will tell you where your daughter worked though, and I suggest you go speak with the administrator there tomorrow. He may be able to tell you more."

The Campbells stared at the captain in disbelief. Did he really think that they were going to sit by idly while the police did nothing? The police had information that the Campbells and the embassy investigator could find useful. They needed to share it.

"So, you see, you have wasted a trip to our station – tonight. Tomorrow, Inspector Perez will meet with you and explain his findings and where they are with the case. As I said earlier, I will put a special team together to work with him. That should show you we are serious about finding Belinda," he said, then looked at the file once more, "I'm sorry, Briana, yes? Now, if there is nothing more for tonight, I have to be getting home to my wife. We will see you back here early in the morning." The Campbells were standing. "I'm sure your daughter is fine.

The Campbells stepped out of the conference room and closed the door behind them. Captain Beritz looked at the folder on his desk, at the picture of Briana, and shook his head. She was very pretty. If they got their hooks into her, she would never be heard from again. As he was about to get up, the door opened and Phil Campbell stepped back into the room.

"Mr. Campbell," the captain said.

"Listen to me. I know you think that we have no idea what we are talking about and that my little girl is shacked up with someone, but I am telling you that is not true." Phil was mad and his anger filled his voice. "Something has happened to her. Someone has kidnapped or taken her for – I don't want to imagine what reason, but I am telling you that beginning tomorrow, I will be working with the weight of the US Embassy and their agents to find my daughter. I'm telling you this so that you can back off, stay out of our way. You never were looking for her in the first place; why start now."

"Mr. Campbell. Do you know how many people go missing in this city each year?"

Phil shook his head.

"Some say 15 people each day go missing. Do you know how many people a year that is? Can you imagine how hard it is to find that many people? Even a fraction of that many people, yes? If your daughter is missing, really missing, she will never be found. It is as simple as that. I understand that you have an obligation to find her, but we do not. We will do our work, like we always do, but unless we find some evidence that helps us find her, your daughter is as good as dead."

Phil stared at the captain. "This is sick," he said. "Is this what you tell everyone who comes looking for their children. Even your own people?"

"I'm telling you the truth. Most people can't handle the truth. It would be good if you prepared Mrs. Campbell for the inevitable, no? Maybe take her for a nice dinner in the nice part of town and explain it to her."

"Fuck you!"

"Be careful, Mr. Campbell. We will tolerate your wife's outbursts, but you are a different story."

"You're afraid to act. Afraid of the cartels. They control everything. Do I need to talk to them to find my daughter?" Phil was livid.

Captain Beritz walked around his desk. "Mr. Campbell. I would not recommend looking for trouble with the cartels. I would recommend that you do not even use that word again while you are here as guests in our country. They will not take kindly to your accusation. They do not control us. We have an understanding, yes?" The captain opened the conference room door once more. "Now, go console your wife. Do not investigate on your own. I have no quarrel with you. Don't make me regret my words."

"Fuck you, captain," Phil said. "We will be back in the morning to see your investigator."

Phil walked across the room to Claire and grabbed her hand as he led her out of the police station.

After the door closed, Captain Beritz picked up his personal phone and dialed a number. When the call was answered, he spoke eight words in Portuguese indicating to the person on the other end of the call that a problem existed and that action needed to be taken. The captain was told he would receive a return call within five minutes.

Beritz hung up the phone and waited. In his capacity, he served two masters: the people of his city and the cartel. It was the latter that paid the biggest dividend and Beritz knew that cooperating with them was key to maintaining the peace. When he sensed that the search for Briana would not quickly dry up, he made the quick decision to alert his benefactors. When the phone rang, he answered quickly.

In Portuguese, the voice asked for information. The

captain answered in kind.

"The subject's parents have sought help from the American embassy and a powerful senator. They are pressing forward with an independent investigation."

"You could not shut this down?" the voice said.

"I tried, but they want answers; answers I cannot provide."

"Then they shall have their answers. Once they are gone, we will arrange for an accident and you will explain to them that their daughter perished in the accident. Do you understand?"

"Yes," the captain said.

"Keep them at bay, captain," the voice said. "We will be in touch."

Captain Beritz hung up the phone. He knew his actions would destroy Briana's family, but he also knew it was better than them ever knowing the truth.

Chapter 22

Briana opened her eyes slowly. The room was foggy and spinning. She blinked to clear her head. Her arms and wrists hurt. She pulled on them. Was she standing? The room became clearer. Standing. Her hands were tied above her head. She tugged on the ropes, grunting. Nothing. There was music and bright lights streamed through the fog as her vision became clearer. She was in the club. She tugged again. No use.

Through the fog, she saw a familiar face. Santana. That beautiful woman that she had met earlier. Santana stepped closer to her. She felt Santana's hands on her breasts. Her soft fingers sliding over her. Briana looked down, realizing she was naked except for her heels. She was standing in the center of the stage. She gasped. Looked around. Rey, her captor, sat at the table, clapping, the sound vibrating in her head.

Santana pulled Briana's head toward her, covered Briana's mouth with her own and then pressed her tongue inside. Briana pulled back, but Santana held her head. She felt Santana's tongue press against her own and then she kissed her back, feeling Santana's arms wrap around her. What was it about this woman, Briana thought? Briana's nipples were hard; her body was excited, all nerves on edge. She remembered drinking the tea. Santana's tongue tasted wonderful in her mouth and when she pulled away, Briana leaned forward wanting more.

Santana smiled her beautiful smile and then she bent down and sucked one of Briana's hard nipples into her mouth. Briana moaned loudly, leaning into her, no longer feeling the pain from where her wrists were tied above her head. She felt Santana's silky fingers on her back as she arched up into her mouth. She had never been with a woman before, and she had never felt like she did at this moment.

Briana looked over at Rey as he sat at the table. He was clapping once more, and Briana smiled. 'You're up on stage next,' she remembered him saying, and she realized, she was the show now.

Santana moved to her other tit, sucking the nipple deep into her mouth, licking it with her velvet tongue. Briana moaned loudly as Santana licked and sucked on her breasts, her hands sliding down over Briana's ass, caressing her, squeezing her.

Then Santana's head was between her legs, and Briana arched her back once more, standing on her toes as her skilled tongue licked down the front of her to her hole. She stared down at the blond head between her legs as the woman licked her. Briana's mind swirled and all she could think about was how her body had never felt like this; never this excited, never this ecstatic. She thrust against the tongue between her legs. Then she stared over at Rey who stared back at her watching her being consumed in the throes of passion.

Phoenix didn't know how long Santana was down between her legs, licking and sucking on her; she had lost track of all time. When she finally lifted her head, she looked up at Briana and smiled. Her glistening face looked beautiful and wicked at the same time. Santana rose up in front of Briana and kissed her hard on the mouth. Briana could taste herself on the woman's tongue; she swallowed it deep into her mouth.

Phoenix felt something hard rubbing up against her stomach as they kissed and then she remembered that Santana was not all woman. Santana pulled away from her kiss and they both looked down at the hard cock between them. She watched as Santana's hand wrapped around her own cock and guided it down between them. Santana's free hand slid under Briana's ass and lifted her up as she guided her cock inside Briana.

Briana felt the large cock slide deep inside of her and let out a loud moan as Santana slowly withdrew and drove into her again. Her legs wrapped around Santana as she leaned back in to kiss her, and they started to fuck.

Every nerve in Briana's body was on fire. It was like this was always meant to be, she thought. This woman, this time. So strange. When they broke from their kiss, she looked over at Rey, smiling as she rode up and down on Santana's massive cock. Santana's fingers and breath were like fire as they touched her, igniting pleasure all over her body.

Santana arched her back, pushed Briana's head down to her chest as she pressed her tit into her mouth. Briana sucked from it as if she was a newborn as Santana thrust into her over again. Briana had never felt so much pleasure.

Then there were hands, other hands, on her back and sides. So many hands on her body. She lifted her head and turned to see Gentry at her side, his hands sliding over her sides and back as he stepped up behind her. She smiled at him as Santana lifted her up and down against herself,

Briana arched her back, driving Santana deeper into her.

Through the fog, she could see Rey clapping, smiling. She remembered smiling back as Gentry leaned his head forward, kissed her, then kissed Santana whose face was next to hers. Gentry's tongue found her mouth again and she felt his hard cock press up against her back.

Briana wanted to turn to him, to feel his cock inside of her, but she didn't want to let go of Santana. She felt his hands on her back, sliding through her sweat and down below her. In front of her, Santana's beautiful face swarmed, her smile lighting up the room as the electricity flowed through Briana. She felt her orgasm rising up inside of her; wondered where it had been hiding. She was ready to give into it. Then she saw Santana's face once more, shaking her head. Not yet, she seemed to be saying and Briana nodded.

Gentry's cock was behind her now, poking her. If her hands were free she would reach down and grab it, drop to her knees and slide it into her mouth. Then she would slide it deep inside of her. She heard clapping, loud clapping and she looked over at Rey. He was on his feet, staring at the three of them as they writhed up and down on the stage. Briana smiled at hi. Her head swirled and she felt good.

Then she felt Gentry's cock press up against her. His hands were on her ass, spreading her cheeks. She was aware of every touch on her body. Her smile faltered as the head of his cock pressed up against her ass.

"No!" she thought. She was not ready for that; not now, not ever.

Santana pulled Briana tight against her, her cock buried deep inside of her, holding her close as Gentry pushed the head of his cock into Briana's ass. "No!" she yelled again, but she never heard the sound come out. Santana covered Briana's mouth with hers, pushed her tongue through her lips just as Gentry forced his way into her dark hole. Briana felt the pain, tried to scream out once more, pulled on the ropes that held her arms up to no avail. She felt Gentry's cock slide deeper into her ass as Santana licked and sucked on her tongue.

Briana looked across the room at Rey. This is what he was waiting for this whole night. The cock inside her ass slid out, but she knew it was only temporary, and then it slid back in, deeper this time. Tears fell from her eyes as she looked at Santana who smiled as she slowly started to fuck her again. They took turns sliding in and out of her, taking their time. Their hands wandered over her body and it wasn't long before the pain subsided, and the drugs pulled her into a realm of semi-consciousness.

Briana's tears dried and she closed her eyes, concentrating on the two cocks that fucked her slowly. Gentry pulled her back toward him, driving himself once again into her ass. The three of them were moaning loudly, Santana and Gentry taking turns sliding in and out of Briana.

From behind her, Briana heard a loud grunt, and she turned her head to see the beautiful Gentry as his face twisted and then she felt him unload inside of her ass several times, his eyes closed as he came. When he was done, he pulled himself out.

Santana then slid herself out, planting Briana's feet on the floor as she stepped back. Her arms reached above Briana and she unclipped her wrists from the rope that help them over her head.

Briana felt the pain in her arms, back and shoulders as she lowered her arms. Santana stepped forward, put her arms on Briana's shoulders and pushed her to her knees. Briana turned to look at Rey one more time before she pulled Santana's cock into her mouth and began to suck on her. Santana's hands slid down to Briana's face and held her head in place. Then she proceeded to fuck Briana slowly and methodically, working her cock deep into Briana's mouth and throat.

When Santana came, Briana choked on her sperm, pushing her away so she could swallow. Santana pushed herself back inside of Briana's mouth and then pulled out, jerking herself in front of Briana as she came all over her chest. When she was finished, she pushed Briana down onto her back. She bent her head down to Briana's chest and began to lick her cum from Briana's tits. Gentry joined her and together the two of them licked Briana clean.

As Briana lay on her back, her body squirming under the silk tongues of the two most beautiful people she had ever seen, she heard two loud claps and turned her head to see several uniformed servants come back into the room. Some brought more food to the table. Three of them walked up onto the stage and knelt down next to Briana, Santana and Gentry. Each held a small wooden bucket and ladle.

"Very good," Rey said. "Excellent."

Gentry and Santana stopped licking Briana and sat up alongside of her. Briana sat up and looked over at Rey.

"A most excellent performance. Drink up."

The three servants each ladled a pink liquid into glasses and offered one each to the three people on stage.

"Drink," Rey said. He held up his own pink glass. "We have a long night ahead of us still."

Briana drank eagerly from her glass, as did the others; they were all parched. The liquid was cold and silky as it slid down her throat. She drank the whole glass down and the servant refilled it. Briana finished half of the second glass and handed it back to the servant. Her head felt light again.

She laid down onto her back on the stage, her head turned to the side. She looked over to where Rey had been, but he was no longer there.

"Very good, all of you," he said. His voice came from the stage this time.

Briana turned to see him standing next to her. Santana stood up from the stage and slowly began to undress him. As she did, Gentry climbed on top of Briana. Her body was on fire, her head swooning. The pink liquid was stronger than the blue; its magic igniting all of her nerves. She felt Gentry slide inside of her and she wrapped her arms around his back. His cock was back. She watched as Santana slid Rey's pants down. There were three cocks on stage now. Rey knelt down next down next to her head on the stage as Gentry started to fuck her. Briana's hand reached for Rey's cock.

For the next several hours, they each took turns fucking Briana and sucking on one another. They used each of her holes repeatedly and she wantonly accepted them. At times two of them were inside of her; at other times three.

They broke at one point for another drink of the pink fuel and then went right back to it. When they were done with her, they left her in a pile on the stage as they slowly got dressed.

Briana watched as Rey walked them to the door of the room and sent them on their way. She was broken and exhausted, but her libido was still on fire. She lay on her side watching Rey as he sat back down in his seat. What they did to her was unspeakable, using her as if she was a piece of meat. Fueling her with drugs for their pleasure and the shame she felt for her participation in the acts. But she couldn't deny the pleasure she had also felt.

Rey stared back at as he sipped his wine. He smiled.

"Get dressed now. It is late," he said. "You may sleep in my bed tonight, Phoenix, instead of that filthy tent. You have earned that right for the night."

He smiled at her. Briana smiled back.

Chapter 23

Lily was beside herself. Briana had not returned to the tent last night and, as the sun was coming up, she was still missing. That could only mean one thing, Lily thought, and it was not good. Actually, she knew it could mean many things, each one worse than the next. Despite her trying to put the thought out of her head, her brain ran through a litany of possibilities.

Briana could have been beaten horribly or even killed. Lily had heard that they killed those who really put up a fight and when she last spoke with Briana, it sounded as if she was going to be as tough as possible with their captors. She could have been sold – isn't that what they were told could happen to them? If she was, what did that mean? Where did she go and how would she be treated? Lily realized that there could be a thousand other situations that Briana could be facing. What struck Lily the most though, was her certainty that she would never see Briana again. That, even though their bond had not been that great, caused Lily to breakdown and cry.

When the guard came to get Lily, she was still curled up on her bed, sobbing. The zipper opened and the guard stepped inside. Lily made no attempt to get up.

"Let's go, Lily," the guard said.

"Fuck you!" she responded.

The guard approached her, standing by the side of her bed looking down at her. Lily looked up.

"Get the fuck out of here! I don't want to be a part of... whatever this is anymore. This is so fucked up... so fucked up!"

The guard reached for her arm to lift her off the bed. She pulled it away.

"Fuck you! Don't touch me." Lily looked up at the guard and spit at him.

His reaction was quick and forceful. He slapped Lily across the face, sending her body down to the mattress. She looked up at him, her hand covering her face where she hit him.

"You coward," she said. The guard reached down to grab her arm, to pick her up from the bed. Lily kicked at him. "Don't you fucking touch me!"

The guard stepped back from the bed so she could not kick him and then he smiled. There were two ways to do this and either way suited the guard just fine. It had been a few days since he really laid into one of the girls. If that was the way she wanted to play it, then he was fine with it. He was a fair man though, he maintained. He would give her one last chance.

"Lily. Get up. I won't ask you again."

Lily stared up at him, her face defiant. She wished she had the drug coursing through her body. Her reticence to ask for it, to ween herself away from it was not going to work in her favor at this moment. It dulled everything and she knew it would be to her benefit to have all her senses dulled as she slowly lifted herself back into a sitting position on the mattress. She knew the guard would not be kind to her when she stood up, but enough was enough. Lily wasn't sure why she chose this minute to take a stand – perhaps it was the disappearance of Briana, perhaps it was a combination of things.

Once seated, the guard waited impatiently for her to stand. When she did, he nodded his head. He sighed; he would not get to hurt her anymore today. He reached out his hand to take her arm, resigning himself to walk her from the tent and to her destination. Lily continued to stare at him. Then she struck out with him with her leg, aiming for his balls. The guard was swift to block her attack, stopping her foot before it reached him. He was just as swift to backhand her across the face, sending her spinning. Lily's hand reached out to stop her from falling. The guard didn't wait for her to turn back around. Instead, he grabbed her by the shoulder and pulled her back toward him. He drove his fist into her back, just above her kidney. Lily let out a loud grunt, dropping to her knees, her head falling forward.

Lily inhaled deeply, trying to catch her breath. Her face and back pained her considerably. The guard grabbed her by the hair and began to drag her across the floor of the tent. Lily reached for his wrist, to lessen the stress on her hair, working her feet to try and get purchase so she could stand up.

"Okay, okay," she managed. The guard let go of her hand, letting her fall back down to the floor.

"Get up," he said.

Shaking and sobbing, Lily slowly lifted herself up to all fours, resting as she tried to catch her breath, willing the pain in her back to recede. She gasped for air before she stood up.

"Up!" the guard said.

Lily shook her head. She didn't know if she had the

strength to get up from this position. She looked up at the guard through her tears, holding her hand up, begging him not to intervene. She would get up; she just needed time.

"Now," he yelled.

Lily used the frame of the cot in front of her to pull herself up. When she was sitting up on her knees, she took one more deep breath before lifting herself onto her shaky legs. The guard looked at her, for the first-time taking pity on her and he helped her the rest of her way to her feet. Lily looked at him and thanked him with a nod, knowing that he could have just as easily driven his foot into her stomach when she was on her hands and knees. The guard led her out.

Lily's face and back hurt tremendously. She admonished herself for taking such a strong stand when she was not strong enough to defend herself. She needed more time to get stronger; needed to be smarter so she could determine when to pick her fights. If she really wanted to resist, she needed to prepare herself rather than subject herself to the casual beatings that the guards were all too happy to administer. Worse, Lily came to realize, the guard was walking her across the compound to the showers. He wasn't even taking her for training. She resisted for no reason, although it was only a matter of time before she would be expected to satisfy someone else's needs.

The guard stared at her as she washed, looking for his own marks on her body. When the shower was complete, he took her back to the tent. He pushed her inside, zipping it back up behind her. Lily climbed onto her cot and sat in the corner, against the wall. She sobbed; that was all she could do as she nursed her wounds.

****

Briana awoke in Rey's large bed. She didn't know how she had gotten there. She wore a silk nightgown; something else she did not remember. She was alone in the bed. Every part of her body hurt, despite the soft mattress that she lay upon. She lifted her head, shook it gently to clear the fog. Her back hurt just from lifting her head. She looked for Rey; he was not in the bed, nor was he anywhere that she could see. Briana breathed a sigh of relief.

She thought back to the previous night and morning. To all that had happened. To all that they had done to her and what she had done with the others. Images flashed through her mind; horrendous images of positions she was in, her willingness to be in those positions, her submissiveness. None of it made sense. She'd been drugged, she argued. But, it was more than just a simple drug. Even now, as she thought about it, her nipples hardened, and she felt aroused. Could they have put something in the tea – those colored teas that made her more willing? An aphrodisiac of some kind. It made sense, because the woman that she was last night was not the Briana she knew.

She sat up on the bed. She looked over her body. Her body smelled fragrant. She must have showered, or they gave her a shower. Her arms were bruised in certain spots, her jaw hurt toward the back of her mouth. Her throat was hoarse. She opened the front of the nightgown. There were marks across her breasts; some red some darker. When she touched them, they hurt. Her nipples were raw. She was sure that she would find similar bruises all over her body. There were so many hands, so many limbs when they were on the stage.

Briana worked her way to the end of the bed. Slowly, she stood up. She was wobbly, but she righted herself. She slipped out of the nightgown, cognizant that Rey could walk in at any moment, but that took a backseat to her understanding her injuries and bruises. Her thighs were bruised much like her arms. Her stomach had similar red and black marks on it. She bent, feeling the pain in her back, to look down at her vagina. It didn't look bruised but touching any part of it sent a small wave of pain through her. She was afraid to look, but twisted herself, despite the pain, to look at her backside.

Her cheeks were red, also bruised in certain spots. She remembered being slapped hard several times on her ass and thighs. The marks were reminiscent of the intensity of their actions on stage. There were marks all down the back of her legs. She didn't care to count them; there were too many and their origin was puzzling. She bent down once more to pull up the nightgown. Bending hurt; a lot. Her ass hurt tremendously, and she knew why, although she pushed those thoughts out of her mind. Briana chose to lock the specific actions that led to the pain in a separate container in her mind; one she hoped to never revisit. The pain was reminder enough.

There was a knock at the door on the far-end of the room. The door opened and a guard walked in. It was the same one who had led her to Rey's room. He walked across the room and handed her a pair of scrubs and some sandals. He nodded and stepped back.

"Please," he said, turning his back to Briana.

Briana slid out of the nightgown and dressed in the blue scrubs. She slipped her feet into the sandals noting that her toes even hurt.

"Okay," she said.

The guard turned around and indicated that she should follow him. Together they walked from the room, down the long hallway and out of the white house. It was hot and humid in the open area of the compound. The guard led her back to her tent. When she was in front of the tent, the guard unzipped the tent and Briana stepped inside. In the corner, on her cot, sat a scared Lily. She rose up to meet Briana as the zipper to the tent closed behind her.

"Oh my God! You're okay!" Lily said. She lifted herself up from her cot and ran over to Briana. She pulled her tight into her arms and hugged her tightly.

"Ow, ow," Briana said, pulling herself away. "You're hurting me, Lily."

Lily let go. "I'm sorry. I didn't think I would ever see you again. Where were you?"

"It was a long night, Lily. A very long night. I don't remember all of it," Briana smiled at Lily who was ecstatic that her friend was okay, standing in front of her. "I hurt all over. In parts I never knew I could hurt."

Briana stepped toward her cot and Lily moved out of her way. Gingerly, Briana sat down on the edge of the cot, noting immediately the difference between it and Rey's mattress.

"Are you okay?"

"Yes," Briana said. "bruised and battered, confused and a little embarrassed. But, otherwise, I'm okay."

"I'm so happy to see you," Lily said.

"What happened to you?" Briana asked, looking up at Lily's bruised lip.

"You should see the other guy," Lily said, letting out a small laugh.

She sat down on the bed next to Briana, gently patting her thigh.

"Do you want to talk about it?" Lily asked.

"I don't know. I don't know if I ever want to talk about it." Briana stared at Lily. "To anyone."

Lily nodded. "We have to do something, Briana. Or they will take everything from us. I was so scared for you, but also happy that you would no longer be in pain – like the rest of us."

"I don't understand," Briana said.

"I thought you were dead." Lily started to sob, loudly this time.

Briana looked shocked and then lifted her arm as Lily slid under it. She hugged Lily against her side, despite the pain, while she sobbed. The poor girl, Briana thought, realizing that Lily was even more broken than she was. The two consoled each other for a very long time, neither wanting to break from the other's embrace.

Chapter 24

The Campbell's were not hopeful that the embassy investigator was going to be any more helpful than the police. The prior night, after leaving the police station, they took a cab to Briana's apartment. The door was locked and they had no way of getting in. Phil Campbell indicated that he was willing to break the door down, but it was his wife this time who was the calming force. The last thing they needed, she told him, was more trouble with the police.

After a hurried breakfast at the embassy, the Campbells were greeted by Agent James Adams one of the embassy's chief investigators. Agent Adams was quick to point out that the Campbells should in no way communicate with the police alone and that discussions with the Brazilian press were not permitted.

"They love the American girl gone missing story," he said. "It makes front page news but does nothing but get in the way of the investigation. Believe me, it is in your best interest. I assure you," he added, "I am your best hope of finding your daughter if she is indeed lost."

"And, your success rate at this?" Phil Campbell asked.

"That's not important, Mr. Campbell. Each case is different. Each person is different. I will give you all of my effort and I will help focus the efforts of the police department. We will do everything in our power to find your daughter." Agent Adams stopped abruptly.

"But..." Phil pushed him to go further.

"But you should be aware that women are taken every day here in Brazil and all of South America. Many of them. Some, we never recover." Claire began to cry. "Your tears will not help, Mrs. Campbell. We need you to be positive and provide us with any information that will help our investigation. Understood?"

Claire inhaled and tried to control her sobbing. Phil put his arm around her and pulled her close.

"Let's go. First stop will be your daughter's apartment."

The Campbells and Agent Adams were met by the police at Briana's apartment door. There was some mingling of bystanders around, but the agent told them to go about their business. Inside the apartment, it became very apparent, that no one had visited the space in quite some time.

Claire began to cry as soon as she stepped through the doorway. She knew instinctively that Briana was not in the apartment and hadn't been there for some time. She could still smell her or her imagination provided that memory. She walked directly into the bedroom, while the police and the agent surveyed the small living space.

Phil followed Claire into the room, knowing that it would invoke many memories of Briana. Her clothes would be in the room; familiar clothes that she brought from home. Claire would be able to picture Briana wearing them. There was nail polish on the counter and her hairbrush. She knew if she looked in the bathroom, she would find her toothbrush. Briana had not packed to go somewhere. She had left the apartment with plans to return.

"She was coming back, Phil. She just never made it," Claire said. "Her pocketbook, with all of her stuff is right here. She must have taken the small one – to go out. Her clutch. Get the agent. We need to tell him."

"Claire, it's okay. They will do all of this. Let them do their work."

"No, it proves what we have been saying. Her sneakers are here, Phil. Her regular shoes." She stared at him as if he was dense. "She didn't leave barefoot – these are the shoes she wore all of the time."

"Maybe she had other sneakers. Maybe she wore sandals," Phil tried.

"And what, she went out in her sandals without her pocketbook?" Claire was forming a picture in her mind. "Her heels. Where are her heels – the ones from the prom. I know she took them; I packed them." She bent down to look in the closet. "They're not here." She looked under the bed. "She was wearing them. She hated wearing them, but they're not here. That tells us she was all dressed up." She went into the other room, calling the agent's name.

Agent Adams followed Claire into the room, reluctantly. He had a method and it paid to follow his method so that he didn't overlook something.

"Her heels are missing. She was dressed up when she left the apartment. Must have gone out – somewhere special because she wore her heels. She hated wearing them." The agent looked at her. Claire looked at Phil. "I'm right, and I can prove it. She only had one nice dress that she took with her. She would have worn that with the heels." Claire moved to the closet and slid the door open. Her hand sifted through the hanging clothes. She couldn't find the dress; that proved her point. "See, it's not here. I can tell you what she was wearing, and she must have gone out that night." She had risen her voice as she made her finding. "She met someone – that's the person…" suddenly her voice went quiet. She had thumbed to the end of the closet and found the dress. She lifted it by the hanger and pulled it from the closet. "I was sure…" she said. "I was so sure."

Claire sat down at the end of the bed, the dress in her lap and proceeded to cry. Phil sat next to her and consoled her while the agent went back into the other rooms. Phil held her while she cried, not trying to stop her. She needed to get it all out. What she discovered proved nothing in particular but being in the apartment was proof enough that something had happened to her. There were too many things that Phil knew his daughter would never leave home without if she was going to stay somewhere else beginning with her hairbrush and her toothbrush. Sure, she could have bought new ones, but that wasn't Briana. He was now as sure as Claire was that something had happened to his daughter.

The police and the agent searched through the apartment for any clues or hints. The agent asked why the apartment had not been searched earlier – when Briana was first reported missing, and the response was simple – they hadn't gotten to it. When they wrapped up in the apartment, they were to head to the school where she worked. Agent Adams asked the Campbells if they were up for the journey to the school. They both nodded their heads. The agent took them aside.

"Listen, you need to keep it together if we go to public places. We do not want to draw attention to ourselves, as I said earlier. If we do, the police will shut down my investigation and nothing will come of it. So, I can have you go down to the police station and meet with the inspector who has been working this case while we go to the school. Or, we can go to the school, but I will ask you to remain in the car. If there is something that we need to discuss with you, we will invite you inside. Which will it be?"

"The school," Phil said. "I don't think it would be a good idea to be at the police station without you." The agent nodded and they left to head to Briana's workplace.

As promised, they stayed in the car as Agent Adams and the police went inside. They spoke to the administrator and even Mrs. Alves. Neither of them were much help. When the agent was about to leave, Mrs. Alves called him back, separately. The agent stopped and went over to speak with her. She told him that she expected something like this to happen.

"She was very pretty. She liked when men watched her, like all American women. She wanted only one thing and she got it."

"What is that?" the agent said.

"You know. They come and get you. I told her to watch out."

"Watch out for who?"

"The cartel, the mob. Whatever you want to call it. They talked to her here. The security men. I told her to stay away."

"Briana spoke to the cartel?"

The police were now walking toward Mrs. Alves. She looked at them and then at the agent from the embassy.

"Tell them what you just told me," Agent Adams said.

"I told you there were bad people in the world."

"Tell them what you said about the cartel..."

"I don't speak of the cartel. No one speaks of the cartel."

Agent Adams stared at Mrs. Alves and then looked at the police.

The police thanked Mrs. Alves for her time, and they walked the agent out. He turned to look at her as she was leaving, and she looked down at the ground. She had given him an important piece of information. What would he be able to do with it?

Outside, Adams asked the lead policeman why they would not consider the cartel as a potential suspect in the situation and he replied that he still believed there was no crime. He warned the agent not to bring the cartel or suspicions of the cartel into a situation that didn't warrant it.

"There is no need to speculate without any evidence," he said. "Are you aware how careful we are not to ruffle the feathers of the cartel. It is best," he added, "not to poke a sleeping bear, yes?"

The agent looked at him and shook his head. Fear, he realized, is what prevented them from finding out the truth. The police waited for the agent and the Campbells to leave before they got into their own cars and left the school. Agent Adams let the Campbells know what happened, leaving out the part about the cartel discussion with Mrs. Alves. It was probably nothing more speculation as the police had said, but he remembered her saying that Briana had "met" the cartel at the school. The Campbells hadn't expected much but hung on the agent's every word.

"Now what?" Phil said. "These are all dead-ends."

"I suggest we go to the police station and then after that, I will take all the information I can get from you so that we can continue this investigation once you head back to the states."

"We're not going back to the states without our little girl," Briana's mother said.

"I'm afraid that is not up to me. Senator Marshall arranged for an emergency two-day visa. You will be returning home in the early morning."

"Why were we not told this?" Phil said.

"That I do not know. I follow orders, Mr. Campbell, just like most of us over here. What I suggest is that we make the most of our time together so that we can continue searching for your daughter after you depart, yes?" The Campbell's just nodded, knowing they had no choice.

At the police station, a little over an hour later, the agent was met by the lead investigator on the case, Gabriel Perez. You can call me Gabe he told the agent and the Campbells. Mr. Perez brought them into a back room and sat them down at a table. He placed a couple of folders on the table and sat down.

"I understand you had a little run-in with our captain, yesterday, Mr. Campbell?" the inspector said.

Phil just nodded. The embassy agent stared at him – this is information that he should have known before stepping into the station.

"I assure you..." the agent started.

"It's not an issue. He's a pompous ass," the inspector said. "Riding out his last couple of years until he retires. All bark, no bite," he laughed. "Very well," he looked at all of them. "I want to show you what evidence we have collected about your daughter' disappearance." He shook his head. "I am afraid it is not much."

He opened the folders on the table to show the pictures that the Campbells had emailed over, as well as snapshots of the apartment, a series of notes, and a printout of the missing person's report.

"You see, there is nothing here. Your daughter has simply vanished without a trace. There is no sign of foul play anywhere. Not in her apartment, not in her place of work. We checked her phone records – with the permission of the embassy. They show her only going from work to home and back again. There have been no new records for more than a week now. If her phone is active, it is not running on our national services. That means, if she is using the phone, it is not in our country."

"What about other carriers?" Phil said.

"We have put a call into them, but that information takes time to gather." He shook his head again. "I don't think her phone is active – but," he added, "it could mean that she lost it and got a new number."

"Wouldn't you have a record of that?" Phil tried again.

"Yes, I suppose we would. Unless she registered it under a different name; perhaps with a friend."

Claire was shaking her head. "She had no friends that we knew of here before she left."

"Perhaps she made one then, huh? Let's be positive. We have nothing to show that any harm has come to your daughter."

"Inspector Perez," Phil said pointedly. "Of all the girls and children that go missing in this country, do you ever have any evidence of foul play?" Perez didn't respond right away. "So, the fact that there is no evidence doesn't mean that our daughter is okay. The more you people continue to believe that, the less I think you try to find her. You see, she isn't just any little girl," Phil said, his voice rising. "She is ours – our beautiful daughter. Smart, strong, and confident. She's not going to become a statistic in your country because it happens all of the time. Do you understand?"

The inspector stared at Phil took a deep breath and then responded slowly. "Your daughter is no different than any other child – or for that matter any person who has gone missing in Rio. We will do whatever we can to find her, and I pray – I really do pray that this is all some silly mistake and she calls you and says she had the best vacation. I just don't know. We will collect evidence and share it with the embassy. If they can help, great. If there is any indication of foul play, we will then bring our Polícia Federal into the search to work along with yours. We hope that not to be the case, but we will use all of our resources if we have evidence that something has happened to her. So, you see, sir, your daughter is just as important as any other person reported missing. I take my job very seriously. I hope you can appreciate that."

Phil didn't respond. Agent Adams took the lead.

"Thank you, Inspector Perez. I'm can assure you that Mr. and Mrs. Campbell appreciate all of your efforts. If you would kindly keep us in the loop on any new findings, we will do the same." He stood up from the table to shake the inspector's hand. The Campbells stood up as well. "It is, in our best interest to work together on this to bring Briana home safe."

The inspector bid the group farewell and closed the door behind them. He sat back down at the round table and opened up the bottom folder. Inside was the report from the taxi driver, who had told them he had not seen Briana Campbell for several days when he came to the station. Inspector Perez had dismissed it then but had since tried to call the taxi driver several times. When he called the phone, it just went to a generic voicemail, indicating the caller was not available. The inspector thought it strange that a cab driver would not be reachable by his mobile phone for several days. He closed the file and pondered his next move.

Back at the embassy, Agent Adams spoke to the Campbells at length, gathered the pictures they had brought for the investigation and collected the names of her friends with whom she had gone to school. It was possible that she hooked up with a girlfriend from school and went on a small vacation. Claire told the inspector that she would never do something like that, and he reminded her that her daughter had told her that she was only coming to Brazil for a short visit even though she began hunting for a job the moment she touched down in Rio.

The Campbells went to sleep early in the embassy that night; their return flight to the states was at 6 a.m. A car, courtesy of the senator would take them to the airport. When they got in bed, Claire cried herself to sleep while Phil held her tight. His mind wouldn't shut off imagining the horrible things that men were doing to his daughter and hoping that whatever suffering she was going through would be short-lived.

Chapter 25

Lily and Briana took their first lunch together in the compound since they were brought to camp. Briana walked slowly feeling the effects on her body of the prior night. It would take more than a couple of hours of rest for this pain to go away, she knew. Lily made a small plate for herself and laughed when she saw the size of the plate that Briana brought to the table.

"When was the last time you ate?" Lily said.

"I'm not sure," Briana responded.

She remembered having eaten at the club, but she could not recall how much, and based on the flashbacks, she did more than work off a simple meal. She was ravenous and she tore into her food. It was nothing like the food at the club, but it filled her up. When she looked over at Lily, the woman was smiling.

"Stop smiling at me."

"I'm happy to see you," Lily said. Then she whispered, "We need to stick together if we are to get out of here. If you were gone, I do not know what I would do."

Briana looked around. Speaking like Lily was speaking could get you a quick beating. Briana's eyes bore into Lily's letting her know not to continue.

"You know what I mean," Lily finished.

When they were done eating, they were escorted back their tent. No one came for either of the two women that day and even after dinner, there was no guard at their tent pulling them away from one another. They slept and talked throughout the day. At some point, in the evening, Briana woke up to find Lily sitting at the end of her bed.

"We have to find a way out before they kill us, or sell us, or worse," Lily said.

"What could be worse than any of that?" Briana said.

"I don't know, but I don't want to find out. I know you are looking at things. I see your eyes, Briana. Always alert, always watching, calculating. We need to work together. To get out of here. I don't know how much more I can take." She looked up at Briana. "I even stopped the drugs."

"Did you?" Briana said, realizing for the first time that Lily hadn't seemed out of it at all since she came back. Lily nodded. "Cold turkey – completely off the drugs?"

Lily smiled. "Well, not completely, but I am trying. Very hard. I don't want to be under the drug's control, but sometimes it helps me to forget."

"We're no good together, Lily if we can't work together. You need to stay focused. Try to erase what happens without the drugs." She looked onto Lily's eyes. "Will you try?"

Lily nodded.

"Good," Briana nodded. "Good. Now, no more talk like this for tonight. We both need to get rest so we can heal. The stronger we are, Lily, the better we are."

Lily leaned forward and hugged Briana, pulled her tight against her. Briana hugged her back even though it hurt to pull her against her. Lily left the cot and went back to her own. Briana lay down on her back on the flimsy mattress and willed herself to sleep. Sleep could heal many wounds, she knew.

In the early morning, Briana was awoken by a guard at her side. She didn't hear the zipper of the tent open. She looked over at Lily's cot; it was empty. The guard waited for her to get up and then led her out of the tent. She winced when he placed his hand on her bicep directing her walk and she felt him loosen his grip.

Briana wasn't sure what her meeting with Rey would be like today. He had been several different people since she met him. The man he was the other night was both strange and gentle. He still was extremely dominant, but he was far from the man she had first met. She wondered if her actions the other night had bought her any goodwill. She certainly was as compliant as he wanted her to be even though she had determined it was the aphrodisiac-laced teas that were the main drivers behind her submissiveness. Perhaps he would be more kind to her based on the way she performed.

As the entered the white house, Briana realized she wasn't shaking. Even as they climbed the steps after passing the guards at the door. Her body remained calm. She was glad it was under control and she hoped it would remain so when she met up with Rey. At the top of the steps, the guard led her to the left. He had always led her to the right before – down the long hallway. This time, they walked about 20 feet before coming to a closed door. The guard knocked and then he opened the door and led Briana inside.

The room was large, but not as big as the first room in the house. Like the other room, there was a large bed in the corner of the room, but this room did not have an office area attached to it. Briana looked for Rey inside the room, but he was not there. Instead a familiar short, fat man walked across the room toward her. He smiled when he came close and his eyes slowly walked down the front of her body and then back up again.

"I'm Oalo, we met back some time ago with Nicolau, yes? I oversee all the camps here in Brazil," he said.

Briana said nothing and he looked into her eyes. She stared back.

"You don't stare at me. Look at the ground when you are in my presence."

Briana looked down at the ground waiting for his temper to cool.

"Hmm, so very pretty. Take off your clothes," the man said.

Where was Rey? Who was this disgusting fat man who wanted her to disrobe? Behind her, Briana heard the door close and she realized the guard had left and she was alone in the room with this man.

"I will say it one more time," Oalo said. "I do not have a lot of patience."

Briana didn't move for a moment and then she slowly reached down to pull up the corners of her shirt. As she lifted it, she watched the fat man lick his lips as her breast came into view. His eyes widened. Briana lifted the shirt over her head and dropped it to the floor.

"The pants now," he said.

"Where is Rey?" she asked. That was a mistake.

Oalo punched her hard in the stomach, doubling Briana over. She tried to catch her breath, but he had knocked the wind out of her. She stepped back, coughing and choking as she gasped for air.

"Rey works for me and I sent him to another camp. You should have been given to me for training, not Rey. Now take off your pants," he said, as she tried to recover.

Briana stepped further back, waving her hand in front of her, warding him off. She bent over, put her hands on her thighs as she sucked in large breaths of air. The short man stepped forward as oxygen filled her lungs once more and she began to get control of her breathing. He smacked her hard across the face.

"Remove your pants!" he shouted.

Still reeling from the slap, Briana's hands worked to push her pants down. She could taste blood in her mouth. What was happening, she thought? She was shaking now. Who was this man and why was he treating her like this? She stepped out of her pants while still retreating, the pain in her left cheek growing. The man grabbed her by the shoulder and pushed her down to the floor. Briana was down on her hands and knees, looking up at him as he circled her.

"Get on your back, Phoenix," he said. She didn't move. "Now!" he screamed.

She was in no position to argue. She rolled onto her back, her body shaking, looking up at the fat man as he stared down at her. As she watched, he unbuckled his pants and slid them down around his ankles. Fuck, she thought. She started to compartmentalize in in her mind. The fat man pulled down his underwear, revealing a small penis that his chubby fingers stroked.

"Stay still," he said to Briana. "Don't you move now."

Briana wanted to kick him right in the balls as he leaned down over her, dropping to his knees between her own.

He smiled at her, one of his hands fondling her breast as he pulled on himself. He looked into her face and then he slid the head of his small cock against her.

Briana's body shook and she turned her head away. She didn't want to watch this sweaty fat man defile her. She wanted to push him away, scream and throw him off of her, find something to smash his head in, but those were not options for her. She could hear him breathing hard as he rubbed himself up and down on her.

He pressed his cock lower down on her, trying to find her hole. He was salivating as he pressed her breast roughly. Briana prayed that he didn't tell her to watch him.

She looked away, tears rolling down her face, forcing her mind to dismiss what was happening to her. Then she heard him grunting, as his weight pressed against her.

He was not inside of her, not pressing against her vagina. His breath came quicker as she listened to him and then finally, he yelled out and she felt him shoot against her. He bounced on top of her two or three more times and then he sat back on his knees.

"Look what you made me do," he said. "You fucking pig!"

Oalo stared at her as she turned to face him. His face was red; he was still breathing hard. He placed his hand on her stomach and pushed off of her as he lifted himself up. He stood over her, pulling his pants up.

"Get up. You are of no use to me now. Get up!"

Briana stood up slowly, grabbing her clothes as she did.

"I didn't tell you to get dressed." Briana dropped her clothes back to the floor. "Come over here and clean me up."

Reluctantly, she stepped closer to Oalo. She looked down at him, his small penis flaccid, his pubic hair filled with his own cum. Did he want her to clean him with her tongue? She thought she might vomit, but she choked it back down. Still better than having him inside of her. She moved closer to him, prepared to drop down to her knees before him. She would close her eyes as she cleaned him, hold her breath if necessary. As she started to bend down, the man handed her a towel, pushing her back.

"With the towel. I don't want your tongue near me now... now that it is over. Clean me up with the towel."

Briana gratefully accepted the towel and cleaned the man under and around his dick. She still found herself wanting to throw up, but she maintained her self-control. She didn't know what was next, but she was tired of being hurt. When she was finished, she looked back up at him.

"Good. Now get out of here. Get out of my sight before I slap you to the floor. Do you understand me?"

Briana shook her head and bent to pick up her clothes. She started to put them on, and he yelled at her once more.

"I don't want to see you anymore. Get out of here! Now!"

She went to the door and knocked on it. It opened and she stepped out into the hallway, naked, shaking. The guard stared at her as she pulled her clothes on. He noted her cut lip and he looked away.

The guard walked Briana back to her tent and placed her inside of it. Lily was not there, and Briana quickly moved to her cot. She nursed her wounds as best she could and then she pulled her legs up under her and waited for Lily or lunch, whichever came first. She wondered what had happened to Rey. She pushed thoughts of the fat man out of her head. He was disgusting, but at least he didn't penetrate her.

Lily did come back before lunch and they ate together. Briana shared the story of the fat man and Lily said that she thought she had been with him once. Be careful, she told Briana, he is a violent man more than anything else. Briana didn't argue with her, still feeling the pain from the slap across her face.

That night they huddled together, hoping not to be pulled out again. They were not and Lily and Briana spoke to each other about what they knew about the compound, its practices and what they had learned of its operations. Briana did not share her time with Rey or the night at the club, at least not in any detail; there was something about him, she thought, that she was not yet ready to share.

The next several mornings, Briana was taken again from her room early in the morning. Each time she was brought to Oalo's room. He would hit her if she didn't listen and after he made her strip naked, he would masturbate on her or try and fuck her only to release before penetrating her. Briana could handle his disgusting advances if he didn't want to physically hurt her each time he was in her presence. He liked to slap her; liked to see her face as it spun away from him. He liked to see the marks his fingers left on her.

The meetings with the fat man happened every morning. The guard would take her to the white building and Briana would hope that they would turn right instead of left in the big hallway. But day after day, she was brought to the same place. During the last meeting, more than a week later, the fat man peed on her after he came all over her stomach. He stood above her washing his sperm from her as he held himself in her hand. When her stomach was clean, he peed up over her chest, smiling as his golden liquid splashed off of her. He finished before his stream could make it up to her face, and he yelled at her for letting him finish before he could pee in her mouth. He kicked her in the side and told her to clean up the mess he had just made.

The only upside to Briana's visits with the abusive man were that they were short. She and Lily often found themselves back in their tents around mid-day licking their wounds, telling each other painful stories about their encounters, searching for a silver lining.

When Briana was returned to the tent that afternoon, humiliated and broken, Lily was already there. When Lily picked up her head, one of her eyes was partially closed, a yellow bruise already forming around it.

"What happened?" Briana said, running over to her,

forgetting her own issues. The question was rhetorical. They had both been beaten in one way or another daily, their bruises sometimes hidden beneath their clothes. Lily's bruise was very apparent.

"I put my foot down," Lily said. "Three of them, over and over again. I just had to do something." Briana saw that Lily's lip was bleeding also. "Two of them held me and one of them punched me – a lot of times," she sobbed. "Then they did what they wanted to do to me anyway."

Briana held her while she cried, consoling her, offering her words of false encouragement. As Lily cried herself to sleep, her head in Briana's lap, Briana thought how horrible their situation was with seemingly no way out. This was their new normal.

During their prolonged stretch of daily 'free time' the pair either slept or spoke about their home life and what measures they believed they would take to get back to it. In these conversations, Briana broke down more than once discussing her mother and father and what they must be going through. Lily told her, it was more than likely that her own parents had given up on finding her a long time ago – stating that she was never a good kid anyway.

"I was a burden to them," she told Briana. "I'm sure a weight was lifted when I no longer presented a problem to them." She looked up into Briana's face. "It was so long ago. One day, I would like to surprise them. Show up at their front door, let them know I was strong enough to come back from all of this. Let them know that they didn't raise a loser."

"You're not a loser, Lily," Briana said. "You're very strong."

That was when Lily held her arm out to Briana, showing fresh needle marks. She started crying. "I can't take it anymore. I tried. I swear I tried."

Briana pulled Lily into her arms and held her tight,

rocking her on the cot. The poor girl, Briana thought; she wasn't strong enough to survive this. They needed to find a way out before it killed her. They needed to escape. They needed to be avenged.

****

The days began to blend into one another. Briana lost all sense of how long they had been held. Her daily routine saw her seeing the fat man who had his way with her in some fashion and then her being delivered back to the room. She no longer expected to be brought to Rey or anyone else. Lily, she had learned, was handed between many people, used for their own sport, especially in her pliant drug state. Briana felt for her and did her best to try and bring her back into line, but the drugs took a deeper hold on Lily. There were times when Lily was not brought back to the tent for more than 12 hours, and when she was, she had a drugged-smile on her face. She was exhausted and often passed out for several hours.

More than a month later, perhaps even longer, Briana was being led to the white building by her guard. He walked her up the steps and brought her to the fat man's quarters as usual. When Briana stepped into the room, she was met by a total of three men, including her fat torturer. One of the men was blond, the other dark-haired; they were tall and light-skinned, perhaps European. They all wore robes, which briefly reminded her of her first visit with Rey. She stepped into the center of the room as she always did, waiting for instructions. She looked at the other two men, then at the fat man, then looked down to the ground as she had been taught.

"This is Phoenix. She is beautiful, no?" Oalo said. "I have

been personally training her. To please people; to be a good lover; a good fuck. That is what men want, no?" There was some murmuring from the other two. "Take off your clothes." Briana slowly removed her clothes, trying to keep from looking at the men. When she was naked, they told her to look up from the ground. She did. "Yes, beautiful. And, she has been all mine to train and to use. I want to share my prize with you. Today will be her first test. Tie her hands behind her back," he said.

Briana looked into the fat man's eyes. Her body started to shake with both contempt and fear. Her mind suddenly concerned that she would be physically helpless with these three men in the room. Her wrists were pulled back behind her by one of the men who started to bind them. Oalo stared back at her and he stepped forward. She knew the slap was coming and she prepared herself. When he hit her, he smiled.

"She is feisty at times, but she can be controlled." Briana recovered from the slap and looked back into the fat man's face. "Follow me," he said. Oalo led them across the room to the large bed. "Up," he said to Briana. She worked her way up onto the bed as best she could with her bound hands. "Very good." The fat man stepped back from the bed and looked at the other two men. "My gift to you both. I will join you after I have my tea." He smiled. "Enjoy... do not leave any permanent marks."

The two men disrobed as the fat man slowly walked away. As they climbed up onto the bed, Briana moved away from them as best she could. She could see that they were both hard and large, not like the fat man. One of them grabbed her ankle and pulled her forward, forcing her to slide down on her back. The other reached for her breast, tugging on it as he bent his head down to her. Within minutes, they had descended on her completely and as she fought them off as best she could, she realized that her attempts were futile. This was what she was being trained for. She closed off the part of her mind that would remember and for the sake of survival, she let herself submit to their needs.

"Okay, okay," she heard herself saying.

Then one of them was inside her. Slowly pushing himself deeper as he spread her legs wide in front of her. The other man's head was on her chest, as he licked and sucked on her. Briana moaned quietly, knowing that was what they needed to hear; knowing that it would keep her from getting beaten. She opened herself up to them physically as she shielded herself mentally. She started to compartmentalize their faces, their weight, their cocks as they pressed them into her and twisted and contorted her body.

She was rolled from her back to her stomach, pulled up onto her knees as one entered her from behind. At the same time, another pressed into her mouth, sliding himself in and out of her as the man behind her grunted. She didn't see their faces anymore; their eyes were blank so she couldn't remember them. When the one in her mouth began grunting, she did her best to encourage him to finish off inside of her so that he would be done. She swallowed what she could and then was pushed down onto the bed while the other finished off deep inside of her.

After a short rest, they were at it again, perhaps trading positions; she couldn't be sure. They pushed into every hole pleasuring themselves, not caring about her needs. She was valueless, a series of orifices for them to fill. They kept at it for a long time before finally rolling on their backs alongside of her and resting.

"Very good, Phoenix. You have learned well," the fat man

said.

Had he been there the whole time watching, she thought? That miserable fuck just stood by witnessing the abuses these men perpetrated on her, over and over again. She could not hate him anymore than she did at that moment.

"Now, untie her," he added. One of the men reached for her wrists, untying them. Briana pulled her hands to her sides, feeling the pain in her arms and shoulders. Her body ached elsewhere, but those pains were almost commonplace for her. "Very good. You are a good student, Phoenix. I think you are ready to move on soon. I will miss you when you do." He smiled at her. "For today, though, we will continue, yes?"

He dropped his robe and crawled onto the bed. His cock was harder than it had ever been during all of the times that she had been with her. It must have been watching that got him so excited.

"Get on your hands and knees," Oalo said. "I want you to feel this in your ass, where my friends have been today." Briana turned slowly onto her stomach and lifted herself up onto her knees. "Excellent," he said. "My friends will rest now and join us later, as soon as they are rested. We have the whole night together."

For the rest of the day, they took turns with Briana, all three of them using and abusing her. She was willful in her submission. They could break her physically, but she would not let them break her spirit. When they broke for food, they brought some over to the bed, where they had bound her by her wrists and ankles. She ate what they offered her and drank down some water. When they were done with dinner, they had their way with her once more, this time taking turns as the others cheered them on. When the men had

had their fill of sex they turned up the physical abuse. She was slapped around and the odd punch was thrown in while they laughed at her head snapping back and forward.

It was dark when the guard led her away from the fat man's apartment. She was physically exhausted; had trouble staying on her feet. The guard helped her along, knowing what they must have put her through. Outside the tent, he held her up with one arm as he unzipped the entrance. Then he walked her inside and placed her on the cot, covering her body with a sheet. Lily was there, out cold on her own mattress. Briana fell into a deep sleep, her mind slowly opening up to let reality in as her body involuntarily shook and shuddered on the mattress.

Chapter 26

Captain Beritz answered his personal phone and a familiar voice spoke to him. He nodded his head as he listened, and he waited until the voice stopped speaking before he acknowledged it.

"Very well," the captain said. "All will be done as you say."

"And you will be paid properly for your efforts, captain," the voice concluded before hanging up.

Beritz sat back in his chair. It had been more than a week since his first call with the cartel telling them that Briana Campbell's disappearance would not easily go away. They had promised they would take the necessary steps to put the issue to rest. During that time, the captain had entertained several meetings with the embassy agent and numerous overseas calls from Briana's parents and their representative. He assured each of them that everything in his power was being done to find the girl.

Now, after the call, he was sure he would be able to give them a more definitive answer and this problem, like many others, could be put far behind him. He reached for the office phone and buzzed Inspector Perez.

"Gabe," he said when the phone was answered, "just got a call about about a burned-out vehicle. Two bodies inside, burned horribly. Body size and age similar to the missing Campbell girl. Don't have any information about the other body."

"I'm on it, captain. Whereabouts?"

The captain provided the location and hung up the phone. If he was right, the cartel would have taken care to ensure that the coroner was properly compensated to make a positive ID through the dental records that were provided. If they did their job well, which they always did, the coroner's records would indicate that there was no doubt that the body in the car was Briana. The other body in the car would be identified as her taxi driver friend; the one who had come to the police station to ask about her whereabouts.

The official story would be that the cab driver had actually kidnapped Briana and reported her disappearance to throw the police off his trail. An inspection of the cab driver's apartment would find articles of Briana's clothes taken from her apartment and a notebook that described his love for her.

Beritz sat back in his chair. Their cover story was good. It always was. He would wait for the inspector to return and they would both reach out the Embassy agent to tell him the sad news.

****

Briana's eyes fluttered; the room slowly came into view. She was being prodded by her arm; her mind telling her to pull away. Her eyes closed.

"Fuck you!" she said. "No more!"

"Briana, Briana," the voice floated through the fog.

Briana blinked once more, curled into a protective coil,

a fetal position.

"Wake up, Briana. Wake the fuck up!"

Briana felt herself lifted up by the shoulders, her head falling forward. Get a grip, Briana, she thought. She remembered the voice telling her to wake up. She opened her eyes once more, her mind gaining purchase on the voice, her surroundings. Flashes of being thrown to the ground. The memories of being slapped and punched hurt her physically. She recoiled from them, from her own memories.

"It's Lily – look at me." Briana faced Lily, one of her eyes partially closed, the other opened a small slit.

"Lily," she mumbled through her bruised, split lips.

"Earth to Briana. Come in," Lily tried to joke.

She had never seen her friend in this condition before. Maybe she had never seen anyone in such a bad condition, she thought. She lifted Briana's head and slipped her arm around her. Briana dropped her head onto Lily's shoulder and Lily pulled her tight against her.

"That's a girl, Briana," she said. "That's a good girl."

It was daylight now. Lily rocked Briana for the better part of a half-hour until Briana fell asleep. Lily held her as she stared out across the tent. What had they done to her? Stupid girl. Why didn't she just give them what they wanted. What would she do, Lily thought if Briana was taken away from her?

It was hours later when Briana finally lifted her head off Lily's stiff shoulder. Lily looked into her eyes and smiled.

Briana nodded her thanks, as best she could.

Lily twisted her so she could lay down on the cot. Then she retrieved some water and slowly fed it to Briana watching her choke it down as she tried to swallow.

Over the next few hours, Briana faded and out of sleep. When she was awake, she tried to tell Lily what happened.

She described the three men and how they treated her. How the fat man got off on beating her and watching her being beat.

Lily listened intently, understanding some of what she mumbled, knowing that it was important to let Briana speak. It was obvious what had happened to her.

Lily brought back some small amounts of food for her and fed it to her later in the day. Briana ate what she could and then threw it all up. Lily consoled her as best she could, holding her hair back off her bruised face as she vomited, giving her small amounts of water when she was awake, and humming soothing songs to her as she rocked Briana in her arms. She knew Briana would do the same for her; probably had done the same for her already.

A little later in the day, the zipper to the tent opened and Briana involuntarily pulled herself into a tight ball. Lily stared at the guard, ready to leap on him if he had come for Briana; she didn't care what happened to her after what they had done to her friend. The guard stepped into the tent, lifted a hand and curled his fingers indicating to Lily to come toward him.

Lily released Briana, watching her limp body slide back down the mattress, her eyes fighting to stay awake as she stared at the guard. She walked to the door of the tent ready to object, to protect her friend.

"We will not take her today," he nodded.

The guards understood the women in the compound better than anyone else. They did their best to protect them while at the same time walking them to their daily sacrifices. Lily nodded back. She stepped back by Briana and told her that she would be back soon. Then, she walked out the zippered door with the guard to do whatever it was they needed her to do, so she could survive.

It was days later before Briana finally began to recover physically. She was able to sit up and hold down food. Lily walked her out to the courtyard one afternoon for lunch and the other women stared at her battered face. The bruises she wore under her eyes were yellow and purple. It was difficult for her to open her right eye all of the way without wincing. She favored her right leg when she walked, the bruises on her thigh to ugly to look at.

Mentally, Briana was not sure she would ever recover. When she heard a loud noise, she jumped and wanted to curl into a ball. She found herself sobbing in the middle of the night, her mind trying to recall and push away memories at the same time. She wanted to forget, but she knew she needed to remember first so she could put it all out of her mind. Briana hid her late-night crying from Lily; the girl had done so much for her nursing her back from health. She didn't want to be a burden.

Lily had stopped asking Briana what'd happened and focused on the healing process. She fed Briana and comforted her as best she could when she was in the tent. When she was away, she thought only of her friend, helping to put the horrors of her physical actions out of her mind. She rushed back to the tent to be at Briana's side.

It was more than a week later, when the guard unzipped the tent and motioned to Briana. She recoiled against the side of the tent and Lily moved to stand in front of her.

"You can't take her. She is still healing from that last time that fuck almost killed her," Lily said. Her arms were crossed as she stared at the guard. He remained silent. Lily continued. "Take me instead. I'll tell that fat fuck what I think of him and maybe give him a taste of his own medicine."

The guard stepped forward, looking down at Briana, his

hand extended. "Please," he said.

"I said she's not going," Lily said. "Take me instead."

"It doesn't work that way," he responded. Looking at Briana, he said, "Please Phoenix. Don't make me hurt you." Briana looked up at the man. Slowly, she started to move. "That's a good girl," he said.

"She's not going with you!" Lily said.

The guard stepped forward toward Lily. He had heard enough from the woman. If she said something else, he would slap her to the ground. She should know better than to stand up or talk back to him.

"I won't let you take her!"

The guard's hand tensed as he was about to strike her.

"Stop! I'll go," Briana said, standing up from her cot.

Lily looked at her, her hand out, as if she was going to stop her.

"You've done enough for me," Briana said. "I can fight my own battles now."

She smiled at Lily, her bruised face contorting. Lily stared back at Briana – she knew her pleas were hopeless. Briana walked toward the guard, her limp almost gone. She followed him out of the tent and took a deep breath as he led her across the grounds. She did her best to stay in control, to erase the past. She had been here many times before she thought. At no time had she returned in the condition she had last time. It was a mistake; it would not happen again. She would do what she had to do and then return back to her tent like she had done so many times before.

Inside the house, at the top of the stairs, she looked to her right as the guard led her to the left. How long ago was it that she had been with Rey, the man down the hall in the big room who, even though he abused her sexually, had also been kind to her. She continued down the hall in the other direction until they came to the fat man's door. Briana did not know how she would react when she saw him, but she hoped her need for self-preservation kicked in.

The guard knocked on the door and it was opened from the inside. Briana kept her head down as she stepped through the threshold. Once inside, the guard left her side and she looked up. Oalo stood in front of her. He smiled at her, his eyes walking over the healing bruises on her face. Then his eyes glanced down the front of her shirt all of the way down her legs and then back up again.

"You have returned to me, Phoenix," he said. "Rising from the ashes, no?" Briana nodded and looked down once more. "They say when the Phoenix rises, she comes back stronger, more energetic. Is that true?" Briana stood motionless not knowing how to answer. "Take off your clothes. Let me be the judge."

Slowly, methodically, Briana removed first her shirt and then her pants. The fat man walked around her slowly, his eyes walking up and down her body. He mumbled something under his breath and nodded his head as he came back to stand in front of her.

"You healed well. Good," he said. "Let's see if your mouth healed as well. Down on your knees."

Briana slowly slid down to her knees on the carpet and the fat man stepped forward as he unbelted his robe. Underneath, his small penis stared up at Briana and she slowly pulled its flaccid flesh into her mouth. She could bite down, she knew. It would be worth it to take his manhood – give her life for his manhood – no, she knew, it was not worth it. She pulled him deeper into her mouth as he slowly hardened.

His hands fell onto the back of her head, pulling her

toward him as he thrust into her. Briana wasn't concerned about choking on him; he was not big enough to cause that problem. As he thrust in and out of her mouth, she closed her eyes, licking and sucking on him. The faster he got off, she knew, the better. She already could hear his breathing changing.

"Look at me," the fat man said, his stomach covering his own view of his cock as it slipped in and out of her mouth. He pulled back hard on the back of her hair, making Briana cry out as she lifted her eyes to look at him. Instantly, when he heard her cry, his cock grew harder. "That's it."

He yanked on her hair once more. Tears slid down her face. He smiled down at her as he pressed himself deep into her mouth. Briana moaned as he fucked her face; she knew he liked to hear her make noise. She picked up her pace, sucking harder, licking faster. She wanted to be through with him as soon as she could. She heard his breath coming in short bursts. She knew his orgasm was not far behind. She doubled her efforts, swallowing all of him, her hand cupping his balls, tugging on them. Just as she thought he was ready to burst, he pulled harder on her hair and stepped back.

"You do not control me," he said, staring down at her. Briana inhaled, capturing air into her lungs now that her mouth was free. Saliva spilled down her chin. The fat man stared into her eyes. Briana looked away a little too late, the last thing she saw was the anger gathered behind his eyes.

When he slapped her, he knocked her off her knees to the ground. Briana lay there for a moment, gathering herself. Flashbacks of the last time she was in the room with him – with him and two other men filled her mind. She thought if she remained where she was, he would spare her any more pain.

"Get up! Get back up to your knees."

Briana used her hands to push herself back up to her knees, looking down at the ground as she knelt in front of him. The pain in her face was tremendous, but she held back her sobs.

"Look at me!" the fat man said.

Briana slowly turned her face up toward the man. He stared at her left cheek, red with his finger marks from where he had slapped her. She watched as he smiled and then his left hand shot out, smacking her on the other side of the face, driving her once more to the ground. Again, Briana lay on the carpet, whimpering as the pain settled into her. What did she need to do to stop him from hurting her?

"Get up, bitch!"

She turned her head to look at him, her hands reflexively pushing her back up onto her knees. There was no use ignoring him; he would have his way. She could only look to minimize the pain.

When she was on her knees, he grabbed the back of her hair and began to drag her across the room.

She cried out and scrambled to get to her feet so she could follow him.

He pulled her close to the bed, throwing her head into the side of the mattress as he let go of her hair.

Briana could feel the pain at the roots of her hair, her scalp burning. Sobbing now, she sat at the side of the bed, waiting for his next direction.

"Stand up!"

Briana stood up, her head down once more as she faced him. She knew better than to look into his face unless he told her, and she also didn't trust herself not to spit at him. She was breathing hard, sobbing in pain as she stood in front of the fat man.

"I see you still have some fight in you, Phoenix. We'll see

about that." As she listened to him speak, Briana saw how hard his cock was. He got off on administering pain to her and others.

"Look at me."

Briana lifted her head. They stood about two foot apart and she did her best to hide her contempt for him. Briana knew it would do no good to fuel his temper.

He extended his arm between them, holding her chin with the fingers of his left hand. "You have so much more to learn, Phoenix," he said. "But I don't have time to teach you anymore. I have better things to do." He stared into her eyes and smiled. "Still... you will serve your purpose."

His right hand, curled into a fist, flashed out and punched her directly in the face. Briana felt the pain as she was driven down to the bed. She could taste the blood as it filled her mouth; she must have bitten her tongue, she thought. For a moment, she thought of raising her head, lifting it to determine what had happened, but as the thought formed in her mind, his fist slammed into her face once more. Her eyes caught a glimpse of his smile before a third blow connected with the side of her face and her eye. The last shot brought on the darkness and all went black around her.

Oalo worked hard to hold off on punching her a fourth time. He stared down at her bloody face. His right hand was in pain from striking her, but his cock was swollen to its limits. Briana was out cold on the bed before him and he lifted her legs and rolled her onto her stomach. He climbed onto the bed behind her, spreading her legs and then he pressed his hard, red cock inside of her, driving deep into her as he grunted. Briana's lifeless body shifted as he drove into her and he grabbed her hips to hold her steady.

Oalo pumped into her repeatedly, feeling first the dry

sides of her pussy dragging against the skin of his cock and then her wetness as he worked himself in and out. He was breathing hard, grunting as he fucked her, watching her ass bounce before him. After a short while, he pulled out, not ready to cum yet. He turned her over onto her back. Unconscious, her head lolled to the side. He turned her bloody face toward him, smiled as he admired his handiwork. He stared at her split lip and swollen eye as he slid himself back into her. His free hand held her hip, pulling her toward him as he thrust into her.

When he was finally ready to let go, he pulled himself out from inside of her and knelt over her, jerking his hard cock as he stared down at her swollen face. The blood that spilled from her mouth was enough to put him over the top. He shot his load over her chest and face, dragging the head of his cock through the silky milk as he let go, prolonging his orgasm. When he was finally finished, he reached down to her mouth and ran his finger through her blood, sliding it through the cum that had pooled between her tits. He slid the finger into his mouth and sucked on it as he bent his head down and licked her tits clean. When he next picked up his head, his mouth covered in blood and cum, he was hard again already.

The fat man turned Briana over and proceeded to fuck her lifeless body until he was completely satisfied. He came two more times over the next couple of hours. When he was done, he left her on the bed while he went to shower. He returned, in a clean robe, poured himself a glass of wine, and sat watching her chest rise as she breathed shallowly, her tits rising only slightly each time she inhaled. She was beautiful. He hoped that she would recover from her wounds quickly, he thought, so he didn't have to wait too long to be with her again.

Chapter 27

Phil Campbell picked up the phone is his home office on Monday morning. The voice on the other end was accented but spoke perfect English. It was the Embassy agent. Phil braced himself for the worst.

"There's been a break in the case," Agent Adams said. "It's not good, Phil." Phil listened, waiting for the agent to go on. "They found her body in a burnt-out car. Badly burned. They identified her with dental records, Phil. There's no mistake." He paused. "I'm so sorry for your loss."

They were both quiet for a moment and then Phil spoke for the first time. "Do they know what happened?"

"The theory is that a cab driver, who she be-friended, kidnapped her. He held her in his apartment – the police found traces of this as well as some of her clothes and notes he wrote about her."

Tears had filled Phil's eyes and he fought to keep it together. "But I still don't understand..."

"The car? The accident? We have no way of knowing what happened. There were no witnesses and no other cars involved. They hit a bridge support at a high rate of speed and the car set on fire. I'm sure she passed quickly from the impact, if that is of any help." There was more silence. "I'm so sorry, Phil."

"I don't know how I will tell Claire," he said, openly crying into the phone now.

"Just tell her it was an accident. She doesn't need to know the rest."

"She needs to know the truth. She needs to know that her little girl didn't just stop calling her. She was incapable of calling her because some madman in that country decided to kidnap her and... who knows what." His voice raised in anger.

"Phil," the agent said. "I'm so sorry."

The door opened to the office and Claire stepped inside. She had heard Phil's mumbled voice from outside the closed door. When she saw his face, she fell to her knees in front of him, sobbing instantly.

"Thank you, Agent Adams," Phil said into the phone, hanging it up.

He opened his arms and Claire fell into them. They hugged each other tight as they cried, consoling one another, neither saying a word. After a long time, Claire pushed away from Phil and looked into his eyes. He nodded his head as if to confirm what they already knew.

"They're sure?" she said, holding out the last thread of hope.

"Positive, Claire. I'm so sorry," he said, pulling her back into his arms as the both wept loudly.

"I want to see her," Claire said, "for myself. I don't believe them." She stood up, pacing the room, her mind wondering whether to fly out there or have her flown home.

"Claire," Phil said, standing, approached her. She walked away, her mind churning. He followed her and took her by the arms. "Claire. There was a horrible fire." He stared into her eyes imploring her to face reason. "There's nothing to see. It will only add to our pain. We can have a memorial here for her – with her spirit present. But what's left of her body is not our daughter." He tapped his heart. "She's in here now. She's always been here."

Claire stared back at him for a long time, her tears rolling down her face. Finally, she nodded back at him, as if she understood. He knew there would be more to this, but he was confident that he could prevent her from trying to go see the body or having it sent back home. It would serve no purpose; no purpose at all.

"I'm going to make us some tea and then I think we should maybe tell the rest of the family. They have all been waiting for news about Briana."

Claire nodded and slowly followed him into the kitchen. Phil knew that he would have to take the next few days moment by moment and stay at his wife's side. She was china-fragile, ready to crack at the tiniest bump and there were going to be many bumps in the road going forward.

****

Lily splashed Briana with water to try and wake her and shook her repeatedly. There was no movement from her roommate, but there was a pulse. Her face was a bloody mess. Whoever did this to her meant to inflict as much pain as possible. She had been returned to the tent to die. Briana would not be the first. Their captors did not hide their ruthlessness from the women in the camp. If someone died in their tents, then others would learn from their mistakes, perhaps not put up a fight and be more compliant. Lily knew how to play the game.

She punched the mattress next to Briana. Why couldn't Briana play by the rules? This would have never happened to her. Take the drugs if necessary. Forget it all. But, as she looked down at Briana's face, this was too much. She didn't even recognize her friend.

It took three weeks this time for Briana to recover. Her face at the end of those two weeks still bore the signs of the beating she had taken. The right side of her mouth hung down slightly, just above her lip. Smiling hurt Briana, but there was nothing to smile about. She knew once she regained her strength, she would only be beaten once more by the fat fuck who got off on beating women until they were unrecognizable.

During her recovery, the guards were hands off to her, waiting for her to regain her strength. They had come in several times to make sure that she was not dragging out her wounds, but one look at her face told them that she was in no position to please a client, much less the fat man who they all knew would only beat her on top of her welts.

As she recovered, Briana bonded more with Lily. She had also made up her mind about how she would be able to handle the routine in the compound.

"I'm going to ask for the drugs now," Briana said, her voice soft and hoarse.

"No, Briana – there's no turning back from them. Look at me!" Lily held her arms out.

Briana smiled at her. "I know, Lily. But, I can't survive this again. Maybe with the drugs I will be better, or easier to deal with. Maybe with the drugs, I won't feel the pain."

"Do you think that will help with that monster?"

Briana shook her head. "I don't know. But, I see no other way around it. You can erase it all, right? I cannot. I remember each time his fist smashed into my face. Each time those men did what they did to me, over and over again. I can't live with that, Lily. No one can. It all makes sense to me now why you take them, who you need to become to survive all of this."

"It's not you, Briana – you are stronger, better than me. You are confident, able to think through this all of this." Lily was crying now. "If you turn to the drugs, then... then," Lily knew what she was going to say, and still let herself say it, "who will take care of us?"

Briana put her arm around the sobbing Lily. She patted her back. "We'll take care of each other. Just like you took care of me these past weeks. And, more than once. Not once in the last month or more have I done anything for you, Lily. And, you have done everything for me." Lily nodded, still sobbing. "We take care of each other, always, forever. Right?" Lily didn't answer. Briana lifted her chin and stared at her. "Right?"

"Right," Lily said.

The two girls hugged, choosing to share the small cot that night as they held each other in their arms. It was a small turning point for the two women under impossible circumstances. They had sworn their allegiance to each other, even while determining the best way to deal with their captors was to hide behind the drugs that would dull their senses to the point where they would no longer feel anything.

A few days later, when the guard came into the tent to retrieve Briana, Lily whispered in the guard's ear. He nodded and took the shaking Briana out of the tent, leading her to the big white house. Briana has almost healed physically, but she was struggling mentally. She pushed away all memories as she walked toward the house. Instead of proceeding directly up the steps, the guard took a small detour to a red house that was adjacent to the larger building.

"Sit," he said. Briana sat. He held a needle up in front of him. "This will take affect almost immediately. It will dull your mind a little and, it is will make you less inhibited."

He reached for Briana's arm and pulled it toward him. In one step, he pulled a rubber strap around her arm, tightening it. He didn't wait for her to respond before he tapped just below her elbow and pushed the needle into the first vein that popped up. Briana started to pull away, but he held her arm firm as he pressed the liquid into her vein. She watched as the drug slid into her body and then as the man pulled the needle from her. Briefly, she wondered if it was a clean needle.

The man stood up, released the rubber strap and placed the needle on the small table. "Come," he said.

Briana stood up and felt her head cloud. She stared back at the guard and he smiled at her. She felt a smile come to her face involuntarily as the drug began to take effect. The guard took her arm and led her into the white house.

When she entered the fat man's room, she removed her clothes as soon as she heard the door close behind her. She watched as his right eyebrow rose and he nodded his head. Her own hands reached up and slowly massaged her breasts, her fingers circling her nipple. She knew not to go too far, or he would take it as an affront and that too could result in a beating. She watched as he slowly opened his robe, his penis growing as he stared at her hands. Briana felt the drug coursing through her, flushing her face as she began to relax.

"You have learned in your absence," Oalo said. "Come," he waved to her, inviting her deeper into the room.

Briana stepped forward, slipping down to her knees in front of him, taking him into her mouth as her hands wrapped around his ass pulling him close. The drugs definitely took the edge off her, she realized. She was not fighting the fat man, in fact, her body was reacting positively to his touch as his hands fell across her shoulders. She heard herself moan as she sucked him deep into her mouth, and she felt his thumbs press into her shoulders, kneading her skin as he rocked slowly in and out of her mouth.

When he pulled on her hair, forcing her to look up at him, she felt herself getting wet, her nipples hardening. She moaned as he pulled himself out of her mouth, smacking her in the face with his dick, smiling down at her. She was his submissive now, she thought. She would do whatever he wanted, willingly; the drug allowed her that freedom.

She slid her tongue down over his balls as she jerked him, her hand running over his wet ball sack, sliding between his legs, her fingers circling his hole. She heard the fat man moan and she pushed her finger deep into his ass as she swallowed him deep into her mouth. His hands moved to the side of her head, sliding her back and forth as he fucked her mouth and she finger fucked his ass.

When the fat man came the first time that day, grunting loudly, he held her mouth on him until he finished unloading into her as she swallowed his cum down. When he pulled out, she slipped her finger out of his ass and he lifted her up from her feet. He kissed her deeply, his tongue swirling in his own cum in her mouth, his hands pulling her tight against him.

Briana fucked Oalo several times that day willingly and whole-heartedly. She came loudly when her orgasms took her, not holding back, reveling in how his small, hard dick tickled her in just the right places. When he took her in the ass, she rocked back against him, holding his hand on her clit as he rubbed her until she screamed.

Hours later, after the two shared a lunch, he offered her

some white wine which she gratefully accepted. The fat man held her hand as they ate lunch, feeding her grapes and other foods.

When they were done with lunch, he had her kneel on the bed facing the wall. He tied her wrists to the bed in front of her. He told her not to look at him as he knelt behind her on the mattress and proceeded to whip her gently with leather flogger while he jerked off onto her hair and neck. When he was finished, he untied her hands and gave her the flogger, asking her to beat him about the chest as she sat on him and rode up and down on his cock.

The day ended with Briana walking out of the room next to the guard. Oalo had only hit her three or four times, and each time, he had held back, almost trying not to hurt her. Her body was still on fire when she was returned to the tent. The guard unzipped the door and pushed her gently inside.

Briana hoped that Lily was there, but she was not. She wanted to tell her about the progress she thought she had made and that maybe, just maybe, they would both be able to get through the horrors of the camp. She climbed up on the mattress, thinking about her time with the fat man, reliving her loud orgasms and how she had let herself go. She slipped her fingers inside of her pussy as she waited for her roommate to return. She was exhausted, but her body was still on fire. When Briana came, she was laying down on her mattress. She closed her eyes as her fingers slipped out from inside of her and drifted off to sleep.

It was hours later when Lily was returned to the tent. She found Briana, naked from the waist down, her hand resting between her legs. She tried to wake her, but Briana wouldn't budge. Lily had been where Briana was many times before. She lifted her arm to see the small pin prick, a tear rolling down her cheek.

Chapter 28

The next several weeks brought much of the same. Almost daily, Briana was walked over to the white house, stopped at the red cabin, drugged and then taken to the fat man. She would perform whatever services he needed, sometimes initiating them and the two of them would fuck for hours. With the help of the drug, Briana was able to 'erase' much of what happened during these trips even to the point where she had trouble describing some of the acts to Lily.

Her sex with Oalo was never the same. Sometimes he would tie her up, other times he would hold her against the wall and pound her from behind while he made her hold a teacup, telling her he would slap her if she spilled a drop. Briana rarely spilled a drop, but she knew that if he didn't get to slap her occasionally, it could get much worse. Sometimes, before he came, she would spill a little on the floor and apologize. He would then slap her ass hard as he finished off inside of her, turning her ass pink.

Other times, he would have her drink large amounts of water during the first couple of hours that they were together when she wasn't sucking on him or being fucked by him. He would tell her that he would hit her if she needed to go to the bathroom. She would have to hold it until he allowed her to go. Later in their day, he would let her straddle him and demand that she pee on him until she was empty. When she was done, he would make her lick him clean as he jerked himself off.

Lily was also being drugged as she was passed from man to man that was brought into the compound. Unlike Briana, she wasn't favored and didn't have a dedicated trainer, so she would have to take on the men that were brought to the camp as her captors saw fit. She often was returned to the tent exhausted from having sex with multiple partners.

When Briana and Lily found themselves in their tent together, their conversations were not about anything of substance. Either one of them was high or both of them were. The drugs were working effective, reducing the two of them to nothing more than sex slaves when they were needed and mindless drones when they were alone.

Lily was returned to the tent one night earlier than usual. When Lily stepped through the unzipped tent door, she found Briana lying naked on the floor in the middle of the tent on her back. Two of her fingers were jammed deep inside of her as she moaned loudly. She looked up at Lily as she continued to masturbate.

"Don't just stand there, Lily, help me."

Lily didn't miss a beat, falling to the floor beside her roommate, covering her mouth with her own as she reached down between Briana's legs. The drugs swirled within the two of them, releasing all inhabitations, and fueling their libidos. When Lily's tongue touched Briana's, Briana pushed Lily's fingers deep inside of her, thrusting against them until she screamed loudly into Lily's mouth. Briana repaid the favor by burying her head between Lily's legs and licking her until Lily came all over her face.

It was the first of many trysts the two shared when they had enough strength. Briana reasoned that her lovemaking with Lily was essential to their surviving in the world of hatred that surrounded them. A few times, Lily and Briana made love without the influence of the drugs and they both agreed it was just as satisfying. They took their time learning the curves and edges of each other's body. If Lily or Briana had returned to the tent with any injuries, they would begin by consoling one another, licking each other's wounds and then making love until they gave into their exhaustion.

It was after one of their exhaustive lovemaking sessions, that Briana was summoned earlier than usual to the fat man's room. A guard came to collect her and as Briana went to stop at the red cabin for her fix, the guard prodded her on to move on into the white house. She turned to him.

"I need to stop here," she said.

"Not today, Phoenix," he said.

She didn't like that he called her by name. She didn't know him, and he was denying her what she needed to get through the next couple of hours with the fat maniac.

"Please," she said.

"Inside," the guard said.

Her body was shaking now. Not only did she believe she needed the drug to handle the next several hours, but her body required the drug as it had every morning for the past several weeks. It wasn't a choice.

She stared into the guard's face, her eyes meeting his. "I beg you. I need this."

The man grabbed her bicep and pushed her forward. Briana looked back at the red building as he guided her up the steps. No! She needed her drugs. She felt her body shaking just thinking about them. She dragged her feet when they reached the top of the steps. She would not go.

She could not face the fat man without the drugs. The guard pushed her from behind. She turned and looked at him. He slapped her in the face. She should have known better. He prodded her along once more and this time she moved her legs so he wasn't dragging her; something she was sure he was capable of doing.

Briana stood outside the fat man's door. She was shaking as the guard opened it. When he did, she stepped inside, and the guard followed her in. She heard the door close and the guard stepped around her. The fat man was nowhere to be found. The guard turned to her.

"Undress, please."

Briana slowly undressed; her shirt first, her pants last.

"Very good, very nice," he said as his eyes slid up and down her shaking body.

"Wait here." The guard walked toward the back of the room, toward the large bed. He positioned himself against the wall and he called over to Briana. "Come."

Briana walked across the room the large bed. She had been in this room so many times; she knew every nook and cranny. If the fat man was in the room, he could only be in the bathroom. She looked at the bathroom door expecting it to open. It did not.

"Up on the bed." Briana climbed up on the bed and pulled herself up to the headboard.

The man held a small black band in one hand and Briana slipped her hand through it. He tightened it, pulling her wrist and arm back against the headboard. He moved to the other side of the bed and did the same with her right wrist. Briana sat on the bed, bound by her wrists, spread wide behind her. She heard the door click in front of her and watched as the bathroom door opened. Oalo stepped out of the room and smiled at the guard. He was naked, his cock

274

was semi-hard.

"Is she ready?"

"Yes," the guard said.

"And, you didn't stop at the cabin?"

"No sir."

"Good, get undressed. You may watch and then you can have her when I am finished."

Briana stared up at the fat man, suddenly scared. He was not acting at all as he had over the last couple of weeks and she didn't have the drugs in her to dull her senses, to prevent her from thinking too deep, too hard about what was about to happen.

"Now," he said, climbing up onto the bed on his knees, kneeling in front of her. "I understand that you have been medicating yourself so that you can be with me."

Briana shook her head. That was not it at all. She had been medicating herself so that she could handle all of this. Did he not understand what they had put her and all of the women in this camp through?

"There is no need to lie to me, Phoenix. I have been told everything. You think it better to be drugged, lost in your head than to face the cold, hard reality of what is happening. That's it, right?"

"No," she said. "That's not it. I'm..."

He slapped her hard across the face. Her head spun to the side, spit flying from her mouth. His finger marks were immediately apparent. "So, it's me then. You need the drugs to be with me?"

She shook her head. No! He had it wrong, she thought. She and Lily had found a way to make it work. Only the drugs had helped.

"Come," he said to the guard. "Look at this beautiful face." The guard stepped around the side of the bed. He stared into Briana's face. "She is one of the prettiest we have ever had. That is why I have her sent to me each morning." His hand traced the side of her shaking face, where he had slapped her. "Maybe she is too pretty, eh?" The guard just nodded. Oalo's hand shot out and slapped her in the face once more. Briana grunted as her face spun to the right.

Briana felt blood pool in her mouth, and she spat it on the sheets. She slowly turned her head back toward him, hoping that the slap was the last of it.

"Would you like to a try?"

"Yes, sir," the guard said.

"Good, come, come..."

The naked guard climbed onto the bed and sat on the opposite side of Briana. He was very aroused. Briana was breathing hard between them as she looked from one to the other. She flashed back to the several times the fat man had beat her. Tears rolled down her eyes. She didn't have to look down at his cock – she knew it was already rock hard. He reached up to her face and ran his fingers down it once more.

"Such a shame, Phoenix," he said as he climbed down off the bed.

Briana stared at the fat man, looking down as his hand reached down in front of him to wrap around his cock. He jerked it slowly as he stared back at her.

"Go on," he said to the guard.

Briana turned to face the guard, her body shaking, not knowing what to expect. His hand shot out and slapped her across the right side of her face. Her head turned, her eyes closed. When she opened them, she was staring at the fat man who smiled and masturbated to her pain.

"Again," he said. This time, the guard struck her from the other side. Briana screamed out in pain. "Once more, harder."

The guard struck her harder, in the center of her face. Briana's head jerked back on her neck as she cried out. She bit down hard on her tongue, and blood spilled out of the side of her mouth. She was woozy from the slaps. Or were they punches? She wasn't sure. Her head lolled to the side and she looked over at the fat man.

"Yes! Now fuck her," Oalo said to the guard. "Fuck her anyway you want."

Briana turned to the guard, hoping to appeal to his better side, but when she opened her mouth, she could only mumble.

"Shut her up first. I don't want to hear her mumble."

Briana watched as if in slow motion as his fist crushed into her face. She lost consciousness, succumbing to the blackness as it took over. She remembered slipping in and out, seeing the guard at times on top of her, and then the fat man's face smiling at her as he cheered the guard on.

At one point, she awoke as she was being dragged by her feet across the carpet, on her stomach, her nipples scraping against the rug, her head bouncing on the floor. She tried to reach out to lift herself, but her hands were bound behind her back. When they lifted her off the carpet, they tied her to the wall, her hands bound above her head. Both men took turns with her and then the fat man approached her and untied her from the wall. She could barely stand up on her own, leaning against the wall for support. Oalo punched her in the stomach, forcing her to double over and vomit.

"Still too pretty," he said, punching her in the face as the guard lifted her back up.

Then they were both on her. One in front of her and one in back. They were inside of her, pounding into her, pulling on her hair, slapping and punching at her. Briana willed herself to shut down, to go into hiding. You can erase it all, she remembered Lily saying. That's what she needed to do. Erase it all. There was another blow, this one to the side of her head as one of them forced themselves into her mouth. She wanted to bite down. No, shut down. Just shut down! Survive!

****

The swing set was the best that money could buy, she heard her father say to her mother. Her mother had just finished yelling at him for spending half his weekly paycheck on something so expensive. The two battled it out in the kitchen as Briana watched through the window, her body swinging back and forth as she sat on the green plastic seat. She didn't like when her parents fought; they yelled at one another and she always felt like it was her fault.

She looked away. She was flying on the swing, rising up high, her feet kicking out, pumping herself even higher. The swing would glide her up – until it reached the maximum height it could with her on it, and then it would hang there for just one quick second before gravity took its toll, driving it back toward the ground, before rising up behind the frame as it started its route one more time.

Briana thought about her birthday, only a day before. She turned seven. Her parents had thrown her a small party and she got everything she asked for. The swing set was not on her list, but her dad decided she needed one. He spent the entire day assembling it before her mother called him to the carpet for spending too much money. Briana loved it. It had several swings and a wooden-attached fort with a slide on it. There was some other yellow thing on the side that her father called the 'contraption'. She didn't know how it worked, but it looked like it needed two people. She would have to wait for her friend Alana to come by so they could try it out.

As her parents continued to argue inside, Briana soared on her swing, up into the clouds, pumping her sneaker-clad feet urging the swing to rise higher each time. She remembered looking down as her father came out of the house. He seemed so far away as her body rose above the top of the swing set. He was waving his hands as her back arched, her feet pumping one more time.

"You're too high," she thought she heard him say.

What did he mean? She looked out in front of her. She felt as if she was over the trees, in the clouds; definitely higher than she should be. How had she gotten up so high off the ground? She watched her legs bend once more.

"...too high, Briana...," she heard in the distance.

And then she panicked. Her body stiffened and for some reason, some unknown reason, Briana released her hands from the ropes that held the swing. Her body left the swing at the peak of the arc and she was suddenly flying out over the yard, toward the trees and bushes that led into the neighbor's yard. She screamed out, as their garage came into view, her body slamming into the concrete side before her scream was even finished.

She remembered waking up in the ambulance on the way to the hospital. Her father held her hand and told her she needed to stay awake. If she fell asleep, he told her, she might not wake up. She did her best to keep her eyes open, but the darkness kept sneaking in, turning everything black. He tugged on her hand to wake her and she looked at him through half-open eyes.

There was pain everywhere. In her head, her shoulders, her face. She tried to move, but nothing happened. She heard her name, opened her eyes. It was all foggy. Then she was back on the swing again, flying through the air. It was effortless, that feeling. She had no cares at all. The wind blew at her as she flew through it, alone, free.

"Briana," the voice called her back.

"Leave me be," she wanted to say. "I'm flying all alone. Drifting... leave me be."

She was shaken by her shoulders once more. Her eyes flittered open. When they did, she felt the pain, in her face, her back, her legs, her head. Everything hurt. Close your eyes, Briana; the pain will go away. If she fell asleep, her father told her, she might not wake up. She opened her eyes – the pain came back.

"Briana..."

It was too much. The pain was just too much. She closed her eyes once more.

She was in a big hospital, doctors all around her. Several of them shaking their heads. Her mom was crying not far from her She reached out her hand; her mother didn't come. She was yelling at her father. It wasn't his fault she wanted to say. It wasn't. He told her not to go too high.

Then she was alone with the doctor. He stared at her with a bright light over his head. He held thread in his hand like he was going to sew a shirt or a sock. She watched as he leaned down to her. She felt the prick of the needle and watched him as his hands moved above her face, the thread slipping in and out as he thread it into her, tying it off and snipping it with a scissors. He said something to her.

Briana looked left and right for her parents. They were nowhere to be found. The hospital was different suddenly. She turned back to the doctor and the nurses, but there was only one man. Was it her father; it had to be. He was the one constant in her life besides her mother. Always there; always willing to do whatever she needed.

"I didn't mean to let you down," the figure said to her.

What did he mean? She stared at the figure of the man once more. Slowly, the man turned to her. It was her father, at least for a moment.

"I'm sorry I let you down. I tried everything to get back here."

To get back? She opened her eyes. It wasn't her father anymore. It was the man from the camp. Not the fat man; the other one. Wait, none of that was real. She was only seven. That was in her imagination. The doctor leaned over her from the other side, speaking to the man.

"They almost killed her this time," the doctor said.

"Will she make it?"

"We'll know in the next 48 hours."

The man nodded and the doctor bent over her again with his thread and needle. He worked on her for a long time she thought, but she wasn't focused on him. What did they mean, will she make it? You didn't die from falling off a swing set. She knew she didn't die. She went onto junior high and high school, even made some great friends. Of course, I made it, Briana thought. She was headed to Brazil, after high school ended. A gap year. Well, that's what she told her mother.

"It's so dangerous, honey," her mother had said. "I really don't think you should go."

But she went, didn't she? She went and got a great job. She was going to stay for several months. She would see all of Brazil in her spare time with the money she made from her job.

"It's very dangerous," her mother said.

It all came flooding back to her. The van, Lily. The fat man. She didn't imagine him. The camp. The drugs. Was that what this was, the drugs? No, she felt tears rolling down her cheeks. That was all a dream; a bad dream. She needed to wake up. Needed to open her eyes. If she fell asleep, she might not wake up, her father had told her. She needed to wake up.

"Wake up, Phoenix!"

Her eyes sprung open. She recognized the voice. She didn't want to hear that name; never wanted to hear that name again.

The room was dark and quiet. There was no one around her. She tied to lift her head, but the pain was intense. She turned it to the side; better.

"I didn't think you would come back to us," the voice said.

It wasn't her dad's voice. She was sure of that. Her head was a ball of confusion, filled with cobwebs and steel wool. She couldn't form a thought. A light snapped on in the corner of the room. Briana strained to see, the gesture causing a sharp pain to shoot through her head. "Ouch," she tried to say, but nothing came out. She tried to move her jaw, but all she felt was pain.

In the light, the figure – the one that was not her father, turned toward her, coming into focus. It was Rey. He was there which meant that all that she dreamed was real. But where was she? Why was he there? Where had he been for months? Lily! Where was Lily? Was she okay?

The man walked toward her.

"Your jaw is wired. I had my doctor do it. We couldn't take you to a hospital, could we?" She wanted to ask why not, but nothing came out of her mouth. "I'm afraid that you were beat-up pretty bad. They almost killed you." The man paused as he came to her side; he shook his head as he looked over her body. "Oalo sent me away for a while on business. Your training wasn't meant to happen like this. We had great plans for you. I would never have let this happen, Phoenix."

He called her Phoenix. That clinched it. It wasn't a dream.

"I won't let them hurt you again. I won't let anyone hurt you again. And when I find who did this to you..." his voice got much louder, "they will pay dearly!"

She felt his hand on her arm. She stiffened at his touch. She needed to go to the red cabin. To the drugs. To forget.

"You need some sleep, Phoenix. Sleep will heal everything."

If she fell asleep, she heard her father say, she might never wake up again.

Briana closed her eyes and let the darkness take her once more.

Chapter 29

For four or five nights, Lily returned to an empty tent. There was no sign that Briana had been there at all and she was beyond worry for her friend. They had gotten into a routine that seemed to work for both of them. They supported one another, comforted and loved each other. Without her, Lily knew, she could never survive. She fed off of Briana's strength. When she was alone, Lily curled up on her cot and cried, listening intently to the sounds in the camp, hoping to hear her friend's voice.

Over the months as the two women became closer, they talked about friends and their families. What they would do when they got out of the camps. Where they would travel to. Lily liked listening to Briana talk about traveling through Europe. She promised to go with her, to be by her side at all times.

Fueled by the drugs, their talks would eventually turn to their escape. How they would go about stealing away from the camp under the cover of darkness and how they would make their way out of the jungle. Lily told Briana of the many different men that she had seen in the place where she was brought each day. She would look out the window of the room as their expensive cars arrived. The men would enter the house and eventually, one or two of them would be brought to her room. Lily performed for them; gave them what they needed for the hours that they needed it. Then they would go. She would watch as they slid back into the rear seats of their expensive cars and were driven away,

Lily's plan involved getting into those same cars, escaping in plain sight. The guards would open the gates for them, Lily said as they were driven away from the camp. All they would have to do is wait until the cars stopped, wherever they stopped. Together, Lily said, they would then find their way to a safe place where they could call the authorities and announce their escape.

There was no way the plan would work without Briana, Lily knew. She wasn't strong enough on her own to pull something like that off. Even if she was, she had no idea how she would get out of the country all alone. She needed Briana. She always needed Briana.

Her cot was cold and lonely without her friend; without her lover. Lily closed her eyes and cried herself to sleep, worried she would never see her friend again. Worried, that she would now have to suffer all alone.

****

It was dark when Briana finally opened her eyes again. She was not sure how long she had been out this time and her body continued to shake and tremble. She tried to lift her head, but was unable to move as if she was weighted down. Her mouth didn't move when she tried to talk, tried to scream. She shook uncontrollably, yet still unable to move. Her eyes darted from left to right; she heard her own moans.

A light snapped on and a familiar face came into view. "Stay with me now..." the voice said.

Her body shook once more. She wretched. Whatever was inside of her had to get out. She tasted the bile as it filled her mouth. She felt her head forcefully turned so she could vomit. Tears rolled down her face. She mumbled through her wired jaw:

"Please."

She felt a brief sharp pain in her arm and then the clouds filled the sky and she closed her eyes and let them take her away. She was flying once more. Safe, free from any care. Flying; that's where she wanted to be.

Rey watched over Phoenix in her condition for the better part of a week. He could see her physically healing, but inside, mentally, she was not there. His doctor told him that there was nothing they could do. Keep her on the drugs he said; make her comfortable if you want. She would never be the same person she was before.

Rey didn't believe the doctor. He focused all of his attention on Phoenix, but he quickly found he was battling more than her physical and mental issues. The drugs had seized her over the last couple of months; their trail evident in her arms. They had hold of her and, unlike a hospital, he didn't have the tools or counter-drugs to ween her off properly. He was reduced to supplying her with smaller amounts of the drug to combat her tremors and vomiting. The reaction from the mix of pain killers and psychoactive drugs was impossible to control and Rey found himself guessing without the help of a trained professional.

More than once, the drug cocktail that Rey mixed for Phoenix sent her into a tailspin forcing her to convulse and vomit before she passed out. He had no tools to revive her and often waited patiently for her to recover, monitoring her vital signs to check that he had not killed her.

The marks on her face had begun to clear by the end of the week. Rey took solace in that. At least something was working. Each time he looked down at the women, one of the most beautiful women he had ever seen, a spark of rage lit inside of him. He had waited too long for information on who had done this to his Phoenix; who dared to desecrate what was entrusted to him. He knew when he found this man – or men, they would pay for the pain they had caused her.

Phoenix lay in a separate bed next to his as she healed. He wanted her close so he could hear her breath. So he could make sure that she was alive at all times. After ensuring that she was comfortable for the night, he walked to the office part of his room and he made some calls.

"What do we know?" Rey said into the phone. The voice on the other end of the phone spoke for several minutes. Rey nodded his head as he gritted his teeth. He took a deep breath. "I would like to see them both, together. Not here. You know where."

He slammed down the phone and then looked across the room to make sure he had not disturbed Phoenix. The men who did this to her would pay. Today. He showered for a long time before he dressed, checked on Phoenix and then prepared to leave. At his door, a guard was instructed on how to watch Phoenix, what to look for and when to contact Rey, should something happen.

Rey met a car at the base of the big white house's steps and was driven out of the compound. Some 30 minutes later, his driver pulled off the road, down a dirt path. They traveled for several minutes through the jungle until they reached a clearing. The car pulled up next to a small concrete-block building that stood all alone in a field. Rey left the car and entered the building flanked by his most trusted guards.

"Strip them down," he said as he closed the door behind him.

In front of him, bound to the ceiling by their wrists stood the fat man and the guard who had beaten Phoenix. Rey pulled on a pair of leather gloves as he looked the men over.

"Wait Rey. You don't want to do this," Oalo said.

"Shut up," Rey said. "You should have left camp when you had the chance and never come back."

"You work for me you fucking idiot."

Rey knew who he was, but it was of no concern to him. He also didn't care that the man's father held a high position in the cartel and ran the UK operations. This should have made Oalo untouchable. But, when Rey looked at him, all he saw was rage. The man had to disappear, and Rey would have to deal with the fallout. No matter. It was something that had to be done.

"Shut him up," Rey commanded.

He watched as the guard reared back and punched the fat man in the face. His head spun and then he shook it, turning back to look at Rey, spitting blood.

"Is that all you got?" he said to the guard who prepared to strike him once more.

"Enough!" Rey said. "Strip them."

The two guards in the room worked the clothes off the two bound men as they kicked and cursed at them. When they were done, Rey stood in front of them, his arms crossed.

"This is about your whore, isn't it?" the fat man said. "She is incredible. What I did to her... what we did to her. She begged for it, my friend."

Rey's temper was rising, but he held himself steady waiting for the fat man to finish. The man disgusted him, but he let him talk, helping to confirm his decision to move forward.

"I had her many times, she should never have been given to you. She was destined to be trained personally by me."

"Enough!" Rey said.

He looked across at his guards and nodded. Both guards ignored the fat man and moved over to the other bound man, the one who had beat Phoenix that day. From a sheath on his belt one guard pulled out a large hunting knife. The captive's eyes stared back at the guard in fear. He mumbled something as the guard stepped forward. One of the guard's held the man's legs.

"Cut it off," Rey said.

"No!" the man screamed.

The guard with the knife bent down to the man's cock and pulled it forward. He looked into the man's eyes as he slid the knife underneath to the base of his cock. Then he pulled the knife up and across, slicing cleanly through the man's penis as the man cried out. Blood spilled from the man into a bucket below him. The guard held the man's cock up in front of the man's shocked face, his eyes bulging as the reality of his fate set in. The man sobbed loudly as he hung from the ropes.

"Very good," Rey said turning to the fat man. "Now, feed it to this fat bastard."

Oalo had been quiet as he watched the man be dismembered. Now, as the guards approached him, Rey stared into his face. He looked down the fat man's body to see that he was erect, his cock at attention. He had gotten off on watching, Rey realized. What a freak.

"Feed it to him!" he yelled, disgusted.

289

One guard worked the fat man's mouth opened as the other jammed the flaccid, bloody cock into his mouth. He fought the guards, forcing another to step forward to help. Three of them wrestled with the bound fat man until the deed was done. Rey stood by watching as they held his mouth closed, the appendage shoved inside.

The fat man stared back at Rey in defiance. He was untouchable and Rey would pay dearly for what he had done to him. When he was free, he would see to it. Maybe he would even do it himself and let that bitch Phoenix watch.

Rey stepped forward, taking the knife from the guards. He reached down to the fat man's still erect cock and tugged it forward as he looked into the man's eyes. He waited for recognition from the fat man.

After a moment the fat man realized that this wasn't just a threat and that Rey wouldn't stop at the punishment of his guard. Seeing his reflection in Rey's cold eyes he realized that he wouldn't get the chance to kill him.

Rey pressed the point of the knife into the fat man's forehead. He pushed enough to draw blood and then drew the blade slowly down Oalo's body until it reached the top of his penis – a thin line of blood left in its wake. Rey paused and circled the knife round his cock. In that moment, when Oalo understood his fate, Rey finally saw the man's fear. Rey slowly worked the blade through his penis as he stared back into his eyes. The fat man screamed and bucked but was held firmly by the guards. Rey finished slicing through his cock and he stepped back. He dropped the bloody appendage to the ground in front of the fat man.

"Release him," he said to the guards.

The guards let go of his mouth and one of them sliced through the ropes that held the fat man's wrists. He fell to the floor, his crotch a bloody mess as he scrambled to reach for his penis that lay before him. Rey stepped back and watched, his arms crossed. At one point, the fat man, cock in hand, looked up at him, sobbing in pain, his eyes imploring Rey to help him. Rey smiled back at him.

"That was for Phoenix. You fucking pig!" he said. Then to the guards, "Let them both suffer until they bleed out, then get rid of the bodies." He looked down at the fat man who had pulled his dick into both of his hands, holding it against his heart as blood pooled around him. "And take his cock from him."

Rey turned and left the small building. The men would clean up behind him. The bodies of the two men would be further dismembered and spread out over parts of Brazil and into the ocean. No one would find a trace of either of them. He sat back in the car and urged the driver to make haste back to the compound. He wanted to check on Phoenix to make sure she was okay and to tell her that the men who had done this to her had paid the price.

Back in the white house, Rey slid into a chair next to Phoenix and lifted her hand. His other hand felt her forehead where a fever had persisted as a result of her withdrawal and a possible infection. The doctor would be by later today to check on her. Until then, he would hold her hand and comfort her, letting her know that the people who had done this to her could no longer hurt her.

****

Briana heard voices at times as she came out of her stupor. Her throat hurt her tremendously and she had a constant pain on the right side of her head. Light especially seemed to bother her. When she opened her eyes in the dark, she tried to grasp control of the situation, but there was no clarity. At some point, her body wracked with tremors, she remembered seeing Rey holding her head, wiping her mouth as she vomited. Why was he helping her? Still, later she could hear his voice talking to her, singing to her. It was the only voice she had heard for so many days, she thought. How long had she been like this?

And Lily. Where was Lily? Why had she not come to see her? She would ask the voice – even if it was Rey where Lily was. She seemed to have no strength on her own that she could muster to help her situation. Whenever she did try, she found herself confused, her thoughts muddled. Briana felt as if she had no control of her body or mind. She would have to focus more to get that control back.

The doctor was present today – yes, there was a second voice. She had heard it before. He lifted her arms and prodded her. None of it hurt, not like the real pain. He spoke to the Rey, the other voice. She heard bits and pieces of what he said, assembled them to try to make sentences.

"Drugs... stop... harder first... needs to get up... she is strong..."

She liked the last part, latched onto it. She was strong. She could help herself if needed. She just needed to focus.

Briana felt them lifting her up, bending her. The pain was back. She opened her eyes and the room came into view. She remembered now; it was Rey's big room. They lifted her onto her feet. She was standing – with their help, one on each side if her. She turned to face them, their faces blurry. She tried to say something, but nothing came out – her mouth still not opening. "Your jaw is wired" – she remembered someone saying that. She lifted her hand to her mouth, slowly feeling around it, slipping her finger between her lips. Her teeth were clenched together.

"She looks like she is trying to figure out what is happening. That's a good sign," the doctor said.

Briana grunted and tried to smile at his words; she wasn't sure if she did. They walked her around the room for a long time, until her body dropped as they held her. She was exhausted when they placed her back on the bed. She fell into a heap. At some point, they were back to walk her around the room again. She listened as they spoke trying to pick up any information she could, storing it for later when she could compile it all together. She noticed she wasn't shaking as much; the tremors were mostly gone. The walks helped. She felt stronger, walked longer.

The next time they came for her, she opened her eyes and stared at them, trying to lift herself up from the mattress as they guided her. She looked first at the doctor and then at Rey. His face was clear to her. Memories of her time with him rifled through her mind. He had mistreated her terribly, but then he had been good to her. Then he went away. He smiled as she stared into his face.

"Welcome back, Phoenix," he said. It was the same voice that hummed and sang to her. "You are doing so much better."

Full sentences. Completely clear. She nodded back to him and his smile grew even brighter.

"Let's get her up."

The doctor and Rey lifted her from the mattress and began to walk her across the room. At one point, Briana stopped moving, resisting their pressure to step forward. She shook her shoulders, shaking their hands from her and stepped forward on her own. Briana walked to the end of the room and back. When she returned, she looked both the doctor and Rey in the eye and nodded. She would show them.

"Incredible," Rey said. "You are amazing. You have truly become our Phoenix, you will no longer fear darkness as you have risen from ashes."

To prove that it wasn't an aberration, Briana turned slowly, almost losing her balance, shook their help off as they reached out to her, and then walked across the room once more. A feeling of confidence swelled inside of her as she turned and walked back. She passed both men and went to sit on the edge of her mattress. Looking back at their faces, Briana knew that she had made a marked improvement from where she had been earlier.

For the next few days, there was more of the same. She challenged the men to let her do things on her own as they tried to help her. Each day showed improvement and ended with her collapsing in exhaustion. Despite her fatigue, she tried to stay awake a little longer every day. Toward the end of the week, she asked for a pad and pen so she could communicate. The first question she asked was about Lily.

"I don't know," Rey said. "She is not my concern."

"She is my concern," Briana wrote back.

"Then I shall see about her, Phoenix. I shall see that she is taken care of."

The next day Rey reported that he had spoken to his men and they told him that Lily was okay. He had arranged for her to be brought to the white house the following day. Rey told his men to make sure that she was showered and not to indicate where they were taking her.

"You shall see Lily tomorrow," Rey told Briana.

"Thank you," Briana wrote on her board. She meant it.

Rey smiled back at her.

When Briana went to sleep that night, her mind firing mostly on all cylinders again, she thought about Lily and smiled. Her friend was okay. Somehow, they were both okay.

Chapter 30

Lily was belligerent as the guard pulled her toward the white house. She had asked for her drugs, but he refused her. Something was different about the guard, about the way that he had forced her to take a long shower that morning telling her to "clean up completely." She knew he often watched her as she showered, but he seemed preoccupied as she soaped up her body.

As they came closer to the house, she dragged her feet. This was the house that Briana had told her about – the one with the fat man who had beat her, tortured her in the past. She stopped as the guard urged her on. Staring at the house, she wondered if her friend had met her untimely end.

"Move," he said to her, staring into her eyes, letting her know he meant business. His job was to deliver her, and he would not be deterred.

Lily walked up the stairs, her mind searching for an out. She noticed that she no longer looked about the camp as they moved her. No longer identified escape routes and tried to build scenarios in her head. No, with Briana gone, her will was also broken and she let day blend into night, the drugs dulling her to the point where nothing really mattered anymore. Self-preservation was still there – in the end, it never really left you, but the will to seek a solution in advance, that was all but gone.

They entered the big white house and they walked up the small set up stairs to the next level. Lily remembered Briana describing the same walk. Her fear and trepidation of not knowing what awaited her at each end of the hallway. One, Briana had told her, was preferred, the other was pure hell. As the guard turned right, leading her down the long hallway, Lily could not remember which was which. She cursed herself and her memory, long-addled by the drugs. This was important, very important. She needed to steel herself somehow if she was to be brought to that monster at the end of this hallway.

Her body began to shake as she got closer to the door at the end of the hallway. The guard pushed her forward as she started to slowdown, urging her not to resist so he could get on with his day. At the door, they stopped. The guard knocked. He lifted Lily by the arm so she stood up straight, His eyes admonished her to be still, obedient. The guard pushed the door open and walked Lily inside the large room.

Her eyes looked out over the massive room. There was a large bed in the distance, and a separate larger space to her right. The bed was canopied with long sheets extended around all sides. The guard walked her forward and they waited.

"You must be Lily," the voice came from a distance, from the open area to their right.

Lily turned to see a large man walking toward her. He was big; not fat. He smiled at her as he approached, and Lily looked down at the floor.

"That will be all," the man said to the guard. The guard let go of Lily's arm and stepped out of the room. When the door closed, the man spoke again. "Follow me, please."

He walked past her, toward the large bed. Lily followed behind him, keeping her distance. She awaited instructions, assumed nothing. That could only get her into trouble. When they were near the bed, the big man turned around. He smiled at her, his eyes walking up and down her body. She would soon be asked to undress, Lily knew. She prayed that he would be gentle with her; she did not have the aid of her drugs.

"I want to show you something."

The man walked next to the bed and he beckoned her over. Slowly, he pulled back one of the long hanging silk sheets that shielded the bed from the outside world. Lily looked through the opening, to the mattress and her heart leaped into her throat. Could it be? No! The figure that sat up on the mattress looked up into her face. It was unmistakable.

"Oh my God!" Lily screamed, then her hands covered her mouth, realizing that she had yelled out loud. Tears rolled down her eyes as she stared at Briana. She looked at the man, sobbing. Her friend was alive.

"You may go to her," Rey said.

Lily stared at the man for a moment and then climbed onto the mattress. She crawled across it until she reached Briana. Briana's arms opened, and Lily fell into them. How was this possible, Lily thought? Where had she been? She pulled Briana into her arms, hearing her groan and released her quickly. Lily looked down at Briana, her eyes scanning her from head to toe. She was all there; maybe a little broken, but she was all there. She turned back toward the man, and watched as he closed the canopy sheet, giving them their privacy, at least for a few moments.

"I thought you were dead," Lily said. "I thought you..."

Briana opened her arms once more, pulling Lily in close.

Lily fell onto the mattress next to her, crying onto her shoulder. She sobbed openly, loudly, as Briana soothed her, stroking her hair. They stayed like that for a few minutes until Lily calmed down. She picked up her head and looked down at her friend.

"Oh, Briana, I am so sorry."

Briana opened her arms once more and Lily fell into them. They hugged for a long time, until Rey returned to the bed and pulled back the satin curtain. He smiled down at both of them and then he held out his hand for Lily. Lily looked at Briana and Briana nodded. She took Rey's hand and he led her off the bed.

"You will go back to your tent now," he said to her as she stood before him. "This is our little secret, until Phoenix is all better. When she is, you will be paired up again. For special appointments. VIP appointments. Do you understand?" Lily nodded. "Good. Please do not start trouble in the meantime. I cannot help you if you do. You are Phoenix's friend and I am doing this for her. It is not a gift. Do you understand?" Lily nodded her head. "Be smart, Lily," Rey said. "Go."

Lily looked back at the closed silk curtain, the bed which contained her friend, her lover. She was alive. Be smart, the man said. She wanted to crawl back onto the bed, but instead, she turned and walked toward the door to the room. When she got there, she knocked on it and waited for it to open. The guard stepped in and looked across the room at Rey who indicated that she should be brought back to her tent. Lily left the room and the door closed behind her, leaving her friend inside; inside and alive.

When the door closed and they were alone in the room, Rey turned back toward the bed and pulled back the satin curtain. Briana remained sitting up on the bed and smiled up at him as best she could. It was an incredibly kind thing for him to do, she knew. She didn't know why he did these things for her, but she knew that it was important that she acknowledged them.

"Thank you," she said, through her clenched jaw. Her words were not completely clear, but her eyes conveyed her message.

Rey slid onto the mattress and pulled himself next to her. He sat with his back against the headboard as she did. He reached for her hand.

"I have a gift for you, Phoenix. I wanted to wait until you were completely back on your feet, but I think you are ready for it. You are so much stronger than you were a couple of days ago and much better than you were a week ago. You should be happy with your progress." She smiled at him, and he handed her a small box.

Briana took the box from him, tears forming in her eyes. It was a square box, wrapped with a red bow on it. In her mind, it seemed so out of place amongst everything that was going on around her, in the jungle, in her life. The wrapped gift contrasted so much with all of the pain and horror that was everywhere she looked.

"Open it," Rey said.

Briana pulled the bow off. She had a brief flashback of opening gifts with her mother and father which she pushed out of her mind. She had no room for their suffering or memories of them. Her fingers pulled at the gift paper until it shredded and rested on her lap before her. She looked up at Rey and he smiled, nodding for her to continue. A romantic gift, she suddenly thought, in all of this chaos? Briana lifted the lid of the small box.

Immediately when she saw what was inside, her eyes widened, and her pulse quickened. She jerked back, dropping the box onto her lap, its contents spilling out in front of them. She turned her head to him, and his smile broadened.

"It's Oalo's," he said. "He will never bother you again."

Briana looked down at the shriveled penis in her lap, the jagged, bloody skin where it was cut indicating that was no concern for the man's pain. She knew she should be horrified, repulsed, but for some reason, she felt a sense of calm come over her. It was a fitting end for the man who had abused so many in such horrible ways. She knew first-hand how he reveled in her suffering and the suffering of others. She had no sympathy, no compassion for someone like him.

"I did it myself," Rey said. "The rest of him is scattered all over the jungle."

"Thank you," Briana said through her braces. She meant it.

She picked up the penis and placed it back it the box, handing the box back to Rey. He took it and put it off to the side. He stretched his arm out and Briana leaned into him as he pulled her close to him. They sat for a long while in the same position, deep in their own thoughts. Briana started to let her mind wander back to the beatings, but she stopped herself, choosing to lock it deep down inside of her. The gift that Rey had given assured her that she would never have to fear the fat man again. She could lock those memories away, suppress them deep down.

Eventually, Rey sat up, kissed her on the head, and slid off the bed. He had work to do. He had made Briana happy which he considered very important to her recovery. He hoped that seeing what had been done to the fat man also allowed her to feel safer. He closed the satin curtains and stepped away from the bed. He would return for dinner with her and nurse her until she was back to full strength.

Chapter 31

It took close to two more weeks for Briana to return to full-strength. As she became stronger, the wiring on her jaw was removed and she was able to begin speaking naturally again. During the time she continued to heal, she had no communication with Lily. There was no vehicle in place for them to be able to talk. Each of them took Rey on his word that he would do the best he could to look after them. Briana went to bed each evening praying for Lily's safety and that she would be okay when she next saw her.

Lily was put back into service as if nothing had changed. She returned to the drugs and was sent out on appointments. Rey took no steps to intervene. She was not his problem. He only cared about her as much as was necessary to prove to Phoenix that he was true to his word. When Phoenix was ready, he would pair her back up with Lily and he would control the appointments for which they were scheduled so that the two remained safe.

The night before Briana was ready to be returned to her tent, Rey presented her with a choice. She could spend the last night with him in his comfortable bed or return to her tent to check on and be with her friend. He made it clear that her time to stay with him had to end and that Phoenix had to get back to fulfilling her role or problems could be created for both of them.

Briana weighed her options for a moment before answering him.

"Rey – you have been incredible to me over these last several weeks, in fact most of the time I have known you," Briana spoke slowly and deliberately. "Without you, I would not be alive today. None of this makes any sense to me, or any woman in the compound, but you have done more for me and I do not know why."

Rey started to say something, and Briana put up her hand, daring to stop him from speaking.

"Please, let me finish."

Rey didn't speak, letting her continue.

"I owe you a huge debt of gratitude." She stepped toward him. "I need to thank you appropriately. As you should be thanked."

She reached down to the bottom of her shirt and slowly pulled it up over her head. Briana's breasts stood out on her chest. Her nipples were hard and swollen. Her hands reached down and pushed her scrubs down over her hips. She was naked underneath, her bush untrimmed. Rey had not touched her once since the beatings. Now, he stared down at her, his eyes wide.

"Let me thank you, Rey," Briana said, reaching for his hand, taking it as she pulled herself toward him.

Her hand reached down between his legs where he had begun to grow. She smiled up at him, a slightly crooked smile, but just as beautiful and then she closed the gap between them. She kissed him gently as her hand traced his shape. Then she pressed her tongue between his lips as she felt his arms slide around her, pulling her in tight. His tongue met hers and they kissed passionately, hungrily as

302

she moaned into his mouth. When they broke from their kiss, she led him over by his hand to the big bed. There she undressed him, knelt down in front of him and took him into her mouth. Everything he had taught her and everything she had learned quickly came back to her as she swallowed all of his length into her mouth.

Rey and Briana made love several times that night. It was passionate and mutual. Neither of them rushed, but when they climaxed it was more than a simple release for both of them. It was the culmination of all of the pain and suffering, all of the attempts at love in such a horrible place, and the union of two souls that knew they should never be together. For Briana, it was her way of thanking Rey for putting his own life on the line for her, for taking care of Oalo, and for protecting Lily. For Rey, it was his way of showing her that he really loved her, that he would do anything for her, anything within reason. He was not a good man; he was good to her.

In the morning, Briana lay on her side in the bed, Rey spooned up behind her. She could feel his large cock resting next to her. She thought of the fat man's dick, rotting in the box on the shelf in the room. How different it was to Rey's and how differently they used them. When she left to go back to the tent, she would leave the box behind. It was the action that Rey took that was important. She giggled to herself. It's the thought that counts.

After lunch, a guard took Briana back to her tent. Briana freshly showered and put on some clean blue scrubs. The guard unzipped the door to the tent and let Briana step inside. When Lily saw her, she ran into her arms and collapsed.

****

303

It took until the next morning before Briana could completely console Lily. She was high on the drugs and she cried uncontrollably. Briana held her in her arms, soothing and rocking her throughout the night. Briana wasn't sure what to expect when they woke up in the morning. Eventually, they both feel asleep, holding one another.

The next morning, Briana and Lily were able to really speak for the first time. Some of the drug's effects had worn off while Lily slept, and Briana tried to get her to focus. She told Lily that they would be together now. She could slow down with the drugs, eventually stop. She described how she was able to do it. She told Lily she was confident she could also.

Lily stared off into space at times seeming to grasp bits and pieces of what Briana was saying. Then she would turn and stare at her friend, like she had just arrived from a long trip. She would smile at Briana, her mind trying to figure out where she had been all of this time.

They spent the morning together expecting Lily to be taken out sometime before lunch. That didn't happen and both women went out to the camp to collect their lunch together. Briana felt strange amongst the women, some she remembered, and some were new. They moved like robots, doing what they were told to do without question. Had she been like that all along.

The food was also different, and she joked with Lily, even though it was dark, that she knew of a way to get better food, but it was a painful process.

"I can't believe you can even joke like that," Lily said.

"Me neither. But, none of his makes any sense so I'm not quite sure how I should act."

They ate in silence for a while until Lily broke it.

"Now that you're back, we can put our heads together and plan a way out of here," Lily said.

"I'm not sure that is productive. Rey said he would help us by getting us safer jobs. Appointments with people that were wealthy and less-prone to hurting women."

"Do you think wealth has anything to do with that?"

"No, no, Lily. But, I do know he is true to his word. He will try to help us."

"Because helping us, helps him. We still have to fuck people! We still have to take it in the ass, live out their disgusting fantasies! We are still slaves... fucking sex slaves, Phoenix."

It was the first time Lily had called her Phoenix and it wasn't lost on her. Lily emphasized the name almost to accuse her of being one of them. She stared at her to make her point.

"I don't want to do this anymore. It's disgusting, humiliating and I've lost all of myself. I don't know who I am anymore," Lily continued.

"It's the drugs, Lily. I know; I felt the same way."

"I know it's the drugs, but without them. I can't forget. Without them I feel things. I don't want to feel anything anymore. The drugs stop me from feeling... and that's good."

Briana had walked over to Lily and pulled her into her arms. The poor girl was so lost. She had been all alone the last several weeks and had totally lost her way. Briana made a commitment to herself at that moment that she would get Lily back on her feet. Make her whole again. She rubbed her back as she held her, listening to her friend sob, her warm tears sliding onto Briana's neck.

"Hey," Briana said. "Who's my girl?"

Lily nodded her head.

"You're my girl, Lily. We're gonna to make you better. All

better. Because you're my girl, baby."

Lily looked up at her, their eyes locking. Briana could see so much pain there. Her beautiful friend in so much pain. She bent her head down and kissed her gently on the lips. Lily kissed her back and Briana pulled her into her arms, swallowing her tongue as she covered her mouth.

They pulled each other's clothes off, their hands, fingers, mouths journeying over one another as they re-familiarized themselves with their bodies, their scents, their sounds. They gave into each other completely, quickly making up for lost time while patiently and painstakingly scouring every inch of their bodies.

They pointed out new scars and never-seen marks that each sported as a result of their trials. They giggled quietly, never losing sight of their passion and the need to drive one another to personal ecstasy while hiding their needs inside this tent in the middle of the jungle. They screamed into each other, their vibrations threatening to make their own noises that could be heard throughout the compound.

When they were done, naked, wet and panting, Lily turned Briana onto her back and gently traced her fingers down from her mouth, and neck, over her chest and stomach and then slowly down to her toes, gently kissing each abrasion and imperfection. Lily took her time climbing back up, repeating the process in an agonizing slow fashion, ultimately burying her head between Briana's legs where she licked her until Briana bucked uncontrollably. When Briana finished cuming, she rolled Lily onto her back and returned the favor.

They slept naked that night, uncovered on a sheet on the hard floor of the tent. When one of them woke up in the middle of the night, they took each other once more, desperate to provide as much pleasure as possible before the light of day brought back the ugliness of their surroundings. Neither of them got much sleep, if any at all. When morning came, Briana silently thanked Rey once more for returning her back to health.

Chapter 32

It was the next day when Briana and Lily were visited after lunch by a guard. They were both taken to the showers and then returned to their rooms. They were each given sexy lingerie, high heels and a dress to wear, no doubt picked out by the little lady. Later that evening, the guard reappeared and walked them in the direction of the white house. They stopped at the red cabin and Lily, despite Briana's protests, stepped inside for her drugs. When she came back out, she smiled at Briana and they were brought to a large black limousine. They were led into the back seat and the guard slid into the passenger seat. Lily looked around, and Briana knew she was thinking once again about how to get away should the opportunity present itself.

They were on the road for a little over 30 minutes when the car pulled off the road, onto a small road and then drove deeper into the jungle. At the end of the road they came to a stop next to a series of massive houses. The driver got out of the car and opened up Briana's door. The guard opened up Lily's.

"Welcome, welcome," a man said to them, approaching from the direction of one of the houses. His eyes scanned Lily and then Briana. "You are both beautiful. Excellent," he said. "Come," he said, waving his hand. Both girls followed, one on each side. "Now, tonight is a birthday party for a very important man. I trust you will know how to make him happy."

Both women followed the man up the steps. He stopped in front of a large set of doors and turned to them.

"Listen. I would like to consider this an audition for you both. If you perform well, I will ask for you by name." He smiled at them, looking Briana up and down once more. "I hope you both perform well. Maybe one time even we can be together."

He pushed open the doors into a massive foyer, similar to the lobby of a hotel. He motioned the girls in and smiled once more. There was a huge party going on to their left and he led them in that direction. Once there, he turned to them once more.

"You may mingle, you may touch and flirt. Excite these men and woman as much as you want. But, only when I give you the signal may you leave with one of them, do you understand?" Both women nodded and he waved his hands in the direction of the party. "Go, have fun, and make fun for our guests. Spread out."

Lily and Briana walked further into the party. Heads turned as they got closer to the larger group. Eyes slid up and down their bodies. Lily walked over to a table and grabbed a small plate. She filled it with a few pieces of shrimp and slowly began to eat one.

"What are you doing, Lily? We can't eat."

"He said to have fun. I'm hungry."

They both looked back at the man who had brought them into the party. He nodded and smiled at them. Briana picked up a dish and placed some food on it. She turned to Lily as they ate, smiling at her.

"Different," she said.

A man was passing glasses of champagne around and Lily reached for one. She handed the glass to Briana and took one for herself. Briana took a sip, feeling the bubbles slide down her throat. She didn't think that Lily should be mixing drugs and alcohol, but she didn't have a chance to tell her.

"Care to dance," a middle-aged man said, stepping alongside Phoenix. His fingers touched her arm as she turned to him.

"I would love to," Briana said.

The man took her hand and led her away to the dance floor on the other side of the room. Lily looked on for a moment, before she too was approached and found herself moving in the direction of the dance floor.

The man introduced himself to Briana as they danced. He led her across the floor and when the dance was over, he asked if he could get her another drink. She shook her head telling him she was good for the moment. He bowed and stepped away from her. She watched Lily dance with a tall, dark man. She liked the way she moved on the floor. The drugs made you very elastic, flexible, Phoenix remembered. It was evident they were coursing through Lily.

When the music was over, Lily looked across the room toward their host, and he nodded up and down almost imperceptibly. Briana watched as the man escorted Lily off the floor and toward a set of doors on the far side of the room. They disappeared a moment later and Briana walked back across to the where the food was.

"Alone this evening?" a deep voice questioned her from behind. She turned to see a small man, maybe a head shorter than her. His hand reached up to her side as he looked into her eyes.

"At the moment," Briana said.

"I would ask you to dance, but that might look awkward."

"How so?"

"You are quite a tall woman."

"I am." She extended her hand. "My name is Phoenix," she said, wincing inside having used the name she'd been told to use.

"Albert," the man said. They shook.

"Why are there so many Americans here?" she asked, not sure if she was saying something she shouldn't.

"Wealthy people come from all walks of life. North American wealth is something they love to see. They pay for us to come here, to spend our money in exclusive clubs like this."

Phoenix didn't want to ask what they got in return knowing that she was probably on that list.

"You are quite beautiful."

"Thank you," she said.

"I saw that you came with a friend?"

"I did, but she seems to be off with someone."

The man smiled, changing the subject. "It's my birthday," he said.

Phoenix looked over the man's head across the room. The host smiled at her and nodded his head.

"Well, happy birthday, Albert. I hope you get some wonderful presents."

"Me too," he said.

Phoenix's hand reached out to his arm, gently massaging it as she spoke to him. "I think everyone's birthday should be special. Did you come all of this way to celebrate your birthday here?"

Albert nodded. "I did. I came with a number of friends, but I can celebrate with them anytime. Would you like to celebrate with me?"

"Very much, Albert. Very much."

Phoenix took Albert's hand and he led her away, out of the far side of the large room in the same direction that Lily had gone. They walked down a large corridor toward a series of elevators. Albert pulled out a keycard and swiped it next to infrared box on the elevator and the door opened. Albert pulled Phoenix inside and pressed the top button for the third floor. They traveled in silence for the quick ride and then stepped out of the elevator and headed down the hallway.

"Should I ask what birthday this is?" Phoenix said. He guessed he was in his 40s.

"Forty-five," he said.

She slipped her hand into his as they walked further down the hall. When they got to the end, Albert opened the door with his room key, and they stepped inside a large suite. He closed the door after Phoenix stepped in and he looked up into her eyes.

"Very beautiful," he said. "Come, I want to show you something."

Phoenix followed the man across the room to another door. He opened it and he extended his hand indicating she should step inside. Phoenix smiled and stepped into the room. The man followed, again closing the door behind him.

She looked around the large bedroom. There was a small door off to the right, which she assumed was another bedroom. As she stood there, the door to the room opened and out stepped a woman, also middle-aged. She wore a black, sheer lace robe. Phoenix looked at the woman and then at Albert.

"This is my wife, Julie," Albert said. Julie nodded toward Phoenix.

Julie walked to a comfortable chair that sat in the middle of the room facing toward the bed. She took a seat in it, looking towards the bed. Albert led Phoenix to the side of the bed and smiled up at her. His hand rested on her hip as he looked over at his wife. Phoenix looked over as Julie nodded. Phoenix was beginning to understand and bent her head down and kissed Albert hard on the mouth. His hands pulled her tight against him and she wrapped her arms around her neck. When she kissed him again, she felt his tongue in his mouth and she licked and swallowed it as his hands slid down to her ass and pulled her toward him.

Phoenix broke from their kiss, both of them breathing hard and reached up to the buttons on Albert's shirt. She unbuttoned it and then reached down for his belt, unbuckling it as his hands reached up to her chest, his fingers moving across her breasts. Phoenix pushed his pants down over his hips, leaving his briefs on. She turned in front of him then, offering him the zipper on the back of her dress which he quickly slid down. She looked over at Julie as her husband slid her dress down over her arms. Phoenix stepped out of the dress and stood in a black basque, hold-ups and high heels. Julie's eyes consumed her. Her nipples hardened under the woman's gaze.

Albert slid up closed to her from behind, his hands sliding up under her arms and over the cups of her basque, cupping her breasts as he gently grinded into her. Phoenix let out small moans as she placed her hands over his massaging her own breasts as her eyes met Julie's.

Phoenix and Julie played with each other, each pretending not to look at the other for a short time. Albert unlaced her basque from behind her and released her from it. Phoenix made sure she turned to the woman as her breasts were revealed, her nipples rock-hard. She watched as Julie swallowed as she stared at her tits, her husband's fingers gliding over them. Phoenix held the woman's eyes as she reached behind her and grabbed Albert's hard cock through his underwear. She let out a loud moan as her fingers circled it in the cloth and she slowly jerked it. She heard Albert's breathing change as she arched her back in front of him.

They stayed in this position for a little while, fondling one another until Phoenix slowly began to turn in front of Albert until she was facing him. She took him by the arm and gently turned him so that his back was to his wife. Phoenix slowly slid down to her knees in front of him, her eyes on the wife. She slid off Albert's underwear and pulled him into her mouth. She slowly sucked on him as she watched his wife open her robe and spread her legs in her chair. Julie played with herself as she watched her husband rock back and forth into the beautiful woman's mouth. Phoenix took her time, licking him up and down his shaft, nibbling on his tip and then deep throating him. Julie never took her eyes off of them.

When Albert came, his cock deep inside Phoenix's mouth, she clamped her lips tight on him to prevent anything from spilling out. She milked him, sucking on him until was dry and then slowly let him slide out of her mouth as he took in large gulps of air.

"Fuck!" he said as he stepped back, turning to look at his wife.

Julie's fingers were buried deep inside of her as she worked herself into a frenzy. Phoenix stepped away from Albert and moved toward his wife. Julie stared up at the woman as she stepped in front of her. Phoenix slipped down to her knees in front of the woman. She leaned forward, kissing the woman deeply, spilling the remaining cum that was in her mouth. Phoenix's hands roamed the woman's body as her mouth slid down from her chin, over her neck, to her breasts and then down to her stomach. She waited to feel Julie's hands on her shoulders as they guided her further down until she was between her legs.

Phoenix filled her mouth with the woman's scent as her tongue slide down the front of her pussy. Julie cried out, holding her tight against her as her hips thrust up into Phoenix's face. From behind, Phoenix felt Albert's hard cock slide up inside of her. His hands fell to her hips as he hardened inside of her, watching his wife as she screamed out in ecstasy.

They took turns for the next couple of hours fucking one another and watching each other fuck. At one point, Phoenix found herself staring at the motion of Julie's large tits as they swung back and forth as her husband pounded into her from behind. Her tits were beautiful, almost perfect Phoenix thought. After Albert finished off inside of his wife, he pulled out and rolled onto his back on the bed. Julie rolled over next to him, both of them breathing heavily as Phoenix sat in the chair and stared down at them.

A short time later, the couple fell asleep, naked and exhausted. Phoenix stood up, went into the bathroom, cleaned herself up, dressed and then quietly left the room.

She rode the elevator down to the first floor where a small portion of the party was continuing. She searched the room for Lily, but she could not find her. Phoenix grabbed a glass of champagne from a passing waiter and drank down the glass slowly. As she scanned the room, she saw their host, in the same place as he was earlier in the night. She tilted her glass toward him, and he nodded back at her, a smile on his face.

Phoenix busied herself at the party sampling some

desserts, talking with a few guests, and gently swaying to the music. Two men approached her at different times, and each time the host shook his head; she was not to leave with either of them. She gently declined their advances as she moved about the room.

Phoenix watched Lily eventually re-enter the main room. Phoenix noted that her hair was a little messy, but otherwise she looked fine. She made her way over to Lily and asked if she was okay.

Lily grabbed a passing glass of champagne and downed it in one shot. "I'm fine," she said, searching for another glass.

"Enough, Lily. They are watching."

Lily followed Phoenix's eyes to the front of the room, to the host. He lifted his hand briefly, alerting them to come in his direction. Phoenix took Lily's arm and led her across the floor. Lily giggled as she looked as some of the men, commenting, perhaps a little too loudly.

"Shh, Lily. Just be quiet for a few minutes." Phoenix knew it was the drugs that were fueling Lily's silliness, but it could get them in a lot of trouble if it wasn't checked.

They finally made their way to the front of the room. The host greeted them and smiled.

"Very good. Both of you. I heard good things," he said.

Both girls nodded. How were they supposed to respond to that?

"Your car is ready," he said. "Thank you. I will be requesting your services again. Very soon." He turned and led the women out of the room and down to their car. They were escorted inside and driven back to the compound where they were escorted back to their tent.

Inside, after the guard had left and they had changed out of their dresses into their scrubs, Phoenix sat down on her cot and Lily sat down next to her.

"That visit was much better, for both of us," Phoenix said, stroking Lily's hair. "Much better."

Lily nodded her head. "There are so many more ways to get away when they take us out of the compound. I thought about it all night. So many more opportunities."

Phoenix ignored her. Lily often got fixated on one concept when she was tired, and the drugs had her in their grasp. She held Lily and Lily just repeated the words over and over until Lily fell asleep.

Chapter 33

Following their first foray out, Briana and Lily were sent on several similar encounters. Always different clientele, but sometimes it was the same large house, other times it was a different place all together. At each location, they were most often paired up with a single individual which became their client for the night or occasionally they were paired with a number of partners. In each instance, the girls were asked to perform a variety of sexual tasks, some more hardcore than others, but all of their clients treated them properly and neither of the girls suffered from any form of beatings.

They were, however, required to perform for the clients. Lily and Briana were required to appear as if they were enjoying the sexual situations in which they were placed, provided that that was what the client wanted. What this meant for Lily was that she was to be drugged for almost every appointment, making her malleable and amenable to the whims of the client. What this meant for Briana was that she shifted her entire mentality and embodied Phoenix. If she was to be forced to have sex, she would embody the persona her captives had developed and assume the pretence of the role.

Rey was given reports of the progress of the women and was happy with the results. Within the first month, he had suggested that the girls be utilized in the same capacity four to five times each week, increasing the level of service to his highest paying customers. He had had several requests to 'buy' Phoenix outright for a huge amount of money and did his best to discourage the purchase as well as bury the request before it was sent up the ladder to his superiors. Rey would do whatever he could to keep Phoenix from being sold off. This also meant, even though he had not been asked, that he would have to do the same with Lily. Protecting her was important to Phoenix.

He summoned Phoenix at the end of the first month. When she was brought to him, he smiled at her and she smiled back. That look was worth all that he had done for her. Her smile was worth everything to him.

"You look well," he said. He was dressed in slacks and a white button-down shirt, she was wearing a blue dress with a flower pattern, specifically chosen by the little lady for her visit to Rey.

"Thank you," Phoenix said.

"I understand everything is going well. How is Lily?"

"She is okay," Briana said, not letting on that the drugs were still consuming her. She would deal with Lily on her own and not give Rey a chance to discipline her – or worse.

"Good. Very good. The reports I've received have all been positive. You two are requested quite often." He scratched his chin. "Hmm. You are very good assets and I will be increasing your availability." He looked Phoenix over for some sign of concern. He saw none. "Is that to your liking?"

"I am here to serve you, Rey," she said. "If that is what you want, then that is what I will do."

"What if I were to ask you to take other women under

your wing?"

"I don't understand," Briana said, suddenly worried that he would take Lily away from him. She was ready to protest.

Rey saw the look in her face. "Lily will be fine. I thought on nights when you were not specifically in service, you could serve as a host for some of the other girls. Perhaps, show them the ropes, keep them in check. Make sure they are doing what they need to be doing."

"And still do what I am doing? I don't see how I could do that," Phoenix said.

Rey smiled. "No, you would serve as a host – a beautiful onsite host. You would not have to perform for anyone during those times." He looked at her hoping she realized that he was providing her with a way out, at least for some of the time.

Briana took a moment to mull over the idea. She wasn't sure how what he was asking of her would affect her overall, but it seemed as if it was to her benefit. She would not be asked to use her body, instead she would be asked to manage the other girls as they were pressed into service. She would be assuming the same role as Rey which she abhorred, but as she thought about it, it would be a way to help control some of what happened to these women.

"Phoenix?"

"Yes," she said. "I think I could be an asset to you and to the women."

Rey saw her thinking; her wheels spinning. She was smart, he thought, very smart. "Good," he said. "I think it will be good for both of us."

He looked down at her body which never failed to excite him. She had recovered 100 percent, gained back the weight that she lost during her injuries and her scars had faded – almost disappeared; she was truly beautiful. Briana saw his eyes and she stepped forward. She would never forget what he had done for her; what he continued to do for her. She slid her arms up around his neck and smiled at him. She winced as she bit the tip of her tongue and then leaned into him and kissed him gently. Rey kissed her back and pulled her into his arms where she melted into him.

Briana slept with Rey and stayed with him overnight. She repeated the process at least once each month, showing her thanks to him by letting him take her as he saw fit, submitting to him fully. She held nothing back when she was with him knowing that he deserved the very best of her for all that he had done for her.

Over the next several months, Rey made good on his promise to utilize her in a hostess capacity as well as the regular services that she was providing. On those nights, when she was taken away from Lily separately, Lily waited for her to return back to the tent and quizzed her about her whereabouts. Briana did her best to explain that she was helping to make sure that other girls remained safe by managing them at the offsite locations.

On one night in particular, Lily having been returned to the tent after servicing someone locally, called out Briana's actions. "So, you are no better than them," Lily said to her.

Briana could tell she was high.

"Pimping out the girls for sex. Like your friend Rey and the others."

"I'm hoping," Briana explained to her slowly and calmly, "that my serving in this capacity will help protect then. They are going to be forced to have sex anyway. If I can make sure they are safe and that I help direct them properly, I think it benefits them."

"Whatever helps you sleep at night, Phoenix. Whatever helps you sleep."

Briana was cross at the use of that name from Lily. She was about to argue, then quickly caught her tongue. It would not be a fair argument in the condition that Lily was in, plus she really couldn't defend her actions. Given the circumstances, she was doing what she needed to do to survive. No one should question her on that. Instead of arguing, she tried to reach out to Lily, hug her, but Lily stepped back.

"Don't try to make this all better," Lily said to her. "You're different. You're giving up. Not trying to help us get out."

"No, Lily, no. That's not true. We just have to be smart."

"Be smart about it. I've been searching for ways out since I got here and every time I mention it, you shut me down. You don't try to help me. You don't offer ideas. Nothing. It's like you don't want to get out of this hell that we are in." Lily was angry, almost in tears.

"Of course, I want to get out, Lily. This place disgusts me. What we do disgusts me. I just know what happens when we buck the system, what happens even when we play by their rules."

"Then help me. Help us. Please," she pleaded.

Briana pulled Lily into her arms, despite her protests, holding her tight, soothing her. "Shh. Shh. Yes, I'm trying to help. Very much trying to help." She stared out across the tent thinking that any plan for escape would be futile.

Eventually, Lily gave up her fight for the night and the two of them slid into a single cot, holding each other until the fell asleep. In the morning, Lily and Briana went on with their business without further discussion about Briana's new role.

****

Briana learned quickly how to be a good hostess and over the next year, learned how to utilize the women at her disposal in the best way to satisfy the clients. At times she was very demanding of the woman, but always ensured that they were safe when they were with a client. She carried herself with an air of authority that let the client know that the girls served at her pleasure, so the clients understood that they needed to heed her requests.

Phoenix, and by association Lily, would be pressed into service themselves for high-powered clients and for special requests. Phoenix never failed to please her clients often bringing them over the edge multiple times. It was her job to make sure that they were happy and making them happy meant that she was safe. On these nights, she made sure that Lily remained focused on making the clients happy and that the drugs were not hampering her performance. She did not want it getting back to Rey that Lily was not pulling her weight.

After a long night, Lily rested her head in Briana's lap on the way home in the limo. She stared up at Briana, reaching her hand up to her chin, gently rubbing the side of her face. Then Lily smiled.

"What?" Briana said.

"I figured it out," she whispered, her eyes darting left and right.

Briana wasn't sure what she was talking about, but she knew it wasn't something they should be discussing in the car. She looked down at Lily and shook her head. Lily giggled. The drugs were coursing through her body.

"I was good tonight. Very good."

"I know, honey," Briana said. "Now, quiet down. We'll be back home soon."

Lily kept trying to start a conversation over the

remainder of the trip and Briana shut her down each time. Finally, they were deposited back at their tent and Briana turned to Lily after the zipper to the tent was closed.

"What are you trying to do? Get us in trouble?"

"I just figured it all out. I wanted to tell you."

"Wanted to tell me what? That you knew how to get us killed? Do you know what they would do to us if they knew you were thinking of escaping? If they caught you escaping?" Briana was raising her voice into a loud whisper and Lily stepped back across the tent.

"No. No. I just..."

"You're a stupid girl. You could get us killed. You don't know what you are doing because of the drugs and because of that – you could get hurt. We could get hurt." Lily was crying now, but Briana was mad. "Do you know how hard I work to keep you safe; to keep all these girls safe." She shook her head.

Lily stared at her with her arms crossed, tears rolling down her face.

"Just stop talking about things that can't happen. Focus on how you can help yourself here, now." She walked toward Lily. "You have to stop with the drugs. Stop with all the talk about escape. You have to understand that this is it for us."

"No!" Lily said. "I won't give up. This is not my life. This is what they want me to be. I didn't sign on for this and, I won't give up."

Briana reached for Lily to calm her, but Lily pulled away.

"Do you know how long we've been here?" Briana asked.

Lily stared at her. "I don't know. There is no such thing as time. Only what they do to us. They have taken everything from me. I won't let them take my hopes and dreams away."

Lily's voice rose and Briana pulled her into her arms to console her, but also hoping to quiet her. Into Briana's shoulder she continued.

"I have a plan. A good plan. I figured it all out. It can work and I know it will work for you too. It will get us out of here. Into a car. A way to escape and get away for good. All we need is to get to a safe place and then we can get home."

Briana held her at arm's length, shaking her head.

"I mean it. Here's what we need to do. I've thought it through so many times. I know it can work."

Lily pulled away from Briana and sat on the floor. She used her finger to make a path in the dirt floor as she explained her plan. Briana tried to quiet her at first, and then realized it was best to let her continue. Get it all out of her system before she shot holes in it. Lily went on for a long time, crossing out her first concept and then revisiting it again. When she thought she had laid out a complete plan, she looked up into Briana's face for approval.

"What do you think?"

"I think it's a good plan, Lily. But crazy. How do you think it will work? There are so many things that can go wrong."

"It can work! It will work! And, I'm not waiting any longer. I can't wait any longer! I'm going to do it the next time we are at that big house. Like I showed you. And," she looked up at Briana, "you have to come with me."

Briana didn't say anything for a long time and then finally, she looked at Lily and nodded her head. She thought it better not to argue, not to make matters worse. She would deal with it the next time that they were sent to the house. She would talk Lily out of it then, telling her it was the wrong time to do it, and continue that line of thought for as long as was necessary.

"Good." Lily said. She reached down and scratched out the plan she had worked into the dirt. "Good." She smiled up at Briana. "I'm happy we will be out of here together."

Chapter 34

When Rey called upon Phoenix late in the month to be with him, she did so willingly, looking forward to his company. She didn't love the man, but he truly cared about her and he treated her well – she felt beholden to him. When she entered his large room in the big white house, she immediately sensed that something was wrong.

"What is it?" she asked.

"Lily," he said. "My men overheard her tell someone of her plans to try and escape."

Briana looked at him. That was impossible. Briana was sure she was the only one that Lily had told. Who else could know? Unless someone overheard them that night in the tent.

"I don't believe that," Briana said.

"Is this true?" he said.

Briana looked up into his eyes. He was deadly serious, He almost seemed hurt that someone he had taken care of would try to escape. Had he forgotten what he asked these women to do on a daily basis? How they were treated? How they lived?

"I don't know..."

"Don't lie to me, Phoenix."

Briana thought before she said another word. Finally, she said, "Of course she has thought about it. I have thought about it. But it's only talk, Rey. There is no way out of here. You have all seen to that. Where would she or any of us go if we were to escape?" She reached for his arm and he pulled it away.

"I want you to let her try and escape. Help her. Go with her."

"What?"

"You heard me. She will expose weaknesses in our system which I will need to address. You are to encourage her to escape and then we will catch you both when you are in the final stage."

"Your men will kill her; kill us! It's suicide."

"You have my word. My men will not hurt you. They will not hurt Lily."

"This is crazy," Briana said.

"You will go tomorrow. First, you will tell me as much as you know of the plan and then you will both try and escape tomorrow. My men will catch you and this will stop her and others from thinking about escaping again."

Briana had let go of his arm and was walking about the room. She was trying to rationalize the situation. Lead Lily to an escape in which they would both be caught. He promised his men would not hurt her. She didn't know what she should do.

"Now, sit down and tell me the plan," Rey said.

Briana sat down, slowly unraveling Lily's plan for Rey. He took notes as she spoke, and Briana realized the futility of the attempt the more she spoke of it.

"I don't want to do this, Rey. Let me talk her out of it."

"It is done!" he said. "Tonight, you will encourage her and tomorrow you will attempt your escape."

Briana shook her head and then ultimately nodded. She knew she had no choice.

"You promise none of your men will hurt her?"

"You have my word," Phoenix. "Now, you have planning to do. I want this situation done and not discussed anymore after tomorrow. Do you understand?"

"Yes," she said.

Rey walked her to the door and knocked on it. The guard led her back to the tent.

****

Lily was crumpled in a ball when Briana woke her a couple of hours later. She smiled up at her friend, her lover and opened her arms. Briana fell into them and they cuddled on the cot.

"I didn't think you would be coming back tonight."

"I'm happy I did, Lily. Listen, I've been thinking," Briana said. Lily stared up at her. "Your escape plan could work. And... I think we should go for it."

Lily sat up on the cot, her legs crossed in front of her. "Really? What changed? Now you think it will work?"

Briana nodded, knowing she was duping her friend, but saw no way around it. "I do. I just realized the futility of this whole thing. It will never change unless we do something. And I think we should try it as soon as tomorrow. Before I change my mind."

"It's too soon," Lily said. She had been ready to go weeks ago, but now that Briana said she was ready, she had concerns. "We're not ready."

"Why not? Everything is the same. I know we will be going to that house tomorrow. There is nothing else we need to do."

Lily thought on it for a moment and then finally said, "You're right. We can do it. We can do it tomorrow. Nothing is stopping us. Yes!" she said, convincing herself. Then she looked at Briana and pulled her back into her arms. "I can't believe we are going to do this. I can't believe we are going to get out of here!"

Briana held Lily tight wondering if there was something more that she could have done to stop these wheels from being put into motion. There really was nothing. She served at Rey's will; they all did. And, she knew she could only put Lily off for so long. Now, at least, when this was over, the concept of escaping would no longer be an option.

Lily hugged and kissed Briana, eventually working her tongue down her neck. She was happier than Briana remembered and despite her knowing that she was setting Lily up for a fall, she let the woman seduce her and willingly made love to her before they fell asleep in each other's arms.

The next morning, the two women went about their business as if nothing had changed and as if there was no planned escape that evening. They both knew not to discuss the plans in any form so as not to let their secret out. When they dressed for their appointments, late in the afternoon, Lily was giddy and giggled as she pulled a yellow flowered dress on.

"I am going to skip the drugs tonight," she said to Briana.

"Are you sure that is a good idea?" Briana said. More than anything she wanted Lily to stay away from the hallucinogenic and libido-enhancing drugs, but breaking routine might draw attention to them.

"I need to be sharp. We..." she said, "need to be sharp."

"Right."

"Good, let's go. You remember everything you have to do, right?" Briana nodded. "Good, because we don't speak about this once we leave this tent."

"Right."

"I love you, baby," Lily said.

"Love you too, Lily."

The two girls left the tent when the guard came for them. They followed their routine, except for when the guard stopped at the red cabin. Lily pulled away from it and he looked at her for a moment before continuing to lead them to a waiting car. They sped out of the compound on their way to their destination.

The plan was simple. It involved each of them moving into a crowd in the center of the party room and selecting a man of their choosing. They would lead the man off to the side, to the wide hallway, as if they were going to go off to a bedroom. The host would see this of course, and object, but there was little he could do about it in the middle of the party. He would have to wait for their return. He would include the indiscretion in his report and most likely blame it on the smaller of the two women – the one who always seemed high. Once Briana and Lily got the men to the wide hallway, each would excuse themselves to go to the ladies' room, leaving the men waiting for them.

While the men waited, Lily would lead Briana down the long hallway and out a service door that she said she had seen when one of her clients led her the wrong way. He had taken her there, thinking it was a bedroom and Lily was quick to notice the door that led outside of the house before he pulled her from the room and led her in a different direction. It was this door she planned on using to escape the house.

Once outside of the house, the plan called for them to take the long path that led them down toward the water. They had each seen this path during one occasion where the party was held out on the docks. They would follow the path and then sneak onto one of the many ships that were used to ferry the guests to the house. They would then hide on the ship until it left port and arrived at its destination. At that point, there would be on their own, but presumedly no longer in the jungle and near a location where they could seek help or call someone.

Lily and Briana knew that the most dangerous part of the escape plan was making their way down the path to the water. If they were seen on that path by anyone, they would have no way of explaining themselves. They just had to be smart and very careful.

Chapter 35

Lily and Briana held hands as they left the car, squeezing them tightly before letting go and entering the massive house – Briana assuming the role of Phoenix. As expected, there was huge party going on. There was a room full of men, a number of women and they both joined the party as if they were standard guests. They separated, smiling at one another, knowing the next time they saw each other, they would be on the run, away from the horror show that they had been part of for so very long.

They both grabbed some food before mingling. It would be wise to eat well like they always did at these events. Lily was asked to dance by one of the men and she accepted, hoping not to see the host nod at her, letting her know she was to eventually take the man to bed. He did not and she continued to dance with the man until the song was over. She hugged him and moved on, drinking a glass of champagne along the way. Phoenix mingled, talking with a few men, accepting a glass from one and also taking her turn on the dance floor. It was still early. Phoenix called it the getting to know each other part of the evening, when she worked with the other girls. It was important, she told them to let the men eat and drink at the beginning of the night, so they were relaxed before they took them to bed.

The two of them worked the room for a while and then Phoenix watched as Lily focused on one man for a short time before slipping her hand into his and began to walk toward the wide hallway adjacent to the big party room. Phoenix looked across to the host, but he was not looking in Lily's direction at the time. She knew that he would be looking for both girls, and maybe others when he turned back toward the crowded party. When he did turn around, he watched Lily slip off the floor, focused on her to get her attention. She knew she was supposed to turn to him for approval, but she didn't, and Phoenix watched as the host turned in her direction.

Phoenix didn't acknowledge the man, looking away before their eyes locked. She moved about the room for another few minutes until the host was preoccupied again and then she took a man and did the same as Lily had done, leading him to the side hallway. She didn't stop to see if the host was watching; it was no longer a concern of hers. After leaving the room, she stopped the man as he urged her in the direction of the bedroom suites. Phoenix leaned into the man and whispered in his ear.

"I need to use the ladies' room, please," she whispered. She let out a warm breath in his ear.

The man stepped back, acknowledging her need and moved across the room to where another man stood, waiting for his own date to return. Phoenix made her way down the hallway and into the service room entrance which was exactly where Lily had told her it would be. She stepped through the door, half-expecting Rey's men to be there, but was greeted by a smiling Lily, who held out here hand. Phoenix took it and Lily led her out of the house.

Both girls stopped outside for a one moment, each of

them inhaling the scent of the air and looking up at the early night sky. For this moment, they were free, away from the animals who had held them captive.

"Let's go," Lily said, tugging on Phoenix's hand.

The two of them made their way along the lush plantings and trees that dotted the well-landscaped house. They tried to stay in the shadows as best they could and when they were required to step into the light, they did so quickly and sought the darkness as soon as possible. Several minutes after leaving the house, the two women found themselves next to the parking area where several cars, including those in which they came were parked.

"We should just take one of these and be gone," Lily whispered.

"Stick with the plan, Lily. Where would we drive to?"

"You're right."

The two women made their way across the back of the long parking lot. Lily tripped at the end, falling off one of her heels and almost pitched headfirst into the ground. Phoenix grabbed her just before she fell, and Lily straightened herself up, slowing down to prevent her from tripping again.

Phoenix was surprised that Rey's men let them get this far. They were out of the house, past the parking lot and on their way to the path that led them down by the boats. She would have thought that he would have stopped them as soon as they were out of the house. For a brief second, she wondered if maybe Rey would let her escape. He loved her, she knew, in his own way, and there was a very slim chance he might help her. Phoenix pushed the idea out of her head as they made their way left of the path that led down to the water.

"It's not a short walk," Lily said. "And, we have to pass under a small bridge just before we get to the boats. That will be the hardest part..." she turned, "... now that we are out of the house."

"Okay," Phoenix said, and the two girls pressed on.

They stayed in the shadows, in single-line formation with Lily leading the way. They walked for at least 20 minutes before Lily stopped and looked back at Phoenix. They were both breathing hard. There was fear all around them and they were both sweating profusely. Phoenix could sense the excitement in Lily as they neared the small bridge. Once they were through that, they were almost home free. Maybe Rey was going to let them go.

"Okay," Lily said. "I think the boats are on the other side of the bridge. If I remember, we go through there and then off to the left. She reached up and kissed Phoenix hard on the mouth and smiled at her as she pulled away. "We're going to make it."

The two girls stared down at the bridge and the path they needed to take under it. There was a tunnel that appeared to come out on the other side of the canal. They stepped down alongside the bridge and then Lily bent her head down to look inside the tunnel. There was no one inside. She waved her hand for Phoenix to follow and the two of them stepped inside the tunnel. They made their way slowly through the tunnel, their backs up against the wall. The excitement between them was palpable. Phoenix now had accepted that they were going to make it.

As they neared the end of the tunnel, a man's voice rang out and they both stopped in their tracks, pulling themselves up tight against the wall.

"Stop!" the voice yelled.

They both held their breath, afraid to make the tiniest noise. Perhaps, he was talking to someone else, Phoenix thought. Lily looked at her as if to ask what their next move was. Phoenix stared back; she didn't know what to do.

"Please, come out of the tunnel," the voice ordered. Neither of the women moved. "Now!"

Slowly, with their hands raised, they peeled themselves off the wall and began walking toward the sound of the voice.

"Did you really think you would get away from us?" the man asked.

The man came into focus as they walked closer toward him. He urged them on, a handgun in his hand. Behind him, were several men, each holding rifles, staring at the two women.

"That's far enough," the man said. "On your knees."

Lily looked at Phoenix, tears rolling down her face. Phoenix bent her knees. Lily did the same, kneeling down on front of the men as they both had done so many times before. The symbolism was not lost on Phoenix. The men had won once more. They always won. Women were their subordinates. They were here only to please the men.

"Hands behind your heads."

Both girls put their hands behind their heads as they stared at the man with the pistol. There was no way out, Lily knew. She had led Phoenix into this mess. She sobbed next to her friend, her lover.

"I'm sorry. I'm so sorry," she said to Phoenix.

"Shh, baby," Phoenix said. She had secured their safety. Rey had assured her that their men would not hurt Lily.

"Now," the man said, waving his pistol in their faces as he stepped closer. "You know what happens to those who try to escape, yes?"

Neither of the girls answered as he pointed his pistol from one to the other.

"Please," Phoenix tried. "We made a mistake. What can

we do?"

The man slapped her with his free hand. Phoenix's face flew to the side. It had been a long time since someone had hit her, and the memories of the last time flooded back into her mind.

"No," Lily cried.

"There are no second chances here. You will die for trying to escape."

"Please no," Phoenix cried out, knowing that it would probably get her another slap. Did he not know the deal she had made with Rey?

"Shut up!"

"Please," Lily said, pleading with the men.

"No! Please! Rey said, you would not hurt her."

"What?" Lily said, suddenly realizing what Phoenix was saying. "What do you mean?"

"Rey knew," Phoenix said. "They all knew we were going to escape. So, I made a deal with them. They wouldn't hurt you if I told them how we were going to do it."

"Briana?" Lily said. "You told on us. You gave us up?"

"It was to save our lives!"

"You may think so, bonita," the man with the pistol said, "but sadly, that is not the case."

"Rey said you wouldn't hurt her."

"That is true," a new voice said, and Phoenix looked up as Rey stepped out of the shadows.

"Oh, thank God!" she said. She looked at Lily hoping she would see that everything was alright. She nodded her head. "I told you."

Rey took the pistol from the man at the front and Phoenix breathed a sigh of relief. She had thought she had made a huge mistake, but here was Rey making everything all better again. Rey stepped forward and smiled down at

337

Phoenix. She smiled back. He extended the hand with the pistol in it toward Phoenix.

"I said none of my men would hurt her," he said. "I am a man of my word."

Phoenix stared at the pistol.

"Take it," he said. "To prove you are truly someone we can trust, you will shoot her."

Phoenix opened her eyes wide. She dropped her hands from behind her head, staring up at him, looking away from the proffered gun. She looked at Lily who stared at her in horror and then back at Rey. He wanted her to shoot Lily. There was no way she could do that.

Rey nodded his head, indicating that he knew this was a hard decision for her. "You don't have a choice. If you do not do it, both of you will die. While I would be very sad to see you go, Phoenix, you need to understand where my allegiance is." He offered her the gun once more. "Where is yours?"

Phoenix reached out her hand, wary of even putting her hand near a gun; she had never touched one before.

"Take it," he said.

Tears rolled down her cheeks.

"Take it. Make it quick. My patience will soon wear thin."

"Briana," Lily cried, "Please!"

"Take it. Show me." Rey said, more threatening this time.

Phoenix's fingers touched the pistol; the grip extended toward her.

"No, Please Briana. I'll do anything, baby. I'm so sorry," Lily stared at her and then at Rey.

"Now," Rey growled.

"Please. Please, Briana, please! I'm begging you!"

Phoenix was shaking, her fingers gripped the handle of the gun. She looked up at Rey who nodded toward her. Her fingers tightened around the handle. She could hear Lily crying next to her, but she couldn't bring herself to look at her. She loved her. The crazy drugged up woman who wanted nothing more than to escape this place; these men; this never-ending horror!

Rey nodded once more, encouraging her.

"Please, Bree!"

Phoenix looked from Rey to Lily. The poor broken girl. Now she had to choose to either die along side her friend; her only friend or live for something else, no, someone else. The name Bree reminded her of her mum and then her dad, and the slim chance that she may get to see them again. In that moment, that split second, Briana made her decision. She grabbed the gun from Rey's hand, turned it towards Lily and pulled the trigger, all in one fluid motion.

"Briana is dead. My name is Phoenix."

Lily's wet eyes stared into hers as the bullet shot through her chest. Her mouth opened as she looked down at her chest where a large red stain began to form on her flowered dress. Her hands covered the area where she was shot, and she looked back up at Phoenix.

Rey reached down and plucked the gun from her hand as Phoenix reached out her arms catching Lily as she pitched forward toward the ground.

Phoenix held Lily's dying body in her arms, her head on her lap as she stared down at the woman who had shared so much with her during this horrific time. She pressed her hand against the wound as if she could make it stop bleeding, take the pain away like they had done for each other so many times. She sobbed as she watched her lover's eyes go lifeless, staring into space. Phoenix's tears fell on Lily as she cried. "I'm sorry baby, so sorry..." her sobs echoing in the tunnel.

Chapter 36

Something died in Phoenix that night in the tunnel with Lily. Another casualty of the jungle and the sex trafficking cult that had already taken so much from her. Now, almost six months later when she looked back on it, she realized it was that moment that changed everything for her. That one moment in time that sent her completely over to the dark side, never considering turning back.

Rey had explained to her that her actions in the tunnel solidified her loyalty to him. It also released Lily from the pain and suffering of the drugs that had taken over her body. Lily wasn't strong enough for this kind of life and now she was free, he told her. Phoenix knew he was trying to placate her, but over time she came to believe it. She had done the best thing she could for Lily, take her away from all of what was happening in the jungle.

Not long after the incident in the tunnel, Rey elevated Phoenix's role once more. For the most part, she had become a full-time hostess. Very rarely was she asked to perform for anyone anymore and when she was, it was something very special; something Rey knew only she could excel at. In her role as hostess, she instructed the women as to how they were to act in various situations. She helped Rey determine those that were ready to be escorts at the high-class parties as well as those that could never take on that role.

Phoenix helped protect the women in the camp also, making sure that they were bathed and fed properly. She was ruthless in her perception of a woman's capabilities, but also kind with regard to what it would take to bring a woman properly into the fold, make them willingly participate with a client.

Phoenix also learned that there was another side to the camp, a much more sinister side that sold some of the women to wealthy suiters who would buy them outright to use any way they saw fit. These were typically young girls, as young as 14 years old who were taken to the camp, dressed up and sent to auctions. It was rare that anyone returned from the auctions, she knew and as much as it bothered her that something like this existed, she was happy to turn a blind eye to it and be spared having any part in the auctions.

Her relationship with Rey had also cooled after the Lily incident. They still remained very close, but it was difficult for her to have sex with him after what he had had her do to Lily. She understood his motives, but she could never completely forgive him for that night. Both of them knew of the change, but they never spoke of it. Their relationship became almost strictly business.

Rey invested his time in Phoenix, leveraging her strengths and ability to communicate to create a strong network of women that he could use as needed for various parties and events. His efforts paid off and those higher up began to take notice of his work noting the money that they brought in and the repeated requests they had received to be serviced by his women. Like every business, data was accumulated to show where high profits were being made and Rey's teams frequently came out on top. This did not go unnoticed by the cartel and those that the cartel serviced.

On a sweltering hot day, in the middle of the hottest part of the year in the jungle, Phoenix was called into a meeting with several men. It was more than two years after she was first abducted when she sat down at the table across from the man who had taken her home that night in Rio Di Janeiro. She stared into his face, moments of that night flooding back into her mind – the food, his touching her on the dance floor, her removing her panties by the bar, the art at his apartment, his naked body. She refused to shake, hardened by the years in the camp, by the beatings from the fat man. This man could not hurt her any more than she had been hurt already.

Esteban stared back at her. His dark eyes looking deep into her. A smile appeared on his face.

"You are still beautiful," he said. "I knew you were special the moment that I saw you at the club."

Phoenix didn't say a word. She held herself together breathing slowly and deliberately. She held his gaze.

"You are strong. Rey tells us very strong... and loyal."

Phoenix looked over at Rey whose face conveyed to her that he was not in charge at this meeting. It was Esteban she needed to listen to now. She turned back to him. She nodded.

"We," Esteban said, looking at the two men to his right, "have an opportunity which we would like you to help us with." He smiled and laughed. "You have done so well here, in the jungle, Phoenix. We want to take your work into the real world. Where you can do so much more, yes?" He didn't wait for a response. "Our plans are to bring you to the UK. London specifically, to start a group that can service the wealthy businessmen there. We want you to be in charge of the girls in this group, to culture them, to instruct them, to show them the ropes, eh?"

Phoenix looked at Rey, who nodded slightly and then back at Esteban. The chance to leave the jungle, to be amongst normal people was too good to pass up. As if she even had a choice. They were not asking her. They were telling her.

"Good," Esteban said. "We will leave in the morning. Alexey and Sergey will bring you from the camp to the airport. There will be people waiting for you in London." Esteban stood up from the table, his face a big smile. "I look forward to meeting up with you again soon, Phoenix. It has been too long." He smiled down at her and then he left the room. The two men followed close behind him.

Rey looked across the table at Phoenix. "This will be good," he said. "You will be out of the jungle. On your own."

"Will I?" Phoenix said.

"It is better than here. I will miss you, Phoenix. Very much. Stay with me tonight, please."

"If that is what you want, Rey. I will stay with you."

"Very well. I have something to attend to now. I will see you in my room for dinner, yes?"

"Yes," Phoenix said.

Back at her tent, she pulled together the few things she wanted to take with her. She owned nothing, but several of the dresses that she wore that she folded into a stack on the cot across from her. Lily's old cot. She ran her hand across the mattress thinking of her old friend and lover. Would she have lasted to this point, Phoenix wondered? Could she have survived this long and followed her to London? She shook her head; she could not think about that. Many things would have been different if Lily was still alive. Phoenix had

343

to think of Phoenix and only Phoenix. With her few dresses packed, she waited to be escorted to Rey's. She would not return to the tent. She would leave directly from the big white house. This would be the last time she would see the place that she had called home for the past couple of years. When the guard came and unzipped her tent, Phoenix took the stack of clothes and went to the door. She turned and spat on the floor before walking out of the tent for the very last time.

Her night with Rey was pleasant and heartfelt. She owed the man so much for picking her out of the rough and keeping her safe, nursing her back to health and elevating her out of the masses. She had changed so much, and he had instigated a lot of that change. She was stronger, more confident, and cunning because of Rey. She was a survivor.

They made love that night, slowly and passionately. She let him come first, deep inside of her. When she came, she didn't hold back, releasing everything into the midnight air of the jungle, hoping to leave it all behind as she started her new life. Rey wrapped his arms around her, spooning her from behind as they slept in his big bed for the final time.

Outside, the next morning the two embraced once more before she stepped into the large black car and headed out of the compound. Sergey drove and Alexey sat in the back with her as the car winded through the roads for more than an hour. Phoenix didn't really take notice of her departure from the jungle until the car they were in turned onto larger, more populated roads that eventually led them to the airport. She was witnessing civilization once more; a vibrant world full of people. She was being reborn outside of the jungle.

At the airport, she was handed a packet with her paperwork including a new passport as well as several other documents. Her new name on the paperwork was Marcy Hammond. She was instructed to memorize her name and her birthdate. Additionally, she was told how she should act and what she should expect. Sergey provided her with a suitcase for her clothes and the three of them approached airport security. They looked as if they were on a business trip bound for London.

Phoenix was nervous as she approached security, but she passed through without issue and made it through customs without any questions. On the plane, she sat between Sergey and Alexey as it lifted off the ground. She stared out the window realizing for the first time that she was finally free from the clutches of the compound and the horrors contained within it. As the plane rose above the clouds, she closed her eyes and drifted off to sleep knowing that when she woke up, she would be in an airport in London and very far away from the jungles of Brazil. Phoenix dreamed about a new life and how she could avenge her captors.

Follow Phoenix's journey in *Primeiro,* the second book of the *Consumed* series.